SHELBY

by
PETE McCORMACK

THE PERMANENT PRESS
Sag Harbor, New York 11963

Copyright © 1994 by Pete McCormack

Library of Congress Cataloging-in-Publication Data

McCormack, Pete, 1965–
    Shelby / by Pete McCormack.
      p. cm.
    ISBN 1-877946-47-8 : $22.00
    1. College students—British Columbia—Vancouver—Fiction.
2. Young men—British Columbia—Vancouver—Fiction. 3. Vancouver (B.C.)—Fiction. 4. Grandmothers—Fiction. I. Title.
PR9199.3.M4238S48   1994
813'.54—dc20   93-27527
                                                                                 CIP

except for the inclusion of brief quotes in a review.

All rights reserved, including the right to reproduce this book, or parts thereof, in any form, except for the inclusion of brief quotations in a review.

First Edition: June 1994 – 1,800 copies

Manufactured in the United States of America

THE PERMANENT PRESS
Noyac Road
Sag Harbor, NY 11963

For my family, who have loved me and encouraged me through an astonishing lack of success.

I

In 1907, on the day after his twentieth birthday, the poet Rupert Brooke wrote to his mother: "I am now in the depths of despondency because of my age. I'm filled with an hysterical despair to think of fifty dull years more. I hate myself and everyone."
But enough about him.

It was a phone call of the confessional nature to my ninety-three-year-old grandmother on April 5th, 1992 that began a conversation which finally raised me from bed. On any given day such an event would appear unremarkable. I, however, hadn't moved since my twentieth birthday three weeks earlier.
"I implore you, Gran," I said, beaten, shrouded in darkness, "no more jokes. I'm desperate for guidance."
"Who's jokin'? Gettin' it yanked curbed the ol' blood flow. By the summer of '55 I was full horsepower again."
"I told you, I don't *have* a uterus!"
"It's that fat girl again, isn't it?"
"Haven't I made myself clear? The family dream is in *peril* and I'm lying here functionless beyond rudimentary discharges, my head pounding from loneliness and thoughts of women contorting beyond natural limitations—"
"Oh hell, Shel, your needs are changin', that's all. Live a little."
"Live? What does that mean? You might as well ask me to do God's will! I ask you: what *is* God's will?"
"Be nice."
"How can I be nice? I loathe myself."
"You do not."
"I was once so sure of my call. Alas, it seems now I am rotting in a tide of my own septic musing. Innocence is snuffed. Destiny unclear. Please . . . my ally, my confidant, if you have

any wisdom from your endless years on this wretched planet, unload it now!"

"Okay, okay. Enough already. First off, this destiny thing is a mug's game."

"A what?"

"As for your marks, I love you and I don't give two shakes of a donkey's dong if they drop—"

"Mom and Dad would sell me!"

"So let 'em."

"U.B.C. medical school awaits my arrival."

"Who cares? Get out of bed! Go back to class. See how it goes. Then you can call me back, okay?"

I awaited further counsel. None came. I was crestfallen. "That's it? That's the advice? 'Who cares?' and then an ultimatum?"

"It's not good?"

"What about the parables?"

"Oh . . . uh . . . okay. You can't milk a dry cow."

"What?"

"I'm rusty."

"I thought you cared."

"Maybe you should stay in bed."

"*What?*"

"I can't win here."

"I feel ill."

"Look, you got any change around there?"

"What kind of change?"

"Nickels, quarters, dimes—"

"What are you up to?"

"Get some change."

"Hold on, I can't see. I have to turn the light on."

"It's the middle of the day."

"The curtains are drawn." I clicked the night-light. There was a nickel on my bedside table. "Okay, I have a nickel."

"Flip it," she said.

"Flip it?"

"Heads you get up. Tails you stay in bed."

"For how long?"

"Forever."

"Forever?"

"Flip it."
"I . . . I'm scared."
"Flip it."
My throat went dry. I flipped it. It landed on my pillow. "Tails," I said with a moan.
"That's it, get outta bed!"
My innards crumbled. "But heads was get out of bed."
"Heads was *stay* in bed."
"Really?"
"Don't try to put one over on your Gran," she said.
"I—"
"Get outta that bed!"

And so, hanging up a few minutes later, I removed my bony frame from my cot and hobbled to my desk. Glancing at the calendar, it was evident that classes were over and the exam period had begun. I dressed myself, draped a knapsack full of lecture notes and textbooks over my shoulder and wobbled into the gray yonder of a Vancouver afternoon. Walking through the Student Union Building, I stopped at a notice board where an exam schedule for the entire university was pinned. It turned out I had an Anatomy exam in less than twenty-four hours and a Zoology exam the day after that. Momentarily shaken, I was soon comforted by recalling my pre-final average to be hovering in the low nineties. Moreover, work done earlier in the year had left me certain I could do reasonably well on any of my five examinations without even opening a text book. Nonetheless, it was time to study.

Sitting at my usual spot on the third floor of Woodward Library at the carrel beside the emergency exit, I removed my Anatomy textbook from my pack and flipped to the index. I fingered my way down the *E's* towards Endocrine System, my eyes darting like a lizard's tongue from column to column. My next recollection was of waking up face down in a pool of saliva, legs tingling, throat parched, temples all a-flutter. To my shock, the clock above my head indicated I had been in slumber for four and a half hours. A needle-like pain shot across my mons pubis and I feared appendicitis. I took a breath and the ache lessened. Wiping the saliva with my shirt sleeve, I flipped to Chapter 4 and began reading about ears: *"The 75 to 100 stereocilia and one kinocilium of each hair cell of the many . . .*

money . . . Minnie . . . in each crista are imbedded in a . . . gelatinous matrix . . . which . . . which abuts a gelatinous jelly . . . imbedded in a . . . imbed . . . in bed . . . "—only to fall asleep again, this time for twenty-five minutes. My mind grappled with thoughts of women wearing avant-garde fall fashions. In a panic I fled the library for the university parking lot, drove to the nearest all-night restaurant I could find—Denny's—recharged on buckwheat pancakes and began studying.

Into the evening I fought off lethal combinations of depression, fatigue and sexual urges with thoughts of academic greatness until the call of destiny once again overwhelmed my senses to where I was, as in days of yore, intellectually titillated by the firing of synapses in my brain. Basking in the rush, I recalled past scholastic successes (projects, awards, newspaper clippings, et cetera) and considered my many options within the medical profession. Naturally research in the form of disease cures intrigued me, but so did Third World relief work and the prestige and financial rewards of several of the specialties—radiology, neurology, and so on. Excited, I returned to my lecture notes and didn't pause again until the course had been reviewed in full. I glanced up to see a gray sun peeking across the Vancouver skyline. Dawn was upon the city, hours having streaked by in a gasp of everlastingness, willpower having obliterated all potentially disconcerting thoughts.

Writing the exam proved more elementary than expected. What answers I didn't know in the multiple choice section became clear through deduction. Written essays were on subjects as natural to me as suckling to a newborn babe. Finishing up the three-hour exam in two thirds the time, I returned to the dorm, confident my academic standing had been preserved, and proceeded to peruse Blake's *Augeries of Innocence* between intermittent naps.

Later that night while in the midst of cramming for the Zoology final, I found myself gulping coffee and cold air and then doing jumping jacks between swigs of peach schnapps in an attempt to remedy what appeared to be some sort of viral narcolepsy. But each time I would return to my desk my eyes would close involuntarily and my head would snap back like a Pez candy dispenser. It was as if the course

SHELBY

material had become allergenic, my eyes watery and red, my skin itchy. Exasperated, I abandoned the struggle and lay my head on my desk. Suddenly Minnie T.'s thick legs and girth appeared, developing like a Polaroid in my mind's eye until they were as real as they had been in the dim light two months earlier when she had me trembling for the removal of her mammoth panties and a mere plunge away from having my virginal ache tossed into that steamy night. Seconds later, after I declined her offer to go out for pizza, the only woman—huge or otherwise—to ever show a carnal interest in me sprang up from the floor, virtually naked, and ran screaming from my room. I was mortified. A letter slipped beneath my door the following morning confirmed my fears: Our three-week *affaire d'amour* was over.

> *Yes I'm big. I'm very big. But you didn't seem to mind that when people thought you were only tutoring me. You didn't seem to mind that when your lips were pressed against mine, when your hands were all over me and my behind behind closed dorm doors. But when I said let's go to a movie or let's go for dinner, you'd make up excuses about eye irritation or food allergies. Don't think I didn't know why you were making up those lies. Now think about what that says about you as a person. You're a worm, and when you grow up enough to realise that, you'll be grown up enough to realise what you missed out on. So much for bedside manner, Mr. Doctor-to-be.*
>
> *Live and learn—and maybe one day love,*
> *Minnie T.*
> *P.S. At least worms can do it with themselves.*

Minnie knew; her rotundity left me abashed at the thought of publicly displaying our intimate involvement—all that in light of me being one of the most unbecoming people I'd ever met. So why did I lack moral fibre? Was the character chasm between me and, say, Martin Luther King or Moses merely genetic? Or had I been flawed by a series of random, long-forgotten traumas in my formative years? Or was it, God forbid, personal choice? Given a second chance, I would now gladly stand in the Student Union Building or atop Gage Tower Residences and testify to the passers-by, "I am proud to say I am attracted to a very fat woman!" Instead, I am forced to live with both my lack of integrity and a realisation that, despite a childhood filled with Biblical foundation, I would have fornicated without question. But by the grace of God did both my soul and chastity remain intact.

* * *

I succumbed to the empty bed, my erection jostling inside my corduroyed crotch like a rat in a paper bag. "Not again," I moaned to myself in mid-writhe, only too aware of Onan and his spilling of semen. "Yes, again," myself replied weakly. I listened for noises outside of the room. All was still. Glancing at the Zoology textbook on my desk, I unzipped my pants, closed my eyes and recalled Minnie's rambling rump. Within seconds I had taken her from behind like a wide-eyed kid riding a two-wheeler for the first time, cautiously peddling, low on the banana seat. Urged on by her sighs, I ventured ever nearer some imaginary G-spot that I knew in reality I would never find. Suddenly consumed with self-hatred, all I could do was apologise to her in spirit for both my lack of integrity and lack of endowment. Then again and again and again and again and again . . .

Winded, I lay silent for a moment before reaching my arm to the back of the bed for a towel. Catching a glimpse of my forehead and eyes in the closet mirror startled me. I sat up, examined arms, skin and hair so ashen and gaunt all I could think of were POWs. Could I be gravely ill? In a fit of denial I snatched the dictionary off the floor, took a deep breath, sat down on the bed and formulated an all-night study plan. Step one, I decided, would involve looking up key terms and fully reviewing my lecture notes. Step two would be text analysis. Step three would be write the exam. Then, aside from the Medical Collegiate Admissions Test (MCAT) which was still two days away, I'd be finished with memorising information that in no way pertained to life as it is lived. Moreover, I'd be back within reach of my dream: to try and aid the world through scientific discovery. I opened the dictionary and looked up *invertebrate*.

1: Lacking a spinal column.
2: Lacking in strength or vitality.

My stomach cramped. I closed the dictionary and whimpered—and what happened next can only be described as pathological. I sprinted out of the dorm, down six flights of stairs, out into the open air and all the way to the parking lot, and before I could compute I found myself in my old Datsun 510, rattling out of the endowment lands towards the city centre with an exhilaration comparable to that which a child would feel sneaking out in the middle of the night and somehow winding up at Disneyland riding the Matterhorn. I gazed at the neon lights and the domed stadium, passing cars and prostitutes, the winds of freedom bursting through my window. I recalled my freshman year when a gang of ne'er-do-wells dragged me from my desk to the Town Pump—my first and still only visit to a night club—to see three bands I can't forget despite all efforts; Skin The Green Monkey, Terminally Dead and Peachfish. The end result was hearing loss lasting the better part of a week and a contempt for University of British Columbia engineers that remains to the present day.

But despite all that, as if by destiny or maybe like a car accident victim whose only catharsis is to get back in a car and drive, there I was again. I opened the door and peeked in. To my surprise, the barrage of guitar noise and the turbulent sea of bobbing heads that had attacked my senses two-and-a-half years earlier had since left. Canned music drifted from speakers barely loud enough to make conversation difficult. The tables were empty. The dance floor was bare. I took a seat to the side, rebelliously dropped my feet upon another, and watched the band set up. What was I doing? It was adventuresome, yes. But practical? I had an exam in less than twelve hours. Contemplating leaving, my guilty pangs were soon alleviated by an awareness that visits of this sort (i.e. into the urban underworld) could well enhance my bedside manner in the coming years. I ordered a beer like it was my nature to do so.

SMEGMA BOMB! was the band's name, as indicated by those words splattered in black capital letters across a pukey green backdrop. On stage was a psychedelically painted chest of drawers with a bedside lamp on it. I observed the guitarist and the drummer in what appeared to be an impassioned tête-à-tête—perhaps, I thought, on the subject of unusual time signatures or musical rhythms from the Middle East.

Right then the guitarist threw a quick jab that snapped back the drummer's head and left him clutching his nose with both hands. The bass player turned around, yelled in what sounded like Japanese, and attempted mediation. The guitar player kicked over a cymbal stand, spat and turned away. The bass player walked over and picked it up as the drummer let go of his nose and pulled out a set of sticks. He pointed at the guitarist while exchanging with the bass player what appeared to be words of disgust. Then the bass player stepped into the red spotlight at the front of the stage and to a house empty save a scattering of employees mumbled into the microphone something indecipherable. I smiled, stunned, intrigued—at first unsure. But the more I looked, the more it was clear: The bass player *was* Eric Winlaw, a high-school Drama classmate known predominantly for reciting defeatist yet joyful lyrics against the backbeat of bongos and bass in the cafeteria during lunch hour. Being a poetry enthusiast myself, I had always found his expression courageous if uninspiring. Most meaningful, however, was the fact that although we had never engaged in dialogue per se, Eric's gestures to me in the form of glances and one-liners had always been friendly.

As it turned out he was the band's lead vocalist, too, and for forty-five minutes howled as though shot in the leg. The drummer and the guitar player were equally discordant and I found myself wondering how music had come to this: from Gregorian chants to the troubadours to baroque, classical and, finally, horrible noise. It was like anti-evolution, and I wondered if perhaps Homo sapiens *wasn't* natural selection's cherry on top after all. Could we be just the latest thing, as opposed to the best thing? Then the drummer toppled backwards off his chair, the band came to an awkward halt and I lost my thought. One song and a brief argument later, they were finished. I approached the stage and nervously tapped Eric on the leg. He looked down and smiled.

"Shelby," he said. "Drama 11. Dug poetry. Couldn't act."

"Wow. I . . . I'm amazed and touched. No one remembers me from high-school."

"I got a thing for faces," he said. We looked at each other until uncomfortable. "You play any guitar?" he asked.

The question surprised me. "Do . . . um, actually, a little."

"Cool haircut."
"Thank you."
"You want to play with us?"
"What?"
"Guitar. You want to play?"
"I'm . . . I'm a novice."
"Don't matter, it's a look thing."
"What about him?" I asked, pointing to the guitar player across the stage.
Eric didn't turn around. He moved in closer to me. "Get this, man," he said, his voice low but escalating steadily. "We're just about finished our damn demo and we've got a couple o' gigs lined up and the dick-head decides he's going to quit and pursue a solo project . . . a *solo* project! Ladies and gentlemen, Mr. Peter Gaaaabriel. What an *ass*hole!" Eric rolled his eyes, smiling. "I gotta pack up. Think about it, okay?"
"I will."
"Hey, we're gonna party later. You wanna tag along?"
I looked at my watch. The Zoology exam was nine and a half hours away and I knew at least five hours of intense study time would be necessary to achieve a first-class score. That left four hours of empty time. I had never actually *partied* before. I pictured my sunken eye-sockets, considered my reclusive behaviour of late and concluded a little camaraderie could only help my concentration. "I'd like that," I said.

* * *

"Shel," a voice said, waking me up. I turned my head to see Eric standing over me, smiling, his right eye bruised and swollen, blood caked around his nostrils. It was daylight outside, and I was lying fully clothed on the floor of an apartment I barely recognized. The smells of beer and cigarettes were pervasive. "Can you play with us Monday?"
"What happened to your face?" I asked, loosening my tie.
"A left hook," he said with a laugh. "So what do you say, man? Monday. The Cruel Elephant."
"Guitar?"
"You said you would, man."
"Eric, I hardly know any chords."
"'Do you know E?"

"Major?"
"Cool. Most o' the tunes are a droning E thing. How 'bout G?"
"I know it, but my pinky—"
"A?"
"The one on the second fret?"
"You got it. D?"
I grinned. "Anyone can do D."
"Great. You're in." He thrust out his hand. "Welcome to SMEGMA BOMB!"
My stomach flipped.
"What's wrong?"
"I feel queasy. I think I overdid it last night."
"Oh yeah. That homemade shit'll kick anybody's ass, man."
"*Oh God.*"
"Brutal, eh?" he said, smiling.
"Oh sweet Jesus, no."
"Are you gonna throw up?"
"What time is it?"
Eric pulled a watch from his pocket. "Ten to eleven."
I sprinted out of the apartment and down a creaky set of stairs before stopping at the bottom, my body twitching, my eyes rimmed with tears of disbelief. It was too late. I sobbed several times before rearranging the keys in my front pocket which were digging into my groin. A piece of paper flicked out and floated to the ground. I picked it up and through blurry eyes read: *LUCY 734–7138*. I staggered back up the stairs. The door was still open. Eric hadn't moved.
"What was that all about?" he asked.
For fear of breaking down I didn't face him. "I've missed my Zoology final," I said shaking, "the infrastructure of my existence is crumbling before my eyes." I felt a numbness in my fingertips. My head dropped.
"Take a deep breath."
"I fear the blood-dimmed tide. Alcohol has ravaged my dreams. Innocence is lost."
"Say what?"
I couldn't respond.
He tilted his head over my shoulder to read the note in my hand. "Who's Lucy?"

"I don't know," I said feebly.

"Yeah, *right*," he said, slapping me in the arm, "and I got a dick the size of a mutant zucchini." I looked up. He had a wide, goofy grin on his face.

"What?"

"Who is she?"

"Who?"

He shook his head, smiling like a proud father. "You dog," he said.

II

> *For there is no real education that does not respond to*
> *felt need; anything else acquired is trifling display.*
>
> —*Allan Bloom*

"All you gotta do is lie, man," Eric said over coffee at Joe's Cafe that afternoon.
 "I'm not going to lie."
 "Then it can't be that important, man."
 "Education is everything, Eric; my calling, my friend—social justice incarnate is what it is."
 "Well tell 'em you . . . you . . . were saving seal pups and you broke a snowshoe or somethin'."
 "I can't *lie*."
 "Everybody lies! You're twenty years old."
 "Age is no excuse. Life awaits us all at every moment. Am I up to the task? Are *you*? That is the question, my friend. For whom does the bell toll? The bell tolls for thee."
 "Look, you missed the test. You tell 'em a lie. You take it again. You get into med school. End of story."
 I stood up, pulled a two dollar bill from my pocket and threw it on the table. "I must go study."
 "So you're just gonna scrap it?"
 I shrugged. "It's one test."
 "This mornin' you were ballin' your brains out."
 "Please forgive that outburst. It was utterly inappropriate."
 "So missing the test is no big deal?"
 "All my interviews were favourable. My grades far exceed that required. All that remains is the MCAT."
 "Okay."
 "Moreover, I truly believe honour to be vital in times of social duress."

SHELBY

"It's your call."

"After all, is a man his marks?"

He raised his eye-brows and smiled. "You ain't, that's for sure."

"What have I done?"

"Hey, you don't have to convince me. One stupid test. So what?"

There was an ache in my chest. "What the hell have I done?"

"Nothin', man. You—"

"What in God's name have I done?" My head flew back and crunched against the wall. I staggered.

Eric grabbed my arm. "Easy."

"Academic *suicide*!" I cried. "That's what I've committed. I feel like Oppenheimer!"

"Hey, it's just a test. Remember? So what?"

"I feel possessed by foreign beings!"

"Take a deep breath, man. Your eyes look funny."

"Why? . . . *Why?*"

Eric put his arm around me. It was soothing. "Hey," he said softly, "it's okay. Take it easy. It's just one day."

I could barely stand.

"Sit down," he said.

I did; and began talking—a startling confession that rolled us out of the afternoon, through dinner and into the early evening. I found myself requesting my own ambitions, my *raison d'etre*, God's hopes for humanity. Moreover, I responded to these questions with answers I was theretofore unaware of feeling. Even the true value of post-secondary education and the motives of my parents' involvement—and in this way their aptitude—came under scrutiny. Only my destiny-filled dreams of contributing to an ailing world remained constant.

Eric chuckled. "You got some sort o' plan?" he asked, snuffing out his cigarette in an ashtray filled with a half dozen stubs.

"Medicine can open up a lot of windows."

"What can't?" he said, standing up, zipping his leather jacket and tossing a crumpled ten dollar bill on the table.

"But, Eric, medicine is the only scientific study of the human being that can be taken to all the world. A gift for the masses that makes some order of this seemingly wacky wonder."

Eric stopped smoking in mid-inhale. "Wacky wonder?" he

said, laughing uproariously. "You sound like Bruce Cockburn."

"Laugh all you want. You wouldn't be here if it wasn't for penicillin or any number of medical innovations. And that's where I come in." I stood up. "I may be unsure of many things, Eric, but I know that academia—or, if you will, thirst for knowledge—is what I do; what I *am*—a yearning I believe to be God-sent."

"Shel," he said, "I hate to be a party-pooper but the big boom is over, man—all the romantic discoveries like insulin and all that are done. AIDS is out o' control. The Renaissance is finito. Syphilis is such a mild disease nowadays we *hope* we get it. Big business is it, man. There's too much cash in the death trade. Politicians have sold us out. We're born too late. The ozone is a piece of Swiss cheese. A degree won't get you a job making toilet seats."

"Eric, that is ludicrous . . . and the only reason I don't just get up and walk away is because I, too, have lately felt fleeting moments of impotence and . . . uncertainty."

He chuckled. "Hey, I didn't say that. I'm happy. I just think we've blown it, that's all."

I shook my head. "How can you believe that and still say you're happy?"

"That's the kind o' guy I am."

"That kind of happiness can't last. You *have* to know why."

"Jesus, man, loosen that tie before your head blows off. Slide a little."

"To what end? Further spiritual decay?"

"Hey, man," he said, "it's you serious types who make the atom bombs, not some loser kid popping qualudes. I have yet to see a fun lovin' politician anywhere, anyhow."

"Well, naturally, it's a difficult job."

He grinned. "Man, I can't wait to see you on stage tomorrow night. Rock 'n roll's gonna kick your ass!"

"Oh . . . uh . . . about the concert, Eric, I don't think—"

"Oh no you don't," he said, "it's just a few power chords. Anyway, you can't say no, Mr. Worldsaver. You owe me for today."

"I can hardly play."

"Oh I get it. You're only into helpin' out the *Third* World."

"It's not that. I just . . . I'm extremely busy right now."
"Bull*shit*," he said, lighting another cigarette. "You'd play if I was some starvin' Biafran and you know it."
"That's absurd."
"I don't think you walk your talk, man."
"What does that mean?"
"It means I don't know if I'm buyin' what you're sellin',"
"I'm not selling anything."
"It means I think you're full o' crap."
"Okay, I'll play."
"You will?"
"Yes."
"I take it all back. You're a man o' your word. Cigarette?"
"Um . . . no thank you. I don't smoke."

* * *

Having dropped Eric at his apartment, I returned to my own hovel feeling dazed. Further reflection convinced me that missing the Zoology final may well have been a sign of my growing dissatisfaction with the current state of higher education. Nonetheless, it was after ten P.M. and I knew that if I was to ever leap beyond Bachelor of Science intellectual psychobabble and be granted a position where I could truly delve into methods of solving general social dysfunction, a fine result on the MCAT was imperative. Moreover, I had been procrastinating and I loathe such practices. I took the guidebook from my desk, picked up a pencil off the floor, turned on my bedside lamp and read:

SECTION 2: SCIENCE PROBLEMS
Time: 1 hour 20 minutes

Directions: In this section, descriptive material precedes a set of four (4) related questions. For each question, use the descriptive material and your knowledge of science to determine the best answer . . .

I woke up half a day later, 11:18 A.M., with the sun streaking across my room, the study guide spread open on the floor, my bedside lamp still on and my body fully clothed. My teeth were caked. I was sweaty. The window was dripping with condensation. Pulling the piece of paper with Eric's phone number out of my front pocket, the piece of paper with Lucy's number fell out, too. I phoned Eric and got his answering machine message advertising the concert at The Cruel Elephant Monday night. A surge of adrenalin surprised me. I picked up my acoustic guitar and commenced playing, occasionally imagining an ocean of perhaps 70,000 bobbing heads, mostly women, chanting my name in abandoned unison.

By the time I broke for a dinner of cream crackers and cheese that filled my bed with crumbs, my knowledge of Henle's Loop remained fragmentary but I'd conquered Gordon Lightfoot's "Pussywillow Cat-tails" at half speed and A Major had lost some of its muffled sound. From then until slumber deep into the early morning hours, my only interruption was Eric's phone call confirming band practice at two P.M. Other than that I was lost in a stream of notes assembling in such a way as to resemble familiar pop songs of the past two decades. Most delightfully, I was the one playing them.

* * *

Arrival at the rehearsal space the following afternoon found my enthusiastic mood in contrast with the rain and the warehouse complex that spread out before me like a sepia photograph of some closed-down American factory in the Depression. I was fifteen minutes early, and the main door was locked. Knocking received no response. Stepping back into my Datsun 510, I attempted with electrician's tape to curb water flow through the sunroof—an endeavour that made matters worse.

About a half hour later a rusty white mafioso-type Pontiac Parisienne with tinted windows pulled up beside me. Out stepped a wooly mammoth of a man—hold the hair—in a jean jacket, Lycra azure sweat pants and a pair of battered brown penny loafers. He surveyed the surroundings as would a King his castle. He had a crewcut and an earring. Thinking he might be involved with drugs and fearing a random knife wound, I slid down in my seat and remained inconspicuous, visualizing his jiggly buttocks lined up through a rifle scope on some African plain in the middle of a monsoon; one bull's-eyed tranquilizer dart from 200 yards and down he'd tumble.

I even imagined the net he'd be placed in being hoisted up by helicopter and escorted to the nearest zoo in Tanzania. I chuckled and stayed low.

Finding the door locked, he edged a few feet to his right, pulled down his sweat pants and urinated on the wall. Hearing footsteps I turned to see Eric running up the road with a guitar in each hand, his trench coat flipping in the wind. Instinct beckoned me to warn him of danger but my head froze at the thought of cross-fire.

"Bryan!" Eric yelled, face grinning, a soggy looking cigarette dangling from the corner of his mouth.

The man, still peeing, turned to Eric. "The door's locked. It's raining."

Eric broke stride. "I know. Hey, man, thanks for coming on short notice." I stepped out of my car. Eric turned to me. "Hi, Shel," he said, out of breath and soaked. "I brought you a guitar. Amps are inside."

"The door's locked!" Bryan cried again, startling me. He pounded his fist against the wall.

"Bad boy, Bryan," Eric said with a smile while pulling a key from his pocket. He shook his head like a wet dog and introduced us while turning the lock.

"It's a pleasure to meet you," I said, extending my hand, "I don't recognise you from the Town Pump."

"Bryan wasn't—"

"Shelly?" Bryan said. "What kind of name is Shelly?"

"Shelby."

"Leave him alone, Bryan," Eric said. "The guy's a genius."

"Then why's he wearing that *fag* tie?" he said, staring as though daring me to respond. I felt my chin quiver. He laughed in my face. We went in and set up.

The rehearsal was nerve-racking. I'd never used an electric guitar before and its heaviness made it cumbersome. Ironically, the strings were more easily pressed down than on my acoustic. Nonetheless, my back ached. Amidst a ruckus that sounded more like a mob of Arabs burning an American flag on the evening news than music, I became plagued with apprehension. Is civility possible in an uncivilized world? How had I allowed myself to be manipulated into playing the music that I loathed? Moreover, was my weakness any different from that seen in many Germans during the late 1930s? Finally, beyond Gran, Mom, Dad and my brother Derek, was it true that I had no friends?

My questioning ended upon hearing a song called "Sally Jean Won't Eat Meat"—in my opinion Eric's only melodic creation. It began with a rambling slur of angry words that burst into bloom with Eric at the apex of his range singing, *Sally Jean Won't Eat Meat* to which Bryan and I replied chant-like, *Oh wo, no she won't*. Eric would then bookend the chorus with, *But she's got legs up to her hips and red and ready lips*, and so on. Humiliating as it is to admit, I found the jaunty, infectious feel libidinous—and demanded we play it again.

Back at the dorm later that evening, with my ears ringing and my head deep into my MCAT study guide, it occurred to me that I'd be returning home to Revelstoke after the MCAT and the Monday concert; back home to await the acceptance response from my medical school application, back home for long talks with Gran and Mom and hours of indulgent, reflective reading, back home for a four-month stint as ditch-digger for Uncle Larry, a man who hates everything but God.

Larry's perception of the universe revealed itself some fifteen years ago, shortly after his wife ran off with his business partner. My Dad, being Larry's brother, invited Larry to move in with us to get support during his time of crisis. We were of little help. Larry, being Christian, had views that clashed with my family's, also Christian. Almost from the day he arrived he started having religious visions by night and come breakfast he'd insist on sharing them with the family. As a six-year-old, I was enthralled. His most frequent caller was Mary Magdelene, and with her visits came short parables loosely based on her salvation from harlotry. At the outset Mom and Dad were tolerant, but with the arrival of Matthew, Mark, Luke and a fourth apostle named Edward Longshanks (who turned out to be a 13th century British King), support diminished.

"It's not healthy, Ed," Mom said, nodding her head towards my older brother Derek and me after Uncle Larry had removed himself from the breakfast table for his ritual half-hour morning movement that would leave the bathroom inaccessible for another thirty minutes thereafter. "And he's getting more and more like your father—and what's he doing in the bathroom that takes so long? Waiting for the second coming?"

"Don't joke about that, Peg. Obviously he's blocked up—and don't bring my old man into this! He's dead, isn't that enough?"

"Larry has no business saying you're on a one-way train ride to hell for reading out the morning horoscope—especially in front of the kids. You've given him a roof to live under, for crying out loud!"

Dad became defensive (guilt-riddled, according to Mom, over having battled with his own father a year earlier only to have him meet his demise before amends had been made). "He's my brother, Peg. He's harmless. You think I'd let him hang around the kids if he wasn't?"

"I guess we'll have to wait and see . . ."

Sometime thereafter came the command from God.

To this day I'm unclear on the details, but I do know a nude Uncle Larry ransacked Mom and Dad's bedroom one night, standing between their separate beds bellowing about redemption and the sins of our household while throwing paintings, photographs, top drawers and, finally, a lit match into a pile on the floor. Dad, so legend has it, after getting out of bed and putting out the fire, stunned Larry with three or four slaps to the head and physically tossed him from the house with a sarcastic promise to write. My recollection is one of terror, partly from the screaming but moreso from the possibility of losing both parents to the hell-fires. I was discovered the following morning, asleep in my closet.

It was two years before we heard another word about Uncle Larry. Late one summer evening we got a call from the Edmonton City Police saying Larry's landlord had found him huddled naked in the corner of his apartment, sweating, the blinds down, gnawing on his own arm.

Uncle Larry wound up in an asylum where he remained for three and a half years—upholding our family's tradition of mental illness. Upon release he preached that only his undying love for God got him through the ordeal (Gran added: The four meals a day, laxatives, sponge baths, a private room and a colour T.V. couldn't have hurt). Repercussions from the arm chewing included sensation loss in his fingertips that to the present leaves his handwriting illegible, the result being banking dilemmas everytime I attempt to cash my monthly summer paycheque. Whenever he can, which is whenever I work for him, Larry reminds me there is a Hell.

* * *

Despite feeling fluish after an all-night study session, my exam adrenalin flowed full throttle as I sat in the auditorium at 8:30 Monday morning and awaited the start of the Medical Collegiate Admissions Test. There were no disrupting thoughts of Minnie T. or Uncle Larry or SMEGMA BOMB! or any other of life's trivialities. Nay, my brain felt poised and clear.

The first dozen questions, general chemistry, were as challenging as chit-chat in a home for senior citizens. By nine-thirty I'd stumbled a few times, but my overall performance exceeded expectation. It came as a surprise when the examiner yelled "Stop" at 10:20. I raised my head to see a room full of would-be doctors seemingly more at ease than tourists tanning in the Galapagos Islands. Panicked, I oozed a cold sweat and pencilled in the last forty blank computer ovals at random.

The situation worsened with Section II. I had become a victim of intellectual paralysis: this time by the ticking clock, performance anxiety, a repulsion for small print and a coughing fit that lasted over fifteen minutes.

For lunch I threw up.

We were back slogging by one and by two I was bored—a boredom that soon turned to agitation. I was fed up answering questions that in no way pertained to the world at large. Disgruntled, I finished the last few questions of the section and slammed down my pencil. Without forewarning intestinal spasms twisted my insides. I groaned, rambling hunched over, clutching my sides, to the front desk where the examiner sat reading *The Globe and Mail*. He tilted back his dandruffed head to reveal the darkest rings-beneath-eyes I had ever seen. His nose twitched rabbit-like.

I held out my exam. "Sir, I know we're not allowed to leave the audit—"

"Hold it, young man."

SHELBY

"Yes?"

"I've noticed you throughout the day *grunt*ing and *groan*ing."

"Pardon?"

"Flipping your pencil. Shaking your head, miserable with life."

"Sir, I assure you it's not—"

"Do you realise that Newton uncovered his fabulous laws only *after* having left Cambridge to avoid the plague?"

"Sir, my stomach—"

"Did you know Einstein formulated his theory of relativity *without* the aid of a laboratory or university post?"

"Please . . ."

"Twenty-seven years ago I stood exactly as you do today," he said, impassioned, his halitosis just then reaching my olfactory glands. "Pasty faced and unpopular and yet yearning to contribute . . . and yet I acted *not*."

My bowel gurgled. "Sir?"

"You adore poetry, don't you?"

"Yes."

"You like William Blake, correct?"

"He's one of my favourites."

"I knew it. Whitman?"

"How do you know all this?"

"It's in your face, your eyes—now go! Pick up the Upanishads, the Koran, the Bible! Read them as myth! James Joyce! Dante! Aldous Huxley! Let it move you!"

"Sir, I'm intrigued but I have to—"

"You have to *throw* down that exam and run far away from this dilapidated sanatorium!" I didn't move, petrified by the panic in his eyes. "Look at these wrists," he cried, turning over his hands to reveal zigzags of scar tissue.

"Good Lord."

"Look me in the eyes!" I looked. "Look me in the *eyes!*"

"I'm looking."

"Can you see yourself?"

"Not in this light."

"You came up here wanting to break from the constraints, didn't you?."

"Actually—"

"Dammit, man, act on your instincts!" He yanked at my shirt and twisted me towards the class. Students looked up, curious at the commotion. "Dead," he said. "All of them."
I turned to the man. "Sir, I—"
"Go! Before the chance is gone!"
"But I haven't finished the exam."
"Lead our children!"
My bowels rumbled. "Sir, I really—"
"Will you be that man?"
"I—"
"Go!" he cried, head dropping forward, wrists flat out before me.
"I'm going . . . but not . . . I have to . . . my bowels . . ." I turned, staggering towards the exit, all eyes upon me. Would I be *what* man? they wondered. Heart cracking in my chest, head spinning with confusion, I dashed into the men's washroom, undoing my corduroys in transit, and crashed into the nearest stall, relieving myself upon landing. My sweaty head dropped into awaiting, trembling hands.

It was awhile before my bowels were emptied. Pushing myself up, dizziness caused my eyes to close. The man's horrific wrists reappeared. How did he know of my fondness for Blake? What right did he have to unload his past blunders on me? especially with the final section of the MCAT still remaining. I pushed the stall door open, revealing myself to a wall of mirrors. Before me I saw misery, confusion and a fiery boil on the forehead of a man who believed that one person *could* alter the shape of history for the better. And the question lingered: Would I be that man?

* * *

I never went back to the auditorium. I returned to my dorm and slept. And later that night, bewildered and frightened, I arrived at The Cruel Elephant to find Eric gulping hard liquor at the bar. He was distraught over SMEGMA BOMB! not getting a sound check because the doors letting in the public had already opened. He was convinced the last band to set up had intentionally stalled.

"Those bastards'll be sorry, man, when they're tuning my guitbox backstage and bringing me fan mail," he said, spraying my face with soggy consonants. "And if that never happens . . . well fuck 'em then . . ."

Four hours and three bands later I was sitting on the edge of the stage shaking. Bryan was slack-jawed and asleep at a table at the back and Eric was crumpled at the bar in an alcoholic haze. It was ten to one and the place was barren. A staff member approached the stage and sat down beside me.

"Listen pal," he said, "I know you guys have been waiting all night to play. But, you see, the thing that makes *rock* really *roll* is the crowd . . . take a look around." He looked around. I looked around. "If there's no one here . . . there ain't no show." He shrugged his shoulders. "So what say we pack up this little Woodstock right now and get the hell home?"

"Rock and roll's got nothing on poetry," I replied.

Suddenly Eric came hurtling towards the stage with his swollen face and his fist thrusting skyward. In a horrible English accent he shrieked: "We are carrying the torch of rock 'n roll! The show must go on! *Anarchy*!" He slipped and fell, badly bruising his thigh. We played. We were awful. And all the while nobody knew that Shelby Lewis, scholastic prodigy, perhaps only in his own mind, was a university dropout.

III

*Surely some revelation is
at hand.*
—W.B. Yeats

By five-thirty the following A.M. as the sun rose outside my window like a flashlight behind a gray sheet, I had packed all of my belongings into four boxes and was startled at how easily I could tie up my life. Pulling the cap off a Jiffy Marker, I scrawled on the wall above my desk:

> IT IS RIGHT IT SHOULD BE SO
> MAN WAS MADE FOR JOY AND WOE
> AND WHEN THIS WE RIGHTLY KNOW
> THROUGH THE WORLD WE SAFELY GO
> —WILLIAM BLAKE

I shrugged and smiled. Gazing out the window, I took a final survey of the campus that had come to be home over nearly three years of toil—good years all in all. The streets were barren save a scattering of crows and the occasional car pulling in or out; the tennis courts were wet, the Student Union Building was dappled in fog. I touched the pane like one would gazing through plexiglass at an imprisoned lover. The coldness on my fingertips was soothing. Goosebumps sprouted across my forearms. I shivered, then lay back on my bed and quietly masturbated in my dorm cot for what I knew would be the last time. Minnie was involved.

I arrived at Eric's apartment just after seven. The door was unlocked. I put my belongings in the corner of the front room and stood there, warmed with sadness—if that's possible. Eric wasn't up yet and I doubted he would be for a few hours. The place was ripe with beer and cigarette odours. I went into the

kitchen to make a cup of coffee but couldn't find any. I scoured through the cupboards for something to nibble on and ended up settling for a glass of water. I went back into the living room.
"*Shelby?*" said a croaky voice.
Startled, I turned my head to see Eric peeking his head out from the hallway. "Hi Eric!" I was happy to see him.
"What are you doing here?" he said stepping into the room. He was in his underwear and surprisingly muscular. He appeared concerned.
"Oh . . . dear God," I said, just then realising what I had done. "I forgot to ask you if—"
"What the hell are you doing here?"
"Um . . . I was in desperate need of lodging and I remembered you had mentioned that your Dad had moved out—"
"Boozed out," he said.
"I'm sorry—"
"Missed three rents. Last I heard he was in the Yucatan selling sandals."
"I . . . didn't . . . I'm sorry about all that. But I've got some news of my own. I didn't tell you at the concert. I've quit university."
"*What?*"
"It's true. And now I'm in extreme need of shelter until I can ramble up a few coins and establish permanent lodgings elsewhere."
"You quit?"
"I'm sorry I didn't call. I don't know what's come over me lately."
Eric rubbed his eye, sighed, and reached down the side of the couch, pulling it out into a bed. "You can sleep here," he said, giving it a wack. Dust mushroomed up in a cloud of mildew.
"Really?"
He walked away. "Yeah."
"Eric?"
"Yeah?"
"Thank you."
He turned around. "Straight up, Shel, are you a fag?"
"Homosexual?"

"I thought so."

"I'm not! In fact I find the whole concept unnatural and . . ."

"Look, man, what . . . I just . . . there's just something about you. My mistake. You got a girlfriend?"

"Not at present."

"Tell me you've been laid."

"I can't. But it's by choice. Abstinence is very common among scholars. Isaac Newton died a virgin."

"So did Fig Newton. What's your point?"

"A man of single-minded pursuit must be true to the call."

"Okay, what's your angle?"

"Angle?"

"Shel, you're built like my ex-girlfriend. You talk like you've got a small house shoved up your ass, you've never been laid and you just B & E'd my apartment. Somethin' ain't right."

"I assure you I am as I appear to be . . . and I didn't *choose* to be an ectomorph. Many a night I've longed for a rippling chest—much as my brother Derek's. As for my breaking in here without calling, I implore your forgiveness."

He grinned. "Look, I'm going back to bed. I'll see you in a few hours. We'll talk rent . . ."

I lay back on the pull-out couch and eyed a stain on the ceiling that was reminiscent of a large fig. Less than a day had passed since I quit school. I was the same person except now the rules were my own. I rolled over and slept.

Popping and cracking sounds from the kitchen woke me up what seemed like minutes later. I peered over the top of the couch. Eric was frying what appeared to be eggs.

"Good morning," I said.

Eric looked over, one hand on a frying pan. "Afternoon," he said back, "how you doin'?"

"Uh . . . Fine . . . you?"

"So you're taking a year off, eh?"

"Hardly. I'm seeking whole new roads. Life is a continuum."

"I thought you said university was your destiny—you want an omelette?"

"You're misquoting me. I was merely referring to the exploits of our greatest visionaries, Newton, Einstein et al., and my desire to contribute to humanitarian causes. I've since

realised destiny cannot be achieved, it can only be experienced. Surely you must have some aspirations of your own?"
"Two-ten."
"Two-ten? What's that?"
"Your rent. I've decided every time you act like an asshole, it goes up ten greenbacks. End of the day I'll give you the total, at which point you can take it or leave it."
"That's extortion. I refuse to change the essence of my personality to get shelter. I'd rather wind up on the streets than succumb to such badgering."
"Two-twenty. So what's it like being an old virgin?"
"Old? Your question is as inane as asking a black person what it feels like having a lot of melanin. It's like asking *you* how it feels having blue eyes."
"Two-thirty."
"Two-thirty. For what? I'm dumbfounded. Your system is Machiavellian. I've booked a room with Josef Stalin . . ."
"Two-forty."
"And I couldn't be happier."

* * *

Much like indigenous peoples throughout the New World who have yet to recover from having their mythology—indeed, their very foundation—slaughtered by the influx of pious Europeans, I, too, had difficulty grasping my new *mode d'existence*. Yes, I still believed my contributions to humanity would be forthcoming. But in the meantime, what was I to do with an excess of leisure time? Where does a free-thinking intellectual go for stimulation? For the first time in my life I found myself absorbed by television; intrigued by soap operas, talk shows and home improvement programs. Not only that, my bed-ridden depression prevalent mere weeks earlier had returned. Only a fear of starving to death urged on a search for part-time employment—a motivation hindered by the alternative fear of becoming trapped into yet another social labyrinth. As for contact with the outside world, I avoided my parents altogether but called Gran on several occasions, confessing to her my dreams and fears without actually admitting to having left university.
" . . . and I saw a Peace Corps commercial that piqued my

interest—sort of a primer in humanitarian causes. Out in the desert digging wells and planting millet and so forth. I wrote the number down."

"Doll, you bruise like a peach . . . you get burned in a well-lit room."

"I could wear a big hat."

"What about school?"

"Oh. Fine. Fine. Why would you ask that?"

"Why would I ask? Last week you tell me the family dream is in . . . what was the word?"

"I believe it was peril."

"That's it," she said, chuckling, "and I didn't even know we had a family dream. Now you're thinking o' signin' up with the Foreign Legion."

"The Peace Corps and school's going fine," I said, ashamed to be lying.

"You sound bored."

"Bored? How could I be bored?"

"Look, Doll, you gotta get out o' that dorm once in awhile and start givin' 'er the ol' Atomic Drop."

"What?"

"Give 'er the figure four leg drop. The pile driver. The half suplex. The body slam."

"What are you talking about?"

"*Life*, Shel. It's like wrestlin'. You gotta get out there and *slam* it. You don't need to dig wells."

"What's wrong with digging wells?"

"Nothing. I just figure that before my little Shelby up and leaves the country he should at least make a few decent friends."

"With all due respect, Gran, this notion of slamming into life head first is at best perilous—what with AIDS and gurus and gangs and drugs. Fact is I'm a little disappointed you're trying to steer me in that direction."

"I'm just trying to help."

"I know that. It's just-"

"Stop thinking so much, Doll. Give your head a rest."

"What's wrong with thinking? I'm a thinker!"

"True. But if it takes away your courage, what's the point? You got no life."

"Thinking does not take away my courage."
"Doll, you never do anything but study."
"I just said I was willing to dig wells in some African hellhole. That's hardly *nothing*. At the very least it's courageous."
"That's true."
"I have a lot on my plate these days."
"I know. You're right," she said, conceding, "and you do have to be careful out there. I keep forgettin' that I was a kid at the turn of the century. Different ball game."
"It's not that I don't appreciate your feedback, Gran."
"I know, Doll . . ."
Denial aside, I hung up knowing Gran was at least partly right. Who was I kidding? I didn't want to dig wells in Kenya. Not only that, I *didn't* do much. Then again, I could hardly be accused of cowardice for not having participated in the boring frivolities of an average twenty-year-old whose idea of fun is sex with strangers and drinking-induced regurgitation. Realising that, my depression deepened.

* * *

Needless to say, days later Gran's advice reared its intuitive head. I had stumbled upon Lucy's number again in the back pocket of my corduroys while doing laundry and, in a rare moment of spontaneity inspired by Gran's attack on my fortitude, ran to a pay phone and dialed without hesitation. A woman answered. After confirming it to be Lucy I introduced myself and detailed to her how I had "Thoroughly enjoyed our brief tête-à-tête at the post-concert soiree two Thursdays ago."
"First off, ass wipe," she said, "I've never heard of you. Second off, I wasn't in town *two Thursdays* ago."
"Wednesday, I mean. Yes, def—"
"Are you one of Frank's buddies?"
"Pardon?"
"Listen, Mac," she said, "maybe I deserve calls like this. Maybe it's the instant karma thing. God knows I'm no saint. But I wasn't in town last Thursday or Wednesday or the Thursday before. What's more, I have a migraine. So please,

do the world a big favour and . . . never mind. Just . . . take your hand off your pud and find a new caller, okay? Fun's up." Click.

I was outraged. How could a woman one night offer me her number and over the telephone a week and a half later deny doing so with the conviction of a Muslim fundamentalist? Suddenly and for the first time I felt truly fearful of my break from academia. Who were these secular people, I wondered, so far from either religion or science—nay, *reality*—that they could lie without flinching?

A phone call from my parents expressing their pride in my academic successes and certainty in my future furthered my downhill slide. I felt like I'd escaped from solitary confinement only to find myself naked in the middle of the Mojave Desert with nothing but a bottle of suntan lotion and a straw hat; there were no lectures, no mandatory reading materials, no fellow seekers, no marks to grade my performance, just me in a rundown front room prostrate on a pull-out couch, paralysed by the state of mankind.

It was in this condition that I came to understand the *pathologically unrelenting urge that exists between the sexes in Western secular society* as what it really is: the side-effect of our loss of wonder with the world at large. I also found out that I was not immune to that loss.

What started out as a bad dream on consecutive nights that the top of my head had been sliced off and converted into a parking lot littered with broken glass and hypodermic needles soon evolved into a condition that made the highlight of my day the freeze-frame ending of the soap opera *Another World*. But nothing was more all-encompassing than a new-found addiction to physical release. The two minute build up was Nirvana; I'd feel vivacious, poised, popular. But the post release letdown was Hell—as were the lonely hours that followed. Denying the urge was equally devastating. Indeed, one battle created such turmoil I experienced a primal flashback.

"Boys like to do it with themselves," Grandfather said. The two of us were fishing, alone, at a creek that I recall only as being greeny. Sweat glistened on his brow, a cigarette dangling between his nicotined fingers. "Always have," he said, "always will." I looked up, strangely concerned for my safety. "Don't do it," he said. "You're a smart boy . . . but idle hands do the devil's work." A sweat droplet rolled off his temple and glided past his bulbous nose as if carrying an urgent message. "Do you understand what I'm talking about, boy?" he asked, dropping a hand on my thigh.

I didn't but I nodded yes.

"I thought you would, you *dirty* kid," he said, moving his face inches from mine. I swallowed and attempted a smile. "Now remember, boy, what I'm gonna tell you. Everytime you pull it, you might as well be pulling God's hair." He squeezed my thigh. "And God gets real mad—I mean God riles up the pits o' *Hell* when you pull His hair!"

That's all I remember.

* * *

It was a rainy late afternoon when Eric returned home to find me prostrate once again. It had been days since I'd had a hearty meal and I had started to suffer from peristaltic shutdown. Not only that, having lost touch with reality, I was communicating by leaving little sticky notes in select parts of the apartment.

"It *stinks* in here, man," he said, crashing into the back of my pull-out couch. As always, the lights were out and the T.V. was on. Eric opened the curtains and stared at me.

Having arrived at the non-talking turn in my cycle of depression, I said nothing.

"What the hell is your problem?"

Flat on my back, a blanket pulled up to my chin, I moved only my eyes in his direction. "Hello, Eric."

"What is it, man? All you do is watch the tube. Are you sick? Your folks? What's goin' on?" I rubbed an eye. "Is it a woman?"

"I'm okay . . . it's Friday, isn't it?"

"Saturday."

"Darn."

"What?"

"I missed the Peace Rally."

"Fuck the Peace Rally! What the hell are you doing with your life, man?"

"Waiting."

"For what?"

"A call."
"From who?"
"God."
"Oh Jesus, Shel . . ."
"I want to contribute."
"Then do something! Christ. You make *me* feel productive." I turned away. "It's a woman, isn't it?" he asked.
"No."
"Your bowels still killin' ya?"
"That's private."
"Private? It's all you talk about!"
"That was when I thought you cared."
Eric laughed angrily. "Look, man, I know it's your life and, frankly, I don't give a flying fuck what you do with it, but you've been a total drag since you moved in."
"I thought we were friends."
"You're very depressing."
"You're my best friend, Eric."
"Shutup." There was a pause. "Look . . ." he said, "if you shower, I'll call a couple of my girlfriends and maybe we can all go for coffee. What do you say?"
I sniffed and turned back to him, feeling strangely calm. "I'm not as smart as my parents think I am," I said.
He shrugged. "Who is?"
"It's a curious feeling to realise you're something other than what they believe you to be."
"Same goes for the kids, man."
"What do you mean?"
"Can you picture your folks moanin' and horfin' and all that? No. But here you are. That's proof enough. They probably suck each other off, too. It's weird out there, man. No one knows anybody. Now get up."
"If we go out would it be considered a four-friend-get-together or a double date?"
"Beats me."
"I'd love it to be a double date."
"I'll see what I can do."
I was touched and my nose ran. I sniffed again. "Thank you for caring in these unclear days."
"Fuck you," he said.

SHELBY

From the kitchen Eric made phone calls, his voice varying between a normal volume and a mumbling whisper. Trying to eavesdrop, I sat up. He walked back into the front room. "The Aristocratic," he said, "ten o'clock, Loretta—you met her before."
"I have?"
"At the party."
"What party?"
"When you missed your exam that night."
"That was when all this madness started!"
"And another girl's coming—Suzanne."
"What's she like?"
"Nice. We leave here at 9:45, we'll take my car. You might have to bus home."

* * *

Tearing down Broadway in Eric's worn out convertible I felt like I wanted to drive forever; bathed in darkness and neon, pals side by side, the wind chilly enough to let us know anything could happen at any moment.

"Relax and be yourself," he said to me as we got out of the car. I appreciated that. "Within reason," he added.

Suzanne and Loretta were there when we arrived and the way they perused me made me wonder what Eric had told them on the phone. We sat in a booth and ordered coffee. Loretta was stereotypically attractive, like she could be one of the blackhaired twins on a Doublemint gum commercial. Suzanne had beautifully expressive hands all covered in silver rings—and the nape of her neck reminded me of velvety Naugahyde. When she told me she was a sculptress my heart jumped. From a purely physical standpoint, 99% of all men would choose Loretta over Suzanne. Not me.

As the evening progressed, Loretta carried the conversation—her most intriguing monologue being fifteen minutes about a steroid user who, on the night she hoped to consummate their relationship, confessed to her that they'd have to wait a couple of months for his testicles to grow back to size. Needless to say, they never made it.

Stories after that paled in comparison and by midnight I was nodding off. Loretta was still talking. Eric sat holding his face up with his hand, dangling a cigarette in his mouth, desperately trying to look interested. Suzanne seemed to be half asleep, too, her head resting gently on Eric's shoulder. I could only watch that and sigh . . .

"Well did you call her?" I opened my eyes to see Loretta in my face. She took a drag on her cigarette.

"Sorry?"

"Lucy? The girl at the party. You told me you couldn't wait to."

"Oh! I . . . I misplaced her number."

"Why didn't you tell me? I'm tellin' you a reading with her will blow your f-ing mind."

"Reading?"

"Psychic readings, Shelby. Christ. I told you all about it. You sure acted interested when you were telling me your f-ing life story—paranormal this and destiny that."

"I *was* interested," I said. "Does she do future telling?"

"Probably."

"Like tarot cards and all that?"

"I don't know."

"Ouija boards?"

"I'm not sure—but you'll love it. She's totally hip with the gods—actually, goddesses. She opened me up a lot. Past lives. Where I was blocking."

Eric perked up. "Is she single?"

"I thought you were working on me?" Loretta said with a smile.

"Like a dog," he said. "I'm asking for Shelby." Loretta turned to me. I instinctively fixed my hair.

"She's a lot older—like thirty-five," Loretta said, "and way out there . . . and a real looker. Anyway, I think she's got a beau."

"Yeah, but she ain't met the Shel-man," Eric said, giving me a wink.

Loretta looked at me and smiled. "To tell you the truth," she said sympathetically, "I think she can pick and choose."

I looked at Eric. Then I looked back at Loretta. I adjusted my tie. "I guess that would make me a long shot, eh?" We all laughed.

IV

*There is a splendor in beautiful
bodies,
both in gold and silver and in
all things.*
—St. Augustine

Over the next few days my emotional clouds began to lift. Eric's very appreciated gesture of friendship seemed to be the catalyst towards rejuvenation. Intellectually, I dabbled through secondhand bookstores, picking up literary masterpieces in paperback for anywhere from one to six dollars; poetry collections, Sartre, Yeats, Nietschze and so forth.

After repeated efforts that helped pass away several nights, I finally got hold of Lucy. On the phone she was amicable despite being mildly concerned as to the present day whereabouts of her psychic abilities. I pictured her with straight bangs, hundreds of bracelets, a diamond in one of her incisors and an embroidered full length frock that causes chafing. We made a date for an afternoon reading. I phoned Gran and shared with her my excitement. She was happy for me. I also chiselled away at what it really means to be successful, accepted some of the variables that stop destiny from happening and, finally, warned myself I may lack that *je ne sais quoi* it takes to enjoy life.

I arrived at Lucy's apartment in Kitsilano around ten to three. From the outside her place was inviting; stained wood stairs leading up to the front door and a calico cat sitting upright and sleeping on the window sill, not to mention a selection of potted flowers. I knocked and looked around. There was no answer. Feeling a moistness under my armpits, I loosened my tie. I knew I was there for a psychic reading but I felt like I was showing up for a blind date. I knocked again and heard footsteps. The door opened and the woman, presumably Lucy, just stood there looking at me.

"Madame Sosostris, I presume?" I said, quoting T.S. Eliot's famous clairvoyant just for fun.

"Wrong apartment." The door started to close.

"I'm here for the reading." The door reopened.

"Oh shit."

"Lucy?" I said to an attractive but weary looking woman in ratty jeans, a wrinkled shirt and disheveled hair. There were no bangs or bracelets.

"Yeah . . . sorry . . . I've been in bed with a migraine and I forgot about the reading." She was squinting. The lights were off. "Look, Steven—"

"Shelby."

"Would you mind if we put it off for today? I'm sorry I . . . I'll give you a discount. I just . . . my head . . ."

"Oh . . . uh . . . sure . . ."

"Look . . . uh. . . . you don't want to come in, do you?"

"Inside?"

She shrugged.

"Um . . . sure . . . my mother gets migraines."

"Sons o' bitches! I've tried everything," she said. "Damn things come and go as they please." Lucy led me in and lit a couple of candles. There were books scattered all over the coffee table and on the floor. "Sorry about the mess."

"No problem."

"I have to keep the lights low for my head," she said lighting a candle.

"Wonderful, I love candlelight." I sat down. "So . . . do you dabble in the future-telling aspects of psychic phenomena?"

"You mean tarot cards and that?"

"Yes."

"Nah." She pulled a cigarette from a pack on the coffee table. She put it in her mouth. "Mind if I smoke?"

"No," I said, our eyes making contact. "My father smokes." Lucy exhaled through her nostrils and with one hand pressed on both temples. "Do you believe in destiny?" I asked.

"Is that a line?"

"A line of what?"

"A . . . never mind. Why do you ask?"

"Oh, uh . . . I was just . . . I've been reading about destiny. Hitler, actually," I said, for some reason lying. "He said he felt he was destined to . . . to do what he did. So did Stalin."

She paused for a moment. "The way I see it anyone who really believes his fate is controlled by destiny—the man of destiny idea—has to be seriously screwed up: schizophrenia, dementia, megalomania, something. I mean it's so *grand*iose. Would you like some tea?"

"Uh . . . no. No thank you."

"And *Stalin*? What a shit-dick he was. Ginseng?"

"Uh . . . no . . . thank you."

"I'm going to have a cup. It helps my head."

"Okay," I said, somewhat rattled by her sweeping generalisation and word choice in describing those who are destined. She left the room. On the coffee table were several books I'd never heard of: *The Dancing Wu Li Masters, The Gospel According to Women, A Confederacy of Dunces, If You Find The Buddha On The Street, Kill Him*, among others . . .

Lucy came back with a cup of tea and our conversation moved along at a fine clip. The subject of destiny, though still on my mind, was not brought up again. Our discussion, revolving around poetry and mythology and sprinkled with psychic phenomena, eventually found its way to our own personal spiritualities. I told her about my somewhat strict Protestant upbringing and we joined in laughter over a few stories about Uncle Larry's fanaticism.

"I'm more into a Goddess thing," she said.

"What religion would that be?"

"Just mine."

"Your own?"

"Why not?"

"Well, I'm partial to Christianity."

"Why?"

"Well . . . it has the theme all the way through it, eh? The seed they talk about in Genesis ends up being Christ. I like that. Plus the prophesies."

"Hey," she said grinning, "some of my favourite mystics are Christian. But please forgive me. It ain't my bag. See, when I was a kid I had recurring dreams that *I* was a Goddess."

"What?"

"Weird, eh? I've even had a couple lately, too."
"What do you look like in them?"
She laughed. "Don't get me wrong. I'm not like a Jesus Christ incarnate. It's a feeling, a connection with the all, the earth, an internal sense of divinity, reliant on faith."
"Sounds wonderful."
"Yeah, kinda nice, eh? It just happens and I wake up very relaxed, all my fears up and gone and I lie their praising myself and my surroundings—as opposed to chanting that western female mantra: 'Fuck I'm fat.'" Lucy laughed. "I can feed off it for a couple o' days—no pun intended." I smiled and glanced at her legs.
"Speaking of matriarchs," I said, "I've got a ninety-three-year-old Grandmother who can make me feel that way."
"Cool."
"Sometimes I fear I rely on her too much. She truly seems to believe in *me*—regardless of my failures."
"Ninety-three? I've got past lives younger than that."
"And she's fat but she doesn't care. Actually she's more chubby than fat . . . and you're not fat at all." Minnie was fat.
The afternoon rolled on.

* * *

By the time it came time to leave, three hours had passed and I wanted to stay. Standing in the foyer, Lucy opened the door for me. Light from outside fell upon a poem that was framed and hanging just inside the hall.

> *The valley spirit never dies;*
> *It is the woman, primal mother.*
> *Her gateway is the root of heaven and earth.*
> *It is like a veil barely seen.*
> *Use it; it will never fail.*

I felt a tingle at the back of my neck.
"Lao Tsu," she said.
"French?"
"T-S-U," she said, "Chinese."
"Oh," I said, "a haiku." My knowledge surprised her; and with such an impression I left, afloat with the joy of connec-

tion. Closing my car door I let out the longest fart of my life, realising then that I'd been trapping gas for hours. What a relief! It came out like a whoopee cushion, and with the expulsion I think a lot of my university anxiety left, too. It didn't smell much. It was pure methane, assimilating easily with the air in the car. I looked up from my window and saw Lucy standing at her door. I'm sure she wouldn't have heard it. I smiled and waved. She did the same.

That night, a newfound self-respect deterred me from acting on my physical urges. Unfortunately, having used the device as a night time soother since leaving school (and occasionally before), I was unable to nod off. Instead I sat muzzled on my pull-out couch with tender thoughts of Miss Lucy Moon; sage, beauty, friend. I had real hope for further involvement and nodded off on such thoughts.

"So what was she like?" Eric said, waking me up.
"What time is it?"
"Two-thirty—you dig her?"
"We have similar interests."
"Did you drop your drawers?"
"What?"
"Did you screw her?"
"*Eric*, I went there for spiritual guidance."
"I'm just buggin' you."
"It was purely business."
"Anytime someone does that braille thing with your mind, man, it ain't purely business."
"We didn't even get to that. She had a migraine. However, we've made plans for a second rendez-vous."
"A second meeting?"
"Yes," I said, grinning.
"Damn."
"What?"
"Uh . . . Nothing. I'm sure it'll be fine." He scratched himself and started walking away.
"What?"
"Just watch out for that voodoo shit, man."
"What do you know about it?"
Eric didn't turn around. "Believe me," he said, "I know."
"What do you know?" There was no response.

Needless to say I woke up the following morning feeling like I'd worked graveyard at an all-night convenience store. The day that followed was spent napping, researching psychic phenomena and circling potential jobs in the classified adds. Paranoia left me wondering if Lucy had read my every thought during our previous day's conversation and perhaps considered me an idiot. Could she have known I had destiny illusions of my own?

Over the next two get-togethers conversations with Lucy reached an alarming intensity. Stories were strewn out like war anecdotes in a British pub; bordering on magical, angry yet funny, loving yet painful. Lucy's veritable potpourri knowledge of alternate thought—mythology, psychology, religion—and her continual popping of vitamin complexes and Tylenol 3's made it for me an experience not unlike talking to a smorgasbord. For every hunger I had, she said something to fill it up. On top of all that, she was genuinely interested in what I had to say—a conclusion I drew from her insightful responses. We didn't do a reading. I considered it a stay of relationship execution.

* * *

On a Sunday evening I drove alone to the university and sat on the steps outside the physics building. It started to rain. It started to pour. Fitting, I thought. Two phone calls on Eric's answering machine from my parents asking if my marks had come had left me aware that whatever vision of destiny I still possessed, it could no longer match my parents'. There would be no Nobel Prize in the future. There probably wouldn't be a magic antiserum for world pestilence, either. I understood why, too. So the following day I revealed the reasons, self-deprecating as they were, to Lucy. Why? Because I was feeling like a house fly spinning in a cauldron of beer, torn between drunken bliss and inevitable demise. For as smitten as I was for Lucy, our relationship was *business*—and once the psychic reading was done, reason told me, so was I. So if I had to go, I decided, I'd go with, if not style, honour.

"I have to tell you this, Lucy. I've discovered some things in the last few days . . . about myself that, well, I know what your opinion is of people with destiny-filled ideas; convoluted, megalomaniacal, split personality and so on. Still, I must confess that I, indeed, am one of those people. Yes, all my life I've believed I was preordained to get closer to God through scholarly pursuits or, at least, something of that nature; perhaps I'd discover the AIDS vaccine or find scientific evidence proving the existence of one God."

Lucy laughed. "Christ couldn't even pull that off, Shel."

"Please," I said, firmly raising my hand and avoiding eye contact, "let me finish. When I was in the tenth grade I decided I wanted to add muscle mass to my concave chest—my older brother had a great chest, hair and everything—so I convinced myself to try and do ten push-ups every morning before school. I knew I couldn't do ten. But I knew that trying to do ten would help me do six or seven and I also knew that if I would have set the goal at six or seven, I only would have done four or five. That's human nature. So away I went. What happened? On the third morning of going through the routine, on push-up number two, I heard a popping sound so loud it woke the neighbors. Turns out I pulled what specialists call the rotator cuff—a shoulder muscle known mostly in baseball circles—and to this day I can't comfortably scratch the back of my head. Hence . . ." I pointed at my boney chest.

"You have an itchy head?"

"Don't you see? Big dreams don't pay! I should have learned my limits and never left them."

"That's a *stupid* attitude. You have to have big dreams."

"How big, Lucy? So big they crush your heart when they don't come true?" Lucy laughed. "You find that funny? I don't find that funny."

"I'm sorry, Shel, but as a little kid you figured your destiny was to change the world and at twenty you find out it ain't that simple and you're eaten up over it. That's funny—I mean what the hell did you expect?"

"A shot at it, Lucy. A plan. Something. Not only did I not get anywhere, I never even constructed an idea of *how* to get somewhere. I never had time! It was hard enough getting A's in calculus without the burden of mankind on my shoulders. I should have known I lacked the necessary ingredients; the dream, the plan, the drive and the talent. The four stars. Anyone who's ever made serious social impact, good or bad, has had them; Josef Stalin. Mozart. Hitler. Albert Einstein. Sir Isaac Newton. William Blake. Albert Schweitzer. Maybe even Wayne Gretzky. The dream, the plan, the drive, the talent. Four aces, full house. Four stars. Three star people are capable of a lot, too. Winston Churchill. They can move small mountains. Two star people are terrific with the space left behind. Sylvester Stallone. One star people are useful, but only to others, and only if that one star isn't the dream. If a person possesses no plan, no talent, and no drive, but they happen to have a dream—especially one of absurd proportions—they become, as my roommate so aptly pointed out, a social burden. And with that I offer you . . . Shelby Malcolm Lewis. One star."

"Shit, Shel, destiny is bullshit. Now you're free to do what ever you want!"

"Destiny gave my life foundation. I am now a man without legs."

"Shel, destiny *is*. That's it."

"That's it? Person A ends up on the moon, person B starves to death in Somalia and that's it?"

"Bad luck, mate," she said in an Aussie accent. "Best o' luck next time."

"But don't you see? I've been shafted, too. I wanted to contribute."

"Shafted? Shel, if you don't contribute—whatever that means—it's only because you're a lazy slob."

"You hardly know me."

"So you're not?"

"I just feel I've been—"

"Close your eyes."

"What?"

"Close your eyes."

"Why?"

"Close your eyes." I did. "Now stick out your finger."

"What?"

"Stick out your finger." I did that, too, and Lucy took it in her hand. I felt something smooth and soft. "Do you know what it is?" she said. At first I thought it was her cheek. Then her chin.

"Your chin?" I said.

"Nope," she said. "My cheek."

"I was going to-"

"Guess this one," she said. It was soft again but a little more solid. I thought it might be her forehead or her elbow.

"Your forehead," I said.

"Nope," she said. "My right thumb nail." I didn't mind being wrong. I didn't think right and wrong was the object. "Turn your face to the left," she said. I felt a little pressure on my cheek. I had no idea what it was, maybe a finger or a toe.

"Your finger," I said.

"My nose," she said, "you sure need some practice."

"You mean there are people who are good at this?" Lucy didn't answer. She just kept throwing out body parts until we'd touched about everything to everything; knee to forearm, shoulder to back of the leg, heart to palm of the hand, cheek to eyelash. I was actually getting better at it. Then she told me to use my lips. I felt something soft. It was her earlobe. I guessed mouth. Maybe I was hoping. Then I felt something soft again. Like a finger-tip. I was getting confused—and aroused. I could feel my erection pushing awkwardly in my pants. My tie was uncomfortably tight; I became disoriented, my eyes had been closed for too long. Body parts were flying through my head.

"Um . . . nose," I said, not really concentrating.

"Wrong," she said. "Nipple."

"Nipple?" I said.

"Yeah. Nipple," she said.

I opened my eyes. It took about five seconds for them to adjust to the candle-light. Lucy was sitting in front of me, cross-legged and naked, covering her breasts with her arms. Her clothes were on her lap.

"You're naked," I said.

"And you think that's destiny? Shit, even if God had written you a script like that, his angels would have edited the crap out of it. It's not destiny, Shel. It's life. And what's gonna happen next is a mystery, too. Do you know how bored God would get if he knew what came next? At best he's an understaffed zookeeper. He can't keep up with the calls on his heavenly switchboard. Take a look around, Shel. Have you seen the papers? The world's a mess. L.A. is on fire! Who in his right mind would plan that?"

"A married Baptist couple and their small child came to Eric's door last week and told us all these miseries have been prophesied—preplanned, if you will—and that we should make some quick decisions."

"Oh geez! Converting the terrified. L.A. has burnt to the ground. What does it mean? And we're here. What does it mean? Luck. That's it. And we should be thankful." Lucy stood up in the dim light. She pulled a record out of its sleeve. "It's this week's favourite," she said. "And while L.A. burns, and the Kurds rot, and another woman is raped somewhere in this big ol' land, and Miss J.W. 1992 walks around door to door saying Armageddon is next Tuesday at four, just like her Daddy did twenty years earlier, and while your dreams of destiny go down the fucking tube, I'm going to play it!" All I could see was the shadow of her back. "Because *I like it*." All I could hear was the crackling of what sounded like an old album. The music started playing.

"*Take Five!*" I yelled.

"You know this?" she said.

"Yeah I know it! I love it! Dave Brubeck! My brother loves this genre—as do I, second only to Baroque! Charles Mingus. Miles Davis. Theodore Monk. Charlie Parker. Derek'd sit in his bedroom for hours blowing on his clarinet—or his licorice stick as he'd call it! Ha! He was good, too!" I got so excited I almost forgot she was naked.

"Good," she said, "then lie down." I lay down and Lucy came and lay down next to me. She held out her hand. "To never knowing what's going to happen next!" she said. "Clink."

"Here, here."

"To Shelby Lewis' brush with reality.... Clink." We were really laughing. Lucy put her hand on mine. My heart started beating out like an African rhythm section. My mouth went dry.

"Dave Brubeck," I said nervously, "who would've thought?"

"Who would've thought?"

"You're right Lucy, if I want to contribute, that's up to me."

"Close your eyes," she said, "and imagine making love. Imagine it's the only place you were ever destined to be."

"Okay."
"Imagine it's destiny."
I closed my eyes and we lay there without speaking. After hours of talking, words suddenly lost their significance. I'd never experienced that before.

V

*I went to the Garden
of Love
And saw what I never
had seen*
—*William Blake*

Much to my surprise, after I finally received a psychic reading (a short-lived affair dealing only with the cleaning of my chakras and for which I was not billed and during which Lucy continually complained she was losing the knack), we still continued with our daily visits. It took an evening of wine in excess for me to finally sleep over, and that meant on the front room floor where I awoke fully clothed. There was a blanket on the couch. I didn't recall falling off. The calico cat was on the windowledge. Numbness in my right leg forced a slow ascent. I checked my watch: ten after five. There was a note on the coffee table. I read it while rubbing my thigh.

> *Morning. I went for a walk. Help
> yourself to anything in the fridge.
> Lock up when you leave. Thanks,*
>   *Lucy*

 Lock up when you leave? Was I supposed to go? She made it sound like I was the plumber—and what was she doing going for a walk in a downpour at five o'clock in the morning? Why hadn't she woken me up? I lay down on the couch and waited for her return. My eyelids started to get heavy . . .
 "Hey!"
 I shot up. Lucy was standing by the front room door, drenched and smiling.
 "You moved off the floor," she said.
 "Yes."

"Listen, it's six-thirty and I'm tired so I'm going back to bed for a few hours. You can stay there if you want or you can join me."

"Thank you."

"I'm just going to towel off a little. It's pouring out there."

"Okay." Lucy left the room. I lay back on the couch and listened for her to finish in the bathroom. Nervous as it made me, I decided to join her and got an erection. I heard her walk out of the bathroom. Then I went to the bathroom and took care of general hygiene; brushing my teeth with my finger and a dab of Colgate, wetting down my hair and so on.

I walked to the bedroom and opened the door. It was dark inside and when I closed the door behind me I couldn't see anything.

"It's me . . . Shelby," I said.

"That's what I figured," she said. "You joining me?"

"If that's all right. As a rule I wouldn't bother you but that couch is as stiff as—" CLUNK. "Ow!"

"Are you okay?"

"I stubbed my toe on the—" CLANG. "Aah!"

"What are you doing?"

I fell on top of the covers, grimacing in pain. "I think I've fractured my shin," I moaned. Her hand touched my arm. The pain lessened. I lay there without moving, nervous, trying to inhale.

"You okay?" she asked.

"Yes. Thank you." Lucy reached out and pulled me into a cuddle.

"Destiny sure is giving your leg a tough time, eh?"

"Yes," I said, trying to relax my arms enough to wrap them around her.

"You don't have to keep all your clothes on," she said.

"Oh, yes . . . uh . . . okay."

"But you can if you want to."

"No . . . I think I'd be more comfortable with some of them off." I undressed with minimal movement, aware only of darkness and my erection. I put my right arm awkwardly around Lucy. She gave me a hug. My left arm was crushed and hurting but I didn't say anything. I modified my position and let out a strange sounding, high-pitched grunt.

"You all right?" she asked.
"Me? Yes. Fine. You?"
"Yeah, I'm good. You wearing boxers?" she asked.
"Sorry?"
"Are you wearing boxer shorts?"
"Me? Yes." I said. "You?" It was a dumb question.
"Am I wearing boxers?"
"I mean, do you ever . . . Have you ever worn boxer shorts?"
"Um, yeah, I guess I have. Why do you ask?"
"No reason," I said. There was a pause. "Should I take them off?"
"Do you want to?"
"What do you think?"
"It's up to you," she said, "they're your shorts."
"Yeah, I guess . . . yeah. I'll just see how I feel." I fell out of the hug, bent down to pull them off and accidentally kneed Lucy in the thigh.
"Oops, sorry, I, uh . . . my leg got . . . I . . . sorry."
"Vee have vays of dealing vis people like you," she said in the worst German accent ever. My armpits started sweating. With her hand Lucy caressed my nipple. It was soon erect. She kissed me lightly.
"Are you sure you're okay?" she asked.
"Yes. Thank you." She put my hand softly on her hip. I could feel her warmth. After a few minutes I slowly tried to lift my leg over her.
"Hang on, tiger," she said.
"Oops, sorry, I . . . I was . . ." I was embarrassed. I pulled my leg off. "I didn't mean anything by that," I said. Lucy rolled over, turned on the bedside light and opened the top drawer of her night table. I froze imagining the headlines: GODDESS SHOOTS IDIOT. She turned back with a condom in her hand.
"You okay?" she asked again.
I nodded. "I thought you were grabbing a gun."
Lucy smiled. "You want me to grab a gun, cowboy?"
"Uh . . ."
"Lie down and close your eyes." I did, and felt the covers come off me. Lucy stroked the base of my testicles and I felt a rise inside that suddenly stopped. There was a crinkling of

the condom wrapper. My heart started to throb, as did the rest of me. I couldn't catch my breath. From behind my eyes I saw flashes of light. I could feel the condom on my helmet. My buttocks flexed and my head flew back-
"Uunnhh."
"Aaah!" she shrieked.
"Ooh."
Then laughter.
From Lucy.
Gasping, I reached down and pulled a blanket up and over my face. Then I felt myself: soft, gooey, the condom loose and saggy.
"You okay?" she asked.
"Could you turn the light off, please."
"It's okay, Shel, just . . . just go clean up."
"No," I said, "I'm fine, thanks."
"Come on, Shel. It's okay," she said. I remained still, numb with humiliation. "Shel?"
"If you don't mind," I said, "I'd appreciate it if you'd turn that light off, bury your face in the pillow and let me leave without looking at me."
Lucy laughed. "Come on, pull down the blanket," she said, "it doesn't matter."
"I'm going to leave now," I said. "So if you wouldn't mind turning out that light I'll be out of your way." The light clicked, and beneath the blanket the red in my eyes turned to black.
"*Shel*, come on. It's okay."
"I'm sorry," I said. Lucy put her hand on my back just as I lifted my ugly body out of bed. I put one hand on the saggy condom that was loose and floppy. "I'm sorry," I said again, "I'm having a spiritual breakdown of sorts."
"It's okay," she said. "Really." I tried to gather my belongings but couldn't find them in the dark. I stubbed my toe twice, actually pealing off a little skin. Lucy tried to talk me into staying.
"I think it's best if I leave," I said. "If you wouldn't mind, could you, with your eyes closed, turn on the bedside light so I can gather my belongings and then be out of your way." The light went on. "Thank you."

Lucy sat up.

"Aaaah! Close your eyes! This is a moment of grand embarrassment!"

She closed her eyes and fell back on the bed, laughing. "Come on, Shel. You're so overdramatic. You're like Shakespeare in a B-Movie."

"First the unmentionable, and now you're reviewing me."

I went to the bathroom, flushed the condom that stole my virginity, dressed myself, and avoided eye contact with the mirror. I knew what I looked like. Then, from outside Lucy's bedroom door, I apologised again. Her reply, although one of understanding, was muffled with laughter, a fact I found insensitive.

My arrival home was greeted by two people sleeping in my bed. I felt angry and violated. Though tempted, and assuming they were two of Eric's ruffian friends, I considered waking them at knife point—just to let them know Shelby Lewis' pull-out couch would not been taken for granted. Instead, I made a cup of tea and sulked, knowing my first two sexual encounters had been rejection by a fat woman and premature ejaculation into a half-on condom. Then I thought about my financial situation and wondered how close I was to standing on a street corner in a yellow chicken suit doing promotions for a fast food restaurant.

Awhile later Eric sauntered into the kitchen in his underwear. When I looked up he laughed as though a film clip of the morning's condom debacle was playing on my forehead; and before I could comment on his offering my pull-out couch to riff-raff, he was introducing me to his friends, who turned out to be his Uncle Mannfred and his Aunt Carol. They had taken Eric out for a birthday dinner the night before, overindulged, and decided not to drive home. They were friendly. They lived in Surrey. They owned a sausage factory there. It was Carol's father's until he had a heart attack getting out of the bath one morning. Carol's Mom heard a crash and ran upstairs to find him beached and dripping and dead on the cold tile floor.

"Three hundred and fifty pounds," Carol said teary eyed, still lying in my bed. "We tried to get him to lose weight. We

SHELBY

tried but he wouldn't listen. Bacon sandwiches for breakfast, ham and sausages for lunch, steak and eggs for dinner . . ."

In his will, Carol's Dad left Carol a sausage factory and a small collection of antique golf carts. She donated the carts to different country clubs across North America.

" . . . including Pebble Beach and Augusta."

She kept the factory. Eric mentioned I'd been searching for employment. They offered me a job. I took it. Eric suggested I call them aunt and uncle, too. They agreed.

VI

*Misfortune comes from
having a body.*
                                —*Lao Tsu*

It became clear that destiny is for those who are, for better or worse, great. All others are at the mercy of fate. Fate is about everyday little things; spotting a celebrity in a supermarket, getting the car towed, being struck by diarrhoea in an elevator, premature ejaculation. It wasn't having fallen from destiny to fate that scared me. What scared me was not knowing if I'd stopped falling.

* * *

After repeated calls I got hold of Lucy the following morning. She never made mention of the day before. I thought that showed a lot of class on her part. We made another plan for a more elaborate psychic reading. She seemed distant on the phone.
"You okay?" I asked. There was no answer. "Lucy?"
"Yeah?"
"You okay?"
"Yeah. Hey, Shel, do you know how many witches were burned at the stake between 1300 and 1700?"
"Uh . . . five hundred?"
"*Five hundred!*"
"I meant five hundred thousand."
"Try nine million. Nine fucking million. And you know why?"
"Um . . . I'd have to think about it."
"Because they were different. Because they stood up for what they believed in. What that means, Shel, is that if you were dull, if you were subversive, you lived. If you were an

SHELBY

original thinker, you were burned at the stake. Imagine the genetic void of brilliance that was left by that?"
"Hey, Lucy?"
"Yeah."
"About yesterday—"
"Don't worry about it."
"But I—"
"Shit, I'm late! I got to go. Give me a call soon, okay?"
"Lucy, how do you feel about pre-marital sex?"
"Good or bad?"
"I'm asking you."
"I'm really late. Call me."
"When?"
"Tomorrow."

I did. But it was another twenty calls and two days after that before I got hold of her again. I had no idea where she'd been and I didn't ask. It was ten after nine on a gray Sunday morning and I woke her up. She wasn't overly friendly but I was able to wrangle a lunch date at the Alma Street Cafe for later that day. It opened my eyes.

In the middle of pancakes and fruit and muffins and coffee we started talking about God and divine inspiration, and then began name dropping our own heros. My mentioning of William Blake and the episode with Christmas future that took place with the teacher in the auditorium when I wrote the MCAT and then quit school was greeted with enthusiasm—as were all other poetical references. Science did not fare so well.

"Newton?" she said. "He's a total asshole."
"Pardon?"
"Him and his buddies; assholes."

I chuckled and picked up my orange juice. "I think you have him mixed up with someone else."

"I think you do, dick-head. Copernicus, Gallileo . . . Bacon. The Scientific Method. They've sanctioned world rape. They make the Serbs look like fuckin' saints."

"I . . . I don't know what you mean."
"Then don't laugh at me like a dick-head."
"I didn't."
"Let me tell you something, ass wipe. The Scientific Method

is the reason we're twenty minutes from being a fucking fossil footnote."

"Really?"

"Shel, if you solve problem B with experiment A, you better damn well know what C is."

"C?" I said meekly, avoiding eye contact. Lucy's voice had attracted attention throughout the resturant.

"Chernobyl is C."

"Hm."

"The Hiroshima survivors are C. Women with PCBs in their breast milk are C. Frogs with fucked up genitalia are C. The repercussions, Shel. Newton didn't care shit about repercussions."

Our eyes fastened and I became self-consciously aware of both embarrassment over the staring patrons and my loins pulsating in needy throbs at her display of passion. "Crumpet?" was my lame retort.

* * *

After the outburst, the meal actually proceeded along with laughter and affection, and walking back to Lucy's apartment beneath a thin drizzle, I could feel the walls of my heart crumbling as would a small sea port in a typhoon; all protection gone, I surrender. Mount me on the sidewalk.

Sitting on the couch, Lucy laid her hands upon me with the warmth of a faith healer. My eyes filled with grateful tears that I hid. Later, with the blinds down in her bedroom, we lay on her bed and I shook. Her kisses were smokey but I was unoffended; dazed, in fact, to be with a lover that wanted to be there—that wanted me to be there!—that took control. It was also an added bonus to be with an older, beautiful woman—out of my league, if you will. In the turn of a short phrase I was protected, and Lucy was on top of me, offering soothing words of encouragement. Just as the head of my erection touched for the first time a woman's juices, I uncontrollably blurted: "Oh my! I'm about to be taken!"

I was in. It didn't last long but it was magical just the same. In short, I transcended religious guilt and subsequently abandoned all I was worth to the woman I loved.

"You okay?" she said in the dim light.

SHELBY

"Wonderful," I said, unable to unclench my body. Lucy bent down and kissed me before climbing off. We lay in silence; no words, no cigarettes, just breathing. I felt deep empathy for those clowns who have sex without love. I thought of my parents and their separate beds and hoped that my dropping out of school wouldn't hurt them too much. I thought of Gran and how much I loved her. I thought of Minnie and wished her well. I thought about Derek and his well-defined chest. My condom started slipping off so I reached down and held it on. Lucy suggested we shower. I agreed, wholeheartedly in voice, tentatively in spirit, and let her get out of bed first for fear of having her gander at my boniness. She turned on the light. Never had I seen her naked in a well lit room before. She had a remarkable body.

I followed her into the bathroom (about a minute behind) and turned off the light. We didn't make love in the shower. In darkness I loofahed her back.

"Lucy," I said, "I'm embarrassed to say this but your body is well sculpted."

Lucy laughed. "What does that mean?"

"Statuesque."

"Well . . . it pays the rent."

"What does that mean?"

"I'm a dancer."

"I didn't know that."

"I thought I told you."

"I thought you were a psychic."

"I'm that, too—about once a month and fading. But I pay my rent dancin'."

"You leave me perpetually amazed. First accepting me into your fold. Now you're telling me you're a diva . . . a ballerina."

"Actually a stripper," she said.

"A stripper?"

"Is that a problem?"

"I . . . I don't think so. Do you enjoy doing it?"

"It's good money," she said.

"Hm."

We were silent for the rest of the shower. I didn't know what to say. On the one hand, I was titillated in that Lucy's job was about sex. Shelby Lewis was dating an exotic dancer. If I'd had

57

friends to tell, they'd have been shocked. On the other hand, the thought of men ogling her every move and then masturbating in public urinals was disconcerting.

We made dinner together—another vegetable stir fry casserole with a little too much ginger. Conversation remained sparse.

Returning to bed neither of us moved. The new awareness of her employment seemed to have put additional pressure on me as a partner.

"Night," I muttered.
"What's going on?"
"I'm just so sleepy."
"I'm the same person, Shel. Take off the fuckin' Vaseline lens. I don't have time for this shit."
"What are you talking about?"
"Don't bullshit me."
"I—"
"I mean it. If you're fucked up 'cause I'm a pealer you can go to hell."
"Lucy . . . I . . . oh god, how can *I* judge? My primordial instincts barking out of the Dark Ages. Please forgive me. I can't imagine anyone more disappointing to God than me. *So you're a stripper? Whitman exalts the form and so do you!*"
"I do it for cash."
"Nonetheless, look at me: I'm uneducated and un . . . un . . ."
"—happy?"
"Happy . . . and un . . ."
"—comfortable?"
"Comfortable . . . and un . . ."
"—usual?"

We both laughed. "Lucy, I apologise. I am grateful to be sharing this time with you."

Lucy took my hand in hers and squeezed. "Come here, my little ex–virgin," she said. We embraced, and sometime thereafter we slept.

We woke up rotating in time. In a dusky daze I was motioned onto my backside as Lucy positioned herself on top of me, balanced herself and inserted me as she deemed appropriate. I smiled a sleepy, half dreaming smile, my engorged

penis, confused at first, gradually finding comfort in what reminded me of a fully inflated water wing. Lucy dropped her hands on my shoulders and accelerated her motion. All at once reality smacked me on the face.
"Stop!" my head screamed.
The virgin and the stripper were exchanging body fluids.
"Stop!" I closed my eyes and covered them with my hands; my pelvis pulsating up and down like a wounded animal.
"Stop!" The stripper's history was now the virgin's history.
"*Stop for Christ's sake!*"
Scenes flashed through my mind.
Test results.
Hospital beds.
Hanging I.V.'s.
Wheelchairs.
Visiting hours.
AIDS.
AIDS.
AIDS.
And through it all I just kept pumping.
When it was over I lay in silence, the darkness my only protection. Then came the self-loathing part. Lucy softly stroked my ugly chest.
"You okay?" she said quietly.
"Me? Yeah, fine," I said as thankfully as I could without giving away the lie. My body ached with an internal scream—and there the scream remained.
Lucy's breathing quickly deepened and I could see the angle of her face silhouetted by a streak of light that had crept in through the partially open blind. I reached over her, lifted the blind a little higher and looked out. It was the moon. It didn't move. It didn't even react. It just hung there offering light for free. "Say something!" I yelled from inside my head. The moon didn't answer. The moon didn't have to.

VII

O rottenness! O
monstrous life!
—St. Augustine

Day one at the sausage factory consisted of eight hours up to my armpits in entrails while putrid slabs of pig with the smell of death hung all around me. After a couple of minutes I made a vow to never eat sausages again. Two hours later I made a vow to never *eat* again. Sitting through lunch watching supposedly intelligent employees inhaling foodstuffs from a huge pot of outhouse-smelling chili dried up my intestinal lining.

By midafternoon my olfactory tract shut down. All I could think about was Lucy. My feminist saviour had turned out to be something far different. On coffee break number two I checked my mouth for sores. There was one. Just before the end of the day I slipped on some slop and, in an attempt to maintain balance, splattered the ground-up, diseased bowel of a heifer across my cheek and lips and down my tie. I dry-gagged and a co-worker let out a jolly laugh.

After work, while the rest of the employees chewed on old meat and bellowed out their nightly good-byes, I thanked Uncle Mannfred and Auntie Carol for the opportunity to work at their factory and apologised for my inability to commit to such a fine profession. There was nothing else I could do. Their reaction punched me right in the sternum. Uncle Mannfred was standing off to Auntie Carol's right, leaning against the frame of the office door, his moribund frown indicating he was close to tears. Auntie Carol seemed disappointed but understanding. Without me even having to ask, she disappeared into a back room for a couple of minutes before returning with a check for $56. My first and last day

SHELBY

and they were already treating me like family. Joel (one of the workers) had mentioned during a coffee break that they'd been trying unsuccessfully to have a child for the past seven years. Infertility. Now they were attempting to adopt but bureaucratic barriers were blocking their every move. If it ever works out, I envy that kid. Auntie Carol oozed maternal instinct. So did Uncle Mannfred for that matter. They were so passionate about their sausage making I feared I was passing up the chance of a lifetime. As I pulled out of the parking lot, they simultaneously wished me well and then waved, with five or six employees following suit.

Arriving home, I collapsed on the pull-out couch, closed my eyes and reminisced about being lost in the short-lived throngs of passionate lovemaking. An errant whiff of weiner seasoning on my hands shut that memory down, and my heart sank at not having worn a condom; there was something grossly immoral about being connected with every lover she'd ever had. Then again, I reasoned, I was in love and prepared to see it through any nightmare.

I called Gran and it was wonderful to hear her voice. When I told her about my day at the sausage factory, she laughed with such gusto she dropped the phone. Henceforth in the conversation I was referred to as "Little Smokey." I further confessed to her that my exam marks would be shattering to Mom and Dad and that I had no intentions of returning to university come September.

"Don't expect me to tell them," she said. She knew I knew what she meant. That was her way of keeping a secret.

* * *

That evening, darkness fell slowly upon the city, the night unsure of whether or not it was late spring or early summer. Thoughts of Lucy and joblessness and future outlook and unprotected sex with a stripper had pummelled me into a corner. I decided, much as I often did in my simpler days frolicking through university, to go out walking.

By eight forty-five I was standing on the corner of Broadway and Granville waiting for a bus downtown. Attractive women were on both my flanks. I smiled confidently and puffed up, reasoning that sex with Lucy might be causing me to be giving off a different aura. I turned to the woman on my left. She was well made up. I nodded and smiled. "Wonderful night," I said. She replied with a blank stare bordering on disgust.

On the bus I thought about how there once was a time when practicality was the key ingredient behind choosing a mate. How effective are her childbearing hips? How easily can he pin a cave bear? Then some ten thousand years ago the first sedentary civilizations cropped up along the River Tigris and people suddenly had time to examine their spouses' physical properties, much as one would study a Monet in the Louvre. Overnight, natural selection became a question of cheek bone structure and charm and the width of one's lips. Homely intellects like myself were ostracized to perpetual bachelorhood, expected to update primitive tools and the like. And here we are today filling up our secondary sexual characteristics with silicone and exercising to improve calf definition while the planet—sadly, still the only one known to harvest this thing called life—goes up in smoke.

Then I thought about how wonderful Lucy was for going against the norms of avant-garde natural selection by spending the last couple of weeks mating with a genetic outcast. Sure enough I became aroused, and wondered if I was now free to drop by Lucy's apartment at will—perhaps even to initiate intimate interactions. In short, were we lovers?

I got off the bus at Davie Street and walked northbound up Granville Street. The city had an electric quality, the most recent disco pop hits bellowing out of record stores, breezes of warm air floating head level and the lighting doing wonders for what was left of Vancouver's pasty winter complexion. I stopped at a Muffin Break for a cup of coffee and gazed at the passers-by. Eventually my coffee made its way to my lap and the table had to be cleared. I was wearing brown corduroys and didn't care. One of the staff, a Mediterranean woman in her late teens, smiled at me in an almost come-hither way. I declined, my returned smile indicating I was spoken for.

By about nine o'clock the crowds began to thin out so I took a left on Robson and walked all the way down to the ocean. Then I wandered back. The breeze was starting to get colder. By ten it was dark out and the wind was blowing hard. I took

SHELBY

a right off Robson and walked up Seymour Street. A dozen or more prostitutes were there taking advantage of the drier weather. One particularly buxom, platinum blond with an appealing face moved right into my path, our eyes smashing like a head-on car crash on a desolate highway. I blushed and she smiled—a warm, sad smile. Instantly I was overcome with the image of her staggering home as the sun comes up to stand for the thousandth time beneath the hot stream of a shower, pounding on mildewy tiled walls with tired fists, vowing to never again be used as a spittoon for semen. Words rolled from my quivering lips:

"Would you care to share some pastries and coffee, my treat?"

Again that lonely smile. "You got wheels?"

"Wheels? Uh . . . well . . . yes, but not here. I . . . I thought we could just go to little yonder bistro," I said, pointing to a quaint cafe just up the street.

She glanced at it and then back at me. "Fuck off," she said.

"What did I say?"

"Fuck you."

I left, the wind calling to me as never before. I crossed streets, noticing mannequins in windows, concert posters, construction sites and parking lots. Heading north up Homer Street I skipped in and out of shadows and talked to myself aloud, feeling less self-conscious with every word. I felt a few drops of rain on my hand as I turned right onto Hastings Street. I was slightly lost. A bus passed and in its wake of noise the rain became heavier. I pushed my pace into a trot and sprinted between awnings. Before long I was running in the eye of a North American monsoon. Another bus passed—the Fraser, my bus!—but I didn't flag it down. I couldn't. I was wet and I was cold but I kept moving, running into the rain like it was holy water, my mouth open and inviting, my heart beating into my throat, my lungs gasping for air, my eyes barely able to see where I was going. Every step became a lesson in trust and geography; at any moment I could have crashed into a telephone pole and broken my nose or smashed my reproductive organs on a parking meter. Still I didn't wipe the water from my eyes. I didn't even squint.

I just ran.

And then I stopped.

Where Hastings Street crosses Cambie Street I stood staring into the face of Victory Square. The plaque read: "THEIR NAME LIVETH FOR EVERMORE"—a salute to the dead. I wiped the rain from my face and raked my fingers through my hair. There was a man lying down on a bench about twenty feet to my left, in as close to the fetal position as space would allow. The sky offered him no relief. I wondered if the heavens would. I sat down next to him and figured there should be a drunk memorial here, too, in remembrance of the contribution alcoholics make to road repair work and street cleaning via liquor taxes.

Reading the plaque again I had a burst of literary inspiration but no pen to write down, *Life is a horror show where everybody dies.* It wasn't brilliant but I'd read worse in published works. I reached into my pocket, pulled out some loose change and slipped it into the bum's wet jacket pocket. He didn't flinch. I hoped he was still alive. How strange it would be to put change into a dead man's pocket—it would make him a sort of a welfare Tutankhamen. Then I wondered, what's the point of being dead?

I started to walk again, drawn eastbound as if by another force. The rain kept coming. I felt like a soldier returning home to no one, but happy to be back just the same. For a moment I feared I was being pursued. My heart kicked in. I looked back but didn't see anybody. I sprinted across the road and stopped by a few wet, empty benches sitting silent and lonely in the rain; no people, no pigeons. I shook my head and smiled—even benches need validation! I moved beneath the shelter of a maple tree and watched the wind-strewn, almost horizontal rain dance in the lamplight. I started walking again, and across the road saw a couple running arm in arm the opposite way. They were laughing and happy. I smiled and moved on. Protective awnings became less frequent. I didn't care. I just kept walking until the traffic from Main Street got so loud it poured into my brain like a mechanical river, smothering my thoughts beyond recognition. I tilted my head backwards and let a few drops of water land on my tongue.

And there it was.

SHELBY

The Number Five Orange, its neon light shining in my eye like the last few embers of a dying sun.
I peeked inside the door. There was a show in progress.
Dripping, I crept into a seat at a back table and sunk low. A thick haired, sandy blond waitress dressed all in black approached me immediately. I smiled.
"I'm not really a regular, I . . . uh . . . a friend of mine dances."
"What can I get you?"
"Oh . . . uh . . . I'll have a . . . I'll have a Sprite, please."
"A *Sprite*?"
"Yes . . . please. With a slice of lemon. Her name is Lucy. Perchance—"
"Lemon?"
"Yes, please. Just a—"
"And maybe you'd like some milk and cookies for later, too?"
"Milk and cookies? No. I . . . would . . . make it a beer." She grinned. I didn't actually see it but I'm sure it was there—one of those internal grins. In a bar for men, she'd crushed one of my balls. Moments later, a man approached.
"How old are you?"
"Nineteen—I mean twenty. Just turned."
"Do you have any I.D.?"
"Yes." We looked at each other.
"Can I see it?"
"Oh, sorry." I removed a damp driver's license from a wet wallet and handed it to him. Back and forth he looked at it and then at me. Then he tossed it on the table and walked away.
I watched a woman with no pubic hair caress her vagina and jiggle her breasts for ten minutes. It was difficult for me to believe that Lucy did that. Then again, she had a wonderful body.
By the time the beer came, I needed it. It cost $3.95 and the waitress gave me fifteen bucks back from a twenty dollar bill and I told her to keep the change. I gave her a twenty-five percent tip for treating me with the respect one gives overchewed gum. Round two and my scrotal sac had been hung from a flagpole half-mast.

The next woman's name was Vulvanna Plenty. She was a flexible, confident dancer, hanging off the pole like an angry anaconda. I thought of Lucy and ordered another beer. After my third beer, I became aware of how cold, wet and uncomfortable I was—and thinking about Lucy and the voluntary spreading of her vulva didn't help. I was disturbed that she'd spit out such educated views to me about metaphysics and goddesses and oneness and female exploitation and then climb up nude on a stage and gyrate her naked loins to some patriarchal backbeat.
I ended up drinking four beers on an empty stomach. At closing, I was wobbly, nauseous and still wet so I remained seated with my chin resting in my hands and my elbows on the table. Everybody left me alone. Maybe I appeared to be waiting for somebody. A man left the bathroom zipping up his fly and I said to myself, "A barfly," and laughed aloud. Right then I received another flash of inspiration, borrowed a pen from one of the employees and wrote on a napkin: *Life is a lunatic refusing to get help.* I liked it more than the first one—and being a non-writer, receiving two gems in less than three hours was invigorating. I folded the napkin over, slipped it in the chest pocket of my Gortex jacket, loosened my tie and stumbled towards the exit. Glancing back one last time at the empty stage, I felt turned on by my lover's profession. It was time to go home.

* * *

Lucy and I spent the following three nights together, indulging in generous amounts of intercourse in various positions that left me feeling both mildly manipulated and more than willing. Several times afterwards I would lie staring into nothingness, wondering what she saw in me. All I came up with was our mutual love for reading.
The days, by comparison, were lazy; ambitions and other social perversions drifting like empty canoes on a placid lake. Mostly we drank coffee and discussed unattainable phenomena; manifestations of God and the potential for human wellbeing. As for her job, for which from a technical standpoint I had a newfound respect, I hinted over sandwiches that an alternate form of employment would in no way decrease her

sexuality. Her response was: "At least I have a job"—and beyond that offered few insights. In the end I concluded that if a thirty-two-year-old woman sees no clash between feminism and stripping, why should I? Truth is it was none of my business.

* * *

Needing answers, on Friday morning I journeyed to the downtown library to research this mobile form of pornography. Unfortunately, all I uncovered were newspaper clippings about pay decreases, attempts to unionize and two poorly written autobiographies that offered nothing more than insight into the writer's superficiality. Only one article offered a theory on the trade's psychology. It was based on castration fear, which, according to the text, is intensified when men see a woman's vulva because the vulva, in its loose-skinned pinky way, reminds men what it would be like to be castrated. Subconsciously, therefore, men feel they have to subjugate women to keep their genitals intact. This is done by making her an object: hence, strip joints. Such an idea had to be absurd. If not, any strip joint on any given night would be a veritable human time bomb capable of erupting at the whim of one man's fury!

* * *

Arriving at Lucy's apartment just before lunch that afternoon, I found her spread out and relaxed on her couch like a modern day Goddess. I sat juxtaposed in a big, soft, greeny-beige chair. After awhile she looked up from her book and smiled. I smiled back. She went back to her book. A minute or so later she looked up again.

"I'm feeling very open today, Shel," she said, "very grounded." I could tell she was. There was a lightness pouring out of her eyes. "I think it's time we did a full reading," she said, smiling that smile that always gives me the impression she knows something I don't. I imagined her telling fortunes in the back of a caravan with bad lighting somewhere in Transylvania—and damn if I wasn't next.

The reading had nothing to do with fortune telling. It was about auras and chakras and pastlives and oversouls. Lucy sat about ten feet from me with her back upright and her feet flat on the ground. She had one hand up at the side of her face and the other one gently waving across the front of her body. She said it was for clearing away energies that weren't applicable to the reading. I found the whole process relaxing and sensual—or maybe that was Lucy. Either way, I got aroused a couple of times.

Lucy said I was having some blockage of energy in my second chakra—the chakra pertaining to my sexuality. That was disconcerting. On a positive note, she also said that my fourth chakra, pertaining to the heart, was open and loving.

"There's a little bit of grayish-blue around the outside," she said, "which is generally an indicator of sadness—the blue being harmony and the gray being fear—greyish-blue being sadness. But for the most part, I see a pinky-red kind of thing which is definitely a sign of love and affection . . ." I smiled. Then she helped me clear away a bit of unnecessary angst that was hanging around. I appreciated the gesture.

After awhile, what with deep breaths and closed eyes, my mind wandered to a time—I was perhaps ten years old—when I walked into the front room of an apartment my Dad was either renting or staying at—I'm not actually sure what it was, but it was sometime during Mom and Dad's trial separation. Dad was sitting in a battered old chair—sort of like the one I was sitting in at Lucy's—staring blankly through a window that overlooked coats and coats of snow that sloped towards town as freely as a white-water river. Dad's eyes were very red. I'd never seen him with red eyes before.

Dads don't cry.

I stood off to the side, about fifteen feet away, just looking at him. For some reason the memory of the image is bathed in wonderfully rich earthtones—a commendable attempt at optimism. The sky appears as an amazingly vivid blue, and for that I am thankful. He let out a little sob.

Dads cry.

"You seem to be coming to me as a woman," Lucy said, her eyes closed, her hand in the air, "a soothsayer . . . the town herbalist . . . you're in your late twenties—twenty-eight, twenty-nine, two children . . . somewhere in the States and I . . . Massachusetts, yeah . . . late 1600s . . . you're in trouble . . .

you're being . . . Salem, Massachusetts, that's it . . . you're being burned at the stake—"

"What?" I yelled.

Lucy's eyes were still closed. "I'm as shocked as you are, Shel, but I'm telling you, this is what I'm seeing." She shook her head. "Do you want me to go on or not?"

"Yes, I want you to go on."

"Okay, you're . . . you're with several other women . . . you've been hounded by religious fanatics on a mass witch-hunt."

"Come on!"

"This is what I'm getting! But it ain't easy with your interruptions."

"I apologise," I said, "but I just can't believe—"

"I don't screw around with psychic ethics, Shel. I have a moral responsibility to be truthful here—and this is what I'm seeing."

"Okay. I'm sorry. Go on. I won't say another word."

"Thank you," she said. "Okay . . . now . . . you're blocking here . . . you've got to relax . . . you've got . . . oh shit . . . God I'm going down the tubes."

"What's wrong?"

"I've lost it . . ."

"Lost what?"

"Wait," she said, raising her hand.

"What?"

"You've got a female guide . . . she's a part-time guide . . . she's trying to show you the way towards yin expansion."

"Towards what?"

"Stop talking!"

"Sorry."

"I see a name . . . Belinda. Her name is Belinda."

"Are you sure it's not Bart?" I asked.

"That's it," she said, "I quit."

"No!"

"I quit—it's all a joke to you."

"No it's not. I'm sorry, it's just that . . . let me explain. Bart was an imaginary friend I had when I was a child. He'd watch over me when I was playing with my chemistry set or lawn darts and so forth."

"We'll do it again some other time . . . my concentration is shot."

"I'm sorry. Were you serious about that witch-hunt?"

"I told you," she said, "I wouldn't joke about this stuff." Lucy's eyes were like two fine crystals. "Believe whatever you want."

"I believe you," I said. Lucy started waving her hands all over the place. "What . . . what are you doing?"

"I'm cleaning the room of any negative spirits and I'm thanking my guides for helping out."

"Thank them from me, too," I said. Lucy smiled. "Hey, Lucy, I must confess, I thoroughly enjoyed that. How did . . . is one . . . what do you see from one person to the next?"

"It depends. As for you, your spirit seemed surprisingly open for an anal-retentive kind of guy."

"*Anal retentive?* I'm a university dropout."

"Why do you wear a tie all the time?"

"Because I . . . it . . . habit, I guess. Why not?"

Lucy shrugged and left the room. I sat thinking about her, and no matter the memory I was filled with glee. This, it would seem, was living; to experience and expand, all the while avoiding social constraints. Lucy returned to the room with a lit candle that she put on the coffee table. She turned off the main light and closed the curtains across the calico cat, the outside lamplight causing a ghoulishly distorted silhouette of its body. Lucy lay down, and when the flame flickered, the highlights on the contours of her body altered shape like a dancing shadow in a house of mirrors. She motioned me to the floor and kissed me. It was then I realised all the truly warm feelings I'd ever experienced had been with women. We made love with our pants half down—a scenario that left me feeling remarkably manly. Afterwards, conversation was comfortable. Even the soggy condom was bearable. Lucy lit a cigarette and the scene bordered on pornographic. Not knowing what to do, I stretched in excess.

Making love half an hour later was a shock to my senses. Never had I even masturbated twice in a day, save during periods of excessive exam anxiety. Stamina fading, I felt like a soldier fallen victim to stimulation overload; out of ammunition and frightened, my war-weary loins soaked in a battlefield of skin-like mud. I closed my eyes and wondered how long I could stand the jungle heat; how one minute I was a young Canadian boy in a small community just north of nowhere collecting empty pop bottles to raise the funds to purchase additional flasks and test tubes for my Junior Chemistry Set and the next minute I was fighting for my life in a country where dogs are a delicacy and the only language is fear. Newsreels from Vietnam flashed like machine gun fire across my consciousness. Then Minnie appeared out of nowhere for three or four flailing pumps before a black-and-white clip of some Indonesian jungle took over. I closed my eyes, straining to hear what sounded like the gentle mumblings of an English journalist:

"Burma 1941. Morale is at its lowest ebb since the war in the South Pacific began. The British troops are fighting a battle that, logically, cannot be won. They are forced to retreat . . ."

VIII

*Love lodged in a
woman's breast
Is but a guest.*
—Sir Henry Wotton

Knowing that mere hours after our lovemaking session Lucy would be parading around as a mobile fantasy for several hundred men was upsetting, and left me feeling all the more alone upon returning home to a dark and empty apartment. There was a note scribbled in pencil by the phone:

> THURSDAY NIGHT
> Your parents called . . . again!! They asked how you were doing. I tried to cover for you. I've got a gig in two weeks. Big shots from Toronto are coming in for it. Might need you to play. Bring home some Bratwurst.
> Eric.

He must not have known I was no longer working for Uncle Mannfred and Auntie Carol. The apartment was speckled in beer cans, cigarette butts and other party remnants, the stench of which all converged at and/or around my pull-out couch. The garbage had gone foul, the sink was coated with globs of what may have once been pasta and the fridge was empty save the imitation syrup spilled all over the bottom shelf and the residue of rotten vegetables in the crisper. I stood with the fridge door open and my eyes riveted on nothing, as if that might make a ham sandwich appear. In the end I ordered Chinese food—high on the gloss—sweet and sour pork with red sauce, two egg rolls, chicken chow mein and rice. I stayed home and read Walt Whitman. I spoke in accents. I drank water and wine. In short, I danced alone. Then I had some peach schnapps and thought I might throw up.

The following morning was spent reflecting on the three

SHELBY

days I had spent in Lucy's company. Never had passing time been so easy—and in that lay our magic. In a sense I was like a late blooming flower, for the first time open enough to enjoy the warmth of life on the *inside*. As a youngster, just reading about relationships had been enough. What amazed me now was how sex—the mere mention of it it, even—could realign the focus of my week.

By midafternoon, grocery shopping had landed me outside Lucy's apartment, smiling at the calico cat in her window. I noticed her front door was ajar. I ran up the stairs and peeked inside to see a suitcase in the foyer.

"Hello?" I said to no response. I stepped inside and walked into the front room. "Hello?"

A "Yeah?" came out of the bedroom. "Who is it?"

"It's Shelby."

"Come on in," she said, "I'm in the bedroom." I walked in to find Lucy sitting on her bed tossing panties into a half-full suitcase. She looked up and smiled.

"Hey, Shel."

"Hi, I . . . I was out shopping and I thought I'd drop in."

"Cool."

"You seem to be packing."

"Road time," she said in a chuck-wagon drawl.

"You're going away?"

"Work."

"Oh."

Lucy stopped packing. "You seem confused."

"No . . . it's just . . . you made no mention of leaving."

"Hmm. I guess . . . sorry about that. I guess . . . Alzheimer's. I'll tell you now. I'm going on the road." She threw another pair of panties in the case.

"For how long?"

"A few weeks." A car horn beeped outside. "Oh, that's my cab," she said smiling.

"Cab? I could give you a lift."

"Oh thanks, Shel. That's okay, though. It's already here." She zipped up her case and walked by without even touching me. Picking up her other suitcase inside the already open front door, she positioned herself to allow me to leave before her. My offer to carry one of her suitcases was declined. She

73

stepped into the taxi. There were no words exchanged between us. No hugs. Not a kiss.
"What about us?" I asked. She shrugged as though surprised by the question. The car door slammed and she leaned forward to say something to the driver. As he pulled out from the curb Lucy smiled at me and waved. I waved back as the taxi drove off. I was stunned. Turning away, I noticed on the window ledge the calico cat perched on its backside, holding its belly, laughing uncontrollably. Suddenly the taxi screeched to a stop up the road and backed up whence it had left. Lucy grinned through the window. Had I not been forsaken? My heart fluttered like a butterfly grappling to be freed from a now useless cocoon. Into slow motion we galloped, lovers about to embrace in a gasping field of daisies.
"I forgot to ask the landlord to feed the damn cat," she said as she sprinted past me and up the stairs. "See ya!"

* * *

Hours into the fourth night after Lucy left I woke up in a sweat-soaked panic, my heart pounding up to my temples, my body paralysed with fear. I got up, turned on the light and examined my penis for spots, twisting it in all directions to see all sides. There were no new blemishes. I lay back on the bed, frozen, and then looked again. I lay back down but couldn't sleep. I paced around the kitchen and into the front room. I gazed out the window and saw streetlights and parked cars, the haunting rumble of the city wrapped up in blue shades of night; seeing the distant apartment lights, I envisioned AIDS sufferers, still awake, annihilated by the reality of their condition. I fell back on the pull-out couch and pounded my fists into the mattress. Reaching across the bed, I picked the phonebook up off the floor and looked up *V.D.*
Venereal Disease Information Line: 872–1238.
I dialed. Six rings. No answer. I looked up AIDS. My temples started to pound again. There it was: *AIDS Vancouver: Information and Counselling. 687–2437.* I dialed. Eight rings. No answer. I crumpled back down on the bed and rolled . . . and groaned . . . and moaned until sleep finally took me.
Halfway through dialing the *AIDS Line* the following morning, I examined my penis and became erect.

"AIDS Vancouver," said a man in the middle of my demoralised groan.

"Oh . . . uh . . . I . . ." Suddenly disgusted, I yanked in desperation as hard as I could on my loathesome erection, agony causing me to yelp simultaneously as the telephone receiver cracked on the floor. Before me, my penis wilted like an old carrot. Trembling, I picked up the phone and slowly brought it to my mouth.

"Hello?"

"AIDS Vancouver."

"I had sex with a promiscuous woman."

"And you're worried about . . . ?"

"I'm phoning an AIDS line! I'm worried about *AIDS*."

"Calm down. Was your partner high risk?"

"She . . . we were sexually active, initiated by her, she seemed experienced. She put a prophylactic on me in seconds . . ."

"So she was using a condom?"

"She did. And then she . . . we didn't. But I just couldn't stop myself."

"Is she a drug user?"

"No. I don't know. Tylenol."

"But no needles?"

"*Tylenol.*"

"Is she a prostitute?"

"No! She's a dancer. She . . ." Beads of perspiration formed on my forehead like tiny turtle shells pushing up from beneath the sand.

"So she's a regular partner?"

"*Was* a regular partner! Now? God knows! And to think I was going to be a doctor. Now I'm a slut, all dreams shattered!"

"Did she tell you she was promiscuous?"

"Oh yes, she sent me a note saying she's a whore! I told you! She's a prophylactic virtuoso—*swoosh* and it was on!"

"Sir, I think—"

"Indeed, the flesh *does* kill! Oh wretched day! Oh—"

"*Sir!*"

Startled, I stood shaking.

"Now I realise you're tense. But please . . ."

"I . . . I'm sorry."

"That's all right. Take a breath."
I did.
"Now, I suggest talking to her."
"How can I? She's miles away cavorting in the nude for strangers!"
"Well, in the meantime, celebrate the fact that she uses condoms. Many people still don't."
"But what if . . ."
"She uses condoms."
"But I—"
"No blame."
"She—"
"She uses condoms, Sir. She practices safe sex. Talk to her."
"I . . . I will," I said.
"Good. Are you all right?"
"Yes . . . I . . . feel better. Thank you."
"You're welcome. Talk to her."

Relieved, I hung up and crumpled onto the bed, tentatively excited and relatively certain I was most likely still uninfected. In fact I was so inspired I packed a knapsack full of essentials, drove west and spent the remainder of the day at Spanish Banks playing my acoustic guitar and reading the Bible. Exodus 22:18 was disconcerting: *Do not allow a sorceress to live.* What about one whose powers are waning? I asked myself. Eerily, at that moment a cold wind shot off the ocean, momentarily freezing me with terror.

By evening and after having spent a day watching joggers running in pairs, lovers strolling arm in arm and parents pushing carriages, it was clear how few good friends I really had. Lucy? No. Gran? My best friend. Brother Derek? There when I'm in dire need, but hardly a chum in the true sense of the word. Eric? Willing yet unpredictable. Beyond that was Carl Tkachuk, a pornography-addicted pal I occasionally chatted with in high-school.

* * *

The most interesting event over the next couple of weeks was a date I bravely initated with Suzanne, Eric's friend I'd met but one time previously at the Aristocratic. On the phone, she didn't even know who I was. Nonetheless, explanation ensued and sure enough we met for coffee at Bino's that very night. It was just what I needed to rekindle belief in intimacy and its essential role in one's journey. But enough about the mystical.

Suzanne: Although somewhat reserved, she showed an extraordinary passion for her creative endeavours. Dressed all in black save a Guatemalan vest of oranges and reds, she said in her deliberate way, and I quote:

"Clay has moved me since the first time I heard that, 'The Lord God formed man from the clay of the ground and breathed into his nostrils the breath of life.' My *God*, what an image. And I, in my humble—humble from the greek *humus*, meaning earthy—way, am doing the same. The breath of life coming, of course, from those who are moved by *my* creations . . ."

Watching her fully-ringed hands express such a testimony, my innards softened to the consistency of corned beef jelly. I was enthralled to hear a women quote scripture. Sensuality had returned to my senses. Was sex a sin? Who cares. Granted, there was no indication from Suzanne that we would soon tumble. Nonetheless, her grounded presence assured me of one thing: There was life after Lucy.

* * *

Two days later, the first of July, I awoke with what appeared to be the flu; sore joints, runny nose, headache and nausea. My anxieties, however, had a different diagnosis. Twenty-two days had passed since I last saw Lucy and I was now more terrified than ever that *her virus* had booked a room in my bodily fluids. A phone call interrupted me in mid groan.

"Yes?"

"Shelby?"

"Yes?"

"You all right?"

I leapt up. "Oh, hi, Dad. Yes, I'm fine—mildly clammy. How are you doing?"

"Good and bad. Here's the bad: Derek and Kristine are talking about breaking up."

"They are?"

"Listen, I've got a couple of letters here from the university adressed to you. We could really use some good news."
"Kristine and Derek are breaking up?"
"Ah damn, I can't talk about that anymore! When are they going to learn marriage ain't some summer vacation? More important, your marks are here."
Out oozed a nervous sweat.
"Did you hear me, son?"
"Um . . . yes."
"So, should I open them."
"I . . . I'd rather you sent them to me."
"What?"
"It's a very personal thing—being judged by peers."
"Come on, don't keep us waiting. Oh, speakin' o' waitin', Larry wants to know if you're coming home. If not he wants to fill your position."
"*Position*? Dad, standing in a four-foot trough shovelling sludge is not a position. Tell him to hire a retarded orangutan."
"*Ha*! That's funny. Anyway, when are you coming home?"
"Uh . . . I'm not sure . . . I'm doing a lot of research."
"Oh great," he said, "that'll cheer up your mother. Let's see. Anything else you want to add? Drug addiction, maybe?"
"*What*?"
"Come on, Dr. Lewis," he said, "let us at least open the letter."
"Dad, I—"
"What's the problem? You fail everything?"
"No!"
"You figure your old man can't read?"
"Of course not."
"I can read," he said.
"I know."
"Don't tell me you dropped out!"
And so rose the opportunity to confess my parachuting from Academia Airlines. But, alas, nary a syllable on that subject plunged from my tongue.
"Dad, please . . ."
"*Ah . . . okay,*" he said, "but let us know, eh?"
There was a pause of relief. "I will. Thank you . . ."
After hanging up, a bout with post-call melancholy and a

yearn for friendship found me dialing Lucy's number. She answered (evidently having returned from her tour) and I hung up immediately. The question, however, of how feelings generated via verbal intimacy and intercourse could be obliterated as though shot with a bazooka still persisted. I had been rejected without consultation.

From bedside over the next five days or so, I enquired through the classified adds for jobs as a waiter, a construction worker, a messenger boy, an inventory clerk and a water filter salesman. None of them offered either medical or pension benefits. I also contacted a couple who were seeking a nanny for their three-and-a-half-year old son. Being male, I didn't get an interview. The process was exhausting—and carrying around the tail end of the flu didn't help. Reality had returned; I was more indispensable than ever to the process of life. Love was a bust. Perhaps only social activism remained. Speaking of which, over another coffee rendezvous with Suzanne I confessed the symptoms of my lingering illness and how scared I was about getting a checkup.

"I would be, too," she said, "the doctor will probably give you two seconds of time and then prescribe a garbage can full of antibiotics."

"I'm not afraid of that."

"You should be."

"Why?"

"*Shelby*, come on. Antibiotics wipe out the immune system long term."

I chuckled. "You make it sound like radiation treatment."

"You said it, not me."

"You're serious?"

"You bet I am."

"Penicillin has saved *millions* of lives."

"Some would say the same for chemotherapy," she said, "but it's no cure for cancer."

"But it's an effective treatment."

"That's the whole problem right there, Shelby: *treatment*. We don't seem to care about prevention. Cancer is about as internal a disease as getting hit by a car."

"My Grandfather had cancer," I said.

"And chemotherapy?"

"I think so."
"And where's he now?"
"Dead."
"There you go. Did he smoke?"
"Yes."
"Meat with every meal?"
I shrugged. "My father's a butcher."
"And I bet *he's* on high blood pressure medication, too, right?"
"I don't know."
"Useless. Did you know over half the patients in St. Paul's hospital are there for drinking or smoking related diseases?"
"Where did you learn all this?"
Suzanne smiled. "It's kind of a hobby. Plus both my parents are doctors."
"Wow . . . Did you know I applied for medical school?"
"I think you mentioned it."
"Last year," I said. "Then I dropped out."
"Good for you."
"Really?"
"Oh yeah. The health system's dying. I'll bet it falls apart inside of ten years."
"*What?*"
"It has to. We just don't have the guts to monitor people's health habits—smoking, drinking, obesity—and billing by the cigarette or the pound or whatever. Even my *parents* say to do that would be a violation of human rights. I say political correctness is killing us and that when the system collapses and we end up like the U.S. of A. where only the rich get care, *then* we've got violation."
"I'm stunned."
"It's all about supply and demand, Shelby."
"Even medicine?" I asked, disheartened.
"Sure. Health and capitalism. N-A-F-T-A. Big business. We sanction the promotion of useless drugs, bad food, cigarettes. It's amoral. Same goes for medical research: I mean how many animals will die before we admit that the physiology of a rat is irrelevant to our own?"
"Millions?"
"*Trillions.*"

"I had no idea how much you knew."
"Hey, I've been in the biz all my life."
"Why does this happen?"
"I'll tell you why, Shelby. Because to a businessman, a dollar saved will never be the same as a dollar earned."
"So you don't think I should see a physician?"
"Are you kidding? You look terrible."

* * *

Fittingly, it was rainy and gray when I slipped into the Venereal Disease Clinic the following morning. I gave the woman at the front desk my real name and then instantly regretted doing so. She didn't ask for identification. I could have said anything. Now I was forever enshrined as one of *those* who consent to sex with people they barely know—a fact that, if leaked, could get me shot should a military and/or moral majority fundamentalist government ever rise to power.

While waiting for my name to be called I browsed through a few pamphlets. *CHLAMYDIA: DO YOU KNOW THE FACTS?* I obviously didn't—I'd never even heard of it. The pamphlet said it was rampant among college students and virtually undetectable in males—no discharge, no irritation—but left untreated could cause sterility and pelvic inflammatory disease.

My name was called out loud enough to be heard stateside. I shuffled into the examination room feeling like I should have been wearing a trench coat and rubber boots with nothing underneath. The room was white and empty. I hung my jacket on the coat rack and sat down. My underarms were sticky. The door opened and I was stunned by the woman who walked in. She had olive smooth skin straight off a Mediterranean Isle, straight teeth, facial hair and a starched white lab coat that, like everything else, aroused me. Cursed addiction!

"Hello," she said, but I knew what she was thinking—what *everybody* thinks when a patient arrives at a venereal disease clinic. I searched my brain for a tactful way to tell her, "It's not what you think."

"It's not what you think," I said.
She smiled. "It rarely is. What can I do for you?"
"I . . . I'd like to be tested for venereal disease, please."
"This is the place to be. What are your symptoms?"

"Um . . . anxiety, headaches, fatigue . . ."
"Any genital irritation?"
"No."
"Discomfort when you urinate?"
"No."
"Have you been with someone who has informed you of having a sexually transmitted disease?"
"No."
She paused, her mouth flexed as though about to speak. "Why are you here?"
"Well . . . it's just . . . I thought . . . as a citizen, it's something I feel everyone . . . should be here."
She put the pad down. "You're sweating an awful lot," she said gently. "Are you all right?"
"Yes . . . good . . . somewhat anxious . . . I understand chlamydia can be difficult to detect."
"Have you been involved with someone who has had the disease?"
"Who can know?"
"So you've had multiple partners?"
"*No*. But I've had sexual intercourse without the use of a prophylactic. We used one at first *and* since but in the heat of a brief moment, my inner reproductive drive outwilled my internal yearn to survive and we didn't . . . and the problem is I don't know her sexual history. I think she's quite . . . well, let me put it this way. She's in her thirties and she dances nude."

The woman cleared her throat. "It doesn't sound like you have much to worry about. But just to be sure, we'll do a swab. Take down your pants, please." My penis slipped into my groin like a sinking ship on a vertical sea. Opening a drawer on the examination bed, the woman pulled out a pair of latex gloves, snapped them twice and slipped them on. I couldn't move, paralysed at the thought of exposing my genitals to a stranger. I'd done that with Lucy and the results were obvious. I hedged my way towards her.

"I must confess," I said, "I'm mildly afraid of Acquired Immune Deficiency Syndrome." She looked up as though wanting me to continue. "I've been run down lately. Actually, I feel relatively healthy today but I've had what felt like the flu for about six, maybe seven, days."

"Are you at risk?"

"Pardon?"

"Do you practice high risk behaviour . . . anal intercourse, needle sharing—are you bisexual?"

"Bisexual? No. Never. I'm hardly heterosexual . . . none of the above. I just . . . high *risk*? Good Lord. Fifteen *million* people have the disease! We didn't use a condom! What does it take to be high risk?"

"Sir," she said, "I'm going to ask you to sit down."

"Oh . . . sorry." I sat down.

"So . . . How long ago did you have sex with this person?"

"A month?"

"Hm."

"I'm not promiscuous. I *loved* that woman."

"Did you know there's a three to six month incubation period for antibodies to show up in testing for the AIDS virus?"

I slumped. "So you think there's a chance?"

"I think you're fine, sir, but we can take a test to ease your mind. Then, if you so choose, you can get tested again in a few months."

"Thank you," I said, "very much."

She smiled. "Now, stand up and take your pants down, please." She turned away and picked up a urethral swab off the table. My pelvis took a step back. I undid my pants and let them drop. She turned around and looked at me—and then at my mid-section. "And your underwear," she said.

"Oh, of course," I said. Not knowing procedure, I had hoped she wouldn't mind if I just let my penis peek through as though not really belonging to me. I lowered my boxer shorts, dismayed to find my penis resembling a withered mushroom. The woman readjusted one of her gloves and I had a flash of her returning home after work and relaying in Italian to a massive extended family the story about the man with no genitalia who came in for a V.D. test.

With the thumb and index finger of her left hand she held my penis. With the other hand she held a urethral swab dart-like and cocked. "This is going to sting," she said.

In it went. I grunted, feeling as if my urethra had been pierced by the fat end of a pool cue.

She pulled it out. "We'll take a culture of that and then let you know." She turned and put the swab in a test-tube and then turned back to me. "Now we'll take a blood test—you can pull your pants back up at any time . . ."

"Sorry."

The blood test was less traumatic. In fact, by its completion we were deep into a non-venereal disease conversation and I, young fool, felt urged to ask her out on a date. Unfortunately, blurting, "It's queer this game of love," was as close as I got. She responded with, "Call next week for the results," and offered a smile (the closed mouth kind) before leaving.

I stood for a moment in silence—save the hum of the fluorescent lights—while my armpits exuded that pungent odour characteristic of nervous sweat. No, I and the nurse would not become lovers; and yet in the sharing of a few brief sentences I felt we'd both gained a greater empathy for the sexual plight of humankind. Lifting my jacket from the coat rack, I slipped it on and walked through the door. I could tell that a pair of nurses at the front desk and a man in the waiting room who undoubtedly had V.D. were staring at me—probably gathering assumptions and judgements to soften the horror of their own existence. Willing to be their temporary scapegoat, I strutted past them, exiting via the main entrance into a dull Vancouver morning.

Arriving home, I stepped on a stack of mail inside the front door; junk flyers, an unemployment insurance cheque addressed to Eric for which I'm sure he was desperate—he and another friend had met Eric's Dad for a holiday in Southern California—and beneath it all, a manilla envelope.

From: *Peg and Ed Lewis.* To: *Dr. Shelby Lewis, M.D.*

Opening it slowly did not buffer the shock of an F in Zoology. The remaining marks were palatable: one pass, two second classes and a first class. There was a letter from the *Faculty of Medicine: We are sorry to inform you that you have not been . . .* Worst of all, however, was a cheque from my parents for two thousand dollars. Their letter, written by Mom, read:

Dear Doogie (Dad insisted),
We hope your exams went well. Let us know as soon as you find out and

SHELBY

don't worry if you don't get in, there's always next year. Very few students get into medical school before they've completed their degree. We've enclosed a cheque to help pay for next year's tuition and books. Try to come and see us before the summer ends. Gran was visited by the police for mooning religious solicitors again.

Miss you,
Love Mom and Dad

Weighing the positives (the cheque would help pay for food and lodging and save me from dressing up in a chicken suit) and the negatives (keeping it would be ethically wrong and make sleeping difficult), I decided to think of the money as an interest-free loan to a son in need. To give the cheque back would be to admit that my academic career had been abandoned for the duration, a display that would cause only pain. On the other hand, my journey to who-knows-what-heights was far from complete and this money would surely aid in its evolvement. That in mind, I mustered the nerve to phone home and confess my non-acceptance into medical school. Mom's response was one of disappointed compassion. Dad, however, blamed it on preferential treatment for minorities. I never made mention of dropping out and they never mentioned the cheque.

Later that night, to my startled surprise, I was awakened by a call from Lucy. She was at work and between dances. She'd got my number from Loretta. She was interested in getting together with me. Potential reasons abounded: admittance of a veneral disease, pregnancy or AIDS.

"Tonight?"
"Okay," I said.
"Were you in bed?"
"Um . . . yes."
"Bad time?"
"No."
"I'm not off til one-thirty."
"Uh . . . okay."
"The Bread Garden? Say, two?"
"Where is that again?"
"First and Burrard."
"Okay."

* * *

It was ten after two before Lucy arrived. I made no mention of her tardiness, nor was I aloof.
"Thanks for coming, Shel," she said, sitting down.
"You're welcome," I replied. And then came her smile. My heart inflated like a hot water bottle, my insides danced the tango and passion bolted towards my capital city until it throbbed like ten thousand peasants in riotous celebration. Life, I salute you!
"You like cheesecake?" I nodded. "Strawberries?" I nodded. "Yeah," she said to the waitress, "can we have two slices of the strawberry cheesecake, an espresso and . . ." Lucy glanced at me. "Hot chocolate?" I nodded.
"Okay, Shel. Here it is. You and me. The story? We were gettin' a little too . . . permanent. I got the chance to go away for work and I jumped at it. It was a cop-out, no doubt about it—but in my own defense, I was confused, like I was scrambling through a pile of laundry but I couldn't tell the dirty from the clean, you know? What's good for me? What's bad for me? I was feeling trapped. That's why I left. Anyway, I figure I owe you at least the honesty I feel you offered me. So what I'm going to do is give you some background. I'll save my childhood for another day. For now, I'll start with Frank. First off, who is he? He's a prick. Second off, I married him. Third off, we're still married."
"You're a married woman?"
"*Easy.* Separated. Here's the line on Frank. Subject to fits of anger and physical violence, he's a drug user with a perverse sort of vulnerable charm, he owns a night club—the Big Dipper—he's the one who got me started stripping, he gets off on lingerie . . . what else? He's a big fucker . . . he's a *dumb* fucker . . . uh . . . get this: He's got a hockey card collection worth about $20,000."
"Wow."
"Now me: I'm roughly the same, hold the cards and the panties."
"You do *drugs?*"
"Did."
My mind flashed to the AIDS test. "*Needles?*"

SHELBY

"No. Coke, hash, uppers, downers . . . I still do cigarettes, obviously."
"—and Tylenol."
"True enough."
"Aspirin."
"Same thing."
"Wine."
"Yeah, yeah, yeah. So anyway, here it is: Three years ago or so I met Marj. She was another stripper. Have you heard of the Rajneeshees?"
"No."
"Well, they . . . she . . . that's another story. But let's just say I saw some alternative ways of two steppin' with this life thing. Remember the Goddess dreams I was telling you about?"
"Yes."
"Well, I started havin' 'em again. I started sticking up for myself. I started wondering about what the hell I was doing, you know? I started feeling . . . hopeful. Naturally, any form of self-examination led to one thing first and foremost: dump Frank. So I did. Since then things have been slowly improving. Reading's about my worst offense these days. Course there's a butt-load of old baggage. Where the hell's my self-esteem? I know I saw it here somewhere . . . that kind of thing. A.A. meetings. N.A. meetings. Oh yeah, I had a rotten childhood, too." Lucy bellowed out a laugh. "And Frank the prick manages to slime back into my life from time to time—if only to show me the battle never ends. Then all my old ways of dealing with shit come back—you know, punching, spitting, scratching . . . House of Commons stuff." Lucy laughed. "But I guess that's the price of history. All events lead to where we are today. Anyway, I'm sorry if I let you down. Enough about me. How have you been doing? You sound a little stuffed up."
"Me? Yes . . . I . . . I've had a cold but I'm doing well. I've been seeking employment, et cetera . . ." I stopped talking, dropped my head in my hands and took a deep breath. "Why must I lie? I've been in turmoil. Fearing death. Fearing life! Out with it! *Who have you slept with!?*"
Lucy cracked a wide open smile. "What?"
"I've had the flu for god knows how long!"
"Why are you yelling?"

"AIDS, Lucy, AIDS! We had unprotected intercourse! Fear has left me without foundation."
"Shel, everything leaves you without foundation."
"How can you joke?"
Smiling, Lucy reached out and took my hand. "You're pretty cool, Shel," she said, "and, yes, I've been tested. After Frank and I broke up. You're the only person I've slept with since."
"*And?*"
"It was okay, you know? You're a little inexperienced. I'm a little neurotic about the whole thing—"
"I mean the *test* result."
"Negative—what do you take me for?"
"What a relief! Of course there's still that new strain that doesn't show up antibodies for HIV—something like eleven cases worldwide. Nevertheless, the odds appear to be in our favour. I think we can both look forward to an angst free sleep tonight."
"I'm glad to hear it . . . Look, Shel, maybe I'm out o' line because I don't even know what you want. But seeing as we're trying to do the honesty thing here and we're talking about sex . . ." The cheesecake came. "I'm just goin' to spit it out: I like you and I want to spend time with you but the thought of getting regularly laid makes me sick . . . no offence."
"None taken. I understand."
"You do?"
"Of course, Lucy. I'm certain we can work out a reasonable timetable."
Lucy laughed. "Uh . . . I don't think . . . what I mean is . . . we can stay lovers, but sex between us is over."
"Over?"
"Yeah."
"Does that include kissing and general affection?"
"Shel, I don't want to get into semantic bullshit. If we can't be mature enough to be sexless lovers, let's just forget it."
"Don't jump all over me. I can do that!"
"Really?"
"Sure."
"You feel okay about it?"
"Yes."

SHELBY

"Great. You know I'm dying for a cigarette."
"So have a cigarette."
"You've got cheesecake on your chin."
"So?"
Our eyes took hold. She grinned. "So wipe it off."
"I'll do whatever I want to do," I said, holding my own.

IX

*Live your life,
poor as it is.*
—H.D. Thoreau

It would appear the short passage of time Lucy and I spent together on a carnal level was God giving me a quick dabble into matters of the flesh so as to save me building up an unhealthy preoccupation with the subject thereby losing my focus to get on with whatever it was I was destined to get on with, which I soon found out to be correcting social injustice.

I dropped by Lucy's apartment late one afternoon to find the curtains closed and the lights out. She answered the door with the chain lock still on. She'd never done that before. Her eyes peeked through the door crack.

"You okay?" I asked.

"Oh, hi, Shel," she said, "yeah." She let me in.

"Do you have another migraine?"

"No."

"Your cheek looks flushed," I said. "Do you have a fever?" Lucy looked up at me. "No . . ."

"What's going on?"

"Me and Frank," she said, shrugging.

"*What?*"

She smiled. "We went at 'er," she said.

"What?"

"It was tit for tat, you know?"

"Tit for tat?" We stared. There was a pause. "Did . . . he . . . he struck you?"

"It was more of a violent wrestle."

"But . . . but he's a *man!*" I cried, spinning around and running into the still open door. "You're not even married to him anymore!"

SHELBY

"Take it easy."
"Lucy, he *hit* you."
"I'm okay, honestly. He won't be back."
"No, no no! This is too much." I turned and ran down the steps.
"Where are you going?"
"This is wrong! I will not allow another voice to be silenced."
"Whose voice?"
"The bell tolls for thee!"
"Shel, come back. It's not—"
"Honour!" I yelled, traumatized, dazed, getting into my car and driving off, Lucy's shouts wailing into an unresponding street.

Arriving at the Big Dipper club and having to double park only increased my frenzy. I stormed through the main door and grilled the cocktail waitress as to Frank's whereabouts. "Stop spitting, you little shit," she said, pointing to a behemoth who was clumping out the door, "he's over there." I ran out the other exit and caught up to him.

"Excuse me?" I said, to a thick boned man perhaps six foot four and 230 pounds, with his suit and crew cut a cross between punk and yuppie.

"You wouldn't be Frank, would you?"
He adjusted a pair of dark glasses. "I might be," he said.
"How could you?"
"Who the hell are you?" he asked. I could smell alcohol on his breath.
"She's a *woman*, Frank!"
"Who the shit are you?"
I moved in a little closer. "You have an anger problem, Frank."
"Who the *fuck* are you?"
"I'm going to warn you but once, Frank. Get help!"
"You just *spat* in my face, you little fuck."
"You're lucky I—" I stopped, suddenly aware of my precarious situation and the change in Frank's general aura. "I . . . I'm sorry if I spit . . . I . . . I'm a little . . ." About then memory fades. My next recollection is of lying prostrate on an examination table, Lucy's blurry hand on my forehead, my eyes flooded with tears.

"You crazy son of a bitch," she said, her eyes warm and thankful. I'd never been called that before. I liked it. I felt like the . . . I felt like . . . his first . . . his first big fight . . . I felt like . . . Madison Square Garden. My hands are taped up with protective gauze, my knuckles ache. The pungent sweaty odour of a dingy locker room seeps in through my crushed nose. I can hear the crowd buzzing fifty feet above the room. The manager's in the corner mumbling salary details to a man with a big cigar and a plaid jacket. A large man with a limp that everybody calls Tiny keeps saying, "Don't worry, champ, you'll be back." I tell him to shut up. He does. Tears are in his eyes. Security tries to keep the press out. I hear Lucy call my name from outside the door. "Let her in, Jake," I yell from the rubbing table, "she's my dame . . ."

"Shel . . . are you okay?" I opened my eyes. There was no security around, no plaid jacket, no Tiny. The smell was that of a hospital, sterile. I smiled.

"What?"

"Are you okay?"

"Sure."

"Your poor face. What were you trying to prove, Shel?"

"I was fighting for freedom, Lucy—yours, mine."

"Fighting? That would mean *two* people threw punches."

"I never saw it coming. Is there a mirror around?"

Lucy took a compact out of her purse and clicked it open. My face was ghastly, yellow and red, eyes badly swollen.

"Your nose is broken," she said.

"I look like a pizza."

"That's one brave pizza."

"I don't understand it," I said. "It's totally against my character. I was incessantly beat up in grade school. Not once did I fight back."

"I guess when it really matters, you're there."

"You think so?"

"I think you should let me handle it next time."

"Next time," I said, "I won't stop until the job is complete." I threw a few punches upwards into the air and we both laughed. Lucy lightly kissed my swollen cheek.

"Thanks, Shel."

"Anytime," I said, throwing a few more.

SHELBY

* * *

After two days of being nursed under the watchful eye of dear Lucy, I returned to my own abode with my ruptured face. Eric was still in California so I had the apartment to myself. I watched copious amounts of T.V., indulged in milk shakes and painkillers, received frequent calls from Lucy and read ten to twelve hours a day. Such meditative solitude—as Thoreau must have experienced at Walden Pond or even Hitler in his lonely jail cell—caused an outpouring of inspiration that peaked while I was perched on the toilet and reading in *The Province* newspaper about yet another massacre in a McDonald's restaurant. In pen just above the towel rack, I scribbled: *Let me feel and love and defend the needy and the hurting, O Punishing God, Holy Creator of the Modern-Day Guilt Trip, or I, too, may open fire in a fast food restaurant.*

Perhaps two weeks into convalescence, my brother Derek called to inform me that he and Kristine had separated on a trial basis. I was deeply saddened and yet somewhat immobilised by his lack of emotion—it was as if he'd phoned to tell me she had gone to the mall to buy Cheezies.

"Are you okay about it?" I asked.

"Yeah . . . Shel, gotta go . . . the game's back on."

"Game?"

"The Lions and Blue Bombers. Overtime. I'll talk to you soon, okay? Shit, I'm sorry. How have you been doing?"

"Okay."

"Great, bye-bye." Click.

A half hour of deep reflection later it came to me. Derek's call was a plea for comfort and advice; the hockey game merely a Jungian type mask used to cover up what appeared to be a sign of weakness in our male dominated—or patriarchal, as Lucy would call it—society. Can a man not reach out for help? Yes, he can—especially if he's *my* brother! After all, when he selected me to be best man at his wedding, despite my being but fifteen tender years of age, I thereby accepted the responsibility of standing by him during troubled times. What a wonderful day it was, too, before God and family and all of the friends he didn't choose. Trisha Blaisdell was the maid of honour—a half-foot and seven years my senior. On the second dance, a waltz, she insisted on jiving. Back and forth I swayed in a cloud of pubescent glory, her breasts bulging before me. She smelled like the perfume centre at Sears; and when I caught a peek at the shaving rash on her underarm it threw me into sexual spasm.

"Hello?"
"Hi, Derek, it's Shel again."
"Did you see that field goal, man? Lui! Lui!—"
"Hide no longer, Derek. I vowed to be your best man and, damn it, I will be."
"What are you talking about?"
"Do you love her?"
"What?"
"Don't give me what, you dodo brain. Do you love Kristine or not?"
"Of course I love her."
"Well then talk to her! Express what you're feeling. Let her know what you think of her. In all honesty, it's hard to figure you out sometimes."
"Bullshit."
"I'm going to let you in on a secret."
"Are you *cry*ing?"
"No! I'm just filled with the spirit! I've quit school."
"What?"
"That's right. School."
"Do Mom and Dad know?"
"No. And don't tell them, either."
"Jesus Murphy, man! Why the—"
"That's not the secret, Derek! Everywhere writers are allegorizing the plight of the twenty-somethings. That's you. That's me. We're lazy! We're without cause! Without direction! Silent. Gasping. Generation X, they call us."
"I can't believe you quit school."
"I'll tell you what that X stands for. *Exhausted. Tired. Sick* . . . of having *those* people tell you and me what it takes to be important in this world. To be relevant. To contribute. Don't they see? We don't want *their* life! We want *truth*! I for one am not ashamed to pick God over a new Toyota!"
"What's got into you?"
"We are not lost, dammit, and don't let anyone tell you we

are! Check it out! Hark, I hear a noise afoot! We are rising up in silent unison! 'Truth!' cried the hippies until their words were garbled by barrels and barrels of bodily fluids and a consciousness of crystalized chemicals. Alas, their movement was blocked. But we are back with their cry, minus the sex, minus the drugs!"
"That's enough! What's going on?"
"Don't you see? It's not a sin to *not* want Swedish furniture. Derek, my brother, my *brethren*, those before us have stretched the elastic band of existence. Honesty, compassion and courage are all that remains. But it has to start from within."
"Shel?"
"Talk to her."
"Shel?"
"Let her know what you're feeling! If you—"
"Shel-"
"—love her—"
"Shel—"
"—you *have* to tell her."
"Shel?"
"For the cause."
"*Shelby?*"
"Yes?"
"Okay."
And in the passing of a few more sentences, Derek confessed he didn't know if they were still in love. He also went on to detail some of the turbulence they'd gone through over the last two years. I hadn't a clue their relationship had unravelled so. I offered unconditional support and told him I loved him. The last thing he said was, "I'm going to take your advice." It was a proud moment.
Perhaps an hour after speaking with Derek, Eric called saying he was back in town, boozing it up at the The Rose and Thorn Pub and in need of an ear. I took mine straight there. Upon arrival, however, he was far more interested in the fact that I had sacrificed my face for the honour of a woman.
"I'm proud of you, man, big time. Seriously—and a little disappointed you didn't land any blows."
"Like I said, verbal jabs to the cerebral cortex. One, two—"

"That ain't the same, man. Look at your mug! Let me take him out."

"No. It's over. My point was made. Violence merely begets violence."

"Y'sure?"

"Certain. Thank you. I want to know what's bothering you."

"I'll do it for you."

"Eric . . . he's *mammoth*."

"Size, shmize."

"Tell me about your trip."

Eric paused, rubbing his fist in his hand. "Okay . . . so . . . the riots broke in L.A. . . . we headed straight north to Reno to avoid being conspicuously white—even though Robbie's black. We get away. Great, we figure, we're safe. Then my old man loses $1,100 playing black jack and winds up drinking himself into an American hospital where he hallucinates for four stinkin' days without medical insurance. Final tab: $8,202."

"Good God."

"That ain't half of it, Shel. Me and Robbie take his wallet so the people at the hospital won't find out he's Canadian, right? We tell them we found him outside Circus Circus and they buy it because he's so much older than us. So then the cops get involved and I swear to God I had the runs for three days from wacked out nerves, man. Look at me." He lifts up his hand. It's shaky. "Meanwhile the old man's seeing mauve giraffes with big balls in his sleep. So in a panic two days ago, knowing we haven't got any cash for the bills, we tell the nurse there we're going to take the old guy out for a stroll around the grounds. Bingo, we throw him in the convertible and hightail it all the way home—17 hours—Dad, a crying, blubbering fool in the back seat. I tell you, Shel, crossing that border I have never shaken so much. But once we're in Canada we're safe, right? Wrong. I've been followed since last night."

"Really?"

"No. My Dad met a woman in Tuscon and he's still there. Robbie and I hung out in Vegas, dried up our savings, booted it here over a three-day stretch and got home last night. I stayed at his house last night and I've been here since noon today . . . drinking."

"So that was all lies about your father?"
"Yup," he said without smiling. His head dropped.
"What's wrong?"
Eric sniffed and took a drag of his cigarette. "Remember that record company I told you about in Toronto?"
"I think so."
"I phoned them this morning and the ass wipe said they'd made a mistake with the demo tapes."
"Really?"
"No."
"Quit doing that!"
Eric looked up at me. Again no smile. His hand was shaking. "I got laid in Walla Walla," he said.
"What?"
"I'm meeting Loretta at ten o'clock tonight and I had sex with a woman in Walla Walla forty-eight hours ago. How am I gonna look her in the eyes?"
"Did you use a prophylactic?"
"I've got to tell her. That's the only thing I can do. It's the stupid 90s, man. Fuck I'm a dildo. Ten years ago you could do this kinda shit, hate yourself and not tell your lover." Eric took a long, nervous drag on his cigarette. "I was really starting to like Loretta," he said.
"Is that why you did it, Eric? Were you getting scared?"
"I've got to tell her."
"I understand, Eric. Lucy got scared, too."
"I have to tell her."
"Even if she despises you afterwards, I'll admire you for being honest. And I think you're a good person. You've been good to me."
"I'm going to spill it to her," he said. "I gotta." He shook his head and took a drag on his cigarette. He was visibly shaky. "You know what's weird, Shel? I spent a month in Southern Cal and Vegas and Reno acting like a friggin' Chinese monk. And driving home I was proud, man, figuring I was out from temptation. I'd passed the test, you know? Next thing I knew I met a woman in a Walla Walla laundromat and then she said we could stay at her house for the night and we drank two bottles of wine and ate bad Chinese food, Robbie fell asleep on the couch and I ended up horfin' her like a damn high-

schooler." The waitress came with two beers and removed the three glasses that were already on the table. Eric reached into his back pocket and pulled out his wallet. It was empty.
"It's on me."
"You're a prince," he said, "and if you change your mind about Frank . . ." We drank and talked for several more hours. The evening ended up costing me about seventy-five dollars; twenty-five for the beers, five for the cab home because I was too intoxicated to drive, and forty-five to pick up my car the next morning. It was impounded for being left in a *NO PARKING ZONE: 7 A.M. to 9 A.M.* For the record, later that night Eric confessed to Loretta his infidelity in Walla Walla. She dumped him on sight.
"What would you have told him to do?" I asked Gran on the phone the following day.
"The best he can," she said.
"That's what he did. He reached within the depths of his conscience and told Loretta the truth. Now look at him."
"There's a price to be paid for experience, Doll. But the good thing is once you've paid that price, it's something you can use forever."
I sniffed and thought about my own lack of fulfillment. "Okay, I've got one for you, Gran. What's the key to a happy life?"
"That's an easy one, Shel," she said. "Enjoy it."

* * *

Other than the collapse of my car's transmission causing a severe dent in the two thousand dollar cheque, the next two or three weeks rolled along uneventfully. I spent most of my time indoors, still recuperating from facial disfigurement. I was again masturbating in excess; identifying career confusion, self-hatred, a lack of physical outlets and the excessive absorption of literature as the root causes. I'd been reading Shakespeare (*Othello*) and Blake (his biography, *A New Kind Of Man*), miscellaneous Jung and Sartre (Lucy's), all four *Gospels*, *Acts* and, most ominously, *Revelations*. If that text is accurate in its prophesying the signs foreshadowing Christ's return, I figured He should arrive in about forty-five minutes. Wouldn't that be something? Interestingly, in reference to the

SHELBY

Hebrew Scriptures, I calculated that it would take 720 feet of rainfall a day for 40 consecutive days and nights to push Noah's Ark above Everest—earth's mightiest peak. The largest 24 hour rainfall on record, however, is a mere 7'2" on some island in the Indian Ocean. Furthermore, it would seem unlikely that a boat 450 feet long and three stories high could carry eight humans, 4,000 mammals (half rodents, a quarter bats), 8,600 birds, 2,400 amphibians, 6,000 reptiles, 1,000,000 insects and ample food all multiplied by a number somewhere between one (some animals are hermaphroditic, humans are accounted for and food doesn't multiply—except in Eric's fridge) and seven (some animals are unclean). Still, it remains unclear if uncovering these facts lessens the credibility of the *Four Horsemen*.

For the first time since Lucy mentioned it, I also had opportunity to research the origin and function of the necktie—and proceeded to put my findings to paper.

TIES

Its original use was of a military nature; a regiment of Croation mercenaries wore ties in the mid-seventeenth century, purpose unknown. From there the French took fancy and passed the fad across the channel at the time of the plague where it caught on more quickly than Newton's discovery of the New Math. How remarkable that two such polar inventions would come out of the same tide of thought—not unlike moon voyages and Hula-Hoops in the sixties. But, alas, ties are just ties, without function, right?
Wrong.
Ties are the closest thing to a hangman's noose that isn't considered barbaric. Ties are the closest thing to a human leash not considered pornographic. Ties are a constant subliminal message to a man that if he isn't strangling somebody's spirit, he's just one shift of a position from being hung up by his own lack of morals. In short, ties are a disguise for the wicked, breed paranoia and I will wear one no more.
A short list of people who wear ties.
Businessmen.
Politicians.
Televangelists.
Wiseguys.

X

*Thank God I was never sent to
school
To be flogged into following the
style of a fool*
  —William Blake

September 4th came and for the first time in fifteen years school began without me. I passed the morning watching T.V. and reassessing options. I got into the devil's water (one beer and a half bottle of peach schnapps) after screening a phone call from my parents wishing me good luck and good fun on my first day back at the university, and asking me if I would be coming home for Thanksgiving. It was the misty-eyed feeling in my heart of guilt and loss that led me wayward. By the middle of *General Hospital* I was soused and titillated (which in my now sober state I can see is the program's objective—as opposed to entertainment). I hid beneath the covers with Minnie—why *Minnie?*—in my mind's eye and so began another episode of *As The Ache Blows.* Alas, drunkenness left me slogging until my thoughts had segued to ways of ridding the planet of Frank. Strangely, this led to insight into the uprisings of lower classes through the ages—be it the English serfs in the Dark Ages, the French peasants charging the Bastille in the 1700s or even the L.A. riots from the 60s through to the present. I realised that having nothing but shabby lodging and excessive amounts of free time will always leave the underprivileged person prone to thinking up violent means of annihilating his or her oppressor. On rare occasions the unemployed layabout (e.g. Joan of Arc) will find his and/or her reactionary ideas being reshaped under the watchful eye of God. This was not one of those occasions. My hand stopped and I lay panting beneath the sheets before eventually pulling them back and reaching out to an empty Kleenex box.

* * *

Desiring structure, I picked up a copy of the *Vancouver Sun* the following morning and scoured the classifieds for employment opportunities. How quickly it bored me. Why couldn't there be a position for an enthusiastic young man to teach poetry to foreign students or the mentally ill? Because the health care system has no idea about holistic healing and even less about the therapeutic potential of 18th century poetry. From experience I *know* a dose of Matthew Arnold can soothe panic attacks better than any amount of high school counselling.

Desiring intimacy, that afternoon I dropped by on Lucy for an hour or so before she had to go to work. It was a remarkable meeting. We sat on the steps and for some reason broke into a discussion of the human condition that must have mirrored Plato and Socrates—answering questions with questions—doing the same thing thousands of years earlier sitting on the steps of the Parthenon in the hot Greek sun.

" . . . haven't we lost the nurturer?" Lucy asked. "Are humans a people without a home?"

"Do people need a home?" I replied.

"Or is *in* the womb the only place humans feel at home?"

"Or is home somewhere we go after we die?"

"Or is it neither, and do we spend our whole lives trying to get something that cannot be gotten?"

"Or—"

Lucy raised her hand to stop me. "Or," she said, "is the earth that womb?"

"And we don't know it?"

"If we did, would we do what we fuckin' do?"

"Who can say what we'd do if we didn't do what we do?"

"I mean it's like what do you get when a drug-addicted mother gives birth?"

"Do you get a baby?"

"Or do you get a *drug*-addicted baby? Extrapolating that to the world, have we made this planet so sick that it gives birth to sickness?"

"Lucy?"

"What about the womb, Shel?"

"Do you think you and I will ever make love again?"

"My friend Marj took primal therapy in L.A. and reexperi-

enced the second and third trimesters of her own gestation period. She said she felt like God in there."
"Not that I want to force the issue."
"That's why I'm quitting."
"I miss it, though."
"Did you hear what I said?"
"I think so."
"What did I say?"
"I'm not sure."
"I'm *quitting*."
"Smoking?"
Lucy glanced at her cigarette. "Stripping."
"Really? Why?"
"Because when I'm up there dancing," she said softly, "it doesn't feel at all like a womb."
"Did you hear what I asked?" I asked.
"Do you know that before God there was the Goddess?"
"I miss it," I said.
"But is what you miss really what you want?"
"I miss *you*," I said.
"I'm right here."
"Yes, but—"
"I'm right here." She smiled. And what could I do? Alas, the conversation had led her to Mother Earth, me to Sigmund Freud. I shrugged, too horny to be rational, and smiled back.

While watching television later that night after Eric had gone to bed, it occurred to me that all the major characters from *Bonanza* were dead (except the foster brother and Hop Sing). Moreover, in 120 years everyone who is now alive will be dead, too. I lay back, closed my eyes and recalled two disturbing statistics that I'd read in *The Sun* earlier in the day. One, 1 in 500 college students in a recent random survey had tested positive for the AIDS virus; and two, 1 in every 23 black men in the U.S.A. is murdered. Turning off the T.V., I felt both thankful to be alive and fearful of the future. My boney chest became covered in goose pimples, my nipples erect. I started to tremble and recited *Dover Beach* in my head, then aloud.

> *Sophocles long ago heard it on the Aegean,*
> *And it brought into his mind the turbid ebb*
> *and flow of human misery . . .*

It was time to start moving. But where? I didn't know. What was my destiny? The phone rang and it scared me. Reaching for it in the darkness I knocked it off the bedside table and onto the floor.

"Hello!" I said, unable to find it.

"Fuck," I heard back. I found it.

"Hello?"

"I've had a crummy night."

"*Lucy?*"

"I was at work . . . and all I had on was cowboy boots—those ones with the tassles—and a cowboy hat—"

"I like them."

"And this front-row dick yells out: 'You ain't no cowgirl, honey, you're just a fuckin' cow!'"

"What?"

"So I laugh and say, 'Hey, aren't any o' you brutes gonna defend me?' I guess I was gettin' used to it with you. Anyway, no one notices—there's a ball game on the big screen. Then the same guy goes, 'Just fuckin' dance and shut up before someone takes your place, you stinkin' whore!'"

"He said that?"

"So I danced a couple o' seductive steps in his direction . . ."

"Why seductive?"

"And kicked him right in the face."

"My god."

"When I was young, like five maybe, my old man used to call me that—'a whore just like your mother,' he'd say. I've never forgotten it."

"Oh my . . . oh—"

"I think I knocked some teeth out. Everything went flyin'. Down he went, crackin' his head like a watermelon. The club was packed. It got rowdy. Some people were screamin' at me. Some were cheerin' for me. I just stood there, naked down to my tassled boots and hat, lights flashing around me like a pinball machine, wishin' there was a Lone Ranger to come ride me home."

"Are you okay?"

"Dammit, Shel! I was sure I'd grown outta those kinda outbursts. I mean I feel *bad*—right in the face. Some poor, drunkin' schmuck gettin' his jollies—oh, I got fired, to boot."

"This is terrible."

"Charges might be laid. Hey, could I come over?" The question surprised me. Lucy had never been here before.

"Of course."

Despite protests, Lucy insisted on taking a cab. I gave her directions and waited.

Upon arrival, she was sad yet calm—less depressed than I thought she'd be. Barely a word was spoken about the incident. We wound up prostrate on the pull-out couch, munching butter-saturated popcorn and watching the late show until five in the morning. Lucy fell asleep just before dawn, her head resting precariously on my chest, her troubled heart seemingly stilled.

* * *

It had been both two days since I'd comforted Lucy and two days since I'd heard from her. Worried, I paid her apartment a visit; the curtains were drawn, the cat was gone and the door was locked. Her mention that she might go to Seattle was all that prevented me from filing a missing persons report. To my surprise, on my drive home I spotted Suzanne in black waiting at a bus stop on the corner of Commercial Drive and Broadway. I offered her a lift. Ten minutes later and despite my admittance to being nonpartisan on the abortion issue, she had convinced me to at least watch from afar the demonstration I was driving her to—if only to get a glimpse of civil disobedience in action. Upon arrival, Suzanne offered a thankful grin, surveyed the crowd of people and stepped out of the car.

"You know, Shelby," she said, "maybe you shouldn't park so close to the building."

"It's fine," I said, stepping out. At that moment the side door of the clinic opened and I was swept up into the throngs of a suddenly enraged mob. Suzanne clasped my hand and I became an uncommitted link in a human chain of Pro-Choicers blocking Pro-Lifers from a group of three or four women seeking abortions. A sudden push from behind caused my link with Suzanne to be broken, and before I could firmly replant my feet, a placard declaring JESUS IS THE ANSWER—NOT ABORTION had cracked me on the forehead with such force I momentarily lost consciousness. In the resulting melee I was literally trampled, punched and kicked by both feminist peaceniks and religious fanatics who obviously cared more about zygotes than me. My arrival to the periphery of the gathering was the result of a sheer will to survive. Before I could inhale, a reporter had swooped down on me demanding explanation and a disclosure of my position. According to the CBC news later that night, and with blood gushing from my forehead, I replied: "Could you spare me bus fare?" Eric deemed me an irreverent hero à la John Lennon, and asked me to play on the sixteenth of September in a new band of his called Void of Paisley. Suzanne in black deemed me an irreverent fool à la Abbie Hoffman and cautioned me on making blanket statements. My parents deemed me an irresponsible young man à la me and were appalled that I supported radical Pro-Choicers. Gran never said anything. My head hurt.

* * *

One week to the minute after I'd last seen Lucy I saw her again. It was 11:05 in the morning and I was sitting on her steps reading *Portnoy's Complaint* and chewing on a cracked nail and a Hershey Bar beneath a sky almost as blue and warm as it probably was in the late 60s. By then, having received nary a word from Lucy and knowing about both her situation with Frank *and* the kick in the face, I feared abduction or worse. It turned out, of course, she had been in Seattle, visiting her oft-mentioned girlfriend, Marj.

"What are you doing here?" she said with a confused smile.

"Waiting," I said, smiling back. After pleasantries, a much needed hug and an explanation of the gash above my eye which led to unbridled laughter from Lucy, we went into her apartment and started up where we'd left off; talking.

The story goes she and Marj once stripped together, and it was Marj who encouraged Lucy to follow her psychic instincts. At the same time, in the late-mid 80s, Marj was considering joining the Rajneeshees, a pseudo-cult-like group based in Oregon and led by the now dead but once enlightened Baghwan Shree Rajneesh. Lucy assured me that this guru was actually on the level, despite rumours of orgies, fondlings and a fleet of Rolls Royces. But on the evening before Marj was planning to move down there, a seventy-two-year-old tycoon from Seattle approached her after she had finished dancing and, with a massive bouquet of flowers and a selection of gifts, proposed to her. After careful deliberation, dinner and three or four Bloody Marys, she consented.

"They got married?"

"Big time," Lucy said with a grin. "You're lookin' at the maid of honour."

"Is the man . . . *perverted*?"

"Marj refuses to talk about their sex life—anyway, who isn't? All I know is they seem happy living in their mansion."

"Mansion!"

"Twelve bedrooms?"

"Wow. Separate beds?"

"Nope. One four-poster beauty made for romantic romping."

"Good God. Does Marj still dance?"

"Are you kidding?" she said, lighting a cigarette. "She now juggles her weekdays between volunteering at a youth centre for runaways and eating chocolate cherry bonbons on the couch with her ugly, overweight chihuahua, Peppermint."

"How cliché and yet fascinating. And you know nothing of their sex life?"

"Okay, Shel . . . one secret," she said. "He's hung like a baboon."

"Is that healthy?"

"I'm kidding. All I can tell you is Marj is a saint. She's got a heart the size of an oil drum."

There was a pause. "Hey, Lucy?"

"Yeah?"

"I don't want to appear childish," I said, "and I in no way want to pen you in, but I worry about you when I'm unsure of your whereabouts for extended periods of time."

"You do?"

"See, I don't have a lot in my life these days; reading, waiting for my calling. Therefore I've fully committed myself to caring for the people close to me—with hopes of expanding that as my confidence grows."

"Thanks . . . I didn't know that it worried you. If I would've, I would've filled you in."

SHELBY

"Really?"
"Yeah."
"Hm . . . Hey, Lucy?"
"Yeah?"
"Nothing."

* * *

Later that evening while Lucy cooked up a stir-fry, I volunteered to go to Safeway and buy some ice cream for desert. Bouncing up the stairs on the way back, I was startled to hear screaming from the front room. I sprinted into the apartment.

"Lucy!"

"*You!*" Frank yelled the moment our eyes made contact, his as angry as a boil. I braked in mid-stride, the ice cream tumbling from my hands.

"You wife-fuckin' adulteratin' son of a bitch!" he screamed as he lurched towards me from the other side of the room. Lucy attempted to slow him down and got knocked out of the way. I turned and ran, sprinting out of the apartment, diving over the railing and tumbling into a juniper bush. Frank pounded down the porch steps to my left, screaming mean things. And there we were; the hunter and the hunted, galloping into the darkness of that Vancouver night, the sound of traffic and the sea upon us; and there I was, bulldozed to the most basic of instincts, survival, and inches from the most primordial of functions, defecation, all the while yelling:

"We're friends! Just friends!"

In the process of sprinting towards my car I opened up a space between us of perhaps a hundred feet—enough, I presumed, to give me time to get into my car and pull away. Getting the key into the door lock while trembling, however, hadn't been calculated into the equation. Frank closed in quickly. Again I was forced to flee, his desperate breaths now within earshot. Perhaps thirty seconds later and without obvious reason, Frank ended his pursuit. I stopped and turned around to see him walking away. The brute had given up chase. I, the victor, bent over and leaned my hands on my knees, gasping for air, keeping my eyes on him. Just when he reached my car he stopped, glanced to his left, and stared at it. There was at that moment the type of silence that allows a person to hear all their own inner workings; blood flow, peristalsis and so forth. I jumped when, with a god-like *tour de force*, he punched out my driver's side window. He then elbowed in the left back window. Before I could react he climbed onto the hood and in a series of frightening kicks with his gargantuan boots, smashed the front windscreen. My reaction was childlike trembling and a welling of tears. Finally, while staring at me, he unzipped his pants and revealed a penis so large it appeared to have a life of its own. Mesmerised by fear and awe, I watched in silence as he peed through the broken window and all over my seat and dashboard, his massiveness silhouetted by the streetlight behind. At that moment I knew what it felt like to be gelded.

* * *

In the days that followed I was so ashamed by what had occurred, I was unable to disclose the truth to anyone. How could a man have his car urinated in by another man and offer no rebuke—and then drive home in it? To myself, I blamed my nondefense of Lucy on the fact that our lack of lovemaking had weakened our pair bond. Although a lie, it didn't come close to what I said to my companions. I told Lucy I pelted Frank with insults until he just gave up. To Eric and the insurance lady, I blamed the damage on unruly teenagers seeking acceptance among their peers. To Gran I made no mention of the violence whatsoever but ventured into the philosophical and asked her: "What does it mean to be a man?" Her reply: "How the hell should I know?"

XI

All that wells up from the depths of the young soul is cast in the old molds, young feelings stiffen in senile works, and instead of rearing itself up in its own creative power, it can only hate the distant power with a hate that grows to be monstrous.
—*Oswald Spengler*

At the Void of Paisley concert on September 16th Eric dropped a Molotov cocktail by telling me he had reason to believe that Bryan was homosexual, and that his anger was probably a result of confusion. Despite my desire to *not* stereotype, I was flabbergasted. Bryan was *so* gruff; *so* big. And yet, ironically, my toosh may be what turned him on.

As for the venue we were playing at, The Big Easy, it rippled with "big hair" women in glossy Spandex pants whose look I would never confess arouses me, but nonetheless does. What is it about wantonness that stirs one's innards and calls to free the individual from sexual constraints? And was this establishment a bastion for ignorance or self-confidence?—for even women with Minnie's dimensions wore form-fitting attire.

To Eric's chagrin the keyboard player never showed up, so essentially we were SMEGMA BOMB! with an alias. An eight-foot banner that Eric designed was suspended at the back of the stage. The words Void of Paisley were cut out of a thick purple paisley material that hung somewhat buckled on a white cotton backdrop. Eric said he used the paisley to emphasize irony. "Pure genius," was my response. I think he took me seriously.

We were the last band of the night after three heavy metal acts. Eric's opening comment through the microphone was delivered with a roll of the eyes: "I assume you've had enough of *glam* rock!" Midway through the opening song (halfway through the set) the banner fell onto the stage in a crumpled heap. Eric's closing comment through the microphone was: "You're all ugly." The crowd was punishing.

Suzanne was at the concert and we went for coffee together afterwards. Her critique was forthright: "The band was horrible but I liked your pants"—which were actually Eric's, and ridiculously big. We went back to her parents' house and she showed me a selection of her sculptures, the zenith being a fabulous series of clay figurines entitled *Modern Genetics*. My two favourites were *Fish-tail* and *Plane Jane*; *Fish-tail* being an old fashioned Chevrolet Oldsmobile that tapered into the back end of a fish, *Plane Jane* a Boeing 747 on top and a faceless nude woman underneath. We chatted on her bed until four in the morning and, to her amazement, I recited select verses from a couple of her favourite poems. Mostly, though, she discussed the impressionists she most respects and her refusal to tolerate relationships that come between her and her art. Upon leaving, an awareness of the chemistry Suzanne and I shared left me mildly guilt-riddled in knowing I was still in some sort of esoterical way committed to Lucy (and indubitably still in love with her). I also knew that continued repression of my sexual urges and an awareness that Frank was thrice my size in every way had affected me enough to speculate on the possibility of other relationships.

* * *

That night I had a dream in which my loins had been replaced with Frank's. But more traumatising was the fact that I ejaculated upon seeing them. It was beyond bizarre, and for three days thereafter I feared sleep. What did it mean? I remember thinking, "I don't want to be mentally ill." But who could I talk to? My fruitless search for answers caused me to justify the happening as a side effect of what I had been through in the previous weeks: the question of Bryan's orientation, degradation at the hands of Frank, seeing Frank's genitalia, Lucy's denial of my needs, excessive amounts of free time, debating the idea of manhood, admitting to a lack of a future, Derek's marital woes, general social strife and perhaps even excessive exposure to bad rock and roll and tabloid news shows. But beyond that, one questioned loomed: Could I be a latent homosexual?

Then came dream number two.
All I recall is that a leg rolled onto my midsection and I awoke with a start, fully erect.
So what?
The confession
Although I saw neither a face nor genitals, I know that *that* leg was not the leg of a woman. I had had a true gay dream. What did this mean? In a desperate attempt to appease my fears, I made a list, trembling as I wrote.

Intercourse with Lucy:	12
Heavy petting with Minnie (mostly kissing):	2
Masturbation: 4/week over 6 years	~1,248
Erotic fantasies: 2/day over 7 years	~5,110
Wet dreams: 4/year over 7 years	~28
Sexual dreams (no ejac.): 1/month 7 years	~84
Hand job over my pants:	1 (Minnie)
Oral sex (blow job):	0 N/A
Total:	6,485

The numbers were relieving. Two homoerotic dreams out of over 6,485, 100% robust, heterosexual emotional and physical eruptions over a seven year period, did not appear to be a threat to my supposed orientation. The fact was I'd never fantasized about a man while awake, and only once or twice had I even considered the option. So I was just over .03% bisexual? It was common knowledge that nobody is 100% anything. Walt Whitman was a 50–50 split and exalted that awareness—in the 1800s no less. Perhaps it was *his* leg. Either way, why had the possibility of being homosexual petrified me so? The current wave of legislated hatred in Oregon and Colorado, the scourge of AIDS, the threat of sulphuric rain, gay bashing and, finally, the fleeting notion of sharing a life with Bryan seemed to be the most logical explanation.

* * *

The following afternoon, packing flowers and an offer for dinner, I arrived uninvited at Lucy's apartment. The door opened.

"What are you doing here?"
"I . . . I thought I'd drop by and see if you—"
"Christ, Shel. I'm in the middle of a psychic reading."
"How long will you be?"
"It's work . . . I don't know."
"I need to spend some time with you."
"Look, come back in ten minutes."
"I . . . flowers . . ."
"Ten minutes."
I trotted to the beach, sat down on a bench, and gazed into the gray yonder.
My rearrival was better received. Lucy invited me in, put the flowers in water and filled the kettle. We both took chairs at the kitchen table. She lit a cigarette and stuck it in her mouth.
"So?"
"Well, we haven't conversed much since Frank chased me out of your apartment."
"I haven't heard from him since, either, so whatever you said to the dick-head, thanks." She grinned.
"I've been doing a lot of self-exploration these days, Lucy, and at this point in my life I'd say I don't have what one would call a useful existence."
"What?"
"And yet a part of me still feels, as if via a calling from a distant mountain or a bad phone connection, that I am still meant to be alive. It is this dying ember that allows me to push forward despite having very few friends, hobbies or goals."
"What are you talking about?"
"In short, I need to know about you and me."
"Sex?"
"In a sense, yes."
"What sense?"
"Well, it's not that I *have* to have sex with you. Many a man has lived without sex; saints, scholars, lepers. But the fact is I am attracted to you *and* emotionally committed. Consequently, I have to continually deny my urges."
"So you need a good fuck?"
"As degrading as that sounds, yes. Ironically, the need is not selfish. Truth is, I'm fearful of the manifestations of continued supressions."

"What the hell does that mean?"
"I've been suffering from a series of abnormalities."
Lucy laughed. "Like what?"
"Anxiety, insomnia, mild skin irritations, mood swings, depressions, self-hatred and I also had ahomaerodeam."
"What?"
"Ahomoeroticdream."
"*What?*"
"A dream . . . I had a dream."
"So?"
"About a man."
"Who?"
"It doesn't matter who."
"A . . . wet dream?"
There was a pause. "Sort of . . . yes."
To my dismay, more detailed confession had her on all fours, collapsed in a cacophony of laughter.
"I fail to see the buffoonery," I said.
Lucy froze in mid-squirm. "You had a dream about a male leg and you woke up with a stiff dick and now you think you might want to fuck men up the ass. That's funny."
"I never said—*aaaah!*" I crumpled to the floor, Lucy having clamped her teeth, through my corduroys, into my calf. Before I could offer protest, she had me pinned, her buttocks crushing my chest, her knees digging into my biceps. I grappled for several seconds without success and then chuckled, pretending I was allowing her to keep me there. Lucy stared at me, her vagina a foot from my face. O how I wanted to combine loins with her in a blitzkrieg of carnal explosions!
"Are you reading my mind?" I asked.
"No, my little faggot," she said with a smile, "but I know what you're thinking."
"Is there a chance?"
"I can only give you what I can," she said. "After that you have to decide if it's enough."
"Do you think I'm gay?"
She smiled. "Are you gay?"
"No."
"Then I don't think you're gay."
"Sit on me forever," I said.

* * *

Yes, we laughed that evening. Lucy even kissed me a couple of times (one bordering on fervent); and in the days that followed physical intimacy advanced in the form of hugs, body brushes, hand-holding and so forth. However, as our (my) needs remained unmet and our (my) questions unresolved, there began to grow an unspoken frustration that had to at some time—and in fact did—reveal itself in an outburst.

Lucy was standing on my shoulders and placing mouse traps in the attic space by the bathroom when I nonchalantly mentioned I hadn't yet confessed to my parents dropping out of university.

"You fucking Nazi!" she bellowed from above, slightly muffled by her whereabouts.

"What?"

"You fucking turd! Put me down!"

"What?"

"Get out of the way!" Bending my knees and moving to my right, Lucy gripped the ceiling space, dangled for a moment, and then let go, crashing to the floor.

"What?"

"You make out like my not sitting on your little cock once a week is the reason you're spiritually hopeless and the truth is you haven't even got the guts to tell your folks you gave up on school!"

"Little?"

"How long's it been? June, Ju—" Lucy counted on her fingers. "What, four . . . five months?"

"I've told my Grandmother . . . and Derek . . ."

"I got my own crapola, pal. My past. My present. My future. Dick-wad Frank. I'm tired o' dancing. Last night in mid routine with my cunt in full parade there was a fuckin' cockroach with the wingspan of a bald eagle climbing up my inner thigh. So I'm *so*, so sorry you ain't got a hole to stick your dick in. *Fuck* you!"

"Lucy, I didn't—"

"You need your dick wet to find yourself? Bullshit! Try looking for the mystic in the shit holes of Vancouver, babe. Dumpin' on me! *Fuck* you!"

"Lucy—"
"Blamin' me for your god damn gay dreams. Get away from me!" She cowered, shielding her eyes with one hand.
"What are you doing?"
"I can't look at you. Get away!"
I reached for the arm covering her eyes. "Lucy—"
"No! Get away! I'm *ashamed*! I can't look at you! Get away! Take your crap! Go!"
She didn't move. "*Lucy*—"
"You're an embarrassment to anyone who's ever tried to grow! Get out! I can't look! Get out or I'll scream!"
"But Lucy . . ." She straight-armed me with her still free left appendage, knocking me towards the front room. "How could I even consider screwing a two year old?"
"Okay, I'll tell them!"
"Get out! I can't look! Get out!"
"I said—"
"Get out!" I tumbled into the street face-to-face with several passers-by who definitely heard Lucy's final demand: "Come back when you're toilet trained, you fuckin' little faggot!'"

* * *

My initial embarrassment quickly turned to self-hatred. Lucy was justified in her ouburst. How could I speak of any kind of emotional evolution when I couldn't even confess to my parents the most significant decision of my life? Clearly, my only recourse was to call them. Instead, I worked for two days on the letter that would let them know I would never be the doctor son they had so yearned for. It read:

Dear Ed and Peg,

Can I ever express the thankfulness I feel towards you both for offering me the gift of life? Granted, I was both a surprise and a mistake. Nonetheless, by your not choosing to terminate the pregnancy, I am here today— hopefully giving at least limited joy to you both.

I have always tried to make you proud. But since I left your loving nest I have been forced to make decisions that will for the rest of my days affect my life. No doubt my second biggest fear was making a decision that would inhumanely disappoint you. My biggest fear, however, was making a deci-

sion that would destroy the essence of my own being. Hopefully I have done neither. With that, I confess, I have left university (last year) to expand the horizons of my innards.

Please do not call for I will not answer. In fairness, however, I promise to come home on Thanksgiving day to discuss this in greater detail. I leave you with a short piece by the famed Irish poet, Patrick Kavanagh.

> *I have a feeling*
> *That through the hole in reason's ceiling*
> *We can fly to knowledge*
> *Without ever going to college*

Constant love,
Your son, Shelby x x x x

* * *

Five days later the phone calls began—all of them screened on the answering machine. On Wednesday there were four, the theme splitting between guilt and disappointment. Thursday there were another four, that cluster moving towards a more threatening tone that culminated in a final threat from Dad: "You're puttin' us through hell. You've been unfair and unrespecting. Your mother's *shattered*. Either call back in half . . . what time is it, Peg? *Peg*! What? . . . Dammit, turn that thing down! ["Seven!" Mom cries from afar] Call back by eight o'clock or I'm driving the hell down . . ."

"You see, Eric? You see that? I'm completely disheartened."

"What?"

"They have no respect for my methods nor my wishes. I told them in the letter I would accept *no* calls . . . but that I'd come home at Thanksgiving to discuss future plans! But nothing's ever enough. Now he's coming down."

"No, he's not."

"What?"

"Oh, come on, Shel," he said. "Ain't you ever been in deep shit, man? I don't even know the guy, but I know he's bluffin'."

"He's definitely not bluffing."

"He's bluffin' . . ."

* * *

Eric's keen insight proved correct. The calls, however, continued for two more days, Dad ofttimes screaming incoherently. As for me, diarrhoea burst upon my bowels, leaving me chafed in the tenderest of places. Clearly, feelings had been hurt and expectations disillusioned. It got to me.

"I'm not going home," I said to Lucy a couple of days before my scheduled departure.

She looked up from across her kitchen. "What?"

I was pacing. "I'm not going home for Thanksgiving."

"Yes, you are."

"I look around, Lucy . . . I see the poverty, the violence, prejudice, pollution, civil strife and so forth. Meanwhile, I've got two knuckle-head parents in turmoil over my leaving an educational system that does nothing to ameliorate the aforementioned. Frankly, I'm appalled by their narrow-mindedness. I will not discuss my dreams with knaves."

"What dreams?"

"There are a plethora of social causes to sink one's teeth into out there. I have to start helping."

"They're your folks," she said, one small nail in her mouth, another being hammered into the wall. "You got to talk to 'em."

"They didn't respect my demands in the letter: I clearly stated no phone calls, I'll be up on Thanksgiving and that this is *my* life."

"You're scared shitless, aren't you?"

"Where'd that come from?"

"That's why you're not going—is this straight?"

"I'm not *going* because my parents have a warped reality of what I am, and I refuse to cater to it any longer. I am me. Isn't that enough?"

"You tell me."

"Nobody knows me."

"I know you—hand me that picture."

"You don't know me."

"Yes I do."

"Did you know I masturbate?"

"D-uh."

"You did?"

"Of course."

"Well . . . Did you know I've considered killing your ex-husband."

"Take a number—and we're still legally married."

"Okay, okay . . . Did you know I had an affair with a *fat* woman?"

Lucy hung the picture and stepped back. "You been gettin' laid on the side?"

"Would you care?"

"I thought I was your first?"

"It was before you. We never . . ."

"How fat?"

"*Fat.*"

"Did you like that?" she asked curiously.

"What do you mean?"

"All that fat."

"I don't know."

"Hm."

"Wait. Dammit, yes I did like it!"

"Hm."

"Surpised you, eh?"

"What?"

"I'm pretty weird, eh?"

"Oh yeah. Big time."

"You don't think so? Okay, that's it. Get *this*: I once stole a pair of my *mother's* underwear and wore them to school."

"How old were you?"

"Seven or eight."

"You're a kinky boy, aren't you?"

"I have my thoughts."

Lucy put down the hammer and turned to me. "I still say you're chicken shit."

"If I'm scared, Lucy, it's for my parents. They see me as some sort of gifted child. When I tell them I'm not they'll be shattered. I don't want to be a doctor. I don't want their life."

"I think that's bullshit. I think you're scared o' your *reaction* to *their* reaction."

"That's fair enough. But it's more than that."

"Oh yeah?"

"It's money."

"Money?"

SHELBY

"Money."

"What money?"

I rubbed my eyes, defeated. "After school ended this year, my parents sent me resources to pay for next year's tuition, books, et cetera, and a few miscellaneous bills. I knew I had no intentions of returning to the campus life. Nonetheless, I was mildly destitute and I deposited the check."

"How much?"

"Two thousand dollars."

"How much do you have left?"

"Couple of hundred."

"I'll lend you the dough."

"What?"

"I'll lend you the cash."

"Absolutely not."

"Look, Shel," she said. "I think you're full o' shit. I think you're scared they're gonna hate your guts. I think you're scared of a lot o' things. So . . . if that ain't true, take the money and prove me wrong."

* * *

The following morning, Thanksgiving, Lucy and I met at Joe's Cafe. It was ten past nine and I was nervous, packed and ready to go home. Lucy offered comforting words and handed me the certified check for two thousand dollars. I thanked her. She winked and lit a cigarette.

"Don't worry, Shel," she said smiling.

I shrugged, somewhat embarrassed by all the hoopla surrounding a trip I should have made months earlier. The fact that I'd borrowed two thousand dollars without the benefit of a job only made the situation worse. "So what plans do you have for tonight?" I asked.

"What do you mean?"

"Thanksgiving dinner," I said.

She made a face of disgust and offered a thumbs down.

"What?"

"Holidays, you know. Crap."

"What do you mean?"

"I . . . I don't like 'em."

"How can you not like holidays?"

"I don't like 'em."
"I don't understand."
"Look, it doesn't matter."
"Why won't you tell me?"
"There's nothin' to tell. Past shit, that's all."
"I told you all those secrets yesterday. Tell me what's wrong."
"Nothing's . . . Okay, Shel, fair enough. Thanksgiving is the day my old lady took off."
"What?"
"You heard me."
"Your mother?"
"One and only."
"How old were you?"
"Five, maybe."
"*Five*? That's so sad."
"Boo hoo."
"Don't make fun of it. Where the heck was your father?"
"All I can remember from that day is standing in a kitchen staring at this thawing turkey on a marbley yellow-white arborite counter—weird how those things stick out, eh?—and blood dripping down the counter. And every few minutes I'd take a peek around the corner at my old man passed out on the front room floor." Lucy looked up at me and smiled.
"Why'd she leave?"
"I don't know."
"What happened to you?"
"I'm sittin' right in front o' you, aren't I?"
"I mean afterwards."
"The usual shit. Kicked around a few foster homes."
"Were they adequate?"
"They were . . . foster homes. Some good. Some bad. Some you get dinner. Some you get love. Some you get fucked."
"Don't tell me that."
"Okay."
"I want to know."
"Okay. Comox, B.C. Franz Belchman and his lovely wife Glenys: pillars of the community. Idle hands and idle fingers. He'd crawl into my bed, sniff my body, rub himself against me,

smell my not yet hairy areas and have me touch him—shit like that."

"Oh God."

"Shel, *every*body gets it sometime."

"Not like *that*."

"One way or another, whatever shit you carry around, Shel, that's your rapist."

"Stop with your tricky words, Lucy. Some things are more wrong then others. That was *wrong*."

"This world is wrong, Shel, even the good stuff. But hey, I'm here, you're here, and we're enjoying a damn fine muffin. She romps along, you know? Anyway, now the son of a bitch has got karma to deal with."

"Lucy, if there—"

"I know. But it's no biggie."

"Oh God. Yes it is! What can I do?"

"You can pay for coffee," she said, offering a blank expression. "I'm broke."

The cheque she'd given me remained clasped in my hand. "But you . . ."

She smiled. "I'm kidding."

* * *

Lucy had stunned me with her confession, and via my prodding and over two more cups of coffee and pumpkin pie she went on to divulge the horror of ritual abuse in more descriptive and less flippant terms. That this tragedy had taken place was nothing new. Nay, such travesties have occurred forever. But to hear it from the woman I loved, and to know about her experience with Frank and the streets and so forth, was deeply depressing. What is this evil world? Who lurks in that distant alley that we are so sure is well lit? Was it any wonder Lucy had temper tantrums that could come and go like a good sneeze? No doubt with my malleable disposition, such abuse would have left me a serial killer—or at the very least a sicko.

"Lucy," I said before leaving, "I can't alter your past. Nor can I control your future. If I could I would. I swear. But I'm here for the duration, and if Frank tries anything, he'll pay."

Lucy smiled. "Thank you, masked man," she said, "now get

on your horse and go." She let out a laugh that seemed really forced.

"I mean it," I said. "He'll pay . . ."

* * *

Melancholy would be the word I would use to describe my spirit as I rattled onto the freeway, before me a sky so white it was as if God had forgotten to colour in the upper part of the drawing. Certainly I was no longer worried about what lay ahead, for expectations deserve to be shot down and life is far bigger than some rebel dropping out of university. I was saddened for Lucy, her being alone on Thanksgiving and having to live with her history. I was also thankful for the joy in my life, and the love offered so freely from Lucy, Gran and, yes, Peg and Ed. I was also ashamed at how, with all life's misery around me, I had done so little for anyone.

Once into the valley I was awe-struck by the fog-covered, medieval looking flats and, higher up, thick clouds that hung like angry black berets above ominous mountains that deepened in colour as I travelled farther east. I passed the seventy-foot Fred Flintstone sign at Bedrock Village. Childhood, I thought. How could they do it to her? Then came the Hope overpass and signs to the Coquihalla Highway. I headed north, soothed by the curve of the road and the warm air from the heater blowing up my pant legs. The big time evergreens, draped in the moody shades of fall, stood proudly against the paved scar that crept slowly upwards to the highway's summit. I was on my way home.

The rain was torrential and visibility nil by the time I reached the bottom of the highway. I turned on my high beams and moved my face closer to the windshield, all the while wiping away the excess condensation.

Driving into Kamloops around four-thirty and still a solid two hours from Revelstoke, I stopped for gasoline. The rain continued its barrage on what appeared to be a town already turned in for the evening; people gathering, I presumed, to celebrate the miracle of family. Outside the day was remarkably dark, the only light coming from a Safeway across the highway. I felt sad all over.

SHELBY

* * *

"Hello?" I said, pushing the door open. There was no response. I heard footsteps. Our eyes met.
"What are you doing *here*?"
"Flowers," I said, handing her the bouquet.
"Is everything okay . . . is your family okay?"
"They're upset."
"What happened?"
"I phoned from a pay phone in Kamloops and told them the truth: that there was a friend that I just had to be with." I smiled at Lucy. "Hi, friend. Oh, by the way, I brought goodies, too." I faced the grocery bag in her direction. "Take a look . . . yams, potatoes, brussel sprouts, corn, sour cream, butter and chicken—they were all out of turkey." I smiled. "Happy Thanksgiving."
Lucy took my hand and hauled me into the kitchen. She put the flowers in a vase and I unpacked the food; everything survived, the butter was of a usable consistency and the chicken, which I had placed by the wheel hub in my trunk, was thawing. Lucy lit two candles on the table, turned out the lights and began pirouetting around the room like a pixie.
"I dance the dance of thankfulness and joy," she said. My eyes moistened. "Hey! Hang on a second, okay?"
"What for?"
Lucy streaked from the kitchen. Exhausted, I sat down and lay my head on the table, as content as I had been as a child hiking through the woods with Gran. Minutes later the kitchen door swung open and Lucy paraded through in a gorgeous black evening dress, her hair disheveled, her face without makeup, her eyes glistening like pristine dew.
"To Thanksgiving!" she said with a pretend glass in her right hand. "And the surprises it brings!" She let out a whoop, tossed off the glass and ran to me, our eyes as one in the candlelight. And then, as though destined, she pulled my head into her ample breast.

XII

*To the sick the doctors wisely
recommend a change of air
and scenery*
　　　　—H.D. Thoreau

That Lucy and I reestablished a sexual relationship was a fact. The respective effects it had on us, however, were markedly different. Lucy was almost immediately dissatisfied—a condition verbally evident. Her most recent outburst took place when in mid-gyration she suddenly stopped moving.
"Get off me," she said.
"What?"
"Get off me!"
"You're on top."
She rolled off. "Get out. I'm bored."
"What?"
"Bored. This is boring."
"What is?"
"Screw, boring, fuck, boring, boring! Boring!"
And so on.
I, on the other hand, was *so* thrilled with our sexual interactions that the hours of my existence outside of lovemaking were as appetizing as a glazed donut breaking out in mold. Incessant phone calls from my parents (most of which I screened) only exacerbated the feeling. It seemed that my fear of telling them I had dropped out of school had been replaced with a fear of facing them since I told them the news. The result was a change in my psychology that left me impotent to any task (other than intercourse) that could result in my being judged. In other words, lying prostrate on the pullout couch staring at the fig stain on the ceiling lacked any expectations and therefore caused no emotional dysfunction.

Washing dishes, however, could paralyse me just by the realisation that I might leave spots. I was so catatonic, I feared a lifetime of failure in excess had shut down my adrenal gland.

As for life around me, or perhaps even despite me, Eric had toppled for a stunning black woman named Nina; full-time teacher, part-time photographer. The relationship, in fact, inspired the behaviour that led to his midnight arrest for tresspassing at the Stanley Park Zoo. Police caught him throwing two large coho salmons into the polar bear pit without permission.

"Why'd you do it?" I asked.

"The subconscious took over, man. Nina's folks took off for Thanksgiving so Nina and I spent the weekend at their place and fucked like crazy on this polar bear skin rug they had in the rec room. It was unbelievable, man."

"Wow."

"Shel, I *totally* dig her. But every time we finished, I felt guilty as shit."

"Premarital sex?"

"No, no. The *rug*. See, it just didn't seem right screwing on the back of an endangered species—you know, with the Inuit and all that. I thought, 'What can I do?' Sort o' like that thing about you always wantin' to contribute."

"Hm."

"Then I thought of those two beat up old bears at the zoo. Could I free them? No. The arctic's like three thousand miles north, I don't have a truck—it'd be dangerous as hell. On the other hand, it's Thanksgiving, maybe I can buy 'em a little treat . . . boom, off I go. What happens? Two fish and a pair o' handcuffs later, I wind up in the joint . . ."

On a less philanthropic front, Eric's song "Better Off Brain Dead (In a World Like This)" had at last report been receiving airplay on both a university radio station and an alternative station in the heart of the city. Although I hadn't strummed on the recording, nor was I still a band member, Eric put together a three song demonstration cassette and asked me to be part of the cover art. So at the beach Nina photographed Eric's face up close while Bryan and I perched ourselves on a rock and jumped around some fifty feet away. The resulting

illusion was two guys dancing on Eric's head. He entitled the cassette: Void of Paisley: WHEN THE FRIENDS IN YOUR HEAD NEED HELP. Driving back from the beach, I told Eric what had happened between Lucy and myself.
"Bored?" he said, obviously perplexed. "Making *love?*"
"I believe '*not moved*' was her exact phrase."
"Wow," he said. "I don't . . . I . . . I've never . . . wow . . ."

* * *

It must have been a day or so later, in the midst of pondering the connection between soap operas (which I was watching), masturbation (whose temptation I was fighting), social demise (if you're not part of the solution . . .) and depression (my own), that I received a surprise call from the Vancouver Public Library (I had applied for a job there months earlier) offering me work as a part-time library assistant. My inability to decline was taken as acceptance.

My first day of training took place at the downtown branch. I spent eight hours sorting through and stacking a veritable sky-rise of books. The day's highlight was an opportunity to stamp cards with a new due date. It was hardly medical school. Then again, there were no exams, they were paying me and I had pending bills. Returning home I found on the pull-out couch a note from Eric.

> *Shel-man: I've been thinking about what you told me about you and Lucy Ample. Here it is. Fucking has nothing to do with sex. Get it? Did you know hookers don't kiss johns? Think about it. Check out the side roads. Check out the cacti. Check out the underground springs. Let me put it this way. You're always saying that crap about heaven in a wildflower, right? Now think of her wildflower as heaven. If you had the chance, would you kiss heaven? See the world, Shel, or get a life.*
>
> *Your pal, Eric.*
>
> *P.S. Fuck you.*
> *P.P.S. Party tonight—be there.*

I believe I understood his intent. What *was* I doing? Had I ever kissed her below the neck? Had I ever rubbed her toes? Lucy Moon has wonderful toes! My god, it was as if I'd been to the Grand Canyon but never left the gift shop.

* * *

There was no answer when I knocked on Lucy's door later that evening. I turned the knob, pushed it open and peeked in. "Hello?" I said to no response. "Lucy?" I said quietly. I popped my head into the front room to see an unkempt looking Lucy sucking on a cigarette. For the first time ever she was watching T.V.; *Three's Company*, of all things. She didn't look up. Smoke blew out her nose. I crept to the couch and kissed her on the cheek. She tapped her cigarette on the ashtray and then leaned back, lifting her bare feet onto the coffee table.

She coughed. "Okay," she said without looking at me. "Let's do it."

I was taken aback. "Sorry?"

"Fuck you! Cut the National Anthem bullshit. Let's get it on." Lucy undid her jeans and pulled them and her panties down.

"What are you doing?"

"Okay, *Oh Canada*," she said without melody.

"Lucy? What are you—"

"I'm prepped, let's go!" Lucy put her hands on her knees and pulled her legs apart. Her eyes never left the television.

"What are you doing?"

"Are you an idiot?"

"Lucy, I don't know what's brought this on—"

"Look, asshole, just fuck me and go, okay?"

"Lucy—"

"What, are you still jackin' off about men?"

"I never have."

"Listen to you, you prissy little cunt." She picked up her cigarette pack. It was empty. "Why do you talk like Prince Dickhead of Lithuania? Let's just fuck and get it over with—or haven't you got what it takes?"

I noticed I was trembling. "Granted," I said, "I may lack charisma. I may even lack the endowment that suffices you. Nonetheless, I do not deserve this!"

"Admit it. You came here to fuck me."

"I most certainly did not."

"Admit it!"

"There's nothing to admit."

127

"If you had your way you'd have me tied to the fuckin' bed all day long."
"Hogwash!"
"I ain't no concubine—can't you say *shit*?"
"What's gotten into you?"
"You want to screw me. Why don't you be man enough to admit it!"
"Sometimes I do, yes, but not now! And not *always*. And never like this! For your information, I came here to explore other options."
"Options?"
"Yes, other erogenous zones."
"Oh you sexy bastard, I can't stop coming. *Fuck you!* What am I? A self-help manual?"
"What is that supposed mean?"
"If you want to experiment, asshole, use your fuckin' hand."
"This is so immature."
"You're a *pig*. Just like all the rest."
"I am about to storm out of this room!"
"Good. Go jack off!"
"Pull up your pants."
"Fuck you."
"You know nothing about romance!"
"You want to fuck me all day long! Tra la la."
"You're making me *angry*!"
"Oh no! He's going to wet his pants!"
"That's it," I said. I turned around to leave and then stopped. "You know, Lucy, there's a lot of unhappiness out in the world today. Crime. Disease. Hatred. We should rejoice in this opportunity we have to be together."
"Oh god, that's so beautiful. I'm coming again!" She fell back on the couch and moaned.
"Shut up!"
"Oh baby, baby."
"That's it. I'm leaving."
"Good."
"I mean it." I left the room.
"You'll be back," I heard her yell. "Your dick'll be back! Back beggin' . . ."

SHELBY

* * *

I drove home dazed, terrified of the years that lay ahead. Despite the hurt, Lucy's insults had left me aware of my pathological need to be in the throngs of sexual liaisons. Truth was, on any given day at any time I was prepared to be taken. Intercourse, in fact, had occurred to me ten or twelve times driving across the Burrard Street Bridge to her apartment. But, then again, so had cunnilingus and various paths toward spiritual growth. Nevertheless, I couldn't stop wondering what would happen if not for that mysterious *je ne sais quoi* that prevents me from acting on every urge. If it wasn't for social normality and women's rights, how far would I go? Who wouldn't I have sex with? When does a rapist become a rapist? When does a murderer become a murderer? Why *didn't* I kill Frank? I wanted to. Why didn't I hire prostitutes? I wanted to. What was keeping it all in? The wrath of God? The fear of prison? Inherent morality? Insufficient funds?

Overwrought with my lack of answers, I opened the door to Eric's apartment to see through the kitchen a half dozen people on my pull-out couch ingesting varied substances; food, cigarettes, alcohol and so forth. On the floor a few feet in front of me was Eric in the lotus position, wobbling his head. He glanced up.

"Ah . . . you are the temple," he said in a Chinese accent. "Fair lady works at shuttles."

"What?"

"Golden cock stands on one leg."

"What are you doing?"

"Tai Chi fridge cleanin'. Step back, slowly . . . repulse monkey." He handed me a beer, pushed himself up, bowed, staggered to his right and took from the oven what appeared to be brownies. "Kids! Dinner's ready!" he said in a high cackle. He put the tray on the top of the stove, turned and spun out of the room, yelling to the crowd: "Darling, where the hell's my squash racket?"

I grabbed his shoulder. "Eric."

He looked around.

"Can I talk to you?"

"Course."

"Do you like sex?"
His face scrunched. "What kind o' question is that?"
"Do you think about it very much?"
"Sure."
"How much?"
"All the time."
"Me, too."
"So?"
"Answer me this: If you could have relations with every women here without repercussions, would you?"
Eric turned back and surveyed the front room. "Like no AIDS and shit?"
"Disease free."
"Look at the onion on her, man," he said pointing. "No pregnancy, no bullshit?"
"Nothing."
He sniffed. "Maybe."
"If you were a world dictator and could have sex with anyone you wanted, would you?"
"Against their will?"
"Whatever you wanted."
"No."
"Why not?"
"It wouldn't be a kick like that." We looked at each other. Eric glanced at the tray of treats in his hands. "Although I wouldn't mind access to a few more babes. Power is a big time turn-on, man. That's why Presidents don't get dick done. Brownie?"
I felt clothed in despair. "I fear nothing is sacred. Does love truly exist?"
"Course it does, you dick. Drink your beer."
"Why do regiments of seemingly normal young men rape and massacre innocent villagers during wartime?"
"What's gotten into you, man?"
"There are men in this world, Eric—men like you and me—who *eat* other people for sexual gratification."
Eric splurted out a laugh and shrugged. "Go figure."
"I'm scared, Eric. What if I suddenly slit your throat with a kitchen utensil?"
"The spatula killings. Pictures at eleven. Ease *up*."

"How can you jest? How can I be sure the women in this room are safe from my kind?"

Eric put his arm around me. "Because three quarters of them could kick your ass," he said. "Have a brownie and keep on your toes . . ."

* * *

The phone woke me up at twenty after six the following morning. I lay crumpled on the pull-out couch, clothes still on, eyes burning.

"Hello," I said groggily.

"Meet me at 3883 Imperial."

"Lucy?"

"3883 Imperial. Quarter to seven. At the pro shop."

"Pro shop?"

* * *

Lucy was standing beneath a clubhouse awning when I arrived. It was pouring. I got out of the car and ran for shelter.

"A *golf* course!" I yelled.

Lucy smiled, reached out and kissed me softly on the cheek. Her breath was warm. She turned my face to hers and looked into my eyes as the rain crashed down behind us. She smiled a soft smile, and then caused my body to shiver with the placement of her hand on my lower back.

"Come on!" she said, clasping my hand and yanking me towards the pro shop.

"I think we should discuss last night."

"I'm sorry about that," she said.

"What are we doing?"

"Guess?"

"Golfing?"

"Bingo."

* * *

Lucy's first swing dug up a divet so immense we could have strung a net across it and called it Wimbledon. The club sprang from her hands, cartwheeled across the face of a monsoon while the ball, without getting touched, toppled off the tee.

"First time?" I asked.
"Yeah. You?"
"Yeah."

By the time we reached the green I was well over what enthusiasts call par and Lucy was prostrate and using the back end of her putter as a pool cue.

"About last night," she said on her belly, knocking the ball a few feet short of the hole. She stood up, soaked. "How can I put this? Last night's geyser—which I'm sorry about—was an example of what happens whenever I get repeatedly laid over an extended period of time. I don't know if it's biochemical or what, but I get . . . I get these streaks of darkness . . . these bullets on my tongue . . . I guess . . . confined. I feel like a concubine."

"I definitely don't think of you like that."

"I lash out. And I know it affects the rest of my life, too. See, anybody can figure out their options when they're left to rot in a damn cage. What else are you going to do? Push-ups? Rot? Shit? But the real test is to do it when you're free, when you have choices." Lucy scratched her cheek. "I gotta feel free."

I paused. "Lucy?"

"Yeah?"

"Do you ever feel *too* free?"

"Too free?"

"Like there's a myriad of potential opportunites; good and bad. So many you're paralysed by the onslaught."

"You gotta be kiddin'," she said.

We walked up the next fairway, silent save the rain and an almost vocal ambush of greenery. Lucy picked up her ball and walked with it.

"I want you to know, Shel, that when you showed up on Thanksgiving, I swear to god I felt like I could come on the spot . . . It was unbelievable. I felt loved, you know? I thought, 'This guy is *A-okay*'—which I still figure."

"I . . . I try to be kind."

She stopped walking. "But I was wrong in thinking I was ready to have sex without feeling like a *douche bag* afterwards—it's the whore thing, maybe. Whatever, I thought I could, with an open mind, you know, make it loving, mystical—do the tantric sex thing, that's what I wanted—to use the tantra and transfer sexual energy to a higher level instead of crushing it."

"And . . . ?"

"It didn't flow."

"Lucy, before you say anything more I'd like to first apologise for my own actions and admit that there were some bonafide truths to last night's accusations. As far as being a lover goes, I *have* been intercourse-oriented, and for what it's worth, I'm committed to change."

"I should have finished what I was saying," she said. "I'm taking a vow of celibacy."

"Celibacy?"

"Sex for me is still power. Control. There's nothing loving about that. So until I figure it out, I need to commit to my needs . . . and I can't feel guilty about it."

"You shouldn't."

"I just can't."

"What about you and me?"

She seemed suddenly sad. "It's too wet for golf," she said.

XIII

> *Be not hasty in thy spirit to
> be angry:
> for anger resteth in the lap
> of fools.*
> —*Ecclesiastes 7:9*

A burst gasket in Sicamous caused me to arrive in Revelstoke at two-thirty in the morning. The kitchen light was left on but all was still. A sense of emptiness coupled with sadness sat like sludge in my heart. There was a note on the table.

> SON
> *There's meat loaf in the fridge.*
> Ed.

Just as I put the note down both Mom and Dad staggered into the kitchen, matching blue polyester pajamas, shading their eyes from the light, staring at me as though I might be contagious. Both squinting, dad rubbed an eye.
"What the hell have you done?"
"I just arrived."
"Three years. *Flush.*"
I reached into my jacket pocket and pulled out Lucy's crumpled check. "I have the two thousand dollars you sent me at the onset of summer," I said, placing it on the table.
"One question, Shelby. Why?"
"Why what?"
"*Why?*"
"We had an agreement," Mother said, jumping in. "We agreed to pay for your schooling. We have. You quit."
"I have quit, yes, but from only a portion of the whole. To the remainder I remain committed to excellence. Surely, life does not end with the dropping out of school."

SHELBY

Dad walked by me gruffly and put on water for coffee.

I stretched. "I'm about ready for bed," I said. "We'll have a good chat come the new day."

Startling me, Dad grabbed the shoulder of my Gortex jacket and twisted me towards him.

"Don't get uppity with us, you yellow son of a bitch," he said. "We are not the one's that don't *get it*. Don't slough off your mother with poetry. You've been a real bastard. Start explaining . . ."

And so, over the next two hours, as exhaustion set in and the general mood wobbled from bitter to frustrated to caustically sarcastic, I tried.

" . . . well I'll be whoopity damned," Dad said. "Hear that Peg? Shelby's working in a library . . . So what do you do there, son?"

"I shelve books."

"He's a book shelver! Great, great. How's the pay?"

"Quite reasonable," I said. "It's union."

"Fifteen an hour?"

"Nine, actually."

"That ain't bad," he said, the timbre of his voice becoming more strained. "Hear that Peg? Fifteen an hour."

"I can hear him, Ed. I'm right here. He said nine."

"Nine?" Dad said. "Lucky nines. Guess you like it, though, eh?"

"For now it's enough."

"For *now*? Sounds like a lifer to me, Shelby."

"Dad . . . I . . . Please understand. I couldn't continue in a situation I didn't enjoy."

"En*joy*?" he said. His grin—which never really was—flipped to a snarl. "You son of a bitch," he said. "*I* do not *enjoy* what *I* do. But that doesn't mean it wasn't the right *thing* to do." He stood up and over me. "Think I enjoyed busting my balls to pay for your three years of university?" He slammed his fist down on the table.

"I appreciate all you've done," I said, "From moment zero to now. And Lord knows I never meant to let you down—either of you."

"If I told you one damn thing it was school, school, school!"

"I still have plans for social contribution."

135

"You know what it cost to pay for the last few years?"

"I could reimburse you."

He stopped in midstep and turned around, leaning his face to my level. "At nine bucks an hour it'll take you fifty goddamn years to pay back thirty-five grand."

"I'll do it."

"In fifty years we'll all be *dead*."

"Too far, Ed," Mom said.

"Too far nothin'!"

"It's five in the mornin,'" she said. "We should get some sleep."

"Oh I see now," he said, "it's all very clear: The power base has split." He turned and walked out of the kitchen, presumably towards the front door. It slammed.

Mom sat down. "What's happened, Shel?"

"A change of priorities, Mom, that's all."

"Come on, talk to me."

"That's *it*, end of story."

"Don't *snap* at me, you little snot!"

I was startled by the attack. Staggering backwards, I mumbled out: "If you don't mind, I'd like to go for a fresh walk—I mean air."

She waved me away without looking up.

Outside I ambled into a sky dappled in cloud highlighted by a low flying moon. "Embrace me restless night," I cried, "for I am momentarily lonely." I ran towards the woods. How could I worry about school with such splendour before me? After all, it was my life, and I was far more concerned with the incessant ache that had managed to lodge itself in my gut like a national landmark for as long as I could recall. As for Dad, I was sorry he was so upset, but there was little I could do for his position—nor he for mine. And Mom? It was so unlike her to bellow at me as she had. Nonetheless, there were more important matters at hand, like moving out from the cosmological void I had for so long claimed as me. "O what awaits? What awaits?" I cried. "I am open to bigger things."

The light of the new day was rapidly ascending and I could just make out the fall leaves, the wondrous surprise of a dark blue dawn. I closed my eyes and smiled. In a neurotic sort of way it was comforting being home. I looked forward to seeing

Gran. A sudden sharp pain in my ribs had me clutching my side and I tumbled to the dank ground. It passed. Morning was upon us all, good and bad, under one moon, one sun. "Without you we are not!" That is what I heard. Sweet Mother of Nature I suck from your ample breast. Every divine second of existence is innately mine—and yet I see not. Why must I be a turd? Why must everybody yell? What have I been thinking? What a fool I have been! I sat on the floor of the woods as precious, tiny gasps of light peeked through her sheltering cover. Moss hung to bark which hung to trees whose roots plunged into the soil like a lover, and the rich ground offered the same in return. I stood up, danced for a moment and then stopped. My heart told me the moment is eternally dancing and all I need is the guts to cut in. So, feeling only slightly self-conscious, I danced some more.

* * *

After spending the morning with Gran, she suggested we borrow Mom's car and disappear on what she'd always called a *road picnic*—essentially a packed lunch eaten while driving. I readily agreed. Nowhere did I feel so comfortable as I did with Gran. She held for me unabashed love, and I loved her for it. In an hour she could be amazed by a wisp of wind, tearful at the state of the world, hilarious in describing Ed's morning habits, and then suddenly silent, for, to quote her, "The only way to have a true conversation with God is to shut your face."

A series of spontaneous dares had us zooming out of the townsite heading towards the sand flats just north of the city dump, Gran convinced to try driving for the first time in her life.

Within minutes of parking, Gran was strapped into the driver's seat and I was explaining the whereabouts and functions of the gas and brake. Her feet barely reached the pedals. I moved the seat forward and stuck my jacket under her to give more height. She said not a word, her hands gripped tightly to the steering wheel, a dark blue scarf wrapped round her neck, her shoulders hunched and her expression one of focussed determination. She leaned way forward, the entire world suddenly an acre or two of sand flats. All she needed, I figured, was a pair of goggles and a WWI flying cap.

"We're not moving," she said.

I went on to explain the *operandus mundi* of the brake and gas pedals in an automatic transmission. "Okay?" I asked.

Gran offered an affirmative *harumph*.

I continued: ". . . and if you want to stop after you start, just remove your foot from that pedal and transfer it to the left and push it down on the other pedal again . . . okay?" She didn't answer, nor did she question anything I said. She pulled her foot slowly off the brake. The car edged a few inches forward. She put her foot down. She did it again. And again. Then she put her foot lightly on the right pedal and pushed. The car lurched forward. By reflex Gran pushed the pedal down even farther. The acceleration caused momentary panic and she slammed her foot onto the brake pedal. We sprang forward before being roughly braced by our respective seatbelts.

"This thing runs like your life," she muttered.

"Are you okay, Gran?" I asked. She didn't respond. "You want to keep doing it?" Her expression remained on the flats ahead. Over and over she repeated the manoeuvre, her confidence increasing with each attempt. The general tension began to dissipate and some fifteen minutes later she was hurtling around the entire area at twenty miles an hour with a wide, smug smile on her face, dust tumbling all around us, her pleasure unbridled.

"Candy from a toddler!" she yelled a couple of times. It was a sight to behold.

* * *

Dinner that evening, to my surprise, passed without upheaval. Having Gran there was the key; if she wasn't the family mediator per se, she was the one that could shoot down an inane argument at fifty paces just by the look on her face—not to mention the fact that, right or wrong, she'd always been one to champion the underdog.

The night was bittersweet, full of quiet reminiscing over a childhood that no longer existed. I rummaged through belongings stuffed into the far recesses of a once magic closet—

a closet that had travelled to the moon, sailed round the globe and been the laboratory of a thousand world shaking discoveries. And what did I find on this night? A Grade Four scholastic ribbon, a set of Dinosaur Cards from Red Rose Tea with drawings and descriptive analyses of certain dinosaurs, my collection of Tintin books and old model airplanes. The fact was I could pour what remained into a shoe box and maybe sell it for a dollar and a half. And the room itself? Its surreality was haunting and yet miraculous; through Vietnam to AIDS, and my own battles with masturbation, graduation, family wars and on and on, it had steadfastly opposed the marching of time.

* * *

Just after dinner the following evening I phoned Lucy. She was packing to go on a two day trip to Seattle to visit her friend Marj, Leonard and their dog Peppermint. I was soothed hearing her voice, and yet pained in knowing the state of our ill-defined separation. Hanging up, I picked a Winnie-the-Pooh book from the bookcase downstairs, sauntered upstairs into the front room, sat down and read.

Two or three pages from finishing and thoroughly enjoying the final chapter, *In which Christopher Robin gives a Pooh Party, and we say good-bye*, Dad walked in, flicked on a baseball game and sat in a chair on the opposite side of the room.

"You watching the series?" he asked.

I glanced up. "No." I looked back down but I could tell he was staring at me.

"They're a helluva team."

"Hm."

"They won't repeat, though, not a chance."

"No chance," I mumbled.

"Do you know what I'm talking about?"

I looked up and shrugged.

"The *World* Series," he said. "The *Blue* Jays."

I returned to my reading.

"Baseball," he said firmly.

I glanced up. "I know."

"What the hell are you reading?"

"Early Milne."

"Never heard of it."
I returned to the book.
"What's it about?"
"A bear."
"What kind o' bear?"
"It's Winnie-the-Pooh," I said.
Dad reacted as a dog does to getting air blown in its face. He shook his head and turned back to the T.V.
I should have ignored him. "Why'd you shake your head?" I asked.
"Huh?" he mumbled, half watching the T.V.
"I'm wondering why you shook your head."
"I didn't shake my head."
"Yes, you did. I said, quote, I'm reading Winnie-the-Pooh, unquote, and your head went back and forth two or three times."
"You want to know why I shook my head?" he said.
"Yes."
He leaned forward. "Because I cannot believe my twenty-one year old dropout son is sitting on a couch in Revelstoke reading Winnie-the-god-damn-Pooh!"
We stared. "Okay."
His face curled up as though his brain had been sucked out from behind. "That's all you got to say for yourself?"
"What would you like me to say?"
"What do you want to say!"
"I . . . I want you to know that my leaving university was no fly-by-night decision. I didn't mean to let anybody down. And yes I'm frightened about what lies ahead. Yes I am aware that I have forsaken the comfortable path. But a man who *hears* a call and ignores it is, in my books, no man at all."
"And what call have you heard there, sonny boy? Call o' the wild?"
"I'm fed up with these attacks! One's *call*ing does not come in the form of a loud scream. It doesn't say, 'Here I am.' It doesn't come with a set of instructions. Nay, it comes like drops of pebbles into water. Yes, and all the seeker can hope for is to somehow make contact with the tip of that ripple and from there follow it to its source."
"You don't have a damn clue what you're doing, do you?"

My ears tingled, my teeth clenched to stop a surge of tears. "Maybe not . . . but I damn well know what I'm *not* doing—no, wait. I know what I'm doing. I am trying to . . . embrace my . . . you're not helping much."

"You want help. Here's help. I ought to *smack* you right in the chops!"

"Offer denied."

"Don't get smart."

"I'm not."

"You think you know it all but you don't really know."

"What don't I know?"

"You don't know shit."

"I know this much," I said, scanning to the bottom of the page. "Piglet asks Pooh . . ." I glanced up and our eyes shook like copulating dragonflies. "Oh . . . to heck with it." I slammed down the book.

"I paid for that table."

"I know. You paid for everything."

"That's right, I did."

"Well . . . I won't be *bought*."

"No one would buy you!"

"I'm not for sale."

"You're already sold!"

"How could I be if no one will buy me?"

The veins in Dad's head began to ripple, rising like swollen rivers, popping on his temples and forehead as he glared at me. "Talk all you want, your damn philosophy will never pay the rent!"

"By the way, I'm not twenty-one, I'm twenty."

And on we went until all family members had been raised from slumber and *Winnie-the-Pooh* was set alight page by page and left for cinder in the family hearth. Gran, for some reason, found the situation hysterical.

I did not sleep that night. How could I? Twenty years old and I was sent to my room. I tried concentrating on my breathing. It didn't help. I read *The Moons of Jupiter* by Alice Munro—a writer Mom loves but who I find tedious. Still slumber was allusive. Despite my best intentions, the one sure-fire soother called from below. So detached I was from my nature, I wound up in heated conversation. "Come on," he said, "it'll take you two minutes and you'll be asleep in five." My hands clenched. "I don't need you." "Maybe not . . . but you *waaant* me." "No!" I leapt from the bed and penned an extravagant letter to Lucy espousing the beauty of our friendship and how I cherished all she'd taught me about the bigger picture. I threw it out and collapsed on the bed, barely able to breathe for the painful urges in my groin. Ellie McMartin, my laboratory partner in Advanced Chemistry 11 and the first woman for whom I ever ached, slammed into my forehead. It was just before the Christmas holidays, 1988, and I had left beneath her Bunsen burner a note with a passage from a love poem by John Donne: *If ever any beauty I did see, 'twas but a dream of thee.* I signed my name and spent the weekend in bed, staring at my three-winged airplane wallpaper, unable to move, filled with terror.

The following Monday between classes, amidst the crowd, I sipped from the water fountain near Ellie's locker and overheard Shirley Derosa (one of Ellie's horrible friends) offering her opinion of me and my gesture.

Shirley: "A love note?" she asked in her Valley girl way.

Ellie: "A poem."

Shirley: "I don't want to put him down, right? But you're my best friend, okay, and I think he's kind of pukish."

Instinct one: Smash my skull into this ceramic fountain and leave myself for dead, unidentifiable even with dental records.

Instinct two: Puncture Shirley Derosa with my compass several thousand times before mercifully bludgeoning her to death with the textbooks I was carrying.

Instinct three: I am a loser. I need to be in bed, wallowing in self-pity and disgust at my own form.

Instinct three prevailed, the first indications of what lay ahead in the not so distant future. But even worse was that without forewarning, Shirley and her loppy breasts and constricted jeans had mysteriously screeched from the hallway and parked themselves in my head like an inoperable cancer of the brain. Oh yes, I despised her for what she had done, and yet there she was, my first ever dominatrix fantasy, yelling: "It's me you really love, isn't it? Isn't it?" And I'd be crying out in my head: "Yes! Yes! Yes!" in desperation until my piston-like hand had finally blasted all my pain drenched gooey stuff into a white rag pulled over my helmet like an Arabian's head gear. Afterwards, I'd lie spread eagled and spent, the wet rag in my right hand, my body and brain draped in an itchy blanket of self-loathing. As late as the following day I would still be walking around hating my every fibre.

Then I'd do it again.

* * *

After a pleasing enough following day and a deliciously oily egg and cheese fry up dinner at Gran's place, I returned home sometime after eleven to find Dad in the front room gazing into the television, hues of blue and purple dancing off his balding head.

"Hello."

"Son—yeah . . . say, I'm sorry about the book."

I shrugged.

"I shouldn't have . . ." He shrugged, lost for words.

"Burnt it," I said.

"Listen . . . you want to have a beer?"

I was surprised by the offer. Never had we drunk together. "Beer?"

"Sure. I got a case o' Black Label in the fridge in the shed. You want to have one out there?"

"The shed?"

"I'll show you the rad."

"The rad?"

"Still leaking," he said.

"Leaking?"

The walk towards the shed was made without jackets. The wind blew cold as though hearkening to the demands of the winter to come.

"Frosty, isn't it?" I said.

"Ten years ago there was snow by Hallowe'en. Makes you wonder if there's some truth to that greenhouse stuff."

"Did you know ten thousand years ago Vancouver was under thirty feet of ice."

"You're kidding me?" he said, opening the creaky shed door. "It musta been hell on rush hour." I stepped in. Dad pulled a switch and a low watt bulb offered a dull glow, as though courteous of the space it was sharing with the prevailing turpentine and gasoline odours that filled the room. The door closed.

"In fact," I said, continuing on, "as late as the Thurass—" A hand on my shoulder spun me round, and Dad, grabbing me by my collar, bulldozed me sprawling into the wall. Wrenches and other tools rattled around my head, paint cans fell to the floor.

"Dad . . . what—"

"Stand up," he growled.

"I'm standing."

"Shut up. Why'd you back out?"

"I just—"

"I asked you why you were backing out."

"I—"

"Put these on." Dad took a shiny pair of red leather boxing mitts off his workbench and tossed them at me.

"Boxing mitts?"

"Gloves, city boy."

"What for?"

"Put 'em on."

"Fisticuffs?"

"Put the gloves on before I knock you right in the nose."

"This is a setup, isn't it?"

"*Put them on!*" he screamed. Terrified, I complied. "Never made you work, never put you in sports, never made you be a man!"

"I've been set up."

"Never taught you courage or committment." Dad started putting on his pair.

I glanced at the gloves on my hands and backed up. "Dad . . . remember when you told me about Orion's belt?"

"Just put on the gloves," he said.

"Dad . . . I . . . I don't even know how to tie these things up."

His hands and head dropped in dismay. The door swung open and there in the dim light stood a toothless Gran and Mom, both in nightclothes, both in gumboots, both staring, void of expression.

"Shelby?" Mom said, looking at me in the boxing gloves.

"There's no beer in here," I said.

"What's going on?"

SHELBY

"Mom, there's no fridge," I mumbled, near tears.
She glanced at Dad. "*Ed?*"
He didn't respond, gloves clutched loosely in his hands, head bowed.
"I was set up," I whined.

* * *

"I'm utterly distraught," I said sometime later, my head laid out on Gran's kitchen table as she plugged in the kettle. "My own father may have pummeled me to death in a back shed."
Gran whistled.
"Where would he have buried me?"
"Good question. The ground's pretty frozen."
"Are all the prophecies coming true? Is the gyre widening; famine, disease, broken men—alas, where even the best lack all sensibilities?"
"Huh?"
"Must I be what others think I should be?"
"I don't know."
"I now truly believe our own lives are mere microcosms of the world at large."
"Come on."
"I feel like an egg!" I cried, thumping the table.
"Scrambled?"
"Is it only through *these* eyes that insanity reigns?"
"Is it . . . Let me tell you something, mister. At forty-two I knew at best I had maybe three childbearing years left. Thing was I'd never met a man worth his salt. *Problem* was, time was running out. So I offered to chaperone a soiree for some of the young soldiers who were leaving for France. This is just before the Dieppe slaughter; the boys were wide-eyed and pimply faced—no fear, boy, they didn't know. No one knew. Right away I spot an attractive redhead. Introduced himself as Pegland Cecil 'Shocky' Dansworth, Private. 'How old are you, Shocky?' 'Eighteen, Ma'am . . .' 'Ay, you're a handsome lad.' Did he blush! So anyway, before the night ends I offer Shocky a lift home. From there I give him the fling of his life, eggs Benedict for breakfast, and the best war story a kid could want. A month later word came back he was dead. Same day I found out I was carrying."

"Mom?"

"And I raised her, loved her, gave everything a single mom could in the 40s. Told her to be proud, to not worry about what the other children said. She grew up beautiful, strong—smart, too. But she still married Ed. You see, Doll, life has always had, between the sheets, between the clouds, between it all, an underlying spirit of insanity."

"My God," I said, "if it wasn't for one virile redheaded young private, I wouldn't be here today."

"And that's another thing, too. Good times, bad times. You gotta give thanks—even for experiences you don't understand."

"That whole story reeks of destiny. I mean what are the chances of ever actually existing? Three or four hundred million sperm per ejaculate. One egg. Miscarriages. Abortions. Out-of-cycle unions."

"Shel, I'm gonna tell you something. Never told anyone else. When I was sixteen I had an abortion."

"What?"

"Ninteen-fifteen. Knocked up by the son of a prominent Toronto politician. Next thing I knew I was on a train into the city. Yonge Street. Old building of bricks. Broken windows. Terrifed, I was."

"I'm stunned."

"I was laying back on a table. Looked over to a wall, stained. Water. Christ on a cross. Not a word was spoken between me and the man. Light in my eyes so bright I couldn't even see the doctor—if he was a doctor. I was sick for three weeks afterwards."

"I had no idea."

"I saw you on the news that night and it brought it all back."

"I wasn't taking a stand, Gran. I have no position on the issue."

"I know, Doll. But let me tell you one thing, if people tell you it's black or white—they're full o' donkey doo. It's pain and fear and guilt and hope and sad and necessary and wrong and right."

There was a pause. "What do you think of sex, Gran?"

"Overblown."

"Do you believe in the *Christian* God?"

SHELBY

"Oh Heavens, the things we done in His name!" Gran shook her head and grinned sadly. "And now in the name of progress. We go to the moon cause we can't make it work down here. What good does it do us? We can't even feed our children. Pollutin' all the world with our big-time factories, keepin' people alive who have the right to be dead and free from all this medicine. See, nobody knows what they're doing, they just know they ain't happy. And it's not about having enough for everyone. Some ghetto kid, what's he want? He wants what those in the suburbs have. But what do they have? Two T.V.'s. A microwave. We gotta learn when enough's enough. Look at Ed tonight. He's got all the comforts. But he ain't got Ed. Never listened to Ed. And we try to blame someone else, or we try to tell everyone how it should be done. Where's it leave us, darlin? All I know is I hear a lot less birds singing songs when the sun comes up than I did thirty years ago—and it's not because of my hearing aid." We both smiled. "It's not that there isn't enough out there," she said. "There's not enough in here." Gran pointed to her heart. "You want to live? Don't let anyone tell you what you should be doin'. You got a big heart. I've seen it a thousand times. And one day it's going to draw you a big map and you'll nod and go, 'Oh, so that's what that old bag meant'." Gran whooped.

"I love a woman back in the city, Gran."

"I know you do."

"She doesn't love me."

"How could a woman not love you? Dammit, Shel, pour it out. Let her know. Take a chance. If it doesn't work, be proud of yourself." Gran sat down and we gazed out the window and into blackness.

"Are you happy, Gran?"

"If I wasn't happy by now," she said with a smile, "I wouldn't be here. At my age you can pretty much decide before bed if you want to cancel your wake up call." We looked out the window some more. "Your old man loves you," she said. I didn't respond. I knew it was true, but somehow it was more fullfilling to be in turmoil.

"Hey, Gran?"

"Yeah, doll?"

"Given everything, is it all worth it?"

There was no hesitation. "Oh God, yes," she said.

* * *

I drove home without saying good-bye the following morning—except to Gran, of course. I snuck away before dawn. What else could I do? I left a note.

Dear Mom and Dad,
It would appear at present we have nothing in common. But what is the journey of a man's life if it is not his own? I feel deep within that within five years we'll all be sitting around a big fire, petting dogs and what have you, laughing about the time Shelby Lewis dropped out of school. But, alas, for now it is all grief. Sorry about letting you down. Love and thanks to you both.
Shelby

XIV

*Son of man, You cannot say, or
guess
for you know only A heap of
broken images*
  —*T.S. Eliot*

The first week back from Revelstoke, I shuffled along without serious mental anguish or physical disfigurement. In one way, I felt more garbled than ever as to knowing the purpose of life—often picturing myself as a spawning salmon swimming back thousands of miles to the source, only to find the river dammed. In another way, I felt more brave than ever, prepared to express both my needs and my shortcomings.

As for Lucy and I, we spent considerable time together and got along wonderfully despite our disagreements on how to deal with Frank (they had a shouting match outside the Cobalt Hotel over past monies), the National Referendum, divinity, the relevance of her flailing psychic abilities, the function of marriage and, of course and most of all, sex. Never was it actually spoken of as a blatant question as to whether we should confer to copulate, but general conversation pointed to the unwavering chasm between our respective wants.

One evening Lucy and I drove to English Bay for a stroll around the sea wall. Upon parking and leaving the car, with the potential for rain obvious by gloomy gray clouds o'erhead, we zipped up our jackets and huddled in close. The sea air was strong, coating my tongue like a salt lick. The tide was in and the beach was as dark as chocolate milk, sprinkled with seaweed and barnacled logs and fishy smells. Just around the first bend, the rains began. By Second Beach, we were soaked. The night had arrived and the pathways were glistening in the lamplight. My pants chafed my tender legs as from deep within I throbbed, yearning to live out a verse or two of the *Song of Songs*.

I knew, however, it was essential that I also be respectful of Lucy's needs, for it takes two wanting souls and a little serendipity to truly share the milk and honey beneath one's tongue. So if Lucy desired celibacy, what right had I to get in the way? Our previous encounters had uncovered me to be spiritually brain-dead. How could I guarantee I'd changed? On the other hand, further sexual suppression could once again tumble me back into a bed of paranoia and questionable orientation. So no matter what, I was a man with a yin that needed to be yanged.

"Lucy?" I said as we walked onwards against the rain.

"Yeah?"

"If I may say, there have been moments, just before I'm taken by slumber, that you've appeared before me as half woman, half fawn or maybe moose, your hair dangling down across olive breasts, and you're bathing in some glacial oasis in the Rockies."

"Really?"

"Yes. And then from the woods I charge like a galloping stud to mount you in a splashy, furious display of such natural anger that you become fully human. Psychically speaking, does such mythology mean anything to you?"

Lucy laughed and then stopped, looking at me perplexed. "I'm not sure," she said. "You ever fucked a dog?"

"Of course not."

"I don't know, Shel."

"Well, answer me this then: Although your path is celibacy, do you still sometimes think about men?"

"Sure."

"Me?"

"What are you getting at?"

"I don't know. I . . ." I gazed into Lucy's wet and smiling eyes. Rain streamed down around us. Blood and hormones rushed north to my chest and head, south to my loins. "I was . . . would you explain to me about tantric sex again?"

Lucy stopped walking. "What do you want to know about it?"

"Just a few of the basic principles."

"Well . . . the main thing is it's not about orgasm—at least not in the blow your wad sense. It's meditation and balance, transcending the physical."

"So it doesn't involve ejaculation per se?"

"It's about a valley orgasm—and there *is* intercourse."

"Oh."

"It's a perpetual kind o' thing, Shel. No highs, no lows. Some call it a cosmic orgasm, too. Sex becomes a means of transcendence."

"That's sort of paradoxical, isn't it?"

"What is?"

"Well . . . you're saying you want sex to help you transcend and yet you don't want to have sex."

"I just . . . I ain't ready to screw on that level, yet. It's still a power game, you know?"

"So you're working towards being able to?"

"Sort of . . . I know I'm working towards something. What I'd really like is to get to a place where sex isn't even part o' the gig, eh?"

"Really?"

Lucy smiled, stroking her wet hair from her forehead. "Hey, it'd save a hell of a lot o' bull."

"True," I said. "And yet . . . with the state of this wacky world, to engage in such primitive ecstasy with the person you love surely remains wondrous in its own right."

"On paper, sure. But with no Goddess? See, look at science. No spirituality. A tragedy. I mean forget emotions and passion or even committment for that matter. That's all bull. You gotta have the Godhead, Shel. You don't have that in your sex—shit, that should *be* your sex—you end up with what we have now . . ."

"Being . . . ?"

"Being AIDS, rape, syphilis, unwanted pregnancy, venereal warts, unfulfilled expectations, herpetic sores, endless guilt and urges that are so out of control no amount of release can shut 'em down, pedophilia, harassment, power, power, power . . ."

There was a pause. "Yeah, *and* . . ."

We laughed, strolling the next few hundred yards without discussion. The rain let up.

"You know," I said, "I think I understand what you're talking about. Granted, my goals have always been less grandiose—but perhaps that was more from a lack of awareness than a lack of desire."

"The tantra has nothing to do with desire."

"Semantics."

"No it's not. Desire has got to go."

"Okay, no desire."

"Shel, this is just my path. Don't get hung up about your own sexuality."

"Thanks. Hey Lucy, for the record, what spe*cific*ally does take the place of ejaculation?"

"I told you, the tantra allows us to transcend the physical."

"Yes, but what does that *mean*?"

"It means the release is ever present. It's like meditation, Shel. You have to experience it to understand it. People say, How do you meditate? You meditate—"

"Holy cow!"

"What?"

"I've had a flash—and upon brief deliberation, I can fully see the side effects of unsacred love. Therefore and henceforth, I, too, will strive for sex *only* as a vehicle of transcendence."

"A flash?"

"And what's more, out of pure and compassionate love for the All, I am willing to let *you* have me as a partner!"

Lucy laughed. "I'm not ready yet—but thanks."

I thought for a few seconds. "This could take weeks, couldn't it?"

"Years."

"Still, once you're there, you'll need a partner—I mean, not *you* necessarily, but *one* would need a partner."

"Shel?"

"Yeah?"

"I'll let you know." She smiled and gave my arm an affectionate squeeze.

"One more thing, Lucy."

"Yeah?"

"Well, I don't necessarily agree with it, but how do you feel

about the notion that every now and then, purely in the name of mental well-being, the male sex needs a damn good lay?"
"I don't buy it," she said.
I stopped. "Why not?"
"There's no evidence it works," she said. We walked on.

* * *

Week two began with a frustration that most rigorously revealed itself just after two o'clock on Tuesday afternoon while I was watching Oprah Winfrey and guests discuss how to keep the sexual spark alive in relationships. Suddenly and without forewarning I found myself closing the front room curtains and masturbating to the image of Miss Winfrey herself strutting before me in pleated pants, demanding my servitude. Ten unreleased minutes and a fiery bang later, I'd slammed Eric's toaster oven through the T.V.—an outburst that left me rattled over potential repercussions, relieved at the death of my 16" x 11" suppressor (perhaps, symbolically, Frank?) and fearful at the state of my mental health. Thankfully, Eric was unaffected by the event, his sole recommendation being the creation of a payback plan. It turned out to be $55 per month for six months concluding with a $70 payment on month seven. As for the television itself, we removed all the inner workings and replaced them with an aloe vera plant from the corner store on Fraser (my treat).

By Friday, I realised T.V. withdrawal was reopening my ears and eyes to the reality of three dimensional life. In fact, after spending my lunch break at the downtown library listening to a cluster of employees dicussing *Murphy Brown* as if it was significant social commentary (even her name is dumb—and Dan Quayle is right, there *is* something wrong with the American family), I penned a short yet luminous letter to *The Province*'s editorial department stating recent revelations:

Dear Editor(s):

QUESTION: *How in this, the media age, can the U.S. government sell arms to Iraq one week and be at war with them the next and still get support from a solid block of the American public?*

ANSWER: *Television. Beyond creating a simpleton society that gets its role models from music videos, gets its God from Jimmy Swaggart and dismisses poetry as passe, T.V. prevents the masses from organizing intelligent uprisings. Yes, Los Angeles was set ablaze by anger over the Rodney King beating. But what good did it do? The have nots now have even less. And is it a coincidence that atomic warfare and television came into being at approximately the same time? Was the Cosby Show truly a sign of increasing racial unity or rather an attempt by television and/or government white supremacists to manipulate the youth into believing the civil rights movement is fait accompli? Is there a link between the Beverly Hillbillies being the number one show of 1963 and Kennedy being assassinated in that same year? And, finally, isn't Madonna taking up just a little too much of our time?*

Take a gander at your T.V. set, Canada, and ask but one question. Who's eyeing who?

Shelby M. Lewis
Vancouver

P.S. The average T.V. watcher is witness to 18,000 commercials a year.

That afternoon, while sorting books behind the circulation desk, I was startled to glance up and see Minnie T. standing at the book check-out, all aglow, as fat and sexy as ever, smiling and frollicking with some misogynist-looking young man in an expensive sweater. My heart pounded with fear. The last thing I wanted was to have her see me and then have me admit to the dismal state of my current life. Ashamed, I bent down behind a trolley full of books and pretended to sort them. Hearing laughter I peeked out to see that same man brush the hair away from the side of Minnie's face and whisper in her ear. Minnie shrieked with laughter, pushed him lovingly away and half yelled, "Steven!"—which looking at him, was probably spelled Stephen. They were proclaiming their love like televangelists on a money run. Stephen's beeper sounded and I fell backwards, knocking a few books off the trolley. "What, did someone's plumbing back-up?" I said to myself with a chuckle. Stephen unhooked the device from his belt and said to Claudia at the front desk, "Could I use the phone, please? I'm a doctor." I couldn't hear what Claudia said but she did a half turn and pointed directly at me. My bowels nearly opened before I realised she was indicating the phone on the librarian's desk several feet to my right. I discreetly turned around, stood up and pushed the book truck towards the exit foyer. I stood there breathless, my heartbeat spiralling up the stairwell in echoey throbs, my jealousy of Stephen's integrity clawing at my insides, my delight at Minnie's happiness jaded only by an awareness that, thanks to my ignorance, I never took her there. Several minutes later, certain they would have checked out their books and been gone, I opened the door and literally bounced into Minnie on the other side.

"Shelby Lewis!" she screamed with a smile.

"Minnie..."

"Do you work here?" she asked.

Embarrassed, I looked away. "Um... part time... a little."

"Wow," she said, "me, too!"

* * *

I arrived that evening at Lucy's apartment with my first installment towards the two thousand dollars I owed her. Her calico cat was in the window in front of closed curtains. There was no answer even after repeated knocks. As usual the door was unlocked. The hallway was dark. Walking softly into the front room, I turned on the light to find Lucy's clothes crumpled on the floor in front of my feet; T-shirt, jeans, sweater, panties. Books were everywhere. I crept towards the bedroom and called her name. There was no response. My heart sprang into my throat. I put my hand on the doorknob, turned it, and pushed the door open. Light from the front room streaked across the floor. Lucy was wrapped up in a white sheet in the far corner of the room, her head leaning on a pillow pushed against the wall.

Fearing the worst I sprinted to her side. "Lucy!"

Her mouth opened slightly, then closed. "Migraine," she mumbled.

"Migraine?"

"Migraine," she said again.

"Do you need a doctor?"

"Migraine," she repeated, still not moving. I reached out to her and then stopped.

"Uh . . . Are you . . . What do you . . . do you need anything?"

"Close the door," she said in a slow, monotoned voice. "The light's killing me."

I ran to the door, closed it and slithered back using the bed as a guide. I sat down next to her again.

"Hi, Shel," she said, her voice scarcely audible.

"Hi," I said, placing my fingers lightly on her cheek. She tilted her head towards them in acceptance.

"Um . . . should I . . . can I hold you?"

"Sure," she whispered. I unwrapped the sheet that was draped around her and put myself in a position to embrace her sitting down. We slid into each other easily on the hardwood floor. I loosely pulled the sheet around us. Lucy turned her head sideways and eased it onto my chest.

"It's going to rain tonight," she said softly.

I cupped the back of her head with one hand and softly stroked her hair with the other. Her body was warm. No more words were spoken. We didn't move for hours.

Sure enough, it poured all weekend. In between our respective workshifts, I nursed her as best I could. It was in that time, in fact, that I was able to see just what it was about her that moved me so. In short, her idiosyncracies; the way she devours her food with gusto, the way she sucks on her cigarettes as if within loom universal truths, the way she thrusts herself into conversation like a human cannonball, the way she gyrates her ideas into my brain until her words climax in a burst of love from her life-soaked, earth-drenched eyes. Even her manic moods tickle my insides. The woman accepts pain like it's a Blue Cross from God.

By the time a cold and rainy Monday rolled in, Lucy's migraine had subsided. We picnicked on a quilt in her kitchen; two candles, a loaf of sourdough bread, butter, a bottle of Anacin, two sliced tomatoes, salt and pepper, two carafes of crappy red wine and no glasses—a pair of romancing tramps. It wasn't long before the first bottle had disappeared. I was tipsy and aroused, eyeing Lucy maybe four feet away as she painted her toe-nails.

"I'm serious, Shel, I'm gettin' totally sick o' strippin'."

"Do that again," I said, unscrewing the top of the second bottle.
"I just painted them," she said.
I took a swig. "No. That thing with your tongue?" I said.
"This?" Lucy said, rolling her tongue into a U-shape.
"Extraordinary," I said. "Praise be to dappled things." Lucy smiled and kept working on her baby toe. "I can't do that," I said.
"Course you can."
"No. Watch. My tongue won't curve." I tried.
Lucy laughed at the attempt. "Come on."
"I can't!"
"Do it.
"It's genetic—a Mandellian acquired trait passed on through the mother. No. Wait. Wait. The father."
"Bullshit," she said, shaking her head and passing me the bottle.
"Why would I lie?"
"Why would something so pointless be genetic?"
"How can I even venture a guess? It just *is*." I took a swig of wine.
"It's got nothing to do with personal choice?" she asked, still painting her middle toe.
"Personal choice? Genes come from parents."
"Some say *we* even choose our parents."
"Oh come on! I have serious doubts that the brain stem of a spermatozoa is emotionally capable of barrelling out of the urethra yelling, 'Stand clear, I am choosing to latch onto this egg!' while three hundred million others exit a step behind, cheering him on and doing the wave."
Lucy folded over her piece of bread and took a bite. I took a swig of wine. She said, "I say not only that, I say *all* things good and bad are essential for cosmological harmony."
"What?" I shook my head and put the bottle back down on the quilt. "How can famine or AIDS be essential for cosmic harmony? How can some psychotic pulling out a machine gun and shooting his family over Christmas dinner be a necessary part of anything?" I blinked and felt the wine rush to my head.
"What came first, the sociopaths or the psychiatrists?"

"What?"
"Wars or armies? Skin colour or racism? Life or death?"
"Are you going to have that last tomato?"
"Don't avoid the question."
"What question?"
"And second," she said taking a snort from the bottle and wiping her mouth, "do you figure some people are more genetically predisposed to being assholes than others?"
"It's upbringing."
"And do they or do they not serve a purpose?"
"Parents?"
"Everyday human atrocities."
"No."
"Then why do we keep having 'em? Why have we always had 'em?" Lucy passed the bottle back.
"To learn."
"Have we learned?"
"Maybe humans is a *we* thing, Lucy, but I am not responsible for Auschwitz or the slaughtering of Indians or Ethiopian famine or any of that. I am responsible for seeking truth—as well as protecting my family's welfare and, on occasion, yours." I took a snort.
"Then who stands up for the battered child and the raped forest and the ozone?"
"Well..."
"And I thought you were Mr. Humanitarian—or is that only when you're sober?"
"Retraction! Retraction! The aforementioned assessment of my responsibilities was naive. Truth is I want to contribute socially. But I refuse to flagellate myself for history's errors because they were committed by ignorant asses who happened to have the same skin pigment as me. Nay I say! Vive la global community! I have guilt to last three lifetimes." I took a hard swig and wiped my mouth on my forearm.
"What guilt?" she asked, taking the bottle from me.
I looked up. "Where do I begin? My God. Dropping out of university. My father is crushed, all parental ties severed. Academic destiny: *gone*. Religious confusion abounds. I've made no major social contributions. Oh, and wanting *you* in a lecherous way doesn't exactly fill me with gaiety."

Lucy grinned. "Don't let that crap bug ya! That's your path. Embrace it."
"Oh, wonderful. Hello, path."
"We're *all* lost! Doctors. Priests. *Library* workers. I'm a psychic without powers. Even those poets you love. Hell, bein' lost, that's where we get the poetry."
"Give me that bottle!" I yelled. Lucy laughed and handed it to me. I took a swig and belched. "There is no poetry in *my* struggle."
"We're babes of the mystery, man."
"Yes, but who really *feels* that?"
"So you were bullshitting when you said the great thing about Whitman and Blake and those guys is they celebrate the uncelebrated?"
"I certainly was not! Did I say that?"
"You're drunk."
"You are! And no, I don't believe every teensy-weensy thing is poetry. Neither are some big things. Top forty music? No. Figure skating? *No.* Hitler? I cannot and will not accept that bastard being compared to Angie Dickinson."
"Don't you mean *Emily*?"
"And I tell you now! Poetry is a divinely inspired art form slaughtered by ambiguity. At best I'd say Hitler's actions were prose. Genocidal tendencies have very little rhythm—I'll bet he couldn't tango to save his life." I burped. Lucy laughed and I yearned to kiss her. I took another swig from the bottle.
"Shel, it's this simple. Some people deliver babies. Some people drive trucks."
"I feel all giddy," I said with a giggle. "Speaking of Germans, Suzanne's art class at Emily Carr has an exhibition on all week that I wouldn't mind missing."
"You mean seeing?"
I lay down on the quilt. "Skinheads frighten me."
"What?"
"Hey, do you want to see her show?"
"Yeah, sure. When?" she asked, taking a bite from her slice of bread.
I shrugged and closed my eyes. "Say you love me a hundred times even if you don't."
"You love me a hundred times even if you don't."

My insides went gooey. "Thanks," I said, eyes closing.
"Let's go tonight," she said, "I'm not workin'."
"Me neither . . ."

* * *

Later that afternoon, after my nap, Lucy and I walked to Granville Island and took in the exhibition. All bias aside, Suzanne's work was to both of us the most accomplished of all. Seeing *Fish-tail* for the second time, I was even more impressed, and planned to ask Suzanne at our next get-together if she'd consider selling it. There were also some splendid ceramic pots with Indian motifs by someone with an unpronounceable name and a set of appealing impressionistic figurines entitled *Bondage*. Other than that, as much as I abhor those who judge art, I'd have to say the creations were *dégoûtant*. The worst piece was a blob of formless clay in a brown glaze called *Life's Turmoil*. When I mentioned to Lucy it should have been titled *Used Pampers*, we giggled for fifteen minutes. In fact, most of the show had us laughing.

On the walk home we detoured to the Bread Garden and stuffed ourselves with cheesecake and cafe au laits while men in khaki pants stared at Lucy and me in wonder. In other words, "Why is she with you?" Finally, when one handsome bronzed man in a turtleneck glanced at her and then me, I glared back with a subtle yet confident smirk that said: "Figure it out, dunce, or I'll be with your woman next." His eyes scampered to the floor. My boney chest puffed with pride.

Lucy and I slept together that night. There was no sex. There was not even a mention of sex. Nonetheless, I felt adored by the woman; I was her confidant. Moreover, I was getting cosmologically comfortable—a burgeoning Thoreau for the 90s, if you will (with a sprinkle of Hemingway thrown in); rejecting social expectations by quitting school, journeying into manhood by facing my father. So I was unsure of my calling? What was Jesus doing at twenty? Hardly changing the world.

I awoke around six A.M., my right arm tingling beneath the weight of Lucy's head. Shaking off the numbness, I lifted the blind and peeked eastward. The sun was rising without fanfare; that same eternal ball of fire that rose over Mesopotamia and the first sedentary civilizations some ten thousand years earlier; that same endless ache of heat that hung above upright footprints in Olduvai Gorge three and a half million years before that; that same life-sustaining star that had overseen every torrid love affair since time began. And there was Lucy and I, stumbling yes, yet nonetheless mapping a new blueprint of avant-garde chastity for young lovers to follow in the disease-plagued, turbulent and uncertain years that lay ahead.

Floating my hand onto Lucy's belly, I stroked her gently. She didn't recoil so I moved in closer and nudged my erection against her leg, my heart against her back. Without opening her eyes, Lucy rolled over and embraced me. Our bodies moved in time and then stopped. My penis throbbed and I contemplated a tug at her panties, thereby initiating the potential for penetration. I didn't, though.

After a morning of quiet wonder, I left Lucy's apartment with a sense of connection; if we weren't lovers by strict definition, we were nonetheless hinting, with nary a word, at that inevitablity. I drove home in control of my genitals, surrendered yet strong, beaming and assured. I slammed the car door with a little more *oomph* than usual. The day called for it. I didn't bother to lock up.

It was just below the steps of Eric's apartment that I first heard the phone ring. I broke into a sprint. It rang twice more as I fumbled in search of the correct key. My third choice got me in. I slammed the door, tumbled over the pull-out couch and rolled to the phone à la James Bond.

"Hello?" I said, panting, laughing.

"Shel, it's Dad."

"Oh . . . hello," I said cautiously, fearing a lecture. We hadn't spoken since he'd lied about the beer in the shed. I decided right then to let bygones be bygones.

There was a pause. "It's Gran," he said.

XV

She who lives out all of her days has had a long life
                              —*Lao Tsu*

It was good to see Derek and Kristine as a unit when they picked me up at the Kelowna airport; death, it would seem, had reconciled them. Our reunion was mildly teary. The utter dread I felt upon hearing the news of Gran's death, however, had dissipated. I felt curiously numb.

Barely a word was spoken on the drive to Revelstoke; I sat quietly in the back seat, reminiscing, sensing Gran's presence (memory, perhaps) as I associated more than ever with crabgrass and trees and other objects of nature that don't give a damn about death. For, indeed, the lake was still filled with water and the rolling hills still rolled; even downtown Revelstoke hadn't changed, the main street looking more uneventful than ever. And then we were home.

Stepping into the kitchen, the first thing I saw was Uncle Larry and Dad sitting at the table, silent, Dad smoking, Larry glancing around like a child. Mom was pouring a cup of coffee. She stopped and we stared. It was unspoken that we were closer than anyone to Gran. Embracing, I felt the wetness from her eyes seep through my cotton shirt and onto my shoulder. I pushed my hand lovingly on the back of her neck and felt a tear of my own trickling down my cheek. I had no idea what I should or could offer. What difference would it make? She pulled away and with a beat-up Kleenex blew her nose as mothers do. Her puffy eyes glanced at me as if to say, "Ain't life a swift kick to the groin?" I smiled back as if to say "Yeah, I reckon it is." Then with an about-face that bordered on the schizophrenic, she took a deep breath, closed her eyes, opened them, sniffed, wiped her eyes, smiled again and said:

"Enough tears, Mom would hate this!"

Mom was back at her post as platoon leader—a thankless job if I'd ever seen one. If my rank had been any higher than private, I would have ordered her to take a week of R & R. She deserved it.

Dad and Uncle Larry, meanwhile, remained slumped and downcast at the kitchen table. When I reached out and hugged Dad, his odour of sweat and cigarettes and generic cologne catapulted me back to cuddling on his lap as a child, *Hockey Night in Canada* blaring in the foreground. Taking a step back, I figured he must be an expert on death; when he was seven, his mother died of cancer; when he was eleven, his younger brother was hit by a bread truck; and his father—the man who told me masturbation was the equivalent of pulling God's hair—passed away ten years ago.

As for Larry, well, he had God.

* * *

The evening's last light coasted effortlessly into darkness and despite the pain that surrounded us all, our collective grief seemed to somehow lessen the individual ache. We even shared a few laughs.

Just before midnight Larry, huffing and sniffing, returned from the washroom and sat down next to me.

"Hair-raising, isn't it?" he said quietly.

I glanced over and smiled, for the first time in memory aware of a bond between us. "I don't know what to feel," I said. "I keep expecting her to walk through the door."

"No," he said, "I mean the afterlife."

"Scary?"

"Well . . . facts are facts, eh?"

"What?"

"Look, first off, let me just say I ain't *God*—never have been, never will be."

"What are you talking about?"

"I'm just saying that, well, according to, say . . . Luke 13:5—you know that one?"

"No."

"Ah, there's a bunch of them—anyway, it doesn't look good for her down the main stretch."

I glanced at Dad who was leaning over the newspaper with Derek and Kristine, then at Mom who was pouring a cup of coffee.

"Eleven down is aardvark," Kristine said.

My insides rattled. "What doesn't look good for her?"

"Come on, Shelby. The Man wears the robe. The gavel's gotta come down."

"Larry ... um ... you're not saying that Gran's going to hell, are you?"

"Two A's," Derek said.

"Of course *I'm* not saying that. I'm saying the scriptures say that."

I became tense. "Let me get this right. You're saying that Gran, because she never took Jesus Christ as saviour by *name*, she's going to be in Hell for eternity."

"It's in God's hands."

"That's the God you believe in?"

"It's in the scripture."

"But you believe that? You believe that this compassionate God is sending Gran to Hell."

"Does it matter what I think?" he asked.

"I want to know what you think!"

Mom glanced up. "What's going on?"

"Larry's telling me Gran's going to burn in hell."

"I am merely a messenger of the word, Peg," he said.

"This is an outrage!" I shrieked.

"Take it easy, Shelby!" Dad barked.

"Take it *easy*? I want to know what he thinks! If he thinks Gran is going to Hell he should come out and say it!"

"Shelby," Larry said, "I have no control over these things."

"Have you ever even said a prayer for Gran, Larry?"

"I've talked to her many a time about her worldly ways."

"I don't want to know *that*! I want to know if you've ever said a prayer for her! Or do you only pray for your own life?"

"Let he who has ears hear," he said defiantly.

I felt frenzied. "You think she's burning in Hell, don't you?"

"Blessed are those who will be persecuted in His name, for *theirs* is the kingdom of God."

"Persecuted?" I said, standing up. He sat staring, grinning.

"Sit down, Shel," Dad said.

"Did you hear what he said?" I screamed.

"Come on, Larry," Dad said, "smarten up."

"I'm only speaking the truth, Ed," he said, turning towards Dad. "You know as well as I do she wasn't one to—"

Right then I punched Larry square in the face with a closed fist. His head snapped back and then flung forward, grimaced expression moving towards shock. He seemed temporarily paralysed in his chair. I, too, was stunned. I had never struck a person before. "Oh, god," I recall thinking, "what have I done?" And then seeing Larry sitting there, eyes all a-flutter, I panicked and punched him again. Dad tackled me to the ground as Larry's nose poured blood. He staggered to his feet.

"For your glory, Lord!" he cried, wobbly-legged, his white shirt speckled crimson, his eyes glazed like a dog with cataracts.

I lay pinned, staring, shaking. Had divine inspired sentences off the tongue of a man I did not respect loaded my right hand with fury, or was I attacking the words of the devil?

"*Burn!*" he screamed at me, staggering out of the room, blood everywhere. "Burn! Burn! Burn!"

* * *

On the one hand, I would imagine it's always troublesome to justify punching a relative in the face. On the other hand (being my bruised right one), I believe in my heart he deserved it. In what must have been a Hell in itself, Gran had to live within walking distance of the man for thirty years. Moreover, one who compulsively talks about persecution would seem to want to be hit eventually. Now he was. As for me, a lack of remorse was disconcerting; but more disconcerting was the unpremeditated outburst. What would I have done had I been carrying a revolver or even a dinner knife?

* * *

Repeated attempts at reconciliation over the phone proved fruitless. Eventually everyone went to bed and I found myself standing on Gran's doorstep, contemplating knocking. A gust of wind slipped up the back of my shirt. I shivered and turned the knob, slowly pushing the door open. The kitchen table was bare and Gran's chair was as empty as I'd ever seen it.

"Hello?" I whispered, glancing cautiously around the silent room. From the watercolour paintings and the worn shag carpet to the firewood and the musty couch, all was as it had always been. I don't know why that surprised me, Gran had been dead for less than a day. I suppose I half expected her to suddenly stomp through the door and yell, "Well, I'll be damned, Shel, I thought you were back in Vancouver!"

I crept into Gran's bedroom and sat on her bed, stroking my hand along her bedspread and then her backrest pillow. Her navy blue, well-worn duffel coat was hanging on the back of the door, garden mud around the edges. I felt my eyes moisten. Her umbrella was in the corner. On her desk was a photograph of me, her and Derek taken a couple of Christmases back. She had her teeth out and she was saluting.

"Hi, Gran," I said, trying to smile.

There was no answer.

* * *

The following afternoon while I was sitting at the kitchen table, I overheard discussion of the funeral plans.

"Pardon?"

"What?" Dad said.

"Did you say closed casket ceremony at the cemetery?"

"Day after tomorrow," Dad said.

"Uh . . . I'm afraid not."

Mom stepped forward. "What are you talking about, Shel?"

"I know for a fact that's not what Gran wanted," I said. "A couple of summers ago we were sitting on her porch and she told me that when she died she wanted her ashes spread across the yard. I remember because she mentioned something about being toasted with a bottle of Maupassant. I had to tell her he was a writer. You know what she said? 'Well then see if he can come.'"

We all laughed.

Mom sniffed. "That's what she said, eh?"

"Definitely—back to the earth."

"If that's what she said, Ed," Mom said, "that's what we'll do . . ."

* * *

SHELBY

As absurd as it sounds, the day of the funeral was magical. Standing in the backyard amongst friends and relatives (save Larry, who left a note saying: *Will not attend, let the dead bury the dead*), I could hear Gran in the wind and feel her in the sun, as if Heaven was only a moment away. The sky was half-filled with floating clouds the shape of farm animals and a breeze that blew the autumn leaves in a manner reminiscent of some blustery day in the heart of Victorian literature. Champagne and glasses were set up on the picnic table with cheese and crackers, a goose liver pâté, homemade antipasto and the vase with Gran's ashes. We didn't use an urn. The funeral director told us that people who are spreading ashes generally keep them in the original white cardboard box that they are put in after cremation. When I brought the box home, though, Mom was so distraught with the shabby look of it that she immediately transferred the ashes into Gran's favourite flower vase.

While Father Fox, a three-hunded-and-fifty-odd pound Anglican with an honourable if not healthy heart, mumbled his sermon into the wind, somehow tying it all up with references to his mother's cooking—*what a soufflé! But, no, it did not always rise to perfection, bless her heart*—and other delicacies. I, meanwhile, found myself contemplating Larry's attack on Gran's soul. Was it Gran's fault she wasn't overtly interested in personal salvation? Fact was, if she arrived at the gates and was being let in while others were being shooed away, I'd wager she'd say something like, "Listen Petey-boy, either we all go or I ain't budgin'."

Glancing up to see Father Fox spreading the ashes, I was immediately upset by his apparent trepidation. "That's Gran in your hand," I recall thinking, "put a little into it. Spread them like you mean it. Put some soul—"

"Excuse me," I said, surprising even myself. All heads turned.

Father Fox looked up. "Yes, Shelby?"

"Um . . . I don't mean any disrespect, Father," I said, "but could I . . . could I do that?"

He hesitated, confused, and peeked at the remaining ashes in his hand. What was there he brushed awkwardly back in the vase.

"The ashes?"

"Yes," I said.

He seemed surprised but unoffended. That was fortunate, for my intention was clearly not to hurt his feelings. "It's not usual," he said, "but neither was your Grandmother." Everybody laughed, a welcome reprieve. He motioned the vase in my direction.

"Thank you," I said, nervously approaching. "I have a sense that this is the only time anyone will ever spread Gran's ashes and, well, she's my Gran and . . . uh . . . to be frank, I think I know how she'd like them to be spread . . . no offense." He smiled as if to say, *none taken*, and handed me the vase. I turned and faced the crowd. The wind picked up. I closed my eyes and took a breath before turning to the vase. "This is it, Gran," I said. I looked at the faces before me: Mom, Dad, Derek and all the rest, and without warning sprung forward.

"Look out!" I yelled. Dad and second cousin Horton from Salmon Arm leapt out of the way just in time to give Gran and me sufficient room to bob and weave through the second and third rows. I reached my hand into the vase and flung ashes like confetti to the far reaches of the back yard and then into Gran's beloved garden. The wind howled out its support. We darted and danced to the call, Gran ecstatic as we ran towards the greenhouse. A quick cut sent me towards the apple trees and the compost pile. "This is the way you do it!" I yelled. The crowd had spread out more, some in awe, others offering tentative pursuit. "Don't you see?" I yelled. "Don't you see?" We turned towards the cherry trees. "She's everywhere! Everywhere!" I spread her on the bird bath. I threw her in the rose bush. "Everywhere!" I rejoiced, spinning like an Olympian doing the hammer throw, the vase out in front, blowing ash into the cosmos as I turned faster and faster, tilting my head back and screaming to anyone or anything that would listen, the wind howling with boisterous approval, autumn flying into the mystic ache, Gran's heart beating in perfect rhythm, the colours of fall twisting before me in a wondrous collage of oranges and reds and yellows and greens and . . .

Black; pumping, breathing, cold, wet darkness. My eyes opened to the blurred vision of my mother's face and an increasing awareness of sky, wild and blue, revolving around her head like a halo. Slowly she came into focus—nose first, at which point Dad's face joined in.

"Are you all right, Shel?" a voice asked. I shifted my eyes from side to side—looking at all the familiar faces.

"Son," Dad said, "are you okay?"

I looked at him from flat out on my back. "Hi, Dad," I said.

"Son," he said again, "can you hear me?"

"Sure," I said. "Why?"

Then I saw Derek's face. "Is he okay?"

"Hi, Derek," I said.

"I don't know," Dad said.

"Who?" I said.

"Should we get him on his feet?" Derek asked.

"Who?" I said again, as they hoisted me up by my arms and dragged me towards the house.

The moment they sat me down in the kitchen, tears poured up from my heart and into my cheeks, the overflow balancing on my eye-lids.

"I guess she's gone, eh?" I said. A few minutes of interrogation and a wet towel on my forehead later, I had gathered myself enough to go back outside. The masses surrounded to inquire about my condition.

"Well, young man," Father Fox said with a smile stretching his rosy cheeks into two red apples, "that was a divine performance. I'm considering hiring you full time. You okay?"

"Yes," I said, "we're both fine, thank you."

"Good," he said, shaking his head and pivoting like an overstuffed turkey towards the picnic table for another helping of hors d'oeuvres.

The champagne was poured and everybody took a glass. Dad said, "To Gran!" and we all simultaneously repeated it. Tears aside, the mood was festive. I sat by myself on the edge of the picnic table, my heart a collage of sadness and anger, numbness and wonder. How Gran would love to be at this party, I remember thinking. And why couldn't she be? She was only ninety-three. Of course I knew that was old, but compared to what? Had Eve done us in with her garden disobedience? Did all hatred and misery stem from such a mistake? Were episiotomies God's grudge against the first sin? I slipped another quick glass of champagne and became acutely aware of Gran's presence; festivity, eros, wind. I missed Lucy. She had offered to accompany me but I, in stubborn haste, turned her down. What a mistake! What could be more wondrous than discussing the relevance of existence with a beautiful woman from the city in front of a group of country folk? I poured myself another glass of champagne. Gran would have wanted my spirits on high. And so I had a fourth. After my fifth glass I stood up.

"To my closest ally, Gran," I said, "who taught me how little I know." Nobody moved. Nobody even noticed. "Fuck you all, then," I said. I didn't mean it.

XVI

Who's who in
Hinterland?
—Lorne Greene

Guided by the revelation that awoke me at four A.M., my decision was an easy one. My confidant, my mentor, my embassy of refuge, my pal, my Gran had returned to the source and the hour was nigh for me to do the same. All that remained was the penning of a short good-bye note to my family and a letter to Lucy.

Dearest Mom, Dad, Derek, Kristine (and Larry, see Matthew 7:3).

Apologies for not waking you. Thought you could use the sleep. Decided to go home early. Hitching a ride into town to catch the bus home. Talk to you soon.
                    Love, Shel.
P.S. Sorry I let you all down with my education.
                    Love, Shel

Dearest Lucy:

I'm writing to let you know I've decided to stuff muffing about and truly seek the source. Gran came to me in a dream tonight and said, "Shelby, I think I left the stove on." In other words, a warm light to guide my way. USE IT!

It would seem all enlightened men (and probably women, too, although none come to mind—Joan of Arc, perhaps?) were at one time or another called into the wilderness; Jesus Christ, John Yepes, Walt Whitman, Moses, Abraham (the desert), Gautama Buddha, Henry Thoreau, most aborigines, et al. You can now add my name to that list. I would first off like to thank you for the love you have shown me over the past few months. You have cracked open my skull to a myriad of ideas and insights. For

> what it's worth, Gran would have loved you. I applaud your celibacy—
> but don't fight the urge, for then everything gets messed up.
>
> > Eternally, Shelby M. Lewis (who dropped out of school and into life. Farewell.)
>
> > P.S. Please do not contact my parents. They believe me to be taking the bus back into the city. It's better that way. P.P.S. Maybe we could get married when I get back. (Just kidding).

* * *

By five-thirty I was packed and standing on the edge of the porch gazing upwards to a parade of stars, considering God. If in fact the world is a mere six thousand years old, I told myself, He would have had to have created the light from the stars already in mid-flight on the way to Earth in order to make their vast distance away make any sense whatsoever. Accepting for a moment that He was capable of such playful buffoonery, I felt unconditionally protected. My first step made a crunching sound on the frozen front lawn and I thought of Neil Armstrong. Free association led me to think of Armstrong, the small cheese-making community just south of Salmon Arm, and finally, to my bag of Cheezies which I quickly devoured. At the end of the path I dropped Lucy's letter in the mail box.

An hour or so into the journey I strutted into Revelstoke National Park with the image of the voyageur dancing across my mind's eye; blazing trails over pristine country, draped in furs, no roads, no bridges, no worries, trading post to trading post, free from homeland tyranny, free to celebrate good old-fashioned life. And I, their progeny, proud in the wake of Gran's call to be doing the same. I wished I had a pen and paper to keep a journal.

By noon (judging by the sun), the forest had thickened to the point where hiking was treacherous. I stopped, yanked off my pack sack, sat on a moss-covered log and beneath a canopy of tree branches ate a banana and three handfuls of peanuts. Taking off my tuque, I could feel the steam rising from my sweaty head. All before me was silent, majestic greens sprinkled in white, beckoning, beckoning . . .

A sharp pain descended from just below my sternum,

gradually increasing until my bowels burned as if on fire. I found a suitable clearing, pulled down my corduroys, crouched and let out a grunt into the wide open space. For the first time in my short life I felt part of the land, part of the cycle. A gust of wind shot up like a wet towel and cracked my cheeks, causing me to flex my sphinctre muscle so abruptly I toppled backwards into the muddy terrain. Pushing myself back up I continued the task at hand. About half-finished, I noticed a distinct lack of toilet paper and/or toilet paper substitute. As far as the eye could see was an infinite supply of prickly-needled evergreens. My legs broke into a quiver. I waddled towards my knapsack, removed Dad's *Wilderness Survival* handbook, tore out several pages at random and wiped. Hurdle one had been overcome. The trek continued.

By late afternoon, each step became a lesson in perseverance. My legs felt brittle from toes pinched by hiking boots a size too small. Looking up *Footwear* in Dad's book, I was dismayed to read, *Footwear is especially important . . . Lost in the bush is no place to get blisters from stiff boots.*

Estimating I'd travelled thirty to thirty-five miles and ignoring the limits of the human body and in particular feet, I grimaced and trudged on, the price for transcendence fully laid out.

* * *

Recoiling out of thick bush at around dusk, I tumbled flat out onto a wondrous clearing of dirt and rock and moss. Before me was a hill descending gently towards a magical creek perhaps twenty feet afar. I threw my pack to the ground and galloped to its edge, cupping handfuls of its sweetness to my thankful mouth. Climbing back up the hill, I lay my head on my pack and smiled into the fading light, the ache of Gran's death soothed with the remembrance of her toothless grin. I was enraptured with the possibility of immediate eternity and the opportunity to harvest my soul in the belly of paradise. Glancing to and fro, I marvelled at the river rocks and the lichens, the bushes and the trees as my eyes gently heavied. Indeed, I had found my Walden Pond . . .

Thunder awoke me with a start. I was shivering and

shrouded in darkness. Fumbling through my pack I managed to find matches, but every attempted strike was met with a far stronger gust of wind. Shivering burst into trembling. Scrambling up the hill on all fours I played braille in the dirt in an unsuccessful search for my gloves and tuque. Despair joined my battle for light. Dragging my pack and sleeping bag onto more level ground, I pulled the tent from its covering and spread it out by feel and, shortly thereafter, was able to join two metal rods together—presumably the centre pole. Confidence increased accordingly and then collapsed completely upon awareness that I had failed to pack pegs. Panic seized my chest and I scrambled towards where I thought the large tree was, in hopes that I could break off branches and make suitable alternatives. I did so until out of the night a branch skewered me in the eye with such abruptness, I fell to the frozen ground, writhing in pain, screaming and fearing death by over-exposure.

Then came the rain—hail-like drops that stung on contact. Clutching my face, I eased down to the creek and pulled from the freezing water a large stone to be used as a makeshift hammer for pounding the pegs. I crawled back up and, numb hands dripping wet, caked with mud, draped the tarpaulin over me. From there I slipped the ties around the pegs and hummed soothing Gregorian chants to the mindset of the voyageur while my eye poured fluid. It was, in fact, in this meditative trance that I, after six or seven successful hits on the peg, pulverised my left thumb with an errant strike. Never had I been so instantly terrorised; flat out and writhing like an epilectic salamander in a mud pit undergoing shock treatment, one eye wide open in the endless darkness, the light pressure of rain drops landing upon my face via a tarpaulin that took on the feel of a body bag, I realised my days—nay, my hours—could well be numbered. Slowly the cold crept in, my screams turning to dull moans and finally silence, my body motionless as though carved from wood.

Sometime into the night, after I'd slithered my battered body into the canvas tent for additional cover, the rain turned torrential. I could actually hear the rising streams of water forming beneath me. My toes and backside were without sensation. I cradled the hand of my crushed thumb into my genitals for extra warmth and wound up erect. All was black. All was silent. I pictured myself frozen, skin as translucent as skim milk, body as stiff and cold as marble, eyes like ice cubes in a blue tray.

* * *

Morning arrived after several terrifying and freezing wake-ups in the night. The light cast hues of orange through the tarp. My thumb throbbed and was functionless; my eye ached and had all but swollen shut. Scratching my head I discovered sap in my hair. I rolled out from underneath the covering and a chilled stream of water poured onto my leg as if it had been waiting all night for the opportunity. My blistered feet yearned for nonuse. Oddly, I didn't cry. I didn't even react. I lay staring at a sky so blurry and white I wondered if it existed at all.

A stomach growl snapped me from my daze. I dug into my pack and pulled out the last apple and Dad's *Wilderness Survival* handbook. It said: *So you're lost. Don't panic. Survival is a state of mind.* I screamed. Scanning further I read: *When you are lost and confused, a fire will give you a psychological boost, help you relax and provide company on a lonely night. Caution: Improperly set, a small one can spread quickly and soon a forest fire is burning out of control, causing additional problems to the person lost in the bush.* No kidding!

I collapsed onto the tent only to have icy, muddy water gush all over the front of my pants. It was France, 1917, trench warfare, the enemy unsighted yet ever present, dead horses and maggots and lice, rats in their glory—and fear like a coat of red paint across the face of a pimply, young Canadian soldier . . .

Then back, thinking of Gran, I sobbed, aware that my only hope was to find a way home before my organs froze. And so I packed up, prayed for strength, and followed the sun. By early afternoon I was emotionally, physically, and hopelessly lost, delirious, seeing myself as part of the food chain; being first ransacked by a pack of migrating wolves, flesh torn from my feet, shins, and then higher, my defenseless body devoured while I looked on in terror. Calming myself slightly, the new image was more gentle as through brown eyes I gazed into an empty sky as the majority ingredient of a wolf bowel movement. Too weak to know better, my feet kept moving until a vision of Gran found me howling into the echoey abyss. My link to life was broken. Lucy was all that remained. Accepting that, I refused to die. But how could I know what lay ahead?

XVII

Though in my fear of hell I had condemned myself to the prison house where my only companions were scorpions and wild beasts, I often found myself surrounded by bands of dancing girls.
—St. Jerome

"So then what happened?" Lucy asked, finishing the bandaging of my thumb.

"Well, I calmed a little and saw myself as wolf defecation. After that the hallucinations started."

"Weird."

"Lucy, there was a moment I truly believed my legs had turned to compost."

"Wow." Lucy rinsed my eye-lid. "Why'd you run from the gargoyles?"

"Wouldn't you?"

Lucy glanced up and smiled. "You should get this looked at," she said, referring to my eye, cigarette dangling from her lip.

"They were huge."

Lucy smiled. "So then what happened?"

"So I ran until . . . well, twilight. Suddenly everything looked exactly as it had hours earlier, and I feared I'd travelled in a massive ellipse. About to give up, I collapsed on the frozen ground. Suddenly, and from not so afar, I heard a rumbling in the distance. With all the courage I could muster I dragged myself up and onwards. Minutes later, there it was."

"Another gargoyle?"

"Hardly! The Columbia River in all its roaring glory! Next thing I know I'm walking along the Number One highway, hitchhiking for the first time in my life. It's eleven-thirty at night. I'm fluish, frozen, insane with fatigue. The *first* car picks me up and this strange character out of some old movie drives me directly to the depot! So there I am, out of funds. What happens? For no reason, after a short conversation with the clerk he offers me a *free* ticket! The bus travelling to Vancouver arrives, I place my belongings underneath; eight hours later, here I am."

"Wow," she said, taking the cigarette from her mouth, tipping the ashes in the sink.

"I tell you, Lucy, I was looked after. I was meant to come back here."

"Are those tights all right?"

"Quite snug," I said, biting my piece of toast.

"The pink is you," she said, "sets off your skinny legs."

"Thanks."

"Do you want to talk or anything?"

"Must you keep asking in that weepy way? I'm not two years old. I told you, I know Gran is *fine*. And so what if my seeking the source was temporarily halted by faulty gear? Alas, it appears the source was with me anyway."

"I could've told you that."

"I had a revelation on the bus trip home."

"I really think you should get your eye checked."

"Just as the chains of abuse are perpetuated through time, beyond genetic barriers, I now realise so it goes for love."

"Feel what you have to feel, Shel. You and Gran were *so* close."

"Would you stop! Anyway, this is about Gran. Listen: In short, there are bits of Gran's love in me, and now, subconsciously, I'll pass them on just by interaction with others. Isn't that wondrous? A meets B, and B, now with a little of A, becomes C. Then C, say C is me and A was Gran, meets you, D, and D, with a little of C, becomes E, and so on for eternity."

"Have you slept?"

"We are products and results of the other."

Lucy smiled. "I am you as you are me and you are he and we are altogether."

"In a sense, yes. And understanding that," I said, "how sad could I be?"

"I don't know," she said, ripping a piece of toilet paper off the roll and blowing her nose, "but just don't get into one of your self-bullshitting trips."

SHELBY

"How can you say that?"

Lucy flipped the toilet paper into the bin beneath the towel rack and shrugged. "I know you."

"Well, I'll tell you. I've never been stronger; aware for the first time that we are all equals, our destiny the waste product of another organism."

"Oh, by the way, I'm going on the road tomorrow."

"What?"

"I'm going on the road."

"What for?"

"Work."

"What?"

"*Work.*"

"You can't. Not tomorrow."

"What do you mean I can't?"

"I mean why? Why would you do it?"

"It's my job, Shel. Rent. *Food* . . ."

"It's the money I owe you, isn't it?"

"Shel, I've been on the road a million times."

"It's Frank, isn't it?"

"What's Frank?"

I grabbed Lucy by the collar. "I'm going to kill that bastard."

"Ooh," she said, turning away.

"What? You doubt me?"

"Your breath," she said.

"What's that supposed to mean?"

"It's bad."

"Always?"

"No. Right now."

"It's always bad, isn't it?"

"Right now! You've been in the woods for two days. You spent the night on a bus. Anybody would have bad breath after that."

"I'll still kill him."

Lucy wiped my chin with her hand.

"Why'd you do that?"

"Do what?"

"Brush my chin."

"Crumbs."

"Crumbs?"

179

"*Crumbs.*"
"What kind of crumbs?"
"I don't know—from the toast, I guess."
"Crumbs on my chin!" I wailed, falling to my knees.
"What are you doing?"
"Don't go!"
Lucy bent down and hoisted me up, my arm around her shoulder.
"What are you doing?"
Lucy didn't reply, instead dragging me into the bedroom and dropping me on the bed. She took off my shoes, giving both feet a tender squeeze. I tilted my head forward and glanced at her through my only good eye. She smiled warmly. "It's gonna take some time, buddy. Do what you have to do. Feel what you have to feel."
"What do you mean?"
"Let it out," she said, blowing me a kiss. "I'll be in the other room. Call me if you need me."
"I don't need anyone!" I cried.
She grinned, and gave my foot a gentle tug as she walked away.
"Don't go! I . . . I need . . . I . . ."
She stayed.

* * *

I slept most of the night, waking occasionally to nightmares and bouts of disorientation. Lucy astounded me with her nursing abilities; she not only cleansed my wounds, she lent me her television, cooked up a huge breakfast and actually escorted me to the bus stop in the morning. I was truly touched, and as the bus pulled out and I waved through the window I had to beat down a swell of tears. Arriving home I called out to Eric but received only silence. There was a note on the kitchen table.

December 7 Noon
Hey, man. Not sure when you'll be back but if you are before I am I'm telling you I've gone to hogtown for a week, seeking fame, cash and whatever else is behind door number three. Sorry about your Granma. Hope you're okay. Your pal, Eric. xoxoxoxoxoxoxoxoxoxoxoxoxoxoxoxoxox-oxoxoxoxoxo

SHELBY

Unable to contain myself, I plugged in Lucy's eight-inch black-and-white television, put it on top of the old T.V., fell back on the pull-out couch and wept through *Mr. Dressup.*

Day one passed. Lucy was gone. Eric was gone. Gran was *gone.* I closed the curtains full-time, shrank from personal hygiene, indulged in physical releases and declined into dankness.

Day two was more of the same with the addition of cold cereal and perpetual wonder at how a young man could one week seek God's call via the rough-and-ready Canadian wilderness and the next be victim to cathode rays and fantasies of television personalities.

Day three ushered in genuine mental illness evident in inappropriate physical responses to the following: Kathie Lee Gifford (*Regis and Kathie Lee*), soap operas (*All My Children, Another World, General Hospital*), *The Oprah Winfrey Show* (Oprah, of course), portions of *WKRP in Cincinatti, Babar,* snippets of dominatrix cross-dressers on *Geraldo* and one of the contestants on *Wheel Of Fortune.* The *CBC Evening News* blew in shame at my lack of reverence for existence after briefly showing starving Somalians and the plight of the Serbs—as did a documentary on the vanishing habitat of the three toed sloth. Crumbling in despair, spent, smelly, my head rife with Matthew Arnold's *We mortal millions live alone* and the bitter reality that Lucy on the road hadn't bothered to phone, I was comforted only by fits of sadness and anger imploding throughout the night. I feared reasons for carrying on were fading subconsciously.

To my astonishment, the following morning arrived with a bizarre sense of mission manifesting itself in the form of bodily shakes. I could not stop wondering: What was it that made me do what I did? Was it from within? Without? Social constraints or predetermined chaos? Does transcendence truly exist? Was I addicted to sex? To self-loathing? To darkness? And, yes, I did turn on the T.V. But all had changed. The seer, it would seem, had become the seen. The new order had arrived. Destiny was a state of choice.

Within two days cable had been hooked up and loose pieces of foolscap ripe with statistics and ideas and questions were scattered to the far reaches of the front room. My working title expressed it all.

AN EXEGESIS OF SEXUAL URGES AND GENERAL BEHAVIOUR AS THEY RELATE (OR INTER-RELATE) TO (OR WITH) MEDIA (SPECIFICALLY TELEVISION YET ALSO RADIO, MAGAZINES, NEWSPAPERS, MUSIC ETC.)

Naturally, two days was insufficient time to put into a cohesive essay my initial findings. Nonetheless, a few realities poked through.

PART I: REALITIES: Data compiled.

1) Premarital Sex and Cohabitation:

Twenty-two of the twenty-seven sexual interactions witnessed on T.V. were between unmarried, vibrant heterosexuals. Fairly rare, however, for unmarried people to actually cohabitate. Very few portrayals of people with sexual dysfunctions: addiction, guilt, immature ejaculation, size, food fetishes etc—except as plot enhancers.

2) Form:

Fat people on prime time T.V. (4) are all more crass than average. Their sexual quotient is wastefully ignored. Obese people on talk shows cry far more than the national average and are customarily represented as being despondent about their rotundity (occasionally there are programs about frail men enchanted by obese woman, but these "circuses" carry the mood of a P.T. Barnum travelling freak show). Clearly, fatism is epidemic and growing. Fat does not exist on any soap operas monitored, save one woman who was only mildly chunky and, as expected by T.V., annoyingly gloomy therefore.

3) Masturbation:

It's as if it doesn't exist, although scientific studies and self-analysis indicate otherwise. Not mentioned in forty-one hours of viewing. Suggested at by the occasional Rock Guitarist mime, but only in the context of metaphoric ejaculation all over the crowd, which in fact degrades any dignity the act might have in the solitude of one's own dwelling (and in fact is not a solitary event at all). Prejudice abounds whereby ensuring further populist anxiety.

4) *Pedophilia.*

No prime time programs where a major or minor character is a confessed pedophile (excluding documentaries and talk shows and the recently discontinued CBC docudrama Boys of St. Vincent's *about the Catholic Bishop who broke his vows by molesting orphans). Perhaps this is for the best.*

5) *Homosexuality:*

Occasional mention. Only judgement was expressed by a late night evangelist/prophesy preacher: "God despises homosexuals . . . oh how disgusted He is!" The crowd, of varying races, seemed generally pleased with this observation (notice the high percentage of ties).

6) *Position on sex in general:*

Rampant yet very clean. Strong performances taken as fait accompli. *Halitosis, flatulence, et cetera not mentioned. Overall, constant titillation leaves me excessively aroused, creatively confused.*

Last minute note!!:   Plagued by ironies.

The "Liberal Establishment", so caring in speech, all tend to wear ribbons in support of people with AIDS for example, and yet never preach abstinence and promote reckless sexual behaviour in the media and antisocial behaviour in film.
Meanwhile, "Conservatives", so plagued by this liberal attitude, constantly claim that these liberals who run the media are warping traditional values. But get this: The media is owned by Conservatives!! For example, General Electric (bomb contracts, anti-trust violations etc.) owns *NBC. And the lists I have found go on and on with people and businesses I don't know (Capital Cities, Warren Buffett, Westinghouse), but plan to uncover. Every step forward may prove more and more dangerous. Why? In short, I smell conspiracy. Truth-seekers may be forced to search outside the accepted spectrum.*

End of Synopsis to date. Statistics in the binder. Holy crapola!

* * *

A rap on the door awoke me from a nightmare in which I was being chased through the Bavarian countryside by Nazis *and* Jews going mostly by the name of Heinrich. I glanced up amidst books and writing tablets strewn across the darkened room, my mouth dry, my skin damp. There was another knock. I rubbed my unfocussing eyes.

"Who's there?"

"It's Suzanne Ehrlich."

"Oh . . . oh . . . just a minute." I rambled to my feet, pulling a pair of crinkled brown corduroys over stained and baggy white jockey shorts. I scurried through the kitchen in bare feet and opened the door.

"Hi, Shelby," she said cheerfully. "I was in the neighbourhood and I thought I'd drop by and see you and Eric—are you okay?"

"Me? Yes, I . . . I've been researching . . . my thesis . . . you won't believe what—never mind . . . Eric's gone to Hogtown."

"Hogtown?"

"Do you know where that is?"

"Toronto."

"Oh."

"You okay?"

"Yes. You caught me in mid-slumber," I said, attempting re-adjustment of my hair. "What time is it?"

She glanced at her watch. "Four-thirty."

"In the *morning*?"

"Afternoon."

"Thursday?"

"Saturday."

There was a pause. "I saw your exhibition at Emily Carr," I said. "Fabulous."

"Thank you."

"*Fish-tail*," I said shaking my head, "would you consider selling it?"

"Shelby, you don't look very well."

"Really?"

"No . . . and something smells."

"Does it?"

"Are you sure you're okay?"
"Yes."
"Have you eaten today?"
"Um . . . I think I may have had a piece of toast."
Suzanne scrunched her brow. "Look, take a shower and I'll treat you to dinner."
"You and I?"
"Sure . . . meet me on the side street. I'll be in my car. Red Toyota."
"Um . . . I'm . . . thank you . . ."
We dined at a vegetarian restaurant on Commercial Street amidst the flavours of multiculturalism and Christmas. Suzanne insisted that I gorge, and I, being ravenous, obliged.

We mostly discussed her creations, which I exalted without refrain; and the function of the artist, which she believes has been lost since the advent of mass consumption.

"See, Shelby, there *is* good and bad art," she said, once again talking with both her mouth and her hands. "The function of the artist is to arouse the looker to check out their own place, you know? Their own journey, their own ideas, even the day at hand. If that's not happening, it's not art. I mean T.V. and radio . . . ?" She shrugged.

"There are *some* good programs, Suzanne."

"True. But the human experience . . . it's this rich, indefinably big collage that . . . should be exposed everyday by the things we do." She paused. "T.V. is this 9″ x 12″ glowing kryptonic eyeball that sucks out our spirit."

"Agreed. And like I said, I only watch T.V. for research. I've made some startling observations."

"I don't mean to offend you."

"I'm not offended. Really. I don't watch—"

"Let me put it this way, Shelby. Two years ago I saw an exhibition of primitive finger paintings from New Guinea. Browns and blacks and reds painted with the chopped up root of some bush, right? A two-toned turtle shook my spirit. To this day I'm a vegan because of it and I don't even know why. Now *that's* art . . ."

* * *

By the time Suzanne dropped me home, I was visually inspired by her words, and eager to get back to my project.

". . . and open the windows in there," she yelled from her car as I approached the apartment building.

"Okay. Thank you."

"And careful with mixing certain food groups."

"I will."

"And wash."

"Okay. Thank you for dinner."

"You're welcome. Tell Eric I dropped by."

"I will. And I'll drop a rough draft of my work by your place some time next week."

"Okay."

"You're going to love it!"

Refreshed and replenished, I reread some new ideas and found myself pleased with the progress. Whether my research would lead to financial security remained, as is the case with all true art, precarious. Nonetheless, I knew the results would speak for themselves, perhaps revolutionizing the way North Americans not only watch television but experience the world. Fact was, they had already caused me to seek more spirit-oriented programs and reduce my masturbatory tendencies by half. For that I was grateful. It was a wonderful night.

* * *

The front door crashed open a few days later. "What the hell's that smell?"

"Eric?" I groaned, prostrate on the couch.

He walked into the front room. "Bryan Adams makes thirty mil a year and I can't get a lunch date with Duke Street Records! I mean, what the shit have they done lately?"

I didn't move. His eyes peered upside down at mine.

"Eric . . . put that pillow over my face and sit on it for ten minutes."

"You kinky bastard."

"Contribution alludes me."

"What?"

"Every last word," I said whining, "bunk, bunk, all is *bunk*."

I tilted my head just enough to see Eric scanning the room.

Papers were everywhere, the television howled from its blurry visage and the curtains were drawn.

"What the hell's this stuff?" he asked, picking up one of the pads and reading aloud: "PETITION TO HAVE TELEVANGELISTS DISCUSS THE DIVINITY OF ORAL SEX, CONSENSUAL BONDAGE AND OTHER SEX GAMES IN THE PROMOTION OF EMOTIONAL and MARITAL FEC . . . UN—"

"—fe*cun*dity."

He flipped to another page. "CONSPIRACY: TUNE IN NEXT WEEK", "WHY THE SON OF MAN HAD NO PLACE TO LAY HIS HEAD—A CRITICAL ESSAY . . ."

"That's it. All I can find are good titles. The text remains silent."

" . . . PETITION TO HAVE AN OBESE LOVE INTEREST ON *GENERAL HOSPITAL*." Eric glanced up. "What are you do—oh shit, I'm sorry. I forgot. Your grandma . . ."

"Dead," I said.

"I know that. How are you doing?"

"I've masturbated four times in the last thirty-two hours."

"Pig. Where's Lucy?"

"Did I ever tell you she was celibate?"

"What?"

"Did I ever tell you Frank urinated in my car?"

"Who's Frank?"

"The man who shattered my nose."

"He pissed in your car, too?"

"All over the dash and the seat."

"When was this?"

"Months ago—I lied and told you it was vandalised by Asian gangs. It wasn't. Frank beat up my car right in front of me. Then he stood on the hood and peed inside."

"What'd *you* do?"

"I no longer know the feeling of being alive."

"What'd you do when he *pissed in your car*?"

I glanced up. "I drove home in it."

"You *sat* in the seat he pissed on?"

All I could do was shrug.

* * *

Finding my car battery dead on Wednesday morning, I had to use public transport to get to work. The result was feeling as squished as luncheon meat while condensation dripped off windows and seats, perspiration oozed from armpits and foreheads and odiferous breakfast expulsions leaked from a myriad of multicultured orifices. On a positive note, the thirty-five minute ride gave me time to further examine Eric's pep talk from a couple days earlier. In short, I conferred with the following: One, running away petrified is an ineffective (yet physically prudent) method of dealing with a man of Frank's nature. Two, masturbation extremus, a lack of hygiene and bad writing can neither replace the sadness of losing one's grandmother nor alleviate the crippling effect of a failing—if not failed—relationship.

Still in dispute, however, was Eric's belief that a series of vengeful attacks on Frank could terminate my aforementioned anxieties. To reiterate his closing argument:

" . . . and I wonder if you're against violence, man," he said, "or just plain gutless. That dick-head *pissed* in your car!"

The morning book sort did nothing to lessen my general blasé. By noon that feeling, thanks to tedium, had evolved to agitation. A lunch break stroll in the rain amidst the exploitive tendencies of Christmas—be it decorations all over the Eaton's Centre mocking the beggars below or just the outright lie that presents can and will usher in a better day—worsened the condition. It occurred to me that the Western concept of work being that which allows one to play during time off, is madness. Play, I resolved, should be an ongoing, meditative process that alleviates perpetual fear. Wasn't that how Gran lived? Even Jesus said, "Only those who play like a child can enter the Kingdom of Heaven"—or words to that effect. Surely he didn't mean get really drunk on the weekend.

Upon returning to the library, I went to the staff cafeteria and sat juxtaposed to a table of chatty co-workers who, it soon became clear, were recounting endearing Christmas anecdotes from days of yore.

"Excuse me," I said, interrupting. Faces turned to me. "Could I perhaps tell a short Christmas tale of my own?"

A collection of *sures* and shrugs and affirmative nods signalled I could.

"Christmas is an aspiritual moment of social psychosis that ends as the last present is opened. Moreover, eggnog causes bowel spasms, fruitcake is a better doorstop than a dessert and, finally, Jesus wasn't even *born* on Christmas day—moreover, he was a Jew. See any Jews celebrating Christmas?" I stared into the faces before me.

Claudia, a soft-spoken front-desk clerk, shook her head empathetically. "You're an asshole," she said.

I sat for a moment until an inner tremble arose, a wrestle locked between frustration and weariness. All eyes before me seemed to freeze over. I feared a witch-hunt.

Pushing myself up, I staggered, stunned, backwards through the swinging door, out of the cafeteria and into the hallway. "It was a joke!" I cried, overcome with helplessness, my skin crawling as if spiders had been poured on my head. I tore into the stairwell and down the spiraling steps.

"Shelby Lewis!"

My head shot up as I stopped in mid-stride. There before me stood Minnie T., her face radiant with joy.

"What was a joke?" she asked with a grin accentuating her ample cheeks.

"Oh Minnie," I moaned, lip quivering, the need for repentance throbbing from my guts. "I . . . I want . . . I *need* to apologise for last year . . ."

"Shelby, it's—"

"Please hold me!" We dove into each others arms. I was aroused on contact. What was happening? Had I said too much? Had I inferred I wanted to try again? *Did* I want to try again? What if she threw me down and began mounting me right there in the stairwell?

"Forgive me?" I asked softly, head on her shoulder.

Minnie pushed herself away and smiled excitedly. "All forgiven," she said, thrusting her left hand in my direction, displaying a diamond ring.

"You . . ."

"*Engaged*," she blurted, eyes a-twinkle.

"Dr. Moth?"

She pirouetted. "If the shoe fits."

* * *

I was lying in darkness when the front door opened. "Bad news, man," Eric said. I sprang up. The light flashed on. "I was talkin' to Terry Pendleton."
"Who?"
"The guitar player." He sat down on the edge of the pull-out couch.
"Do I know him?"
"I don't know, man, but he's an unbelievable player."
"Really?"
"Yeah. And I told him about the project I'm putting together. Picture this: Desert country. Big *blue* sky. In the distance, clouds thick like mud."
"I don't understand."
"Highway 52 revisited," he said, "back to basics. Free love meets AIDS. A lava lamp meets global warming. REM hold the drummer. Nirvana in a blackout." He raised his brow.
"What's the bad news?"
Eric scratched his head and took a drag on his cigarette. "Straight up, man, the Paisley's dead and this new gig's a two-man show. Bass and guitar. I'm sorry."
"What about?"
"You're out," he said, his face contorting as if he'd taken a swig of sour milk. "What the hell's that smell?"
"What smell?"
"What do you mean *what* smell? Something showed up in the last five seconds that's makin' my eyes burn and my bet is it came out o' your asshole."
"Oh . . . uh . . . gas."
"What a stink, man."
"Okay, I admit it. I've had fetid flatulence for a day and a half now."
"*Man*, air vomit is more like it."
"I'm all knotty inside," I said.
Eric grinned. "That's disgusting. *God.*"
My insides gripped tight. "I'm sorry!"
"What a stencheroo!"
"I said I'm *sorry!*"
"Easy. Christ."
"Do you think I enjoy smelling like this?"
"What?"

"My insides loathe me. I can't go on."
"You got the farts, man, that's all. Take it easy."
"Don't tell me to take it easy!"
"You're pissed about the band, aren't you?"
"What?"
"Just say it."
"Say what?"
"That's why you get gas, you know. *Anger.* You don't deal with the real issue. Never have. You lie in bed all day. You whine. You stink up the apartment. It's that asshole *Frank* that you ought to be screaming at."
"I resolve my wrath my own way."
Eric picked up a piece of paper from the floor and read aloud. "*The Fallacy of Christmas: Fruitcake as metaphor.*" I snatched it from his hand. "You're fucked," he said.
"Since when are you a psychologist?"
Eric rubbed his eye and stood up. "I tell you, if you don't start dealin' with your shit, man, it's gonna tear you up." He walked towards the kitchen.
"Where are you going?"
Eric stopped and turned back. "I gotta go tell Bryan he's out. Oh . . ." He pulled a piece of paper from his jeans pocket, unfolded it and let it drop onto the couch. "Here's some band names," he said. "Let me know which ones you dig."
I glanced at my watch. "It's a tad late to be going out, isn't it?"
"What are you talking about? It's nine-thirty," he said, disappearing into the kitchen. The front door opened. "By the way," he said, "I'm havin' a party here Saturday. Invite whoever you want."
"It's cold out," I said. "The roads are—" The door slammed. The room went silent. I glanced at the slightly crumpled piece of paper.

   HAPPY SLAVES
   SUN DOGS NEVER BARK
   THE ERIC WINLAW PROJECT
   WINLAWFULLNESS
   WINLAW
   WHAT STINKS?

* * *

The next morning, and for the first time since I'd returned to Vancouver, my parents phoned to see how I was doing. Dialogue was laboured, every breath or mumble saying the same thing: Gran is dead. Ironically, it took a story from Dad to transform the dialogue from cliché to comedy.

"... so Mom sees Larry out the kitchen window throwing Gran's garden tools, hoes, rakes, shovels, into the back of his truck, right? It turns out, without asking Mom, Larry planned to donate them to his church."

"The Kingdom Hall?"

"Uh... I think it might be a Baptist thing, now. Some end o' the world group. Anyway... I don't hear any of this, right? I'm snoozin' on the downstairs couch. Slam! goes the door. I run upstairs to see what the hell's goin' on. I look out the kitchen window and there's Larry—get this—in his truck revvin' it, spittin' gravel, and Mom's got her hand through the window gripped around his collar and she's yellin'—and get this—'Don't make me pull a Shelby!' I tell you son, I was on the floor. *'Don't make me pull a Shelby'* ..."

"What happened?" I asked.

"Guess," he said.

"I—"

"Larry starts to drive off and she plants him one right in the snoz."

"I pulled a Shelby," Mom said, "but in my own defense it was more of a cuff than a punch ..."

I smiled, feeling slightly remorseful for my own smacking of Larry a few weeks earlier. "You know what I wish?" I said.

"What's that, son?" Dad asked, still laughing.

"I wish I could have been present at the moment Gran, lying in bed, finally abandoned life as we know it. She let go, poof, pouring her all into the cosmic void ..."

There was a response but it wasn't verbal. The conversation reverted to its stilted form until sputtering to a full stop. We hung up.

That evening Suzanne also called. She invited me to her parents' house for a private unveiling of her most recent work.

SHELBY

Yearning for female companionship—and by now utterly disillusioned with Lucy's lack of compassion—I leapt at the offer.
"I think you'll really like it," she said upon my arrival. She took my jacket and led me through the kitchen and down a corridor bathed in Gothicism. "It's *Fish-tail*'s companion piece," she said. Through a rounded door Suzanne flicked on the basement light. "The studio's downstairs," she said. I followed, surveying the paintings and family knicknacks.
"We're having a soiree of sorts tomorrow night if you'd like to drop in," I said as she turned on another light.
"Oh thanks. Eric told me about it already. Sounds fun." She stopped in front of what appeared to be a barbecue covered in tarpaulin. "You like living with Eric?" she asked.
"It's all right."
"Is he still seeing that woman?"
"Which one?"
"I can't remember her name. She's black."
"Nina. Yes, I believe he still is."
"Hey, how's that paper going?"
"Paper?"
"That thesis you were working on about television. I was hoping to get a copy."
"Oh . . . um . . . I haven't . . . the results are unclear. I have to make sure all the data is correct."
"Hm," she said, rubbing her hands together nervously. "Well, this is it," she said. She yanked the covering as though doing a magic trick. "Ta da. *Fish-tail Pie*."
I was stunned.
"You like it?"
Glazed in natural hues and between the size of a standard dessert pie and a meat or chicken frozen pie one occasionally purchases for a quick dinner, it had a slice removed, slightly less than a quarter, and dangling were five or six fish tails. I could literally *smell* trout. "It's wondrous," I said. Our eyes met and I sensed her craving me, perhaps wondering if she'd lose all control if she laid an impetuous wet one on my puckered lips. A sigh through my nose resulted in a faint whistle.
"What was that?" she said.
"What?"
"That whistle?

"Whistle? I didn't—you *should* have heard a whistle," I said. I whistled as a construction worker would watching a slinky working woman walk by. "*Fish-tail Pie* is *so* good."

"You know I think it came from your nose," she said.

For a second I could not move. I felt suddenly ashamed. "It did," I said.

XVIII

Are you still so dull?
—*Jesus Christ*

Eric and I battled over the next few days until Saturday morning landed me at work snapping at people who didn't deserve such behaviour. Even the walls bothered me, especially the one in the bathroom whose graffiti asked: *WHAT DOES GOD DO ALL DAY?* Whatever the answer to that was, I knew it was whatever he wanted to do, which was more than I was doing. And then I wondered: How does God keep a positive outlook on life? No answers were forthcoming, but in the midst of stamping due date cards I paused to pen some provocative prose:

(Religious fanatics + secularists)x(false compromise) = CHRISTMAS.

To The Weary Who Loathe What They Do But Can Find No Immediate Alternative:

It is, I am certain, the need to smother the reality of one's mind-numbing job with sit-coms, narcotics, masturbation and all other addictions—not a fear of castration—that ultimately causes men to frequent strip joints. Lucy is a victim of the male-invented work week! I say free the stripper! O woe! O woe! I am shackled to the misery of nine to five (8 to noon today) menial labour. Free the stripper and bring her home! Free the shelver, too! Up yours. God help us. Good luck.

Shelby Lewis, December 1992

Returning home at just after one o'clock, I proceeded to collapse on the pull-out couch, only to be rattled from slumber by the door crashing open. Leaping up, I saw Eric balancing two grocery bags and two cases of beer.

"Could you be a little more considerate?" I asked rhetorically. "I worked all morning."

Eric stopped in mid-movement, turning his head as far as he could in my direction. "Okay, man," he grunted, "that's it." He put the bags on the kitchen table and the beer on the floor.

"What's it?"

"Look, I know you're hurtin' over your Grandma. I understand. And I know your old lady's a dead fish, too—"

"She's celibate!"

"Whatever. I feel for you. But see, man, I'm a happy guy. Things are going pretty well. I got some people diggin' my tunes. I've got a great woman. So stop trying to drag me down with your depression."

"You're upset because I didn't like your band names."

"You never told me that."

"Well, I don't. What's more, I think your belief that violence is a reasonable solution to whatever problems you perceive me to have really stinks."

"Not *violence*, you ass-licker. I told you to deal with your crap, that's all. If that means having some balls? Okay. But do you fuckin' listen? No."

"I—"

"Maybe you have no *balls*."

"I—"

"But giving you the benefit of the doubt," he said, putting up his hand to stop me talking. "I've brought home Plan B." Eric reached into one of the grocery bags. "A twenty-sixer of rye," he said, displaying the bottle's logo, "for medicinal purposes."

"Alcohol?"

"With a capital A."

"*Medicinal*? Carcinogenic is more like it."

"Not with mixer," he said. "Anyway, what do you care with a life like yours? I got vodka, too—two mickeys," he said, holding them up. "Add a dash of vermouth and we're doing lunch in L.A. A bag of ice for mood. A bottle of tequila to keep the guts rollin'." He wiggled his buttocks. "Beer, of course. And, last but not least, for you, *mon ami*, Island Treat."

"What's that?"

"Pina Colada mix," he said, "for your tender tummy."

"Eric, I'm not going to drink. In fact, I think you have a drinking problem."

Eric turned and faced me. "Look, man, you're really startin' to *piss* me off! What the hell you got up your ass?"

"Your language is apalling."

He looked away and then back. "Okay, Shel," he said gently, "if you want to be an asshole, go ahead." He started to walk towards his room.

"Eric, wait."

"What?"

"I detest my body."

"Where'd that come from?"

"I don't know. I'm sorry."

"So you wanna beer?"

"I swear a rewarding life is not beyond me!"

"Do you wanna a beer or not?"

"I shouldn't."

"If you ask me, Shel, your main problem is bottling up your anger. Also you jack off so much it makes you hate yourself. You need a woman to chew you up."

"And then what?"

"Spit you out. You wanna beer?"

"Yes, please."

And so, three hours later, after apologies, toasts, resolutions, confessions, beers, vodka, Island Treat, one headlock and an attempt at songwriting, the two of us were closer than ever. Eric stood up from the kitchen table.

"Pee?" I asked.

"Full up," he said.

"Eric, *muchas gracias* for helping me feel better."

"Hey, it's better than breakin' your neck," he said, staggering away. "I just hope it's for real."

"It is," I said.

A few seconds later he wobbled back into the kitchen, pulled his chair up next to mine, put his arm around me and showed me a brown bag. I peered inside.

"For my pal," he said, "Island *Treat* number two . . ."

"What is it?"

He grinned. "Vancouver Island one hundred percent guaranteed to blast your fuckin' mind hydroponic skunkweed."

"Marijuana?"

Eric lifted his arm off me and pulled a lighter from his pocket. "The best bud I ever had," he said glassy-eyed. He lit one of the joints and took a few drags, coughed and passed it to me, obviously unaware that I'd never smoked before.

"We could be arrested."

"For what?"

"This isn't right, is it?"

"We ain't fuckin' each other, man, we're smokin' a doobie."

"Children are shot in the trafficking cross fire. Are we not, as users, also accomplices?"

"It's skunkweed."

"Is it legal?"

"No, but that's a load o' shit. I mean cigarettes are legal! Have you read the package lately? Marijuana couldn't hurt a fly. It's no worse for you then a good lay."

I looked at the smoldering joint. "I shouldn't."

"So don't."

"Will I get flashbacks?"

"That's acid."

"I'm nervous."

"Well, don't do it."

"But I want to! I'm not afraid to live."

"Great."

"But I'm afraid to die. I could become an addict."

"Look, Shel, whatever."

"Dammit, I'm going to give it a go."

"Are you sure?"

I lifted it to my lips and took two tentative drags.

"Shit, man," he said grinning. "You gotta give it a little more suck than that." I took two more inhales, swallowed and gagged. My eyes watered. I coughed. We did it twice again.

"Actually," he said, "some people get flashbacks."

"Really?"

"Nah."

Eric lay down on the kitchen floor. I sat at the table, unable to focus. "What should I feel?" I asked, just as the doorbell rang.

"Oh shit!"

"What?"

"Cops," he said.
"Are you serious?"
"Nah," he said. "Come on in."
The door opened and a few people I didn't recognize peeked in and stared at me.
"Hey, man," Eric said. And so began the party. I didn't move, sitting, instead, glassy-eyed, staring at the fridge as the apartment turned into a veritable beehive of activity. I spun between fatigue and excitement, rich perception and incoherence. Sometime thereafter Eric came and sat down next to me.
"I just threw up, right?"
"I don't know."
"Why is it always spaghetti?"
"What?"
"Puking," he said. "Nobody ever chucks up a salad."
"I have," I said.
"No you haven't."
"Caesar salad. I distinctly recall the pungent combination of bile and garlic."
"And spaghetti, though, right?"
"*Caesar salad*—all on its own. The Revelstoke Keg."
"Bullshit."
"My eyes feel funny."
"But are you happy?"
"I feel funny."
"Happy-funny?"
"I think so," I said, just as nausea wobbled my innards. "Ooh," I said, pushing myself up. "I feel suddenly ill." I wobbled into the hall and towards the bathroom.
"Shelby!" I heard from behind. I turned to see Suzanne standing just inside the doorway, her face smiling and glowing from the cool December air, a shopping bag under her arm.
"Hello."
She grinned coyfully. "Can we go somewhere private?"
The proposition surprised me and I stumbled, crushing my ear on the door frame of the bathroom. "Uh . . . of course . . . um . . . Eric's bedroom?" I asked, pointing, attempting to gather my wits.
Draped in a thick black coat and a red scarf, resembling a

model turned baglady, she nodded. In we went. We sat down on the bed. "I brought you something," she said with a continuing grin. Feeling my arousal level rise, I moved as near to her as I could without seeming obvious. Her neck looked mildy sweaty. I yearned to move my nose nearer.

"First off," she said, "I want to—what are you doing?"
"Sorry, I was . . . moving closer. I couldn't hear you."
"I'm a foot away."
"I can hear you now."
"Okay. So here it is: Pie looks great from the outside, right?"
"What pie?"
"Let me finish. So you see it and think, 'God, this is going to taste great'. Yummy pie, right?"
"Okay."
"Then you cut a slice and fish tails fall out all over the place . . ."

I sat bewitched by her beguiling eyes, fully erect and throbbing to tell her so in a more poetic manner.

"So you stare at this gross pie for days and days and you start to get hungry. So you take a bite and you realise it's not so bad after all. In fact, if you were starving you'd be more than grateful."
"Hm."
"That's the way of the world, Shelby. Everything depends on the vantage point, what your basic needs are and, to a lesser degree, what you desire after that. It's all just Fish-tail pie." She looked at me sideways and from the corner of her eye. "I couldn't sell it to you," she said. "I want you to have it . . ." Out of the paper bag she pulled *Fish-tail Pie* and placed it in my hands.
"Me?"
She laughed. "Yeah, you." I sat silent. "Say something."
"Oh Suzanne . . . *kiss* me."
"What?"
"Please. No more games."
"*Shelby* . . ."
"Let us slam our naked bodies against the madness."
"You look weird."
"Cast our fates and morals to the high sea!" I wrapped my arms around her and we tumbled backwards, me on top.

"Get off me!"
"You and I!" I cried.
"*Shelby!*"
Holding her down, I pulled my face back to kiss her on the lips. At that moment her hand grabbed onto my cheek and dug into my face.
"Get off me!"
My head jerked back in pain and I tumbled away as a few stinging wacks pounced off the side of my head. My face and eyes burned.
"*What are you doing?*"
I peeked through my arms to see Suzanne staring at me aghast.
"You're sick," she said, teeth clenched.
"Suzanne, I—"
"Get away from me!"
"Suzanne . . ." She ran from the room. "Suzanne!" I screamed again, swinging out at the air. All was still. Hyperventilating, I leapt to my feet having joined the ranks of the sexually deviant; the abusers, the molesters, the harrassers. Suzanne had offered me her spirit incarnate and I'd thanked her as would a rabid Rottweiler with his jaws around one's nose. Sprinting towards the door I stumbled on nothing as if tripped by God Himself, crumbling headfirst into the wall. Prostrate and dazed, a sparkle to my left caught my eye. There was *Fish-tail Pie*, upside down, two broken tails inches away. I let out a sob and forced myself to my feet.
"Suzanne!" I cried again, running out of the room, scanning the hallway and then tearing into the kitchen. "Suzanne!"
"What the hell happened to your face?" Eric said, twisting from his seat at the kitchen table.
"Nothing. Honest."
"What do you mean nothing?"
"Oh Eric! What have I done?"
"What *have* you done?"
"I've . . . I've assaulted a woman, okay!"
"What?"
"Suzanne. She declined my kisses and I fell on top of her and she clawed my face."

"And?"
My breathing quickened. I could not speak.
"You bastard!"
"I didn't mean to break it!"
"What?"
"She clawed my face. I tumbled away. *Fish-tail Pie* must have fallen. Suzanne stood staring at me, aghast. Before I could apologise, she was gone."
"Did you hurt her?"
"No."
"Where is she?"
I shrugged.
"Okay, man, that's it. I'm getting my gun." He pushed me out of the way and strutted towards his room.
"I didn't mean anything!" I said, whimpering a few feet behind.
"Not for you, asshole! We got to deal with Frank."
"Frank?"
"You want to deal with this guy? We'll deal with him." Eric reached to the top of his closet and pulled down a revolver.
"No violence!" I shrieked.
Eric turned and glared.
"I've seen too much already."
"Who do I look like? Gerry the Gent? We're just gonna warn the bastard."
"Why now? I need to find Suzanne."
Eric cracked me on the side of the head with an open hand. "The guy shattered your manhood—all your courage. Look at you, man! Assaulting a woman! I ought to beat the shit out o' you right here."
"This is where it happened," I moaned, turning, staring at the bed. I fell to my knees, gathering up *Fish-tail Pie* in my arms.
Eric took a last look at the gun before stuffing it in his pocket. "She needs a good polish," he said, "but she'll still do the job."

* * *

"I'm more than a little nervous," I said.
"626 Cordova," Eric said to the cab driver as we sped to-

wards the city center. He turned to me. "You sure this is the right address?"

"There was only one Frank Sagan in the book. Anyway, Lucy told me he lived down in the bowery."

"Okay then," he said, leaning back in the seat, taking a long drag on his cigarette, "on with the show."

* * *

"What a dump," Eric whispered as we stumbled inebriated up the fire stairwell in search of 201. It turned out to be the first door on the right, second floor. "Bingo."

"What?"

Eric pulled the revolver from his pocket and held it by his side. "Now we knock. Then we give Frankie-boy the only kind of talkin'-to he'll listen to. Stand over there." Eric pointed me off to the side, rapped on the door three times and leaned his back against the wall. We waited, listening. Silence. Eric leaned forward and knocked. Again no answer.

"I'd bet he's at his club," I said, "it's Saturday night."

"Yeah. Shit. 'Course he is."

"We should get back to the party, shouldn't we?"

"Au contraire, mon ami." Eric dug into his jacket pocket and removed a Swiss Army Knife, clipped open the nail file and began prodding at the door handle.

"*Eric*, please. Already my night . . . illicit drugs, Suzanne, now breaking and entering. The widening gyre is spinning beyond control. I need—" *Click.*

"Got it." Eric pushed open the door and crept inside.

"I cannot go through with it," I said.

"Okay, man."

"Okay? You're . . . we're going home?"

"You can. I'm gonna wait for Frankie-boy and let him know what it's all about."

"On your own?"

"Well, me and my lover," he said, raising the pistol.

"You'd do that for me?"

"*God*, it stinks worse than our place in here." Eric clicked a light switch just inside the door, revealing a virtually unfurnished apartment littered with fast-food wrappers and

clothes and glass bottles. "Needles," Eric said, pointing to the coffee table. "Does he deal?"
"Does who deal?"
"Frank! Does he sell?"
"I don't know," I said with a shrug as I surveyed the room.
"So are you stayin' or goin'?" he asked.

* * *

"... and I literally fell on top of her," I whined, brushing tears from my eyes. "I've become a truly rotten person."
"What time is it?" Eric asked. I angled my watch into the lamplight that shone across the room.
"One-thirty."
"How long we been here?"
"Eighty-two minutes."
"Hm. If he is at his club he probably won't be here 'til after two."
"I feel ill."
"Nerves?"
"I'm not sure. Squeamish."
"Shut up."
"What?"
"Footsteps..."

* * *

"... I don't know why I've always felt such a need to be relevant to my fellow humans. Granted my parents believed me to be somewhat of an academic prodigy in my formative years. Nonetheless, how it all manifest—"
"What time is it?"
"Uh... five after two."
"Okay. You gotta stop your yappin', man. Frankie-boy should be showin' up any second..."

* * *

"... it wasn't so much his urinating on the dash that bothered me. The fact is I was floored by his massive endowment. Suddenly there was a whole new—and perhaps paranoid— reality to Lucy's dismissal of my sexual advancements."
"What time is it?"

"Twenty after three."
"Where the *hell* is he?"

* * *

". . . the irony being that dropping out of university I assumed I would find unbridled freedom and instead wound up addicted to television. And what now in the wake of my assault on Suzanne?"

"What the hell were you thinking?" he said, cigarette end glowing in the darkness.

"I . . . I don't know. I pray she'll forgive me. I think I was desperate to be sought after and for the briefest of moments actually thought I was."

"She sure skinned your face. Does it hurt?"

"That's the extraordinary thing. In light of such a grave mistake on my part and now my waiting to threaten Frank with a deadly weapon, here I sit shrouded in a sea of infinite calm."

"Weird."

"And how long can it last? Surely it isn't *true* peace."

"What time is it?"

"You just—good God. Twenty past four."

"Jesus. Maybe he ain't coming home."

"What?"

"It's four-thirty. Where the hell could he be?"

"I sup—"

"Shut up." We both froze in the darkness as a door slammed in the distance. Eric grabbed my shirt and yanked me behind him. "This could be it," he said, bracing himself, the gun firmly grasped at his side.

"Anything?" I whispered.

"I gotta take a leak."

"Nerves."

"Beer."

There was a pause. "It doesn't sound like whoever was there is there anymore."

"I tell you, man," Eric said matter-of-factly, "I don't think he's coming."

"What should we do?"

"We'll write him a note. Let him know he might lose an eye or something if he doesn't back off."

"An eye?"

Eric clicked on the light. "Got any paper?"

I felt through my Gortex jacket and found a pen in the breast pocket. Eric picked up a slightly stained brown paper bag off the coffee table and tore it down one side.

"This'll do," he said, handing it to me.

"What should I write?"

"Uh . . . *Hey Frankie-boy, just thought we'd leave you a little warning* . . . hang on a sec, I gotta take a leak. Keep an eye on the door." Eric disappeared around the corner.

"For the record, Eric, I fear threatening him may only serve to—"

"*Oh God.*"

"What?"

"Oh shit."

"What?"

"Come here, man."

"No."

"Come here."

"Why?"

"Come here."

I nervously walked to the end of the room to see Eric standing frozen in the doorway, staring. I peeked over his shoulder. "*Aaah!*"

"Easy, jeez."

On the bed lay Frank; still, nude, horribly white, a peach towel around his hairy waist, his genitalia unavoidably exposed. He had one leg bent, the other straight out. There were what looked like hockey cards stacked all over the floor. The room was muggy and stale.

"Look at that thing," Eric said.

"Is he dead?"

Eric shrugged and gingerly approached the body, brushing Frank's hand as a game warden would fearing to wake a tranquilized bear. "Stiff," he said.

"Is he breathing?"

"I don't think so."

"Are those hockey cards?"

He bent down towards Frank's hand. "Look at this, man, a Bobby Orr rookie card."

"What are we going to do?"

"He musta been playin' with 'em when . . . when . . ."

"*Eric*, what are we going to do?"

Eric turned to me, his eyes glancing left and right as though seeking possibilities. "Split."

"What?"

"You got a better idea?"

"What if he's still alive? We should call 911."

"He's *stiff.*"

"We have to report it."

"*Shel*, we broke into his *place*."

"We can't abandon him."

"We have a gun, man. You *already* assaulted Suzanne tonight. They'd find out in about two seconds the guy punched your face in. It might even come out about what he did to your car."

"So?"

"So what are we gonna do? Make him dinner? Look at your face. It's a mess. What would you tell the feds? A birthmark? You'd be revenge suspect number one . . ."

"Suspect . . ."

"We gotta split, man."

"And go where?"

"Home."

"*Home?*"

"Where else we gonna go . . . ?"

XIX

Razis tore out his bowels with both hands and flung them at the crowds. So he died, calling on Him who is lord of life and spirit to restore them to him again.
                                                                —*II Maccabees*

"I can't make it on my own."
"I got you the glue," Eric said, tossing it on the pull-out couch.
"Oh wretched humanity!" I cried, perched on top of the covers, slightly fetal, leaning over *Fish-tail Pie*, its two broken tails resting on my thigh. "Man-made decisions will be the end of us all!"
"You still got the runs?"
"I surrender to God, Eric. Right here, you as my witness."
"Look, man, you did nothin' wrong. We were protecting Lucy. Frank was dead when we got there."
The phone rang. Eric picked it up. "Yeah?" Eye movement. "Oh. Oh . . . hi . . . yeah, just a sec." Eric covered the receiver with his right hand and groaned. "It's Lucy," he said.
"Oh no. What does she want?"
"You."
I took the receiver. "Hello?"
"Can you come over?"
"You're home."
"I need you to come over."
"Really? Is everything—"
"It's Frank."
"Oh . . . okay. I'm on my way." I hung up.
"What'd she say?"
"She wants me to come over."
"Does she know?"
"I think so."

"About us?"
"I don't know."

* * *

The door opened. There was Lucy. "What happened to your face?" she said.
"Oh . . . uh . . . Eric and I were wrestling."
"Frank's dead," she said.
"*What?*" A police officer stood in the hallway.
"Shel, this is . . . sorry I forgot your name."
"Kravchuck."
"Officer Kravchuck."
The officer extended his hand and offered a tight-lipped nod of acknowledgement as we shook. "Well, Mrs. Moon, I'll get out of your way. My deepest sympathies."
"Thank you. Thanks for your help." Lucy escorted the man out, closed the door and turned to me, her face expressionless.
"What happened?" I asked.
"He O.D.'d."
"Really?"
"The dumb bastard," she said. "He never shot up while I was with him."
"He killed himself?"
"Smack, they figure. There's some super potent shit goin' around," she said, raising her hands to her face and rubbing her eyes. "They found a strange note on the floor outside his bedroom."
"Hm. What kind of note?"
"Some sort of half-written warning. Cops asked me if I could name any enemies. I said it'd be easier to name friends. *None.*" Lucy walked into the front room and picked up a packet of cigarettes from the coffee table.
"How do you feel?"
She shrugged. "They found him on his bed. He'd been dead for two days."
"I'm sorry."
"I was married to the man! I should at least be crying."
"You never cry."

"They got tipped about the body from a couple of strange phone calls at dawn this morning."

"Strange?"

"Some guy. Very high strung. Maybe another user, they figure."

"I bet he wasn't that strange," I said, disgusted at my inability to own up.

Lucy put her cigarette in her mouth. "Well . . . I'm *back!*" she said.

An acute pain gripped my lower intestine. I winced, and actually felt the colour drain from my face. "Could I use your washroom?"

"Of course."

Due to the speed of the attack, I had to wobble with my cheeks clenched just to keep it all at bay. Skirting around the corner and into the bathroom, I turned on both the hot and cold taps in the sink, yanked down my corduroys and sitting down on the bowl let the rest happen voluntarily.

Amidst noxious fumes, it came to me that life does not last, love is eternal and humanity, in its urge to have The Answers, has made blunder after blunder. Denial of this had already left me unable to accept Suzanne's wondrous gift. My God, she came offering her soul and I, terrified by honesty, lashed out like an animal. And why? Because just as God cannot stomach sin, liars despise honesty. It would seem general confusion exacerbated by drugs and alcohol had left my troubadour within trampled by his very own horse. And now in the front room stood a troubled Lucy, my one love, relaying to me police details that I already knew!

And so, prostrate on Lucy's bed sometime later that evening I confessed to the previous night's commotion at Frank's apartment and begged her not to make me go to the police. Lucy was a combination exalted and appalled—much like life itself, I thought to myself, suddenly aware that all was coming to me as metaphors of existence. I told her Eric and I had reason to believe the last thing Frank did was read Bobby Orr's scoring statistics. For fear of overload, I made no mention of my attack on Suzanne, instead carrying that guilt around as bursts and bubbles of intestinal spasm. I was shocked that both the person I most loved and the person I most despised had died within months of each other. What did this mean? Exhaustion eventually freed me in the form of slumber, the drift of rain in my ears, the taste of Pepto-Bismol in my mouth.

Awakening heavy headed before dawn, I heard the patter of bare feet on wood. Paying heed, they gently waned, to be replaced by a door squeak, running water and, finally, silence. Anxiety gripped my chest and I shook. I was as loathsome and angelic, it would seem, as all the rest. I lay back and concentrated on listening, becoming aware of the household hum and the heater, electricity in general and then sounds I didn't recognize—life going about its business, I presumed. Still fully dressed, I got up and tiptoed towards the kitchen, untangling my underwear where necessary. The apartment was warm, both in temperature and ambience, not unlike a child's sense of Christmas Eve. From the hall, the gentle peep of the stove light on the front room floor and the familiar odour of Lucy's cigarettes indulged my senses. One more step and I saw Lucy, the door frame blocking all but her elbow on the table and the side of her face leaning on her cigarette hand. Creeping closer, I could see her eyes were closed and, save for her bra, she was unclad. For fear of either waking, frightening or embarrassing her, I remained silent. Every minute or so, without opening her eyes, she'd take a long drag of her cigarette and then maybe scratch her shoulder with her cigarette hand or rub her eye. I figured one day soon I would confess being so fond of her that it would be in both of our best interests—and perhaps our children's—if she abandoned cigarettes altogether. I smiled at the thought of her reaction to such a notion. She stood up and walked to the sink, filled a glass with water and took a sip, the kitchen light warm across her back and down her legs.

"Lucy," I whispered. She turned around, briefly trying to cover her nakedness, and then for a lack of hands, gave up.

"Hi, Shel," she said softly, "what are you doing up?"

I shrugged. "Restless, I guess. Are you all right?"

Naked to her bra in the stove light, Lucy gave me a double thumbs up. It was beautiful.

"Is there anything I can do?"

"It's so strange," she said. "Frank's dead. Kinda closes a

book, you know? I don't know how to react; sadness, guilt, fear, anger, relief—in all honesty, the guy was a prick."

"I wish I could help but I gave up having answers this morning."

"Running from your past is like running from your legs," she said.

"Do you want some juice?"

"And how can I judge him? I ain't exactly Mechtild of Magdeburg?"

"Who is?" I said, realising I didn't know who that was.

"Listen to this," she said, putting her cigarette in her mouth and picking up a paperback that was folded open on the table. "'Under heaven all can see beauty as beauty only because there is ugliness. All can know good as good only because there is evil'."

"What's that?"

"The Tao Te Ching," she said. "It's dicks like Frank that make flowers so damn beautiful, you know?"

I pictured his stiff body; white, large, dead—hardly a blossoming iris.

"He wasn't so bad," she said.

* * *

Back home the following evening, still nauseous, *Fish-tail Pie* pieced together and in view on top of Lucy's little television, I read over my attempt at restitution with Suzanne.

Dear Suzanne,

As I sit gazing at Fish-tail Pie, I realise you offered me a seal pup and I clubbed its furry head. Why? Amidst tears, vomit (yesterday) and diarrhoea, one reality pushes forth.

Truth. That is, a lack thereof.

At three days, surely the infant boy must wonder, why have they clipped my foreskin? At five we discover the tooth fairy is a lie. At seven or eight, Santa Claus. Adolescence is a time of intense self hatred over abstract ideas that only have meaning because of more lies; weight, complexion, body hair and so forth.

But it is at twenty years of age that I have seen how pervasive society's lack of truth really is: education, success and sex—mainstays, if you will—have all crumbled before me as illusion. And I ask: from what spring do answers spew forth? Science? God? Indeed, I have done well in neither works nor grace. Since I was a child I have been taught that it is more important to believe Jesus Christ died and rose than it is to live a life of harmony with all that surrounds us. This troubles me greatly.

I never told you, but my Granmother died a short while back. She was my closest ally. Bussing back from the funeral, it was revealed to me that the soul is a big ear. Where was mine when you offered your gift? Filled with wax, I presume.

There is no satisfactory excuse for my behaviour. Perhaps I am a reflection of general social decay. More likely, though, the outburst stemmed from an ever increasing fear that women find me sexually repugnant. If you have any ideas or agree, please let me know. Again, I am sorry. I HAVE NO ANSWERS.

And if you have any plans to charge me for assault, call first and I will turn myself over to the authorities, with whatever written statement you would deem appropriate.

Finally, your artwork is a gift in every sense of the word. If you should want Fish-tail Pie returned, I would obviously understand. If you choose to let me keep it, I would cherish it always.

My deepest repentance,
Shelby M. Lewis

p.s. Not meant as an excuse but I was really drunk.

Humbled, I slipped the letter back into my binder, placed the pen between my teeth and leaned against the pull-out couch. My guts gurgled and I returned to the bathroom for perhaps the fifteenth time that day. While there I decreed to no longer deny any feelings, specifically ones of sexual frustration—even if Lucy insisted on remaining celibate. This didn't mean I was about to search elsewhere. Nor did it mean I would act physically on every (or any) impulse. The Suzanne debacle had been, if not a crime, a grave *faux pas*. Clearly, it was time to embrace my sexual self. Taking the pen from my mouth I wrote three spontaneous proverbs in small print on the bathroom wall below the one about opening fire in a MacDonald's restaurant:

If thou hath low self-esteem, do not love thy neighbour as thyself.

If you think you know THE ANSWERS, shoot yourself in the head. If you miss, call me.

Be nice.

* * *

Later in the week, Lucy had the ironic and unfortunate task of having to orchestrate Frank's funeral. His mother, it was revealed, went insane in Ontario some years earlier and his Father, a longtime remarried priest in the Maritimes, had both verbally and legally disowned him. If he had friends, none stepped forward. I, too, was of little help, suggesting to Lucy that to put too much into the proceedings would be hypocritical. She ignored me, ordering flowers and the like.

As it turned out, the service was brief and sparsely attended; me accompanying Lucy while three other slovenly characters sat in different spots towards the back of the chapel. My first reaction to the emptiness was chuckling, but upon reflection I became haunted at this cavernous metaphor of Frank's soul. It soon became clear: the difference between Frank and me had nothing to do with our respective body shapes. Nay, the difference was Frank had never been liked.

Two or three minutes into the scripture reading a small squeak peeped out. Glancing at Lucy, I convulsed two or three times before breaking down into sobs so loud the priest twice had to stop his sermon, finishing only after Lucy had carried me distraught and wailing down the aisle and out into the fresh air. Swaddled in her arms, I knew—but because of hyperventilation could not explain to her—that my distress was in knowing Frank's attacks on my face and car were as indiscriminate as a tornado searching for a place to stop. The man was literally dying for attention—an absence that finally killed him. And what did I do when he called out to me from yonder field? I hid in yonder cave.

After the funeral and still outside, one of the men who had

SHELBY

attended the service nervously and apologetically asked Lucy if Frank had ever mentioned the five hundred dollars he owed him. She said he hadn't and we all dispersed, me enmeshed and amazed by the mystery that allows a man to break down at the funeral of a man he loathes. Indeed, we are brothers after all.

Dropping Lucy at work and then returning home, I was both surprised and terrified by a phone call from Suzanne. Having received my letter, she said she accepted my apology. From there I suggested we meet just to see if we could somehow return to the way we were. Although skeptical, she concurred. Less than an hour later we were face-to-face over cheese pretzels at Granville Market.

Although it was evident some of the warmth between us had dissipated, Suzanne actually apologised for not having seen me for what I really was. Unfortunately, now seeing me for what I was, she felt compelled to admit she liked me less. She seemed sincere, however, in hoping the scratches on my face healed without scarring. Nervous, I did most of the talking.

" . . . and to cap it all off," I continued, "I made the fatal error of combining deep depression with flagrant drunkeness—a lethal combination for even the most pious people. Lot, for example, after taking on a belly full of wine, slept with his daughters and denied any knowledge of it whatsoever. Granted, there are writers who excel in such a state: Faulkner, Tennessee Williams, Hemingway—although Hemingway put a bullet though his head—Bukowski, Fitzgerald, perhaps even you . . ."

"I don't drink," she said, and we shared smiles as one would with an in-joke.

"How could you," I asked, "and produce works of such calibre?"

She shrugged.

"I truly love *Fish-tail Pie*."

"You can keep it," she said softly. There was a pause until she recommended we leave. Standing up I continued talking.

"For what it's worth, Suzanne," I said, "I'd like you to know that while attending a funeral for an old friend today—"

"Oh, I'm sorry."

"Thank you. I think he's happier."

"Was he young?"
"Thirty-fiveish."
"Sick?"
"Drugs."
"Ooh."
"Sad. But while there it came to me that when I hurt you, I hurt myself tenfold. For although I find you enchanting, and have since our initial meeting, there is another who has arrested my heart. So what was I doing making advances? Well, like my friend now embalmed, I was crying out for affections; but my actions were merely the twisted reflections of yearns unanswered. Being dishonest, I was blinded by your honesty. In short, my bad struck out to kill my good."

Suzanne smiled. "You look tired."

"Strenuous week," I said.

"Take care of yourself," she said as we stepped outside into a brisk breeze.

"Suzanne, do you think we could be again as we were?" I asked.

"Probably not," she said, "but we know a little more now, so maybe something else'll come out of it." She smiled, turned and walked away.

"I'm sorry," I said. Without turning round, she threw up a hand and kept walking.

So haunted by loneliness that night, it seemed, not even sleep wanted to be around me.

"Excuse me?" I whispered around three-thirty A.M., pushing open Eric's door. There was no response. "Eric?"

"Hm?"

"You asleep?"

"Yeah."

"REM?"

"What?"

"A deep sleep?"

"What do you want?"

"Um . . . I . . . How would you feel if I climbed in beside you?"

"*What?*"

"I need to hear you breathe."

"Listen, Shel, whatever you . . . I'll stand by you. But straight up, I'm not your man."

"Friendship, Eric. That's all. I need to be near to life. I need to embrace it. Exalt it. Believe in it. And I need you to know you can come to me for anything."

"Great. How 'bout a quick blow job?"

"I meant of a spiritual nature."

"I *know*. Left hand side. Don't yank the covers, no talking and don't touch me."

I got into bed and lay staring at the blackness. "Thanks, Eric."

"No prob, man. Go to sleep."

"Can you hear that?" I asked.

"Hear what?"

"Life."

"What?"

"Dancing. Listen."

"This is getting kinda weird. Get out."

"Really?"

"Look, shut up, man. It's all gonna be okay."

"I don't want to die alone."

"Well, do a murder-suicide thing."

"I mean without being loved."

"Oh geez."

"And loving."

"Don't worry about it."

"Do you love me, Eric?"

"Come on, man."

"You can tell me."

There was a pause. "I like you, okay?"

My heart trembled. There we lay, two heterosexual men, shrouded in darkness and religious taboo, inches apart in a warm bed. Why was I there? I knew that by confessing I *loved* him, which I did, I could blast open the social envelope, exposing a better world for all. "I . . . I like you, too," I said.

* * *

"Come on, Shel, I got brutal cramps," Lucy said at four twenty A.M. with her hair in disarray, her feet bare (red toe-

nails) and a wrinkled pink T-shirt hanging over wrinkled black tights, me standing in her doorway.
"This won't take a minute . . . I just—"
"What's wrong with you?"
"Were you asleep?"
"It's five o'clock in the fuckin' morning."
We stood staring. "Sure is wet out," I said limply.
"Look, get in here. Five minutes. That's it." She turned around, staggering slightly on her way to the couch, sat down and closed her eyes, one of them covered by the hand she was leaning on. I followed and sat down in the big chair a few feet away.
"Well, it's an assortment of things," I said. "I can't seem to regulate my feelings; anger, sadness, love, fear, frustration, loneliness."
Lucy opened her eyes, picked up her cigarette pack, pulled out a cigarette and lit it. "This ain't about your prick again, is it?"
"You say that like I'm just another guy with a hormonal problem."
"I'm just—"
"When are you going to *fuck*ing well see our meeting each other was predetermined!"
Lucy seemed stunned. "You swore."
"Gran is *dead*. Frank is *dead*. I've abandoned my academic calling. You no longer have an interest in your vocation. I feel robotic. I feel furious. I feel yearning. We're nearing the end, you know."
"What?"
"Can I quote Yeats?"
"You look tired."
"Tired? I haven't slept in fifty-four hours. *Fifty*-four hours. Mere anarchy is loose around the world. The blood-dimmed tide! I don't even know what that is but I do know that everywhere innocence is drowned—take a look: *I* feel that. Young children are abused by the second. Old growth forests cut up for chopsticks. The best lack all conviction. I'm not saying I'm the best, but my heart has no conviction. I spin like a car in mud, messing up everything for miles around me. And politicians? Leaders? The riots in L.A. Earthquakes. Pestilence.

SHELBY

There's no Four Horsemen, Lucy, it's a friggin' cavalry! That's the truth. The Gulf War. The Vancouver Stock Exchange. Tabloid television. Scandals of every type. All is rotten to the very core—and only the worst are full of passionate intensity. Saddam Hussein? Thank god for George Bush and the American people. They figure he was worse than Hitler, you know—"

"Have you been eating?"

"Rising Antichrists and—"

"I think you need some sleep—"

"Don't *patronize me*!"

"Listen to yourself!"

"I held a gun the other day, Lucy . . . ooh—just a little revolver . . . black, so small. And you know what?"

"You liked the feel of it."

"How'd you—yes I did."

"You need sleep."

"It gave me a sense of calm, Lucy. Comfort and power as I cradled its tender shaft."

"Fuck, Shel, it's the news. It makes everyone want to be a vigilante. Sometimes I wish I had a couple o' hand grenades in my bra when I dance. You know, send 'em flying to some corner o' the room. *Kaboom*—"

"This goes way beyond that, Lucy. What were the odds of you and I ending up in each other's arms? *Zero*. Heed the signs! I say we get a couple of plane tickets, head to the place most likely to survive a nuclear holocaust, take provisions—canned goods, weapons to blast out mutant beings that survive the radiation. Then we start having kids. Hundreds of them—"

"Shel?"

"We can't give up, Lucy. So even if Christ doesn't come down we'll repopulate the earth with loving, caring, tender human beings—"

"And cousins who'll have to *dork* each other and then what? A bunch o' mutant sadists more crazy than ever."

"I never thought of that."

"I'm joking, Shel. Jesus. I'm going to say this once—"

"On Gran's honor, Lucy, I vow to you that no one will ever harm you again."

"Listen to me. You've blown a gasket. You need some R & R. You're over-stressed—"

"Look, Lucy." I grinned, unzipping my Gortex jacket and pulling out Eric's revolver that I had stuffed partly down my corduroys.

"Jesus Christ, Shel."

"I want to fill the walls full of plugs! Ha ha ha! I want to *scream* out my rage!"

"Is that thing loaded?"

"I don't know."

"Give it to me." I handed it to her. "Now listen. I need some sleep," she said. "I got a migraine. I got my period. You come over here totin' a six-shooter, talking about nuclear holocausts. You either go to bed here or get the hell home."

"I can't sleep with you, Lucy. I can't be trusted."

"I trust you, Shel, okay?"

"Don't trust *anybody*! I could be Ted Bundy."

"He's *dead*."

"Were you there?"

She covered her eyes for a moment and then stood up, handing me her cigarette. "He's dead." She kissed me on the forehead. "I'm going to bed. I'm taking the gun. And I'm betting we'll all be here and happy when the sun comes up."

"But what's being planned in Communist Angola?"

Lucy walked away.

"I'm not leaving, Lucy."

"I'm not asking you to," she said, disappearing.

"Facts, Lucy, facts!" I yelled, her cigarette smoldering in my trembling hand. "Why'd you give me this cigarette?" There was no response. "I'll extinguish it if you don't answer!" I smudged it into the ashtray just as the light in Lucy's bedroom went out, darkening the front room. Her door closed. I was wet and scared. I crumpled to my knees, bent over and prayed for direction.

Lucy woke me up just before noon. My jacket was still on. My back ached and my arm was numb. She made buckwheat pancakes that were heavy and filling. We giggled like Japanese exchange students seeing a cute guy in a mall. Strangely, I felt far less fearful of either the surprise communist attack or the coming apocalypse that had so haunted me only hours before.

SHELBY

As for Lucy, a few ibuprofen tablets had eased her menstrual cramps and her head was tolerable as long as she didn't speak too loudly or move too quickly. Upon leaving, she gave me back Eric's gun.

"It wasn't loaded," she said.

Holding it in my hand it felt unpleasant, dangerous. "Thank god," I said, "I had it stuffed down my pants." Lucy laughed. I felt my eyes tingle and feared tears. Lucy smiled. I thanked her for breakfast.

"I'm glad you stayed," she said.

So was I.

XX

Blessed are the man and the woman who have grown beyond their greed, and have put an end to their hatred and no longer nourish illusions.
—*Psalm 1, liberally*

A few days later Lucy realised she was late for work and dashed away, leaving me alone in her apartment for the first time ever. Having felt more united with her than at any other time in our relationship, I was overcome with an urge to snoop through her belongings. Thankfully, decency prevailed. I did, however, flip through a photo album I stumbled upon on the top shelf of the closet in her bedroom. The majority of the photographs were of her and Frank; a particular series of them vacationing in Java affecting me most adversely. I lay back, imagining myself as the profile study on *A Current Affair: MILD MANNERED MED-SCHOOL DROPOUT OR DOCTOR OF DEATH?*

Reporter: "*The couple in happier times*" (*cut to Frank and Lucy slicing their wedding cake, swimming in paradise, et cetera*), "*before he came along*" (*black and white still of my face, sombre, eyes pained, showing signs of a thin-man's complex*).

Me: "*I'd do anything . . . anything . . . to win her love!*" *Macabre laugh.*

Reporter: "*Even . . . kill?*"

Me: I smirk. "*She's mine, isn't she?*"

Cut to weathered waitress at the Big Dipper: "*Frank was never the same after she left him.*"

Cut to trailer house.

Lucy: "*I don't know what to believe*" (*puts her arm around me as we sit on a polyester couch, her dangling left hand showing off the huge ring on her finger*), "*but I love my man . . .*"

Strangely, there was but one photograph of Lucy as a child; a small, faded black-and-white snapshot tucked away, after four blank pages, on the final page of the album. She was perhaps five or six, with bangs cut on an outrageous slant (excuse enough for her present-day temperament). She was sitting on outside steps, gently squinting into the sun, her crooked smile as delightful as ever. The moment I saw it, I was convinced getting it enlarged and framed would make the perfect Christmas gift. I removed the casing, pealed it off the sticky backing, and for safekeeping slipped it inside *T.S. Eliot: Selected Poems*, which I was carrying in my breast pocket.

* * *

The following day, December 20th, I did a one-to-five shift at Brittania Library and despite attempting to remain loving felt spiritually lost amidst Christmas decorations, kids, cakes, fruit punch and so on. Couldn't people see the gift of giving had been hunted to the brink of extinction by consumerism? Not even communication as an unconditional offering is taken at face value. And why? Because without a price tag, value is unknown to the Western boob. Where deities were once vehicles for expressing thankfulness for the gifts of existence, God is now a device for manipulating the consumer into buying bushels of dull presents. Wake up! I cried out. Unfortunately my mouth never opened save for three quick glasses of eggnog that took my bowels at gunpoint, a spasmodic reaction intensified by an awareness of two medical students at a nearby table discussing internships and billing numbers while I struggled with the Dewey decimal placement of a book called *Geraldine And The Wind Up Mouse*. In the washroom, I wrote in felt pen my first ever public graffiti: *Cover up, homeless man, in the wasted wrapping of my shiny new presents. God is yet to be found at the shoe department at Sears. Love will and must prevail. SML.*

A post-work staff Christmas gathering at Claudia-the-front-clerk's apartment was, despite good intentions, tedious. With every valueless comment, my heart sank deeper into darkness until all I could do was devour hors d'oeuvres; nachos, brownies, crab pâté and on and on. It was the punch cocktail, I believe, that led to a collage of crude thoughts bouncing around my head; nasty comments and sexual innuendo culminating in a far too real fantasy of me lying face down, naked and fully bound on the tiled floor beneath Minnie T.'s magical mass.

Fighting off the image as one would if his head were aflame I suddenly feared winding up in the back row of an adult theatre gazing at XXX-rated pornographic movies beside equally lewd, slack-jawed men whose idea of art is pumping miserable childhoods into unwashed hankies. Frazzled, I stormed from the house. My voice had to be heard, I cried to no one, and my lover had to hear it. Lucy's nonsensical denial of me was against the ways of nature, as evident in my resulting behaviour; fantasies of Minnie T., wet dreams, masturbation, the attack on Suzanne and so on. Lucy had to understand! Minutes later I was clanging on her door.

"You got my message?" she said before I had spoken.

"Lucy, I fear that if we don't compromise I'll soon be giving my pearls to pigs."

"Did you get my message?"

"What message?"

"I left a couple on your machine." Lucy sucked nervously on her cigarette, ashtray in hand.

"I've been at a party."

"I quit," she said.

"You quit?"

"Well, I was *gonna* quit. I even called the club."

"What did they say?"

"Oh man, get this: Calvin—he's the owner—picked up the phone. I had it *all* ready. Reasons. Thank yous. Everything. Suddenly I feel like I've got piano wire around my fuckin' neck. Out of nowhere comes, 'Can't come in, can't come in, I've got chickenpox.' *Chickenpox!*"

"Chickenpox?"

"Chickenpox. What the *hell* was I thinking? I'm already having a bitch of a time getting work in this damn town. I mean what the hell else could I do?"

"Anything!"

"Grab a brain stem."

"You could do anything. Your life experience . . . your psychic readings—"

"I'm a grade nine dropout and I haven't given a decent reading in six months."

"Your knowledge of Eastern philosophy."
"So what?"
"Lucy, people *need* to hear what you have to say! A word from those who have lived through foster homes and the street and managed to move towards the light."
"You're nuts."
"I'm serious. Tell the world! Open up that window and tell the world how you did it!"
"Did what?"
"Go on!"
"Shel . . ."
"We'll write your biography. I'll cap every chapter with brilliant quotes in Gothic print. Robert Frost. Gerard Manley Hopkins. Christ, even—no wait, female writers only."
"Nobody wants to hear my story."
"Are you *mad*? Of *course* they do!"
"Are you drunk? You're acting like a fuckin' bozo."
"Of course I'm not . . . oh God."
"What?"
"I think I am."
"Am what?"
"I think I drunk and driv—I mean drank and drove."
"You look fine."
"I could've killed someone."
"How much did you drink?"
"God knows. Glass after glass."
"Of what?"
"What am I doing? I'm supposed to be here for *you*."
"It's okay."
"Is the biography a possibility?"
"No."
"What about you and me? Is there room for growth?"
"I can't talk about that right now."
"Okay."
"I'll think about it, all right?"
"Yes."
She rubbed her eye with an open hand. "What am I doing?"
"Maybe you just need some time off."
Lucy's shoulders slumped. "I'm not an accountant, for Christ's sake," she said shakily. "I'm a stripper. Time is . . . you

know . . ." She put her hands beneath her breasts. "Perky tits . . . it's a young gal's game, Shel, think about it." She pulled her cigarette to her mouth and looked away.

"Where's the mystic, Shel, where's the magic? That's what I want to know. Mechtild and Hildeberg and Eckhart—they weren't survivors, they were livers—walkin' along the Rhineland, thankful in the face of hatred and fear. This city? It could take your soul at twenty paces. This world? Fuck this world." Lucy put out her cigarette in the ashtray that was in her hand. She took a few steps into the front room, put the tray on the coffee table and lay down on the floor. I followed, lying next to her. We clasped hands. Shrouded only in darkness, it fringed the romantic.

* * *

In light of recent events, having Lucy invite me to a *special* dinner a couple days later—in which no explanation was offered beyond suggesting I dress formally—was thrilling. But to then arrive at her apartment and find her absent was disconcerting.

Hanging off the outside railing, I peered through the front room window and pounded on the glass. The only light seemed to be from the kitchen. I sensed trouble, a feeling compounded upon discovering the door was unlocked. I crept inside and called out to no answer. I ran towards the kitchen and thrust open the door. Shattered glass was scattered across the floor as steam rose up from a huge mound of rice and vegetables and Jumbo shrimp—some sort of casserole—that was splattered in front of the stove which was still open and on. The room was muggy and the windows dripped with condensation. A closer look at the mess revealed drops of blood. I yelled out and ran towards Lucy's bedroom. A crack of light under the bathroom door caught my attention. Pushing it open I found Lucy huddled against the bathtub, arms crossed in front as though trying to warm herself. She had on her stunning black evening dress. Her left hand was wrapped in a blood-stained towel and she was rocking herself to and fro.

"I cut my hand," she said, "I cut my hand." She reached

towards me, exposing a ballooned blister across bloodied fingers. In an instant I was on the floor, my arms around her. "I cut my hand," she said again.

"It's okay," I said, not knowing if it was.

"My head," she said. "All day my head wouldn't let me think and I wanted to make a special dinner for us and I couldn't see and I burnt my hand and dropped the jambalaya on the floor and the bowl smashed and I couldn't think and I tried to pick it up and I cut my hand."

"It's all right," I said.

"I cut my hand," she said again.

I drove Lucy straight to St. Paul's Hospital where we sat in the emergency waiting area amidst Christmas decorations, magazines and the other Monday night injuries; two or three drunks, a woman with abdominal cramps, a limping man and his wife, the incoming stretcher brigade and a petite elderly man with streaked hair who pranced around hysterically yelling, "I've been raped! Doesn't anybody care? I've been raped!" Lucy sat beside me with her eyes closed and her head against my chest, in a mild state of shock, the blood-stained towel still wrapped around her hand. I remained placid, protective, fully embracing my role as guardian.

It was over two hours before the doctor on duty got to Lucy. He put twelve stitches in her pinky and some sort of antibiotic cleansing ointment on her burn. She hardly even flinched, and spoke nary a word on the trip home. Back at her apartment she thanked me and went directly to bed, sleeping until two the following afternoon. At that time I brought her lemon zinger tea in bed and we chatted and laughed, the mood warmed by sunlight through her window, dappling the sheets in gentle shadows. For dinner and while reading we had toast and hot chocolate in bed. It would seem to me that events had led us to a new mutual reliance in which, yes, we knew we could survive without each other, but why bother?

To my surprise, Derek telephoned me that night—he got the number from Eric—to tell me that he and Kristine had not only moved back in together but that I was seven and a half months from unclehood! My joy was unbridled. Deduction revealed the infant to have been conceived in Revelstoke during the time of Gran's funeral—evidently willed by her spirit. I was the only person he'd told, and I was not to mention it to Mom or Dad. Lucy's enthusiasm was wonderful. Later I demanded she join my family for Christmas in Revelstoke with all the traditional trimmings; chestnuts, stockings, turkey. She declined without hesitation.

* * *

The following day I left Lucy's apartment two full hours before my shift in order to explore toy stores for Junior. Lucy, bless her, remained in bed, a migraine now added to her blistered hand. Beyond cooking and comforting, there was unfortunately little I could do for her. Nonetheless, with taking care of her, talk of children and the notion of family togetherness being a theme still visible beneath frenzied Christmas consumerism, I could not help but occasionally imagine us married.

Outside, I was unbothered by the falling rain, mesmerized instead by a mother carrying a heap of presents while waiting at the bus stop on the corner of Yew Street and Cornwall with her two young children in tow. We shared a smile as I took a portion of the bench. I figured one of the children to be newly born (although he was so swaddled in a snugly I couldn't even see him. Does life, I wondered, ever get better than that?). The other was a handsome boy, maybe three, with a mop of dark hair and blue eyes, stepping in puddles with his gumboots and tiny legs that *grow*, gazing all about, babbling to the passing cars, at ease with the rain and with himself—still years from hating his body and the rest of the world. The mother glanced at me and smiled when one of his stomps splattered a spray of dirty water just far enough to catch the cuff of my corduroys.

"Cute kids," I said.
"A handful," she said with a warm smile.
"I'm going to be an uncle."
"Congratulations."
I looked at the boxes in her arms. "Christmas presents?"
"Yes."
"They enjoy it?" I asked.
"He's getting the hang of it," she said, pointing to the older one.
"Christmas *truly* is a time for children, isn't it?" I asked. She

nodded. "For the record," I added, "I'm opposed to Nintendo, television and board games based on the occult."

She smiled.

"As presents, I mean." There was a pause. "Cute kids," I said again. The bus came. I helped them on. We said our goodbyes.

Over the next hour and a half, it was evident that the baby news had instilled within me a newfound ability to shop. Although Dad doesn't golf, I bought him a golf glove and golf balls. For Derek and Kristine I purchased a snugly—$49.99 at the Bay. Ward's Music had a sale on so I picked up for Eric a *Pink Floyd: The Wall* stained songbook for $1.99 and an equally cheap kazoo. And for Mom I bought a few secondhand paperbacks. The *coup de finis*, though, was picking up a card, wrapping paper and the framed and enlarged childhood photograph of Lucy—its beauty shaking my foundation.

At work I was swamped by books in circulation, my only respite being ten minutes of casual conversation with Hans the custodian about the joys of motherhood and marriage. I did most of the talking. Upon asking his thoughts, he replied, staring straight ahead: "Vell, it is alvays quvestinabull vhat is best for ze soul, yah?"

Despite having arranged to go to Lucy's right after work, I first returned to Eric's apartment to pack my Christmas presents and take them to Lucy's so as not to have to stop off at the apartment again before travelling home for Christmas. The place for no obvious reason wreaked of fish. Eric, as expected, wasn't home. Evidently he'd left for his two-day Californian holiday. I left his presents on his bed.

Arriving at Lucy's, she told me Eric had phoned in the morning to tell me he cancelled the California trip due to a lack of funds and that if I wanted a lift back to Revelstoke I should call him by noon. I was too late—not that I'd have called anyway. After all, I had a blue canvas hockey bag full of presents on my shoulder, Lucy an arm's length away, the spirit of childhood in my heart and, finally, the delightful awareness of my love and me sharing one more day together before the bus trip home. Standing in the doorway, she didn't invite me in, instead grinning as would a child with a secret aching to be told.

"May I come in?"

"Of course."

I put the hockey bag on the floor, kicked off my shoes, walked into the front room and sat down in the big green chair. Lucy sat across from me, on the couch, and continued to stare, her grin intact.

"Are you all right?" I asked.

"Fine." Her smile widened.

"I'd like to say it was awfully fulfilling looking after you."

"Thanks," she said. Maybe a minute passed.

"Lucy?"

"Yeah?"

"What are you looking at?"

"Who's looking?"

"You are."

"Can't I look?"

"You can *look*."

"You sound paranoid."

"No."

Lucy stood up from the couch and exited towards the bathroom humming a few bars from "Have Yourself a Merry Little Christmas"—nary a week after she'd expressed her ambivalence towards the season.

"You can't sing that and walk out!" I yelled.

"La la la."

"What's going on?" I followed her into the bathroom. "If I guess will you tell me?"

"Tell you what?" she said, breaking off a piece of dental floss.

"It's love, isn't it? You want to tell me you love me."

"I hardly know you," she said, flossing.

"Ha ha."

"No more questions or I'll kill you."

We spent the evening in a state of quiet euphoria: talking, reading, smiling.

* * *

"Get up!"

Heart pounding, I sprang forward to see Lucy roll off the bed and run out of the room, clothed only in a bra, socks and her gauzed hand. I turned to the clock. It was five past six in the morning.

"Close your eyes!" she yelled from outside the room. I closed them. "Are they closed?"

"What are you doing?"

"Close them."

"They're closed."

I heard her steps get closer. "Okay," she said, "open them."

And there before me was an unusual looking black case on the bed about the dimensions of a bassoon.

"Open it," she said with an enthusiasm reminiscent of when she lent me the money to reimburse my parents months earlier.

Unclicking the buckles, I was shocked to find inside a saxophone—judging by the case and a few dents an old one, but nonetheless in excellent condition, lined in pinky-purple shag carpet, its body like buffed gold. I gingerly touched a couple of the keys. "My God."

"You like it?"

"For me?"

"No kidding."

"*God*. I adore it!" Inside was a note:

Merry Christmas
Thanks. A sexy instrument for a sexy guy.
Love Lucy xoxox.

"Me?"

"Of course you," she said with a laugh.

I glanced up at her. "I'm not sexy."

"Can *I* pick presents?" she asked proudly. Sighing, my nose whistled. It made no difference. There was a poem, handwritten at the bottom of the note.

If your house catch on fire, Lord, and there ain't no water around,
Throw your trunk out the window, and let the shack burn down.

"I'm stunned," I said.

Lucy beamed. I reached over and hugged her. "Now you can jam with your brother," she said doing something disco-like.

"Derek?"

"He plays the clarinet, doesn't he?"

"How did you know that?"

"You told me about it months ago—when we first met."

I didn't recall. I glanced back at the card. "Lucy, I . . . don't know what to say. What does this poem mean?"

Lucy tilted her head to read it. "I saw it in a book of Spirituals I was flipping through in the store where I bought the sax. It sounded cool. The card was there . . ." She shrugged her shoulders.

I gave the saxophone a squeaky blow. "Three months," I said.

Lucy smiled.

"I'm not kidding," I said. "Music is very mathematical and I have a gift for math. Speaking of that, I have a gift for you, too."

"Really?"

"Yes. It's not much. It's . . . I'll get it." I trotted out of the bedroom and into the hallway by the front door, and removed from the hockey bag the wrapped photograph of Lucy. My heart momentarily fluttered. I walked back into the room and offered it to her gently.

She unveiled it face down, flipped it over and stared.

"Well?"

She looked up, her face without expression. "Where did you get this?"

"I borrowed it from your . . . photo album."

She looked for a few more seconds. "Oh yeah," she said, her face lightening, "that's where I've seen it."

"What does that mean?"

"I found it on the top shelf of the bedroom closet when I moved in here," she said.

"*What?*"

Lucy shrugged. "Homely little thing, isn't she?"

"It's not you?"

Lucy laughed and glanced back at the photograph. "Of course it's not me," she said, "look at her." Lucy turned the photograph my way. She was still laughing but it seemed forced.

"I don't know," I said, "I think there's a resemblance."

"Really?"

"Of *course*. I thought it *was* you! Why do you think I had it enlarged?"

"Sorry," she said with a smile. The saxophone glittered at my side.

"I thought it . . ." I shook my head. "Give it to me and I'll smash it."

"*No*. I'll put it on my wall."

"What for? How stupid."

"It's great."

"I feel like *swearing!*"

"I love it, Shel, really," she said, "it's a beautiful photograph." She leaned her face towards me, offering a smile and a kiss. We collapsed backwards on the bed and she caressed my ribby back with her bandaged hand. I was soon soothed.

* * *

The morning was shrouded in the possibility of lovemaking. We had tea and toast in bed while outside the white sky sent forth snowflakes the size of cotton balls. Floating down, they'd land in the alley and then, *poof*, be gone. Lucy sat watching them for a good hour while I lay on the front room floor perusing Sartre's *Anti-Semite and Jew*—Lucy's book and surprisingly readable (albeit an unusual choice for Christmas Eve). Every quarter hour or so I'd peek into the bedroom and watch from behind Lucy gazing out the window. Though curious, I didn't ask her what thoughts she held. I had a feeling they weren't for sharing.

Sometime into the early afternoon the snow stopped and the sun shone white through the clouds like a bright reflection off a silver tray. Lucy and I bundled up and trotted to the Safeway at the corner of Fourth Avenue and Vine. The trees and bushes were covered in a pristine inch of snow. The roads were clear. The air was cold on my face but my body felt wonderfully warm. Without provocation, Lucy slipped her hand in my jacket pocket and for the first time, I knew without question we were lovers.

"Come to Revelstoke for Christmas," I blurted. "We'd have such larks."
"Larks?"
"*Fun*. George Bernard Shaw. We'll go tobogganing."
"Yippee!"
"You'll come?"
"No way."
"Don't be afraid."
"I'm not."
"Come or I'll kill myself," I said. She laughed.

XXI

*Sail forth—steer for the deep
waters only!*
—Walt Whitman

Groceries were irrelevant with the hand of the woman I loved in my pocket. We wandered aimlessly and contentedly around the store for a half hour or so and ended up with a box of Japanese oranges and two purple candles. Once home, we walked directly into the front room. Lucy lit one of the candles, put it on the coffee table and poured the oranges all over the floor.

"*Din*nuh is served," she said. I ate four of them and I think Lucy ate two. We split a bottle of Muscadet, swig for swig. Towards the end of the meal we simultaneously lay down on the carpet and rolled oranges wrapped in green paper back and forth in the faded light; sometimes the paper fell off, sometimes an orange rolled under the couch, sometimes they rolled out of reach. Gorging the last one, I remembered the Christmas card I had bought for Lucy was still in the hockey bag I'd brought from home. Cheeks bulging, I offered her a one finger "Just be a second" gesture. Lucy rolled an orange beneath her hand and gave me a thumbs up. Entering the hallway, candlelight flickered, landing upon the wall like the shadows of a thousand ballerinas. And in that light I read:

> *The valley spirit never dies;*
> *It is the woman, primal mother.*
> *Her gateway is the root of heaven and earth.*
> *It is like a veil barely seen.*
> *Use it; it will never fail.*

I started to tremble. That poem had moved me the first time I saw it, too, seven or eight months earlier saying goodbye to a Lucy I did not yet know, a migrained Lucy, a Lucy I did not yet love—or did I? I'd always reacted to it since, but suddenly the feeling was all-consuming. I turned back to the front room.

"It's time," I said.

Still rolling the orange, Lucy looked up. The candle flickered her shadow on the wall. She smiled. "I'm playing with an orange," she said.

I lay down and softly kissed the tops of her feet and then her ankles before standing up and undressing in front of her, my boney frame now only mildly embarrassing.

"Look at you," she said.

I walked into the bedroom and lay on the bed. The mattress, at first cold on my back, warmed quickly.

Lucy came in with a candle flickering in her hand. She placed it on the bedside table. Her footsteps were soft upon the hardwood floor as she undressed naked to her bra. I stood up and undid it, gently holding each breast, one at a time, kissing her nipples. And when we were on the bed I kissed her everywhere else I'd never kissed her before.

If forced abstinence had taught me anything, it was that lovemaking was not about paying ten dollars at a toll booth on the way up the Coqhihalla Highway. Indeed, Lucy's foreplay comment from months earlier had rung a true chord—and for the first time I knew it was not about connecting dots. It was about not knowing. I knew nothing. It was about timelessness. I took off my watch. It was about faith in the mystery. We had no destination. There was no map. There was no manual. I was lost, words from the *Song of Songs* playing over and over in my head, *Do not arouse or awaken love until it so desires, Do not arouse or awaken* . . . Had I done that? What was right for my spirit? Was this the tantra? *Let go,* I said over and over, *I mean hold on, I mean let go* . . .

Every time I'd begin to speed up, Lucy would put her hands around me and slow me down. Barely moving, I could hear our sweat breaking forth just as primordial sludge must have done, splitting in two, deep in our ancestry; separate, together, separate, together, the rhythm meditative, spreading outwards from the center, beyond the bed, into the night and farther. I moaned with pleasure, pulling my body upwards,

SHELBY

gazing at Lucy. Pulling me in tight, we began to speed up. This time, Lucy didn't slow us down. Collapsing forward, alive with exhaustion, our bodies inseparable and indecipherable, the only movement came outwards from the tips of my soul, pumping, yearning, flailing . . .

I screamed at the moment of ejaculation; feeling both fully helpless and fully alive. Afterwards, we lay flat-out and exhausted, somewhere in the valley, our bodies gently moving, our mouths softly moaning, one step into the gateway (the root of heaven and earth), motionless for what seemed like hours . . .

I woke up with a different kind of scream. It was quarter past eleven and I had to catch the 11:30 night bus to Revelstoke at the downtown depot. Lucy jumped out of bed, ran into the front room, ran back into the bedroom and threw assorted garments at me. A half-minute later I was half dressed and tumbling down the outside stairs with a saxophone in my hand, a bag full of presents over one shoulder and soiled laundry draped over the other. Lucy was milliseconds behind, fumbling to find the right key to lock the door.

Driving was treacherous; I had to continually wipe the front window inside and out—a precarious stretch—and keep the side windows fully open to minimize condensation build-up. Lucy burst forth in song, singing "Leaving on the Midnight Bus to Revelstoke" to the tune of "Leaving on the Midnight Train to Georgia," and when I attempted to add the background parts but became confused with their rhythmic placement—the *his world is my world* proving particularly difficult—fits of laughter took us both over. In a moment of reckless bravado I stuck my head out the window and, hair blowing, screamed for several seconds.

We arrived at the depot three minutes before departure and just before my reserved ticket was transferred to an affable looking old man with a bulbous nose and a curious limp. I felt like Ebenezer Scrooge snatching a crutch from Tiny Tim Cratchet (as a pensioner). Truth is, if I'd have had reliable tread on my tires I'd have offered him the seat right there. Instead, all I could do was shrug and apologise. In disbelief he stared, dropping his cane when the bus driver verified me to be who I said I was.

Lucy and I embraced in transit, a painful situation falsely romanticized by perfume commercials. Our hug, however, was suggestive of a force that could not and would not be denied. I turned away, climbing into the bus and taking the only seat I could find, six rows back. Wiping away the condensation, I saw Lucy through the hole, some twenty feet away, grinning. The bus lurched forward. She waved and turned around before suddenly yelling:

"I can't drive a standard!" Her hands slapped down on her thighs and she fell into a paroxysm of laughter. The bus pulled away; my eyes welled with tears of joy and sadness. I sat back picturing her wonderful smile, and proceeded to lambaste myself for not having coerced her into accompanying me.

Within minutes, the woman next to me was snoring erratically while her Walkman projected its tinny sound at a level reminiscent of a pestering mosquito. Twice I lovingly asked her to turn it down. Half an hour into the trip and fed up, I reached over and clicked it off. She opened one eye and snarled at me. I retorted with a blank stare that seemed to unnerve her. The person in front of me was bothersome, too—his seat just far enough back to cut off the circulation below my knees.

The rest of the passengers, however, most notably those sitting towards the back, were in festive spirit. We all bellowed out a cheer at midnight—and why not? It was Christmas. On the way back from the washroom a drunk man looking about as fun as a glass milkshake offered me a drink from a paper-bagged bottle. Hoping to avoid a knife wound, I smiled graciously and declined.

"Come on, asshole," he said, spitting and slurring, "it's Merry Goddamn X-mas!" That was true. I took a quick snort and asked him what it was. He didn't answer, instead throwing out his hand and yelling. "Puda here, asshole! Merry fuckin' Christmas!"

We shook. "And an injury-free Christmas to you," I replied, which seemed to delight him even further. Returning to my seat and closing my eyes, I was soothed by the Hope-Princeton's curvaceous route and the warm air vents blowing up my pant leg. As much as I despised *having* to ride the bus, there was something curiously romantic about hopping a lift on

Christmas Eve with an assembly of other vagabonds going who knows where. Tilting my head to the side, a deep breath uncovered for me an awareness of Lucy's fragrance all over; in my hands, my hair, my clothes, a reality enhanced with every inhale. I closed my eyes and recalled kissing her in mysterious places, wondering how at one moment life could feel as comforting as being sucked out of an airplane with its back end blown off in mid-flight, and at another like the earth and the sky are a uterine wall and our mutual existences are two and the same. Oh the good fortune to be hanging from that mysterious chord!

A jerky stop awoke me in Keremeos. It was ten minutes to five and dark. Slapped by the freezing wind, I shivered as I made my way outside for a quick stretch. Snow abounded. The womb, it would seem, had frozen over. Returning for a second snort from the drunkard's bottle, I was disappointed to discover he'd reached his destination an hour earlier. Glancing around, it was apparent there were two or three others capable of taking his place. I suppressed the impulse. Sitting back down at my own seat, I accidentally stepped on the foot of Walkman Woman and got snarled at a second time.

"Idiot," she said.

"Sorry," I said, with as gentle a smile as I could manage. I closed my eyes and thought of Lucy.

"*Idiot*," she said again.

Opening my eyes we locked horns like disgruntled caribou. "Excuse me," I said, "would you mind moving your thigh over a wee bit, please?"

She glanced down at her leg which was as far over as it could be.

"Oops, I'm sorry," I said, "I mean your fat arm! Ha ha ha! Mind if I call you Redwood?"

Tears erupted, reminiscent of Pompeii. And like those mortified Roman peons, I ran but could not hide—smothered by guilt at my inability to turn the other cheek and see in her eyes the divinity I had failed to see in Frank's. An apology was my only recourse, and I proceeded to give one. The effects were remarkable. Within minutes barriers crumbled to where she was expressing to me in soggy detail the anguish of adolescent obesity. I sympathised, confessing I'd once been rejected by a fat woman—to whom I was wildly attracted—merely because she'd perceived my failure to rise above the neurosis of social stigma. An hour or so later, still engaged in our therapeutic tête-à-tête, I felt blessed to have witnessed the effects of a few kind words. Sometime thereafter, we drifted into slumber, Doris' head on my shoulder, our bodies no longer an issue. Her subsequent departure in Osoyoos, although allowing me greater leg room, was bittersweet.

Arrival in Revelstoke was a nonevent. No one else got off the bus, no one appeared to be in the depot, and no one was there to pick me up. It was twenty minutes to noon, the bus ten minutes early. I stood for a moment, stiff, punished somewhat by the beef jerky, coffee and Nibs in Salmon Arm, gazing afar as "God Rest Ye Merry, Gentlemen" with flutes, strings and electric piano floated out of the backroom. A nippy draught from the doorway slipped up my sleeve and snapped before me the reality of what I was soon to face: Christmas without Gran.

* * *

Mom and Dad picked me up a few minutes later. Pleasantries were bathed in melancholia and the drive home was, although tender, strained. Back at the house I called Lucy several times without success. Derek and Kristine showed up a few hours later and announced the baby news to Mom and Dad (and me, pretending). It was a joyous happening, everybody ecstatically teary-eyed. Larry wasn't around, having boycotted (except for personal emergencies) the family and our worldly ways. Ironically, I missed him. He wasn't so bad.

Gifts were opened after dinner amidst sadness, laughter, Gran anecdotes and Dad and Derek, both having overindulged, breaking out in the theme song from *Hockey Night In Canada*.

"Is that show still on?" I asked sarcastically and to much badgering.

"When that *Hockey Night in Canada* ceases to be part o' Saturday night," Dad said out of context about twenty minutes and two more rye-and-Sevens later, "the elephant has rolled over. Free trade has squished our duffs. Canada: the fifty-first state." He erupted into spontaneous song: "*Oh say can you see*

..." We all joined in and got the words wrong. Mom insisted it was only proper we sing "Oh Canada," also, and began it in her strangled soprano. We flubbed those lyrics, too, and nobody dared attempt the French translation.

Later on I did a load of wash and took a shower. By midnight, alone in my old bed, I envisioned a wet stream of life connecting Lucy and Gran and Derek's new baby . . . everyone, in fact; an infinite thread of interconnectedness blossoming out of one big cosmic navel, exposing us all for what we really are: mass murderers, gluttonous swallowers of life—be it plants, insects or the ground itself, living and dying, ingesting and regurgitating with every moment. And on that thought I fell asleep, smiling and thankful, thoughts of Gran swirling. No life: no death. No death: no pain. No pain: no brain. No brain: no joy.

Waking with a start, I considered how wonderful it would be if the hormones essential for fertilization could only be released through the process of true love—a cosmological definition that no level of debate could ever alter. One either learns to love, or the species dies. Truly, then, by our fruits we would be known. Perhaps, I added, that's happening, anyway. I thought of Lucy, and wondered if she'd used protection. Then I thought of Gran and had a little weep.

* * *

Boxing Day arrived for me just before noon as I stumbled into the front room dressed only in underwear, dress socks and a T-shirt. I'd never been so casual growing up. Dad and Derek, watching football in the front room, turned and gawked. I stood in the doorway, nervous.

"*What?*" I asked.

"You . . . you look different," Dad said. "D'you get your haircut?"

"On Christmas night?"

"I don't know . . . you look different."

I shrugged as though ignorant to his questioning. I knew, though; I'd exposed to them the real Shelby Lewis; rebellious, unpredictable, half naked.

"Nice hair," Derek said.

"Where are Mom and Kristine?"

"Out walkin'," Dad said.

Derek looked down. "Nice gonch."

"Have there been any calls?" I asked.

"A few . . . why?"

"Just wondering. Any for me?"

"No."

"Oh."

"Were you expecting some?" Dad asked.

"No, I—"

"*Sheb*by got a girlfriend," Derek said with his goofy grin.

Dad, seemingly startled by the revelation, turned to Derek. "Does he?"

"*Yup*," Derek said, "nice girl, too. Couple o' heads and one eye. Shame about the foot odour."

Dad turned back to me. "Son, I'm happy for you."

"You seemed surprised," I said.

"Dad thought you might be a fag," Derek said.

"*Derek*," Dad said.

"Sorry, Dad. Homo*sexual*." Derek grinned, stroking Dad's ear.

"Why?" I asked. "Because I'm skinny? How Revelstokian." I walked away.

Awhile later as I flipped through an old newspaper and munched away on a bowl of Shreddies at the kitchen table, Dad came and sat down. I continued reading. He stood up and opened the fridge door.

"No damn leftovers," he said halfheartedly.

I didn't respond.

"See that, son," he said chuckling, "no damn leftovers."

"You can have the rest of my cereal," I said, knowing I'd finished the box.

"About that gay thing," he said, "I just wondered what was wrong when we were goin' through all those troubles." He sat down again. "I didn't mean anything. I asked him a lot o' things."

I shrugged. "Doesn't matter."

"You got a girlfriend, eh?" he said as warmly as I'd ever heard him speak.

I smiled. "Yeah."

"Like her?"

"Oh, yes."
"What's her name?"
"Lucy."
"Wow," he said. "So . . . uh . . . had any luck with your calling?"

I looked up. "My calling?"

"Yeah."

"Um . . . still unclear. I'm hopeful, though."

"You know, sometimes I wish I'd . . . I just . . ." He shrugged. "Kids, marriage—I used to carve a lot, you know?"

"Carve?"

"Wood stuff. Little people and that. Whittlin' away. I spent days doing it."

"Do you have anything I could see?"

"Nah. Went into a rage in '62—maybe '63, built a fire and burnt it all."

"I never knew." He shrugged, smiling, and I, looking into the eyes of the genetic pool from which I'd liberally borrowed, felt suddenly overcome. He'd asked me about my calling!

"You thinkin' about settlin' down?" he asked.

"Pardon?"

"Settlin' down. With Lucy . . ."

"Dad," I said, edging towards him, "as cliché as it sounds I believe our meeting was predetermined."

"Wow. What's she do?"

"Uh . . . well, she's between jobs. She's very talented. She used to be a dancer."

"Hm." Dad scratched behind his right ear. "Thanks for the golf stuff, eh."

"You're welcome. I hope you take up the sport."

He stood up and opened the fridge door again. "You ever think about going back?"

"To Vancouver?"

"To school."

"Oh . . . sometimes."

"You could do it," he said, pulling the tab on a Fresca. "There's no doubt in my mind you could do it without missin' a skip."

"Thanks."

Dad took a swig from his pop and made his way towards

the basement. "You could do whatever you want," he said, not facing me.

"Dad?"

He stopped, glancing over his shoulder. "Yeah?"

"Thanks," I said.

"Ah," he said, sloughing me off with a wave of his hand. "Oh," he said, reaching into his pocket and pulling out a rustic looking jackknife about six inches long. "Here."

"What's that?"

"That's the knife I used to use. I want you to have it." Before I could respond he'd disappeared downstairs. I sat, flabbergasted, when to my shock my boxer shorts shot up my anus.

"I want answers!" Derek yelled, hoisting me in the air. "*Where is she?*" The jackknife clanged on the kitchen table.

"Who?"

"The mystery woman."

"Let go and I'll tell you."

Upon release I yelled "Ignoramus" and attempted to bolt away. My socked feet, however, offered insufficient friction to keep me in pivot and I crashed into the kitchen table, pole axed to the floor like a collapsing giraffe. Derek landed on me and twisted me into a quick half nelson and then spun me into a headlock.

"This is going to hurt me a lot more than it hurts you," he said, throwing me face down, spanking me and laughing without constraint.

"Knave!" I cried.

He swung me over and sat on my chest, crushing his knees into my biceps.

"No!" I yelled.

"'Fraid so, Shel," he said, "for your own good—and you're still my little brother."

"I'm twenty years old!"

"Well, cowpoke, Happy dang birthday!" He laughed and precariously dangled spittle inches from my face, slurping it up at the last moment. "It's really an art form," he said.

I flexed every muscle in an attempt to break free. "I'd kill you at *chess*!" I screamed.

"Checkmate," he replied, slapping my forehead.

* * *

Getting in touch with Lucy was a grand relief. As it happened, she'd been out walking all day as she had on Christmas, too. I asked her to pick me up when I got back into Vancouver. She was obliging.

"How's your family?" she asked.

"All events considered, quite well. It's strange without Gran around but the baby news was thrilling—even a second time. How's your hand?"

"Uh . . . still a little swollen."

"I miss you."

"I stalled six times on the bridge driving home," she said.

"Lucy, I had a wonderful Christmas Eve."

"Yeah, me, too."

"What does it mean? How can such joy and confusion come from the interactions of lovers?"

"Buddhist Noble Truth Number One: Life is hell."

"Really?"

"No—hey, guess what?"

"What?"

"I quit my job."

"For good?"

"Yes—well, I haven't sent in my resignation or anything, but I've worked out all the plans."

"You're really going to do it?"

"Well, I'm a little anxious about it. It's the toss-up between a lack o' skills and a lack of excuses. But it's like take a shit or wipe and get outta there, you know? I mean why the hell should I be afraid? Screw fear."

"I've had some revelations, too. I can't wait to share them with you."

"Like what?"

"They're just . . . right now . . . *ideas*. Life. Death. Love. How such an awarenesses effects the look of other issues. Oh, and my Dad, too . . . I . . . I'll try to make some verbal sense of them before I return."

She laughed. "You're *so* corny."

* * *

That night I had a dream. Lucy was singing in her kitchen. A crash of glass and a scream sent me sprinting in there to find her sitting on the floor, naked save for her bra, her face buried in her hands, blood dripping through her fingers. Scattered across the floor was glass and assorted vegetables, much as it was the evening I found her in the bathroom with her cut hand. But in the dream, she lifted her head from her hands and gazed at me with eyes and haircut identical to that of the little girl in the photograph I gave her for Christmas. It was truly haunting.

Not being able to sleep, I watched out my bedroom window the sun's gentle ascent, and as the grays and pinks dappled above the mountainous skyline it occurred to me that, metaphorically, life runs on an identical revolution. In other words, just as the sun *appears* to live and die every twelve hours or so, it could be that Gran (being at the same time an example of life and death) never really died, either, but rather travels on the outskirts of some eternal ride that will eventually spin her back into my life.

* * *

Derek and Kristine left for home later that morning. It had been a wonderful visit, the rebirth evident, Derek and I perhaps closer than ever despite the thrashing he gave me on the kitchen floor. As they drove away the phone rang. It turned out to be Eric wanting to wish me a Merry Christmas.

"By the way, I'm going home tomorrow," he said. "You need a lift?"

"No thanks, I'm going home on the bus tonight. How was your Christmas?"

"The bus?" he said. "Why would you do that when you could come back with me tomorrow?"

"I just need to get back."

"Work?"

"No, I just need to get back."

"Say no more, man, I getcha," he said. "Are you going to bring her to the New Year's party?"

"Who?"

"Fuck you *who*."

"Lucy?"

"D-uh."

"Um . . . I doubt she'll come."

"*Snob*. Why not?"

"I . . . We've got several things to discuss."
"Oooh. Sounds like el cruncho time."
"What does that mean?"
"Nina and I had that exact yap before I left."
"What yap?"
"The Love Yap. Listen, man, I gotta ask you a favour?"
"What love yap?"
"It doesn't matter. Remember Terry Anderson?"
"The guitar player."
"Yeah. I gave him a call this mornin' and his girlfriend said he'd gone on the road with a Top-Forty band—Thunder Frenzy—what a stupid fuckin' name. Anyway, man, he's left me dry for the Pig gig on Thursday night. Can you sub in?"
"I don't know any of the songs."
"Sure you do! We'll do some SMEGMA BOMB! material and maybe a couple tunes from the Void. Just the cream, though. I've got a rehearsal booked for Wednesday night. What do you say, man? You and me, old times? Be your best friend."
"Eric, I haven't practiced in weeks. All the callouses on my fingers are soft."
"Come on, man. I'll give you woman advice."
"I don't need any advice."
"One piddly night. Two at the outside."
"Okay."
"Atta boy!"
"Hey, Eric, what was that pungent odour in the apartment?"
"What . . ." Eric barked out a laugh. "Oooh, sorry about that. I bought a couple o' big cohos to give to the polar bears."
"*What?*"
"Coho salmon-"
"I heard you! You're talking about the polar bears at Stanley Park, aren't you?"
"You know any others?"
"You were *arrested* last time, Eric."
"Yeah, by hypocrite assholes. Screw *them*."
"But we're talking about your *free*dom, Eric."
"Shel, I can't believe your attitude," he said, sounding disillusioned with me, "it was fuckin' Christmas . . ."

* * *

After ten o'clock and less than an hour and a half before the bus to Vancouver was scheduled for departure, Lucy was finally home to receive my call.

"If you're never home, how am I supposed to let you know what time to pick me up?"

"Hey, Shel?"

"I hate taking things personally."

"I quit work."

"I know, you told me that yesterday."

"No," she said. "I *did* it. Twenty minutes ago. From a pay phone on second beach. I just picked 'er up, phoned my agent and said, 'So long, no can do. Sayonara. I'm outta here!' My agent says, 'Lucy, what are you talkin' about?' Listen to this psycho-babble. I say, 'I can't do it anymore. I'm going off to find myself. I quit.' She thinks I'm *nuts*."

"Well she's wrong."

"But I ain't nuts, Shel—but I'm *free* and I am *done*. Officially and unconditionally unemployed . . . with no skills. Ta-da!"

"I'm delighted for you."

"I thought it'd kill me."

"No way."

"It didn't kill me."

"I'm very happy for you, Lucy," I said.

"I can't believe I did it. I can't believe I *fucking did it!*"

"I never doubted you."

"I know it—and you know how scared I was about havin' no skills?"

"Yeah."

"I don't even know what that was. Tell you the truth, I don't *give* two shits!"

"I knew you'd do what was best for you."

"I know you did."

"So . . . uh . . . I'll see you in the morning?"

"Yeah," she said, her excitement reaching through the phone and tugging at my innards.

"About seven-thirty . . ."

"Great." I could feel her smiling. It made me happy.

XXII

The world is ruled by letting things take their course
—Lao Tsu

With my parents waiting in the truck, I slipped on the ice outside the bus depot door, bruising my hip and biting my lip. But the serious injury happened inside: thirty-two buffoons from Golden were travelling to the city to see a Vancouver Canucks ice hockey game and, consequently, there were no seats left for the midnight bus. I was enraged. Didn't they understand? Couldn't they have chartered a plane? I *had* to get back to Vancouver. I immediately called Eric from a pay phone and told him I'd need a lift after all.

"Vell, Herr Lewis," he said, "it vood appeuh zee situation hass changed. Now who needs who, hmm?"

"I have no time for jokes, Eric. Just remember I was there for you without a moment's hesitation last night."

"True enough. Pick you up at nine."

"*Nine?* Come on, seven. I've got to get home."

"Ten."

"Eight?"

"Eleven."

"Okay, nine . . ."

I went out to the truck and explained the situation to my parents. Arriving back home furious, I telephoned Lucy immediately.

"I loathe ice hockey!" I cried.

"Shel?"

"The bus is booked! I can't get home until tomorrow afternoon."

"Okay."

"Assuming Vancouver doesn't have a soccer team!"

"Shel, it's no biggie."

"Thirty morons from Golden! I've nearly bit my lip in two. My hip? It's a miracle it's not fractured. I have to drag it behind me like a club."
"It's okay. Settle down."
"I want to get *home!*"
"You'll be home in the afternoon."
"God willing."
"I just remembered, I can't meet you in the afternoon."
"What?"
"I've got some business stuff I've got to take care of."
"What kind of *bus*iness?"
"Just stuff—and I'm working tomorrow night. The last waltz!"
"Well when will I see you?"
"Did you hear what I said, Shel? My *last* dance."
"Terrific, splendid—*damn* I wish I was on that bus!"
"Jesus, Shel, relax. Look, I'll leave the key for your car under your seat. Can you take a cab from the bus depot?"
"I'm driving back home with Eric."
"Oh, perfect. That'll be way better than the bus."
"Lucy, can we get together for dinner tomorrow night?"
"I *can't.* I've got stuff I have to do."
"Like *what?*"
"Like working, for starters."
There was a pause as I considered my options. "Okay . . . I'll call you tomorrow night, then."
"I'm *working* tomorrow night."
"Afterwards?"
"What the hell is your problem?"
"I want to see you! Both of us *free.* We should be together."
"Look, Shel, go to bed. You're acting like an idiot. I'll see you when I can . . ."

* * *

Eric was late arriving the next morning, and to make matters worse, on Mom's insistence he came in for coffee. I was livid. It was gone ten before we left Revelstoke. The roads were atrocious from the outset. Just outside of Salmon Arm, Eric's convertible roof top blew off backwards and crashed against the back end of the car—a problem remedied on the highway

shoulder with duct tape and a couple of guitar strings as eighteen-wheelers squealed by, compounding an already mortifying wind chill factor.
"I can't feel my fingers," I cried, clutching my wrist and stepping back into the car.
"I could fix anything, man. MacGyver don't know shit."
"My lip. My hip. Frostbite. Lucy's going to think I've just returned from war."
"Christmas with the family," Eric said, "same thing."
We laughed. There was a pause. "Between you and me, Eric, I feel an incredible urge to nest."
Eric glanced at me queerly. "What?"
"To nest."
"What do you mean *nest?*"
"Nest. Build a common dwelling. Create progeny. Surely you and Nina have discussed it?"
"The word *nest* has never come up."
"You two don't get along well enough?"
"We get along great—well . . . the pill."
"What pill?"
"Birth control. They were making her sprout the ol' third eye. So she stopped poppin' 'em and started using a cervical cap instead."
"So she's better now?"
"Depends on how you look at it."
"What do you mean?"
"Ever seen a cervical cap?"
"No."
"Let me tell you, man. It looks like a rubber flower pot only it's the size of a contact lens and it's all that floats between havin' sex and havin' Junior."
"That wouldn't bother me," I said.
"Are you nuts?"
"Eric, I *yearn* to commit. With Lucy. With life. With a call to call my own."
Eric glanced over and shrugged. "It's got nothin' to do with committment, man. I don't want kids, that's all."
"Ever?"
"It's big-time bazooey out there, man. If the environmental-

ists are right, we're toast. If the religious nuts are right, we're toast. If nobody's right, then we've really had it."

"Would you marry Nina?"

"*Why?*"

"Just picture it! The big gown, her dark skin against the white—she'd look beautiful."

"Marriage don't mean *shit*."

"It can lead us back to the garden."

Eric laughed. "A society so out-there, man, that it can't stop a woman from feelin' she has to walk around at night with a rocket launcher hidden in her pants to feel at ease ain't gonna be asked to sanctify *my* love."

"Good Lord! It seems even *you* have been duped into believing that walking on the flip-side of corporate America is a sign of rebellion."

"What are you talking about?"

"Don't you see? The prodigal son always returns! What matters, then, is to *what*? To *not* understand what marriage is *truly* about is to fall victim to society's lack of spirit. See the light, friend, I implore you!"

"Why don't you get into Lou Reed or something?" Eric cracked his hand on the steering wheel. "Hang on ... I get it now."

"You do?"

"Lucy wants a rock on her hand, doesn't she?"

"Pardon?"

"I thought she was frigid?"

"*Celibate!*—and I refuse to be coerced into discussing her sexual idiosyncrasies. Suffice to say, Eric, three nights ago we were one flesh and she craved me as no woman ever has."

Eric bellowed out a laugh. "She *craved* you?"

"I bet you don't even know what tantric sex is."

"And she wants to marry you?"

"I never said that!"

"But does she?"

"I don't know."

"What the hell's goin' on with you two?"

"I ... I don't know. But we're compatible on many levels. My next few moves could prove crucial."

"Meaning?"

"I love her completely, Eric . . . and I feel she may be on the verge of absolute surrender."
"Really?"
"My instincts have been wrong before."
"What if they're not?"
"To tell you the truth . . . I see no limits."

* * *

It was dark and just before five P.M. when Eric dropped me at Lucy's apartment. From the sidewalk I could see a light was on in her front room window. It was raining and the curtains were closed and although she had told me she would most likely not be home when I arrived back, I hoped she would be. I knocked on the door twice. There was no response. I left a note in her mailbox telling her to call me whenever she arrived. That done, I took the key from under my car seat, drove home and waited. No call came.

Unable to sleep I started doing push-ups to tire myself, but wound up reinjuring an old shoulder wound on two-and-a-half. All physiological complications aside, the reason for my insomnia was indisputable: My head screamed to expose myself to Lucy to the point of disintegrating all preconceived notions of who and what I was. For what was I? I didn't know, and therefore not what I thought I was. One thing was evident, I had transcended material needs to where my requirements were barely more than sustenance, lodging, collaborating bowels, several books and Lucy within striking distance.

Awakened by a 7 A.M. phone call from the personnel department at the Vancouver Public Library, I was asked to work at circulation from 9:30 to 6:00 for the next three days. In a fatigue-riddled, eye-burning stupor, I agreed, fell back into deep slumber, and woke up in a panic at ten to nine.

Lucy wasn't home when I called on my coffee break at ten. A quick calculation told me she'd been gone the entire eighteen hours since I'd returned from Revelstoke. Coupling that with both her having danced her last dance and an admittance of affection for me, I could understand why she might need time to herself. Nonetheless, shouldn't she have called just to say so? Surely I warranted such courtesy. And how far could she walk?

With no success getting hold of Lucy on either my lunch or afternoon coffee break, I was truly concerned. I called Eric to inform him of the situation and to tell him I'd in all likelihood be late for rehearsal—if there at all. After work I called again, to no reply. Our time without verbal contact was approaching twenty-four hours. Visions of foul play, smelly dumpsters and back-alleys ravaged my mind. I telephoned 911 to report a missing person and hung up at the last second, instead dashing to my car and heading to Lucy's apartment for clues.

A traffic accident and heavy rain on the bridge increased my trip time sevenfold from the usual six minutes. Finally arriving, I immediately noticed that, like the previous day, the front room light was on. Whether or not that was a positive sign remained unclear. Stepping out of the car, my feet were drenched from the flooded floor panel, my heart was pounding and my armpits were pungent. All that and my hip notwithstanding, I triple-stepped it up the stairs and clanged the door with closed fist. There was no answer. Resisting the urge to break in, I hoisted myself up on the porch railing, reached out to the window, lost my footing and tumbled into a soaked juniper bush. Clambering back up to the railing I tried to yank myself over, tearing my shirt in the process. Hanging there, I recalled the note I'd left in her mailbox when I'd first arrived back. If the note was gone, she was still alive. I let go of the railing, fell to the ground and hobbled back up around the stairs—hip reagitated—one at a time. I lifted up the lid. The box was empty. She'd been home.

* * *

"Listen up, ass-picker," I heard Bryan yell from a few feet outside the rehearsal space, "you told me you'd give me forty bucks for the gig—twenty now and twenty tomorrow. Now you're tellin' me you ain't got it." I peeked around the door. Bryan and Eric were in opposite corners of the room, Eric nervously tuning his bass.

"Come on, man," Eric said, "you know I'm good for it."

SHELBY

"I don't know dick. All I know is if you don't pay, I don't play."

"Hi, guys," I said. They turned to me.

"Well, if it isn't Shitby," Bryan said, before turning back to Eric. "I guess you already paid your scrawny little bum-hole-buddy his forty, eh?" he said.

"Shut up, you fat fuck!" Eric blurted.

"That's it, I ain't playin'!"

Eric rolled his eyes. "Actually, *Bryan*, Shelby's offered to do the gig for a split of the gate."

"Well that's him and this is me," Bryan said as he lifted his huge leg and farted. "A cut o' the gate? A cut o' dick-all, that's what that'll be. Cough up or I'm AWOL."

Eric shook his head in frustration and turned to me. "Did you find Lucy?"

"No, but I have reason to believe she's all right."

"Did you hear what I said?" Bryan yelled. "*AWOL!*"

"Look, man, I said I'd pay you, didn't I? I just don't have the funds right now." Bryan reached down, hoisted up his bass drum and walked towards the door.

Eric glanced at me. I shrugged. "Hang on," Eric said. Bryan turned around. Eric looked at me again. "Can you lend me a twenty spot, man?"

I put my guitar down. "I've only got . . ." I removed my wallet from my breast pocket and flicked through it." . . . eight dollars, I've got eight dollars."

Eric looked at Bryan and raised his eyebrows. "That's a start, eh? Eight bucks should at least get us talking."

"This is bullshit," Bryan said, "but because we're friends, I'll play for ten today if you pay me the thirty tomorrow."

"Okay."

"Make it thirty-five. And I want the ten right now."

Eric reached into his black canvas bag and sifted through it. "Look," he said, "I got a buck and a quarter . . . wait, a buck forty-one, two . . . a buck forty-three. Plus the eight bucks from Shel. Nine forty-three and I'll pay you the rest tomorrow. How 'bout it, man?"

"All right," Bryan said. I transferred the eight dollars to Eric.

"You're a saint," he said, funnelling that and his change into Bryan's stubby hands.

Bryan shoved it into his front pocket and picked up his bass drum. "It's business," he said.

"What is," Eric asked, "bein' a dick-face?" Bryan turned round and glared at Eric, towering over him by probably three inches and a hundred pounds. Eric didn't flinch. No words were spoken. The stare broke. We set up.

By midnight we had flushed out four of the ten songs. Eric was hoarse, Bryan's flatulence knew no bounds and I was desperate to see Lucy.

* * *

From a pay phone I called Lucy and got a busy signal. It was the closest we'd come to contact since my return. Relieved, I drove home. As it turned out, Lucy had left a message on Eric's answering machine. It was as follows:

"*Hi, Shel . . . This is Lucy. I really have to talk to you . . . Come by when you can. Anytime. Don't bother calling, I'm not answering. Thanks.*" I phoned. There was no answer. I drove right over.

Seeing Lucy when she opened the door split my heart as would a radial arm saw; her hair was in disarray, her eyes were weary and hollow and her skin pallid. We stood gazing at each other like confused war children.

"Hi, Shel," she said, voice quivering.

"Oh Lucy," I said, "I've been dying to see you—to talk to you."

"I quit," she said.

I smiled. "I know you did. You told me."

"I quit," she said again.

"I know."

"I told you I would."

"I know you did." I reached out to bring her into my arms. She flinched and pulled away.

"What . . . what are you doing?"

"I . . . I've got some news."

I reached out a second time.

"No!" she cried.

"*What?*"

She crossed her arms around herself. "I'm going away," she said.

"On the road?"

"No."

"What are you talking about?"

"I've been thinking about it for a long time, Shel. Forever. And the last couple of days I—since Christmas Eve . . . I . . . I'm going to Seattle tomorrow and I'll see Marj and then . . . then I'm going to go to Bingen and after that I-"

"Bingen? What are you talking about."

"I'm going away."

"For how long?"

"Forever."

"What?"

"I'm going away."

"What . . . forever . . . Bingen?"

"It's . . . uh . . . a town in Germany—on the Rhine . . . where all the mystics came from. I'm going to walk where the mystics have walked, Shel. Eckhart. Mechtild. Hildegard . . . she's the one from Bingen. People that lived by their conscience doing whatever they had to do no matter what the consequences. Brave, brave people, Shel. That's what I'm going to do . . ."

"I . . . I don't understand."

"What don't you understand?"

"I don't understand."

"I'm going away."

"But Lucy I . . . look . . ." I pulled a piece of paper from my breast pocket. "'If ever any beauty I did see, 'twas but a dream of thee'! *Thee*, Lucy. That's you!"

"I'm sorry, Shel."

"But we . . . I . . . why?"

"I'm sorry, Shel. I . . . I know it must seem kind of sudden—"

"*Sudden?*"

"You're right," she said, "it is sudden. But I can't tell you how freeing it feels. Fuck off job! Fuck off pain! Fuck everything that ever stopped me from feeling good!"

"Lucy . . . you're not going anywhere."

"I'm going."

"You're staying!" I cried out.

"I can't, Shel."
"You *have* to."
"I have to go."
"But our love, Lucy . . . it's . . . it's . . . Dammit, I can't think. I had so much to . . . what was I going to say?"
"This is what I have to do."
"*No.*"
"Yes."
"I've put too much pressure on you, haven't I?"
"Shel, you've been wonderful—"
"Okay, no marriage—but a committed relationship . . ."
"Shel—"
"Okay, no relationship, nothing . . . just—"
"I can't stay, Shel."
"Please . . ."

Lucy stepped forward and put her arms around me. "Come on," she said softly, leading me. I froze in mid-step.

"There's . . . where's . . ." We both stared into the empty front room.

"Packed," she said.

"When did . . . why didn't you . . . oh God."

"It just happened, Shel. When I phoned and told you I quit . . . well, afterwards I couldn't sleep. I just lay on the floor hyperventilating. I thought I was going to die—that's just like you, isn't it?" She smiled. "I went out walking . . . it was about five in the morning and I walked and walked and walked and at eight o'clock I was standing outside a travel agent office, standing there . . . By nine-thirty I had a one way ticket to Frankfurt and by ten I was home packing."

My eyes skirted around the room; no books, no candles, no old green chair, no couch, one box in the centre.

"I saved some things for you," she said pointing at the box, "the rest went into storage. I told my agent that if I don't get in touch with her in the next six months, she can sell it all and keep a cut—fifty percent." Lucy smiled. "I gave her your number for the other fifty."

Staggering into the bedroom together, dazed, dumbfounded, Lucy clicked the light. Her telephone and quilt were all that remained, save her suitcase. "There's nothing here, either."

"I know," she said.
"No bed."
"It doesn't matter." She unzipped her suitcase and took out two sweaters, laying them side by side on the floor. "Pillows," she said softly, almost to herself. She stood up and looked at me as though too fatigued to smile or cry. She turned out the light. Our hands touched and together we crumpled to the floor and into each others arms. Pulling the quilt over us, she buried herself into me, her face resting on my upper chest like a captured wild animal finally giving in to undeniable exhaustion; her legs and arms like adjustable clamps around my body, holding on like a parachuter fearful of jumping. I was in shock.

I woke up in the night to the hum of life and Lucy's breathing. I was sweaty and my left arm and leg were numb, crushed between Lucy and the hardwood floor. An attempt to stretch was met with resistance; Lucy gripping on like a child afraid of darkness, afraid of dying, afraid of disappearing—or maybe that was me. Outside was darkness. Gently I pulled away, flexing until circulation recurred. I caressed the side of her face with my hand, then her hair, and pictured this madwoman, my lover, strolling along the Rhine river, draped in rags, flowers in matted hair, chanting Gregorian hymns from the Middle Ages. Suddenly she started to breathe very rapidly. I lowered my lips like rose petals upon her cheek, slowing down her panic without waking her up. That was all I knew. I closed my eyes, dreaming of love—for me, for Lucy—coasting over us like the night.

We woke up simultaneously, before us the soft, hopeful glow of morning. Neither of us moved. We just looked. Lucy put her hand on the back of my head and pulled me in close until our noses touched. She kissed me and smiled, her breath warm. I leaned my cheek on hers and closed my eyes.

"Hello," I whispered.

She placed her hand softly on my cheek and left it there, saying nothing.

"You're going, aren't you?" I asked.

I felt her nod. We lay awhile longer. I opened my eyes.

"How are you getting to Seattle?"

"I'm flying," she said softly.

"What time?"
"Three-thirty."
I phoned the library and left a message on the personnel answering machine saying I wouldn't be in because of a family emergency.
"Does that make me family?"
"Only if you stay," I said.
"I can't, Shel."
"I want you to know you've really gone and blown all my plans."
"What plans?"
"I'm not sure, but I know you were in them."
Lucy closed her eyes, touching her fingers to my cheek.
"Lucy . . . I have to tell you something. You have to stay."
"I can't."
"You *have* to."
"I *can't*."
"I . . . I have cancer."
"*What?*"
"That's a lie . . . but *please* stay . . ."
Lucy laughed.
"*See?* That's the kind of fun we could have if you stayed."
"Fun?" she said grinning. "I need turmoil."
"Why do you have to go away?"
Lying on her side, she shrugged her shoulders. "I just know I have to."
"But . . . isn't it . . . I think it's good here, you know?"
"It's not that, Shel," she said. "It's just that . . . I've never actually been anywhere where it felt like it was where it should be. I've always felt like either I'm in the wrong place or the place is in the wrong place."
"And Nazi Germany is the answer?"
"I'm going everywhere."
"I don't think going away is the answer. You can't just walk into the Amazon River and say, 'Hi, I'm here, I'm your new Goddess.'"
"I can't?"
"No."
"Why not?"
"Well . . . because . . . well . . ."

We both laughed.

"I'll be hittin' the Rhine first, anyway," she said, "then maybe the Nile. Rumour has it the Amazon's crazy with wannabe Goddesses this time of year."

"Hey? Why don't I come with you? I have no immediate plans. I could probably hear my calling in India just as well as Vancouver—maybe better."

Lucy closed her eyes and touched two fingers from her right hand to my lips. Her eyes opened. "I'm going on my own," she said.

"Lucy, if you can't find yourself here, I don't think you're going to be able to do it anywhere else."

"Maybe."

"Wait," I said, "you can't go. I still owe you a thousand dollars!"

"A gift."

"*What?*"

"It's yours."

"I can't take it."

"Too late."

"What are you going to live on?"

"I've been stripping for eight years, Shel," she said. "I've saved a bushel of money—stashes of it everywhere." She grinned. "Accounts all over the world. Even with Frankie-boy I saved a fair chunk of dough."

"Lucy, I have to pay you back."

"Look, keep me in my old age."

We stared at each other.

"I would," I said.

"Thanks, Shel."

"In fact it was one of my plans."

* * *

Just before leaving for the airport, Lucy bestowed on me a cardboard box full of things she wanted me to have, books—*The Flowing Light of the Godhead, Myths to Live By, Original Blessing, The Family, Tao Te Ching, The Book, The Transmission of Doubt, Thou Shalt Not Be Aware*, candles—purple, blue, red, some half melted, some new, the poem she had hung and framed inside the door: *The valley spirit never dies; It is the woman, primal mother . . .* , a small stack of photographs, a pipe, a record—*The Best of Dave Brubeck*, two bracelets and a worn out Raggedy-Ann type doll with a few strands of orange hair, a loose leg and one of her teeth blacked out with blue ink.

Stepping outside, the street—our street—was amazingly quiet; it was chilly, an overcast sky hanging with the threat of rain. I put the cardboard box, the quilt and Lucy's suitcase in the back seat of the car. Lucy put her other bag on her lap. And so I drove, due south, overwhelmed; two days earlier I had been seeking ways to bridge the gap between us, confident, yearnful, unknowing that a finger snap into the future I'd be driving her to the airport so she could venture off on a spiritual safari to someplace called Bingen.

Boom and we were standing at the departure gate watching faceless passengers walk through the metal detector, all of them oblivious to the significance of our situation. Nonetheless, there we were, the gestation period of our relationship about to come to term, only to have us separated at birth. The last call for boarding had come and gone.

"This is it," she said. I glanced at Lucy. She appeared anxious.

"Are you all right?" I asked.

She turned and looked at me as though about to burst. "I think so," she said, half smiling. I was overtaken by a wave of sadness, without warning, rising like a storm front. I turned away and looked out towards the landed planes. A few snowflakes fell. Lucy took my hand and squeezed it softly. My eyes trickled with moistness. I swallowed and took a deep breath. Several more people went through the detector. Lucy squeezed my hand a second time.

"Well, I guess this is it," she said. She threw her arms around me, stroking the back of my neck with her bandaged hand. I closed my eyes, trying to memorize the feeling. Lucy fell away, looking up at me. For the first time ever I saw tears in her eyes. She quickly rubbed them with the wrist of her bandaged hand. "Damn allergies," she said.

"Do me a favour," I said, "learn whatever it is you have to learn and then get the hell back here." Tears were starting to roll down my face.

"Okay." There were no more people going through. "I have

SHELBY

to go," she said. She hugged me again and turned away, putting her carry on bag on the conveyor belt.

"Wait!" she yelled, snatching it back. The customs lady jumped away. Lucy crouched down, unzipped the bag and pulled out the framed photograph of the little girl I'd given her for Christmas. She ran back and handed it to me, her eyes alive with tears and sadness and hope. "It's me," she said.

I looked at the photograph. "Really?"

"Nineteen sixty-five," she said. "Nothing but fear. Thanks for everything, Shel." Tears everywhere, she smiled. I smiled back and looked down at the little girl with the bad haircut, eyes squinting into the sun.

I looked up.

The big girl was gone.

XXIII

O powerless is the brain to pierce this mighty mystery!
—Walt Whitman

I didn't do the concert with Eric that night. I left the airport and drove to the banks of the Fraser River. Pulling Lucy's quilt from the back seat, I draped it over myself and watched the water flow by; pregnant from all the rain, muddy and brown against the light fall of snow, clouds above her reminiscent of sleeping old dogs, factories and the squeals of rush hour traffic dancing around her like a huge golden frame from the Smithsonian Museum in Oxford or some other place I'd never been. Pollution on the shoreline told a tale of its own: a licence plate, two aluminum cans and a plastic bag. Gazing out to the other side and as far east and west as vision would allow, I could see no Goddess.

I watched the river until long after the sun had disappeared, changes abounding, light to dark, altering noises, all of it dished up like soup, rolled out like carpet, unstoppable, source unclear, destination blurry. And then I drove across town, still draped in the quilt, and parked the car outside Lucy's apartment. I knew I hadn't yet grasped the reality of her leaving—whatever that was. I half expected to see her in the window, or dancing, or yelling, or smiling.

In the lamplight I flicked through the books she had left me in her box. In one by some guy named Bubba Free John— poor kid—there was a bright red bookmark with a tassle. I opened to that page and read what had been highlighted in yellow felt pen, presumably by Lucy:

> *Rather than settling down to an adolescent life of complaint, you should kick your ass out of the house and submit yourself to the bare facts of existence. Wander until you find it. This was an obvious course for me. There was no way I was just going to take a profession or a job and settle*

SHELBY

down to a middle-class life. To do so was insane from my point of view. I did not see any Happy people. I only saw people burdened with their lifetime occupation, their dumb ideas about existence, and their endless neurotic fretting. What is the purpose of organizing that into a career? What is the purpose of devoting yourself to a life of preserving that?

I couldn't decide if the passage had been highlighted as a way for Lucy to explain to me her leaving, as a piece of prose that moved her, or as a note for me to reflect on. Either way, I read it several times. I cried, too. I stared at her window for hours; the darkness of glass, the emptiness of a memory of a calico cat. And sometime into the wee morning hours I unravelled myself from the quilt, wandered shivering down to the beach and peed into the ocean. At that moment it seemed, with a golden umbilical chord glistening between us, I and the sea were one; and as I breathed out visible breath I thought, where does this breath end? Where does the air I take in end?

Dawn arrived in a downpour, a cacophony of natural applause, and to this curtain call I did a U-turn on Cornwall Street and parked in the beach parking lot perhaps 100 feet away. Traffic peaked to where its roar—beeps and squeals and all—was indecipherable from the crash of rain. Tilting my seat back, I was swaddled in the quilt, my thoughts as intermingled as Christmas decorations, lights included, after a year in storage.

Save a late lunch across the street at *Mama Gold's*, I remained in the car for the day, wrapped and warm in Lucy's quilt, my sunroof mysteriously not leaking. I thought about the Neo-nazi groups that had spread across the Canadian horizon in the past year or so and the anti-rascist groups that had sprouted up in defence with large rallys and signs like KILL NAZIS. Naturally I took side with the latter group, but were either of them doing any good? The same went for the Pro-Life and Pro-Choice factions. The end result? Individual human ideologies and angers so ingrained that on a large scale differing opinions—indeed *people*—seem incapable of one thing: getting together and chatting it out—or just getting together! *Are* Pro-Choicers really murderers? Does the conscious aborting of a fetus hint towards a human species' subconscious hatred for existence? Is it a feminist reaction to subjugation? As for Pro-lifers, the majority of them also believe that capital punishment is warranted and killing in war is justified. Therefore, I concluded, in the depths of what we call civilization, psychosis abounds. And religion? Jesus appeared to be onto something with his *Do not judge* concept, but look what happened. Moreover, now He has a group of fifty million *ardent* followers in North America who, I am sure, if it weren't for the grace of the times would slaughter homosexuals and wipe out nonbelievers. In short, be it nations or lovers, eventually somebody always stops calling. Perhaps the answer for me was to take no sides and have no opinions. But then how could I still enjoy poetry? Or was the answer to not follow anybody, *including* myself? Dammit, who could I turn to? Lucy had the Goddess, but that for me was not a natural inclination. But what was? What had I accomplished in my twenty years? Nothing. Had I made a difference in anybody's life, including my own? No.

The sun had been set for about five hours by the time I backed out of the parking lot. The rain had stopped and the temperature had dropped to where bits of ice were forming on the windscreen. The Molson Brewery clock said: 11:38—HAPPY NEW YEAR! I was cold and I had to defecate. I drove across town, observing crowds celebrating in the streets and coming and going from different establishments, be they public or private.

Parking outside Eric's apartment, I heard the noise of the party before I left the car. I picked up my box of gifts from Lucy.

Inside, the apartment was enveloped in a smoky blue screen of self-induced oblivion. I felt a twinge of pain in my lower back. Coughing, the pain leapt into my chest. Eric's face popped through a maze of faces.

"Shel!"

"Hi."

"Where the hell have you been, man?"

"Sorry about the concert last night."

"The . . . oh yeah, where the hell were you?"

"How did it go?"

"We kicked the shit out o' that place, man—you look terrible."

I shrugged.

"What's in the box?"
"Stuff."
"You want a beer?"
"No, I'm okay, thank you."
"Y'sure?"
"Yeah."
"Where's Lucy?"
"Seattle or Frankfurt."
"Okay, man . . ." Eric smiled and did a *cheers* gesture with his bottle before sinking back into the quicksand. I pushed my way into the front room, knelt down into something wet, picked up Lucy's photograph from the top of the box and held it to my breast. A knee kicked me in ribs. I didn't respond. I didn't even care, instead getting on all fours and searching through the paraphenalia I kept beneath the couch. Tapped on the shoulder, I looked up to see Eric smiling at me with a beer in his hand and a cigarette dangling from the side of his mouth.

"Hey, hombre," he said, his words slightly slurred, "you sure you're okay?"

Pushing myself up, I embraced him with all the regard I had, kissing him on the cheek, shaking his hand. "Thank you for everything, Eric."

He seemed confused. About to put his beer to his lips, he stopped, offering it instead to me. I shook my head in the negative.

"You sure you're okay?" he asked again.

I nodded, crouched back down and reached under the couch, scattering books until coming up with my red-bound, New International Version, slightly weathered Holy Bible. It fell open to where I kept the photograph of my family: Gran, Derek, Mom, Dad, me. I took the picture out and stuck it in the lower left corner of the framed picture of Lucy. I stood up with the photographs in hand and picked up *Fish-tail Pie* from the top of the television set. Then I put both into the box of treasures Lucy had given to me. Turning around, I borrowed a packet of matches from a man I didn't recognise. I hoisted the box up, now of considerable weight, and pushed my way through the labyrinth of people and into the cloudy hallway. There was a winding line-up for the bathroom. I surveyed the situation and readied myself. The door opened, I barged in, slamming the door with my foot. I placed the box on the yellow bathmat and turned around to lock the door.

"You asshole," somebody bellowed from outside, "I got to take a shit!"

I pulled down my corduroys and did just that. The music stopped and through the barrage of voices somebody yelled, "Countdown!" I smiled, pulled two candles from the box and lit them. Then I wiped, flushed, got up and placed the candles on the toilet seat. I turned out the light and ran the bath. Steam started to rise. I kicked off my shoes and undressed slowly, letting each article of clothing drop to the floor on its own accord—a strip-tease of sorts. Gently I caressed my goose bumped body, stopping for a slightly longer time on my nipples and the base of my testicles. There was a thumping on the door.

"Hurry up for Christ's sake!" Thump. Thump. "Fuckin' hurry up!"

I was pleasantly surprised at how much noise from the pandemonium the running water could block out. The flickering candlelight was brilliant across the bathroom walls. I picked up the picture of Lucy and my family and balanced it on top of the toilet against the wall. I looked at it. The warmth of the candle flame was soothing under my chin, the waxy aroma floating through my senses. There was more pounding on the door, barely audible, over the flow of water and music. I positioned *Fish-tail Pie* next to the candles. I stood up and stuck my toe into the water—the heat firing emergency synapses in my brain—and slowly ventured in.

"What the hell are you doing in there?" mumbled through the flowing water. I didn't answer. Thump. Thump. "What the . . ." I kept my eyes on the photographs, flickering in the light.

"Open the damn door, asshole!" I closed my eyes and let out a deep breath. I slipped my shoulders under the water, opened my eyes and lay motionless. Beads of sweat started to form on my temples. I was amazed at how perfectly designed the bathroom was for setting up a shrine on the toilet. Flat out in the tub I could see everything—Gran, Lucy, *Fish-tail Pie*, the rising steam reminiscent of some ancient medicinal hot spring carved into a mountainside. I closed my eyes and

SHELBY

went under. I pictured a river and then a calm little inlet where the rapids had ceased—rich greens and yellows brilliantly dancing off the rippled surface like some cosmic trampoline. I pushed my nose just above the surface of the water and took a deep breath. There was another thump. I smiled into the darkness.

* * *

When I woke up the water was tepid, the party was still furiously loud and the music was back on. Climbing out of the bath, I dried off, giving my hair a particularly good swaddle, and put the photographs and *Fish-tail Pie* back in the box. I left the two candles on the toilet seat, still alight. Opening the medicine cabinet, I took out Eric's razor and, testing its sharpness, nicked my thumb. Blood oozed freely out of such a fine and wet laceration. Wrapping the cut with toilet paper, I proceeded to shave without incident. I also flossed and brushed my teeth. Then I folded my clothes—jacket and shoes included—and put them on top of the box as a makeshift lid. I undid the bathroom door lock, picked up the box and stepped out.

In the hazy, smoky light everybody stopped and stared as I strutted my clean body down the hallway, big box in hand. I asked a young woman putting on her coat if she'd open the door for me. She obliged. A burst of cold air chilled me. I walked down the steps into the night.

"Shel?" a voice yelled from the doorway just as I opened my car door. I turned around to see Eric's head among many. He was grinning widely. "What the hell are you doin', man?"

I shrugged.

"It's fuckin' freezin' out there."

"There's a quilt in the car," I said.

"You're butt-naked!"

"I know."

"Where are you goin', man?"

I stopped, thinking. "I don't know," I said. "Does anyone want to come?" Nobody moved. I was glad. I stepped into the car, wrapped myself in the quilt and blew them all a kiss. Eric gave me a thumbs up. I drove away.